DATE DUE #3

MAR 2 8 2014	
APR 2 2 2014 *DR*	
MAY 9 - 2014 *AB*	
MAY 2 3 2014 *JL*	
JUN 2 9 2014 *CH*	
SEP 4 2014 *MN*	
DEC 1 3 2015 *DD*	
FEB 2 4 2019	

BRODART, CO.   Cat. No. 23-221

OTHER NOVELS BY
MARGARET BROWNLEY INCLUDE

A Lady Like Sarah

A Suitor for Jenny

A Vision OF LUCY
A ROCKY CREEK ROMANCE

MARGARET BROWNLEY

THOMAS NELSON
Since 1798

NASHVILLE   DALLAS   MEXICO CITY   RIO DE JANEIRO

Published in Nashville, Tennessee, by Thomas Nelson. Thomas Nelson is a registered trademark of Thomas Nelson, Inc.

Thomas Nelson, Inc., titles may be purchased in bulk for educational, business, fund-raising, or sales promotional use. For information, please e-mail SpecialMarkets@ThomasNelson.com.

This novel is a work of fiction. Any reference to real events, businesses, organizations, and locales are intended to give the fiction a sense of reality and autheticity. Any resemblance to actual persons, living or dead, is entirely coincidental.

Library of Congress Cataloging-in-Publication Data

Brownley, Margaret.
    A vision of Lucy : a Rocky Creek romance / Margaret Brownley.
       p. cm. — (Rocky creek romance ; 3)
    ISBN 978-1-59554-811-5 (trade paper)
    1. Women photographers—Fiction. I. Title.
PS3602.R745V57 2011
813'.6—dc22   2011010643

Printed in the United States of America

11 12 13 14 15 RRD 5 4 3 2 1

For Robyn
Beautiful, gifted, loving, and kind
God gave me everything I wanted in a daughter—
and so much more.

Only the stoutest of hearts and bravest of souls should take camera in hand. In case of client dissatisfaction, do not waste your breath explaining that the camera only reveals what's there. In such cases, a quickness of foot may be your best defense.

— THE TRIALS AND TRAVAILS
OF A WOMAN PHOTOGRAPHER
BY MISS GERTRUDE HASSLEBRINK, 1878

One

Never climb higher to take a photograph than you can afford to fall.
— MISS GERTRUDE HASSLEBRINK, 1878

Rocky Creek, Texas
1882

Drat!" Another skirt ruined. Lucy Fairbanks straddled a branch of the sprawling sycamore tree and arranged her torn skirt as modestly as possible. Everything she owned, except for her Sunday-go-to-meeting best, was either patched or hopelessly tattered. At least she hadn't ruined her stockings, having left them at the base of the tree along with her high-button shoes.

"Pa's gonna have a fit," her brother called from the ground below. Thumbs tucked into his red suspenders, sixteen-year-old Caleb Fairbanks stared from beneath a straw hat.

"Pa's not going to have a fit," she called back.

"Will too!"

"He can't have a fit unless he knows what I'm doing." She shot him a warning glance. They shared chestnut hair and clear blue eyes, a gift inherited from their mother. Their stubborn chins came from their father's side.

"And you, young man, are not going to tell him," she said sternly. Four years his senior, she still felt protective of him, though lately he'd protected her more than the other way around. "Quit wasting my time and pull on the rope."

To her relief Caleb did what he was told without argument. His feet firmly planted, he took hold of the rope with both hands and leaned back. Lucy's prized camera rose slowly from the ground until it dangled precariously in midair.

"Don't let it drop," she called anxiously.

She grabbed hold of the bulky black leather box and sighed with relief. "I have it!" Working quickly, she pulled the extra rope from around her waist and secured the camera. "There. That should do it."

Caleb wrinkled his nose. "I still don't understand why you have to take photographs from a tree."

"I told you," she said patiently. "Mr. Barnes promised me a job at the newspaper if I capture a picture of the wild white mustang."

She'd badgered the bullheaded editor of the *Rocky Creek Gazette* for months before he'd reluctantly agreed to print her photographs in the newspaper. At last he'd given in, though he showed no enthusiasm. Obviously, he hoped she'd fail and go away.

"Pa says there's no such thing as the white mustang," Caleb said.

Pa was probably right, but the myth of a white horse once ran rampant among the Indians. They claimed it was the reincarnation of a beautiful woman massacred years earlier in an Indian raid. The Indians had since been moved out of Texas to Indian Territory but the legend remained.

For the sake of her job, she prayed the animal really *did* exist. Some people claimed to have spotted it in the nearby meadow, which is why she chose this particular spot. "No wild horse is going to make an appearance with you around. Now scat."

"When should I come back and get you?"

"Just after the sun goes down. And Caleb—not a word to Pa."

Caleb hesitated. "Don't forget, you promised you'd talk to Doc Myers."

"I haven't forgotten," she said, dreading the thought of, yet again, going against her father's wishes, this time on her brother's behalf. All she seemed to do lately was defy her father's wishes.

Since her brother made no motion to leave, she made an impatient gesture. "Go on, be gone with you. If you don't hurry, you'll be late for work, and you know how Papa feels about tardiness."

Caleb's face grew somber as it tended to do whenever anyone mentioned his job at his father's store. A surge of sympathy rushed through her. Caleb wanted to be a doctor in the worst possible way, but Papa was dead-set against it.

"I'll talk to Doc Myers, Caleb. I told you I would. Now scat!"

"Promise?"

"Promise."

Caleb sauntered back to the wagon a short distance away and, out of habit, checked the mule's leg. Moses had originally been owned by the pastor, who couldn't bear to see him put down when he became lame. Instead he gave the mule to Caleb, who nursed it back to health. The animal had served the family faithfully ever since.

"That a boy," Caleb said, patting the mule's rump.

He scrambled up the side of the wagon and hopped into the seat. *Fairbanks General Merchandise* was written on the wooden sides. Whooping at the top of his lungs, he grabbed the reins and drove off, making enough noise to raise the dead, and probably scaring away every living creature within miles.

Lucy watched her brother with a fond smile, then immediately went to work setting up her camera. That annoying Mr. Barnes and his wild mustang. Next he'd have her chasing after ghosts. Of course, she wouldn't mind chasing after the rumored "Rocky Creek wild man," who was as elusive as a ghost, if he really existed. Anything would be better than spending long hours trying to get a photograph of a stallion that might be nothing more than a fanciful legend.

Sighing, she released the brass lock of her camera and carefully pulled out the folding lens. The maroon-colored bellows stretched out a full fifteen inches, and she secured the extended part to the branch as well. Once she was satisfied that her precious camera was safe, she reached into the satchel attached to another branch for a dry gelatin plate. Though such plates were expensive, they saved her from having to worry about them drying out before they were developed. They also saved her the hassle of having to cart along her darkroom tent and chemicals.

She inserted the dry plate into the camera, then pulled a black cloth from her pocket and draped it over the back of the camera to prevent light from reaching the focusing screen. Squinting through the viewfinder, she made a few adjustments with a turn of a knob.

From her perch, she could clearly see the meadow, a favorite grazing spot for wild horses, deer, and elk. Behind her, the Rocky Creek River wound its way through the valley, its fast-moving waters tumbling over a series of small waterfalls as it elbowed its way to the river below.

What if her father was right and no such white stallion existed? If she didn't find the mustang, her career as a newspaper photographer was doomed before it began. Unless, of course, she found something even more impressive to photograph—like the so-called Rocky Creek wild man.

"Just you wait, Mr. Jacoby Barnes," she muttered. "My photographs are going to make your newspaper the most popular one in all of Texas."

Contemplating success, she surveyed the far horizon. May was her favorite time of year. The meadow looked like an artist's palette, and red, yellow, and blue wildflowers filled the air with sweet perfume. Sweeter still was the high, thin sound of a warbler's song.

A cloud of dust in the distance caught her attention. Moving a leafy branch aside, she could just make out the silhouettes of three horsemen racing toward her.

The horsemen drew nearer. Strangers, by the looks of them. Instead of passing on the road below, they cut across the meadow and disappeared into the nearby woods. Definitely strangers.

Sighing, she leaned back against the trunk of the tree, grateful for the thick green foliage that protected her from the warm sun. As usual, she'd forgotten her hat. She hated anything confining. Hair piled on top of her head in the haphazard way that she favored, she impatiently brushed a wayward tendril away from her face.

She waited. A blue jay flew into an upper branch and protested her presence with a harsh jeering *jaay, jaay* before taking to the skies. A bushy-tailed squirrel started up the trunk of the tree, spotted her, then ran back down and vanished in the brush. A bee buzzed in her ear.

A rumbling sound alerted her. Peering through the branches, she realized it was the Wells Fargo stagecoach, two days late as usual.

Sighing, she wiggled into a more comfortable position and restlessly swung her bare legs. No wild stallion would make an appearance as long as the stage was in the area. She had no choice but to sit and wait.

The rumbling of the stage grew louder, as did the impatient shouts of the driver urging his team of six horses up the slight incline. To while away the boredom, she decided to take a photograph of the stage as it passed below.

She adjusted the camera so that it pointed to the road and peered into the viewfinder. The image, though dim, was clear on the frosted glass. No black cloth was needed. She moved the lever to adjust the shutter speed to high.

Fingering the leather bulb in hand, she waited. The bulb, attached to a rubber tube, allowed her to take photographs without jarring the camera. *Steady, steady*—

Startled by voices, she pulled away from the camera and blinked. The stagecoach had stopped directly below her and the driver disembarked, hands over his head.

It was then that she noticed the three horsemen she had seen earlier, their faces now hidden beneath bright-colored kerchiefs. She had been so focused on the stage she failed to notice their presence until now. The sun glinted against the barrel of a gun and she gasped. Covering her mouth with her hand, she watched the drama unfold below.

The stagecoach was being *robbed*. Shock soon turned to delight. She couldn't believe her good fortune. A wonderful photographic opportunity had practically fallen into her lap— or more accurately, at her feet. Just wait until Jacoby Barnes hears about this!

The gunman came into view below her, yelling, "Get the box!" He was no doubt referring to the green wooden Wells Fargo money box strapped next to the driver's seat.

Praying the bandits would not notice her high-button shoes strewn at the base of the tree, she peered through her viewfinder.

The lens was focused on the driver, but if she moved it to the right, just so . . . with her heart pounding from excitement, she leaned forward and readjusted the camera, tightening the rope that held it.

A twig snapped and one of the robbers looked up. She quickly pulled back and lost her balance. Arms and legs flailing, she fell through the air, letting loose an ear-piercing scream.

She landed on the stagecoach roof with a thud, sprawled facedown.

The startled horses whinnied and the stage took off, taking her with it and leaving the startled gunmen, passengers, and driver in the dust.

Two

Never say "shoot" when you mean "photograph," especially when
talking to a trigger–happy gunslinger.

— MISS GERTRUDE HASSLEBRINK, 1878

Stuck amidst a bewildering confusion of baggage, Lucy held
on for dear life. A large canvas bag had cushioned her fall and
probably saved her from a broken bone or two.

The wine-red stage bopped and rattled along the narrow dirt road, the horses gaining speed with every stride.
The coach swayed from side to side, its leather-thong springs
tested to the limits. The scenery was little more than a blur as
the stage raced by.

"Stop!" she yelled. "Whoa!" Her yelling did no good.
The horses continued to run along the river's edge at break-
neck speed.

"Help!" she cried, but no one was around to save her. Her
only chance was to reach the driver's seat and grab the reins.

Flopping about on the roof of the stage like a rag doll, she
grasped the rope holding the baggage in place. The rope dug
into her flesh but still she held on. Inhaling, she forced herself
to calm down.

"I c-can do-do-do this," she bit out between teeth-rattling
jolts. She had to do it.

Taking a deep breath to brace herself, she tightened her grip. Hand over hand she slowly pulled herself forward. She reached for the guardrail but the stage hit a bump, throwing her backward.

"Ohhh!"

Gasping for air, she waited for the coach to stop fishtailing before clawing her way back. It took several tries before she could finally grab the brass rail.

Fighting to hold on, she lifted a bare foot and heaved her body over the top, landing in the driver's box. She banged her elbow and tears sprang to her eyes. Her slight frame bounced up and down like water on a hot skillet. Grimacing against the pain, she pulled herself upright and searched frantically for the reins.

The leather straps had fallen between the horses and now dragged on the ground beneath the flying hooves. The horses' flanks glistened with sweat, but they showed no sign of stopping. With a cry of dismay she fell back in the seat.

The coach careened dangerously around a sharp curve, thrusting her to one side. At the last possible second, it righted itself and followed the road along the river's edge. Surely it would only be a matter of seconds before the stage went off the road and plunged into the water.

Trembling with fear, she forced herself to think. She had to do something fast, but what? Her only hope was to climb over the front boot and lower herself down to the yoke between the horses to gather up the reins. Not a good idea. It was the only way. *Yes. No. Ohhh.*

A shiver of panic threatened her resolve. Heart pounding, her throat felt raw. Her hair pulled loose from its last hairpin and whipped around her head. Dust stung her eyes.

"You c-c-c-can do this," she stammered in an effort to calm herself. She blinked rapidly to clear her blurred vision, then searched for a foothold. Momentarily frozen by fear, she closed her eyes and said a silent prayer.

Lord, help me. It wasn't the first time she'd faced almost certain death while trying to capture the perfect photograph, but if God saved her one more time, she promised to mend her ways.

Her hands sweaty, she waited for the stage to round a curve and straighten. She then turned her back to the horses and prepared against her better judgment to lower herself over the front of the stage.

A loud popping sound whizzed through the air. Craning to look over the roof of the swerving coach, she stared in horror at the three gunmen close behind. Another popping sound and she dove to the floorboards. Pain shot through her shoulder where she hit it but that was the least of her worries.

Those fool men were shooting at her!

"Stop the stage!" someone shouted.

She peered over the side, her knuckles white from holding on. Wasn't that what she'd been trying to do?

One of the horsemen hurtled past her. His gelding neck and neck with the runaway horses, he managed to leap onto the lead animal. After much shouting and cursing, he finally brought the stage to an uneasy halt.

Lucy's relief lasted only as long as it took for the highwayman to slide off the lead horse and walk back to the stage.

"Stand with your hands up." His voice was slightly muffled by the red kerchief that covered half his face, but there was no mistaking his menacing tone. He was dressed in black from his wide-brimmed hat to his dust-covered boots. A black leather holster trimmed in silver hung from his waist.

With a nervous glance at the gun he brandished, Lucy did what she was told.

His dark glittering eyes narrowed above the kerchief. "Why were you spying on us?"

"I . . . I wasn't spying on you, sir," she stammered. "I was only trying to—"

Before she could explain, the other two horsemen galloped up and the leader sent the short, heavy man after his horse.

She eyed the man with the gun and gulped.

"Come on down," he said. When she showed no sign of moving, he nodded to the other man. "Help her down."

"I don't need anyone's help," she said primly. Lifting her skirt above her ankles, she lowered herself to the ground and brushed herself off. Shaken from her spine-tingling ride, she lashed out at the bandit.

"You should be ashamed of yourselves," she stormed. A strand of hair fell over her eyes, and she brushed it aside with an impatient flick of the wrist. Her knees threatened to buckle beneath her but she had no intention of dying until she gave the outlaws a piece of her mind.

More words tumbled out. "Just wait till Marshal Armstrong gets hold of you. You'll wish you never heard of Wells Fargo. Have you no conscience? Have you no—"

"Quiet!" the man thundered. Startled, she fell silent and he looked her up and down. "That was a pretty good trick you pulled back there. I never thought of hiding in a tree to rob a stage. Too bad you're a woman. I could use someone like you."

Lucy bristled. "How dare you accuse *me* of trying to rob the stage. I have never stolen a thing in my life." No sooner were the words out of her mouth than she corrected herself. "Well, maybe once. There was that little incident with the penny candy. I snuck it away from my little brother but only because he'd already eaten half a bag and I didn't want him to get—"

"Quiet!" he roared again, his red kerchief practically in her face.

Lucy drew back, hand on her chest. "I was only trying to tell you why I took the candy from my brother."

"I don't care."

"I'm not a thief," she said, glaring at him. "And I'm not a spy either! I was only trying to shoot—"

He drew back. "You were trying to shoot us?"

"No, no, I . . ." She described as best she could her reasons for being in a tree but the bandit quickly grew impatient. "Of course it's possible that the white mustang doesn't—"

He grabbed her roughly by the arm and shook her. "Enough!"

She covered her mouth with her hands, and he released her.

The other bandit sat on his bay and watched her from over his kerchief. Thinner than the leader, he looked twice as menacing. "What are you gonna do with her?"

The leader considered for a moment. "I'm 'fraid she may have seen us without our kerchiefs."

She shook her head. "I didn't see—"

The leader swore beneath his breath, his finger practically on her nose. "Don't say another word." He nodded toward the man on the horse. "You get the box while I figure out what to do with the lady."

Oh, Lordy.

The third man rode up with a second horse in tow. The leader nodded, then turned to her.

Just then a shot rang from the distance.

Reaching for his gun, the bandit spun around. "What the—"

A bullet whizzed by, hitting a nearby tree. The horses whinnied and stomped the ground in protest. The leader cursed, grabbed the horn of his saddle, and mounted. "Let's get outta here."

"What about the box?" the heavy man asked.

Before the leader could answer, more gunfire sounded. He took off in a fast gallop with the other two men close behind.

Lucy barely had time to thank God for the narrow escape when a stranger charged out of the woods on a coal black horse.

Three

A lady must never be photographed next to a man
with whom she's not fully acquainted.

— MISS GERTRUDE HASSLEBRINK, 1878

The stranger thundered past her as if to make certain the bandits were gone before reining in his horse. He slid off his horse's bare back and circled the stagecoach on foot. Checking inside and finding no one, he stood with his hands on his hips, feet apart, as if trying to figure out what had happened to the driver.

Apparently recalling her presence, he strode toward her. Up close he was even taller than she had initially supposed, and her gaze froze on his long, lean form.

"Thank you for s-saving me," she stammered. She didn't want to seem ungrateful, but what if he was a bandit too? Or . . . or worse. The thought made her more nervous, and her mouth responded accordingly.

"That man was about to sh-shoot me." Or something like that. "If it hadn't been for you, I don't know what I would have done. If that's not bad enough, he accused me of trying to rob the stage and spying on him . . ."

She talked on and on, doing exactly what she was prone to do whenever she was nervous or scared, and, at the moment,

13

she was both. He was the tallest man she'd ever seen, towering over her own five-feet-eight by another six inches or more. His fringed buckskin shirt barely contained his broad shoulders and strong chest. Muscular thighs bulged beneath buckskin pants. A knife hung from the leather pouch at his waist, and a rifle was slung over his shoulder.

"He thought I saw his face without his kerchief. I did see him but, of course, I wasn't about to admit that. Besides, he was too far away to identify and . . ." Words poured out of her a mile a minute. Random thoughts. Half sentences. She couldn't seem to stop herself. "My brother had eaten half the candy and . . ."

The stranger continued to watch her from a handsome square face, his deep-set eyes flecked with gold and ringed with dark lashes. Smooth bronzed skin stretched over his high cheekbones and perfect straight nose. His eyebrows rose steadily as she rambled on.

" . . . if it wasn't for that white mustang . . ."

Power and strength seemed to emit from him with every breath he took. Like the deepest woods and ever-changing weather, he held an aura of mystery that intrigued her.

Could it be? Was it possible? No! Still, the rawhide clothes, the large black horse. Oh, dear God. The wild man really did exist! Only—only he didn't look all that wild. By now she was talking so fast, her tongue practically tripped over itself.

He cocked his head to one side and frowned. His bronzed skin was lighter than the bold brown eyes that impaled her. A lock of thick dark hair fell across his forehead. She couldn't make up her mind if he was Indian or white—maybe he was both. *Please, God, whatever he is, don't let him be hostile.*

A puzzled frown spread across his face as she rattled on, his eyes dark and unfathomable.

Without warning, he clamped a hand around her wrist and pulled her close, as if he had every right to do so. The nearness of him made her words come faster. Gasping for air, she pressed against his hard chest with her free hand.

"Let me go at once, you hear? You have no right to hold me against my will. Just because you saved my life doesn't mean that you can have your way with me. I'm grateful to you of course, but—"

Some inner light blazed in the depth of his eyes before he lowered his dense lashes and gazed at her mouth.

The whole time she cajoled, threatened, pleaded, and downright begged, the man stared at her with a curious look on his face: disbelief or confusion, maybe both.

Thinking the man either deaf or just plain dim-witted, she lashed out again in a louder voice. "And furthermore—"

As if exasperated, he yanked her against his chest and stopped her tirade with the crush of his lips on hers. Too surprised to react, she let him kiss her—kiss her like she had never before been kissed.

Held captive by the warm currents that rushed through her down to her toes, she might have stayed in his arms indefinitely had he not pushed her away, grounding her in reality.

Shocked as much by her own behavior as she was by his—and more than a little confused—she gaped up at him. She had let a perfect stranger kiss her. Worse, she had done absolutely nothing to stop him. For once in her life she was speechless. Her cheeks were hot as the still-burning fire on her lips. What was the matter with her? It wasn't like her to be dumbfounded, but she couldn't think of a thing to say.

His gaze traveled the length of her. "Sorry, lady," he said, without sounding the least bit apologetic. "I wanted to give you the last word, but I'm afraid you'd never have gotten to it."

"So . . . so you *can* talk."

He arched a dark eyebrow. "When I can get a word in edgewise. I swear you could talk the legs off a mule." Hands on his hips, his mouth twisted slightly. "Now would you mind starting over? This time slower."

She took a deep breath and willed her trembling knees not to give out beneath her. "My name is L-Lucy Fairbanks," she stammered. "They were going to kill me. I'm sure you can imagine that I wasn't quite myself when I allowed you to—" She cleared her throat. "I can assure you that under normal circumstances, nothing of the sort would have happened. Furthermore . . ."

She wanted so much for him to show some sort of understanding. He had to know that an ordeal such as hers would make someone act rash—perhaps even rash enough to let herself be kissed by a stranger.

Something in the arrogant way he looked at her made her temper snap. She pulled herself together, straightening her attire. But it was hard to look dignified when one's hair and dress were in disarray.

"How dare you take advantage of a woman in distress!"

Her outburst brought no signs of remorse. Instead, he stared boldly at her bare toes peering from beneath the hem of her tattered skirt. Of all the rude—

Enough was enough. Intent on making her escape, she turned and began walking away as quickly as her wobbly legs would carry her. She'd taken only a few steps before her bare foot landed on a sharp rock.

"Ow." She lowered herself upon a fallen log and grabbed her foot.

"Now what's wrong?" he asked, much like one would speak to a demanding child.

She shot him a warning look as he approached, her palm held out to ward him off. "Don't touch me."

He grinned. "Lady, you're making it hard for me not to." He dropped down on one knee and lifted her foot. His fingers warm on her ankle, he examined the jagged cut.

After a moment, he pulled his hand away. "Stay!" he ordered.

He turned on his moccasins and followed the trail of his horse, his strides long and confident, his neatly cut hair floating over his broad shoulders. She stared after him until he vanished from sight among the trees. Since his horse had no saddle in which to hold supplies, she assumed he lived in a nearby cabin.

"Oh dear!" She glanced around anxiously. As disturbing as the stranger's presence was, his absence was even more nerve-racking. What if the bandits returned to claim the Wells Fargo treasure box? Suddenly every shadow, every moving leaf seemed fraught with danger. Though the sun was still high in the sky, she shivered.

Her foot hurt, her shoulder ached, and her hands were raw with rope burns. Walking back to town was probably not a good idea. Perhaps she should drive the stage back to the scene of the crime. She'd never driven a stage before, but a woman had to do what a woman had to do.

She was also anxious to see what kind of damage, if any, her camera had sustained. She squeezed her eyes shut. *Please, please, please let it still be anchored safely to the tree.*

Trembling, she hobbled over to the stagecoach and tried to reach the reins beneath the horses.

She picked up a nearby stick and kneeled down, wincing against the pain in her shoulder. One of the horses neighed and stomped its hoof restlessly.

"There, there," she said soothingly. "I'm not going to hurt you."

She had just about reached the reins with the tip of her stick when a nearby rattling noise made her heart nearly stop.

Moving ever so slowly, she turned her head and gasped. A coiled rattler posed within striking distance of her one good foot. A horse nickered and the snake's tongue darted in and out of its mouth.

A bolt of lightning streaked out of nowhere, and the head of the snake dropped to the ground. Her gaze glued to the knife sticking out of the snake, she flinched when a shadow fell over her.

She lifted her lashes and almost lost herself in the velvet brown eyes staring down at her. Pulling her gaze away, she told herself that a man who had saved her life twice was probably not going to do her harm. Even though it was a comforting thought, she trembled, but whether from fear or a delayed reaction from her ordeal, she couldn't say. She refused to think it had anything to do with the unexpected kiss that still seemed to linger between them.

"T-thank you," she stammered.

"My pleasure," he said.

He reached for his knife, lifted the snake up, and examined it. "Handsome critter, don't you think?"

She shuddered.

He shrugged and tossed the snake to the side of the road. Taking her by the hand, he helped her to her feet. The nearness of him overwhelmed her. Something passed between them like a light or a secret message. A wave of warmth rippled through her, followed by a shiver. Shaken, she quickly pulled her hand free and sat on a rock.

He dropped down on one knee in front of her. Lifting her foot ever so gently, he wiped it with a clean square of buckskin, applied a soothing salve, and affixed a piece of gauze over the wound.

"I'm not sure I understand why you were in a tree," he said.

"What?"

"You said you were in a tree when the highwaymen stopped the stage."

"I was looking for the white stallion," she explained.

He drew back in surprise. "In a tree?"

She couldn't resist the opening he gave her. "It was a horse chestnut tree."

He laughed out loud, and she watched him with open curiosity. This couldn't be the wild man that had the town on edge. Still, his clothing, hair, even his black horse matched the description the Trotter boy gave after his encounter.

"I better go," she said.

"You best not walk on that foot."

"I'll drive the stage back." She glanced with uncertainty at the six horses. *Six*.

He frowned. "Have you ever driven a stagecoach before?"

"Not exactly," she admitted. "At least not while holding the reins."

His smile revealed perfect white teeth and her heart did a flip-flop. "If it was just a matter of holding on to the reins, I reckon an infant could drive it."

He was obviously enjoying a joke at her expense. No matter. He wasn't the first man to underestimate her and probably wouldn't be the last. "Just don't stand in my way," she warned.

"Lady, standing in your way while you're in the driver's seat is the last thing I intend to do. But you'd be doing Wells Fargo a favor if you wait till you've calmed down a mite."

She was momentarily tempted to take his advice. Her whole body ached and it was painful to move. What could it hurt to rest for a while before starting back?

Never one to fuss with her appearance, she was suddenly aware of how dreadful she must look. Her hand involuntarily flew to her mussed hair as she cast her gaze downward. Horrified to find her shirtwaist open in front where a button had popped off, exposing her chemise, she quickly clutched at the fabric. Fortunately her heart-shaped locket had not been lost during her ordeal.

She tried to remember the precise words the Trotter boy

had used. *"The wild man almost killed me."* Could he have been exaggerating? She wouldn't put it past him.

"I better go," she said.

"I'll take you back to town."

His offer was tempting but prudence prevented her from accepting it. Her already tarnished reputation would suffer if she were to be seen dressed as she was in torn clothes—in the company of a man.

"That won't be necessary," she said with a determined toss of her head.

He raised a brow but didn't argue. Clutching the front of her shirtwaist with one hand, she allowed him to help her to her feet with the other. His gaze was steady as a camera lens and she felt her cheeks blaze.

Conscious of his touch, she withdrew her hand quickly and started toward the stage on shaky legs.

The full repercussions of the hair-raising ride and brush with death suddenly hit her full force. The sun was warm but still she shivered, her arms covered in gooseflesh. Worse, her head began to spin. Shaking off the dizziness that threatened to overcome her, she stumbled.

He caught her before she hit the ground. She looked up at him with tear-filled eyes and he quickly drew her semi-limp body into his arms. Comforted by the warmth of him, she rested her head upon his chest. His manly scent of leather, woods, and sunshine overwhelmed her senses.

Being in his arms felt so . . . nice. She couldn't remember ever feeling so safe and protected. But it scared her, too, and she panicked.

She pulled away and ran, but her injured foot slowed her progress. He chased after her and grabbed her by her sore arm. The pain caught her by surprise and she slugged him hard. He growled like a bear and released her, hand on his cheek, his eyes leveled beneath dark, knitted brows.

God, forgive her. She had never before raised a hand to anyone, and she hardly knew what to say. What a mess she was: crying, hitting, *kissing*. Where was all this strange behavior coming from? And why was the earth spinning around her?

He held up his hands, palms facing her. "Calm down. I'm not going to hurt you. I'm only trying to help." When she made no reply, he continued, "Sorry, lady, but you don't give me a choice." Without another word, he picked her up and heaved her over his shoulder.

"Let me down." She pounded on his back with clenched fists. He said something but she was yelling too loud to hear. "How dare you! If you don't let me down I'll—"

He lifted her into the stagecoach as if she were weightless and slammed the door shut. Before she had a chance to regain her composure, the stagecoach took off like a flash, sending her flying back against the hard horsehair seat.

More angry at herself for her wanton behavior than she was at him, she stuck her head between the leather curtains, leaned out the window, and yelled at the top of her lungs, "Stop this stage at once!" The least he could do was let her explain her behavior. "Do you hear me? At once!"

He ignored her, and at last she gave up. She sank back into the seat, arms folded across her chest. If he told anyone about her behavior, she would deny it. Better yet, she would plead temporary insanity.

Her mind went back to her camera. If it was damaged, her career as a newspaper photographer might possibly be over before it had even begun.

With this thought came another. The man wasn't really wild. Trotter had obviously lied to impress his friends or get attention. The Rocky Creek residents had lived in fear these last few weeks for no reason—that in itself was a story. All she needed was the stranger's photograph and—oh dear, in all the confusion she hadn't thought to ask his name. Or where he was from. She hadn't asked him anything. What kind of newspaper reporter was she?

Just as suddenly as the stage had started, it stopped. She flew to the window and was surprised and relieved to see the stranded driver and passengers hurrying toward her.

Arranging her clothes as modestly as possible, she opened the door and stepped outside. Her mind was filled with questions as she looked for the stranger but he was nowhere in sight. Momentarily disappointed, she shrugged.

No matter. She failed to get the photograph she'd gone after, but she had something better. Wait until the newspaper editor heard about her encounter with the so-called wild man of Rocky Creek!

David Wolf crouched behind the bushes and watched. He had hoped to keep his arrival in Rocky Creek secret, but that was no longer possible. First he found that boy going through his belongings, now this encounter with Miss Fairbanks. Judging by the way the passengers and stagecoach driver kept looking around, remaining undetected just got that much tougher.

The stagecoach should have been long gone by now, but still it lingered. The crazy talkative woman still hadn't run out of steam and she held the passengers and driver captive with her long tale. Never had he known anyone to talk so much or so fast. Or have sweeter lips.

She had looked so vulnerable, bare toes poking from beneath her hem, hair tousled, lips trembling. Rambling on and on nonstop. If she were a man, a slap on the face might have brought her out of her shock. But a woman . . . he could never strike a woman, not even under those circumstances. Still, he had to do something to bring her out of her alarming state. The kiss succeeded, or at least rendered her speechless.

He could justify his reasons for kissing her. What he

couldn't do was figure out why she had *let* him. Him of all people. *A half-breed.* Unless, of course, she was too frazzled to know what he was doing. It was the only thing that made sense.

"Go!" he muttered impatiently toward the crowd. There was no way he could leave his hiding place without being seen, but it wasn't only his own predicament that worried him. The stage sitting in the middle of the road was at risk. Should the bandits return, the coach wouldn't have a hare's chance in a foxhole of escaping.

And still the woman talked. He couldn't hear her from this distance but he could see her hands moving, could tell from the way the others leaned toward her that she had mesmerized them with her tale every bit as much as she had captivated him.

At long last, the driver ushered everyone inside the stage and took his place on the driver's seat. He drove the stage in the direction of town, presumably to report the attempted holdup to the marshal.

Wolf watched until it was out of sight. What he would give to see the look on the marshal's face when Miss Fairbanks explained her ordeal. The lawman better have a couple of hours to spare.

The thought made him chuckle. Of course, riding into Rocky Creek was a luxury he could ill afford. He'd learned long ago that the best way for him to ride into town, any town, was with a fast horse and a ready gun.

The last time he left Rocky Creek was not of his own accord and almost cost him his life. He wasn't so foolish as to think things had changed. It was imperative that he keep his whereabouts secret until he had accomplished what he had set out to do. The town had taken something from him—and he intended to get it back.

Four

When photographing stampeding cattle, charging bulls, or blazing gunfights, use the fastest shutter speed possible.

— MISS GERTRUDE HASSLEBRINK, 1878

Later that day Lucy sat dead center on the divan, feet together, eyes lowered, and tried for all the world to look appropriately remorseful if not altogether repentant.

Her father, Whitney Fairbanks, stood before her, hands clasped behind his back. A thin man who appeared taller than he actually was, he looked and acted older than his thirty-nine years. His hair was still black except for the white at his temples, and his craggy face reflected years spent as a peddler, traveling from town to town to sell his wares.

His traveling days had ended when Lucy's mother died, leaving him alone to raise her and her brother. He took what little money he had managed to save and opened up Fairbanks General Merchandise—a store he dreamed of one day turning over to Caleb.

Now he stood in front of Lucy with that all-too-familiar look of disappointment she'd come to dread. News traveled fast in Rocky Creek, especially if her name was attached. So it was no surprise that news of her latest escapade had quickly reached her father.

Any concern he might have had for her safety seemed to evaporate as soon as he walked through the door of their small cabin and took in her disheveled appearance.

One look at his stern face told her she was in big trouble this time. Lord help her. She wished she'd had time to change before he saw her.

"Do you realize you could have been killed?"

She flinched at the tone of his voice. "Yes, Papa," she said, holding her bodice together with one hand.

"Or seriously injured?"

"But I wasn't," she said in a rush of words. "I saved the stage from being robbed. You should be happy—"

"Happy? That my only daughter goes from one dangerous situation to the next? Every time I turn around you're in trouble. Last week, you almost got yourself mauled photographin' a bobcat—"

She tightened her hold on the front of her waistcoat. "I know but—"

"And two weeks before that, you plumb near got trampled to death tryin' to photograph a stampede—"

"Yes but—"

"Then you almost got yourself shot by Malone—"

"That wasn't my fault," she protested. "The man was beating his poor wife, and would have gotten away with it had I not taken a photograph and shown it to the marshal."

Her father threw up his hands, looking suddenly tired. "I don't know what to do with you. Your ma . . . she would never forgive me if she knew how I've failed."

"You haven't failed, Papa," she said.

"You're not married," he said, as if that was the sole criteria for judging success or failure as a parent. "You're twenty years old and don't even have a beau."

Her fingers tensed in her lap. Convinced that marriage would cure her wild ways, her father never missed a chance to harp on the subject. "That's not your fault, Papa. I haven't yet found anyone who . . . interests me."

Her thoughts drifted back to the tall dark stranger, and her lips burned with the memory of his kiss. She didn't even know his name or from where he came. Yet she knew the feel of his mouth on hers, the warmth of his arms, and the hard-muscled strength of his body.

"Lucy, are you listening to me? What's wrong with your mouth?"

"What?"

"Your mouth. You're rubbin' it."

"Oh-h." She quickly pulled her fingertips away from her face, but there was nothing she could do about the sudden rush of heat to her cheeks. Why did the memory of the stranger's kiss continue to hold her in its grip? "You were saying?"

"I asked why you don't marry Jim Spencer. He's a good man. He'd take care of you—if you'd let him."

Lucy made a face. She couldn't help it. Spencer was as old as the hills, and had already been married twice, both his wives having died in childbirth.

"Or Richard Crankshaw. He's asked for your hand several times. He's not gonna wait forever."

Lucy shuddered. The way Mr. Crankshaw leered at her gave her the creeps.

She stared at her father in open defiance. "I have plans for my life. Big plans. They do not include marriage."

In a softer voice, she beseeched him to understand. "Papa, I have a job with the newspaper." Or at least the promise of a job. "I thought you would be proud of me. Even Jenny Armstrong has a job." The marshal's wife was about to open a Ladies Emporium on Main Street.

"You know how I feel about you traveling out of state. A woman alone."

She'd talked about traveling to Chicago or New York in

search of a job as a photographer but her father had been so appalled at the idea, she decided against it.

"No, no, Papa. A *local* job. Mr. Barnes said he would hire me if—"

"Barnes!" Her father's face turned ashen. "You're working for that . . . that . . ." He stepped back as if she had assaulted him physically.

She rose, her hand still clutching the front of her waist-coat. "Papa, don't look at me like that. You know how important my photography is to me." More than that, her job could provide a much-needed source of income. Her father's store had seen a drop in business in recent years due, in part, to the increasing popularity of the Montgomery Ward mail-order catalog. A more serious problem was the end of the cattle boom. Few herds traveled through town anymore. Without the constant stream of cattle drovers, her father's profits had plunged.

"There's only one newspaper in town," she said. "What would you have me do?"

"You can do what God meant women to do."

She sighed. It seemed like every conversation with her father lately involved her lack of beaus or marriage prospects. "If I got married, I would have to give up the one thing I most want to do."

He shook his head. "That's not true. You could still take your photographs."

"When would I have time?" she asked. "What wife has time to indulge in her own interests?"

"Your mother found time to paint," he argued.

"But that's only because you were away so much," she countered. "My job at the newspaper requires me to be away from the house. Mama was able to work at home, after Caleb and I had gone to bed."

Her father's eyes clouded over as they tended to do every

time they talked about her mother. "Why can't you be an artist like her?"

He indicated the oil painting of a young woman holding a child that hung over the stone fireplace. One of her mother's earliest works, it wasn't as detailed as her later paintings. Yet her mother's brush had deftly captured the woman's dreams for her child, the hope for a better future.

Like her mother, Lucy felt compelled to capture the world around her and preserve moments in time that would never be repeated. The only difference was their choice of expression.

One of her mother's better paintings was hidden away in the hall cupboard, and her father steadfastly refused to let Lucy hang it. He declined to give an explanation for his refusal and she continued to be mystified. It was, after all, just a landscape. She failed to see why it should affect her father so, except maybe it had something to do with the fact that it had been her mother's last painting.

The look on his face as he stared at her mother's painting filled her with apprehension. She understood the sadness, of course, the heartrending loss of a woman he loved to the depths of his soul, but not the other. Not the emotion that turned his face into granite whenever he gazed at the picture. That came from a part of her father she didn't know, was afraid to know even as she ached to understand it.

"Papa," she said softly, desperate to wipe that look from his face, though it meant having to endure his anger and disappointment in her. Anything was preferable to the dark bleakness.

He drew his gaze away from the painting. The expression she had come to dread disappeared.

"I *am* an artist," she whispered. "Can't you see?" Her father wasn't alone in thinking photography was nothing more than a passing fancy. Few people considered it art and she was accustomed to critical comments, but none hurt as much as her father's disregard for the thing that meant so much to her.

He shook his head and started for the door. "I have to get back to the store."

"Papa!"

He stopped, his back toward her.

"I am an artist!" His failure to acknowledge that part of her felt like he was rejecting the very essence of who she was.

Without a word he walked outside, slamming the door behind him.

After he was gone she reached for the portfolio of her latest photographs. She pulled out a picture of her father.

He stood by the back fence, one foot on the rail, staring across the corral at some distant memory. He hadn't seen her take his photograph, hadn't even known she was there. She traced his profile with her finger. "What is it, Papa? What do you see when you stare like that? What is it that keeps us apart?"

Five

*While posing for a photograph, spinsters should avoid looking
desperate or deprived. A serene smile will show that your
circumstances are by choice and not for lack of beauty or character.*

—MISS GERTRUDE HASSLEBRINK, 1878

News of the stagecoach robbery put the little town of Rocky
Creek in an uproar. By the time Lucy had bathed, changed her
clothes, retrieved her camera and shoes from the tree where
she'd left them, and driven into town to give her statement to
Marshal Armstrong, Main Street was cluttered with wagons,
shays, and buckboards. The line of vehicles extended from the
Grand Hotel at one end of town to the Wells Fargo bank on the
other. A mob of worried citizens bombarded her with questions
as she pushed through the crowd and into the marshal's office.

The crowd was still waiting for her when she emerged more
than two hours later. This time, however, Marshal Armstrong
came to her rescue.

"Miss Fairbanks has had a harrowing experience. For that
reason I ask that you address your questions to me."

Everyone started talking at once. Her brother Caleb sidled
up to her. "Are you all right?" he whispered.

"I'm fine," she said.

"What did Papa say?"

"He said I should get married."

Caleb shook his head and grinned. "Does he really think a husband's gonna keep you out of trouble?"

She grinned back at him. Caleb knew her better than her father did. Better than anyone did, for that matter.

The crowd grew louder and the marshal's patience was spent. "Quiet!" he bellowed. "One at a time."

His command made no impact, but a blast from Timber Joe's rifle did. Dressed in a tattered gray uniform and faded kepi hat, the former Confederate soldier stood on the wooden sidewalk next to the marshal, brandishing his weapon. A tall thin man with a coppery mustache and hair tied at the nape of his neck, he would have commanded attention even without his rifle.

"The marshal has something to say," he shouted.

Though the War Between the States had been over for some seventeen years, Timber Joe still carried on like a full-fledged soldier. This was considered both a curse and a blessing. Some thought he was crazy. Others, including Marshal Armstrong, knew he had a soldier's heart and tolerated his bizarre behavior. No one could deny Timber Joe's ability to control an unruly crowd or convince a reluctant churchgoer to place a generous offering in the plate.

Taking full advantage of the silence that followed, Marshal Armstrong addressed the crowd. He had little tolerance for anyone who broke the law, though some said his recent marriage to Jenny Higgins had made him soft.

"I have already contacted the US Marshal, and I can assure you that the perpetrators will be tracked down and tried in a court of law."

Old Man Appleby yelled out, "I don't care about no perpet'ators, I want to know what you're gonna do about the stage robbers."

Armstrong glanced at Appleby. "If we play our cards right,

we can kill two birds with one stone," he said without irony. "The first thing we need is volunteers for a posse. We have a lot of ground to cover."

Redd Reeder stepped onto the boardwalk. Owner of the Rocky Creek Café, his shock of red hair looked more orange than red next to the ketchup stains on his white apron. Since discovering F&J Heinz's tomato ketchup, he used it with such great abandon that some complained eating at the café was like "eating on a bloody battlefield."

"Marshal, I believe you're going about this all wrong," he said.

Marshal Armstrong pushed his hat back. "How is that, Redd?"

"Times are a-changing. We gotta stop doing things the same old way. Air, that's the wave of the future."

Marshal Armstrong hung his thumbs from his gun belt. "Air?"

"Our very own Eugene Gage is in possession of a gas balloon." Eugene was always causing a ruckus with his wild inventions and modern ideas. Redd held up a sketch of an aerial ship. "From the sky, you'll be able to see for miles. Once you spot those robbers, they won't be able to escape."

Appleby grunted. Apparently he lumped gas balloons in the same category as the telegraph and train, which he considered the start of civilization's downfall.

Marshal Armstrong gave a polite nod. "I appreciate your suggestion, Redd, but I don't aim to lift these boots any higher than it takes to mount my horse." Without further ado, he pointed to every able-bodied man in the crowd. "You, you, and you."

By the time he was done, twenty men had "volunteered," including Redd, Kip Barrel, the town barber, and Lee Wong, who ran the Chinese laundry.

Caleb's mouth drooped when the marshal overlooked

him, and he started forward. Lucy pulled him back. "Oh, no, you don't," she said.

"I want to help," Caleb argued. "They tried to hurt you."

Lucy felt a tug in her heart. Following her mother's death, she had taken care of her father and brother. Not only had she cooked and cleaned for them, she oversaw Caleb's lessons and made him practice his reading and writing every day after school.

Now he suddenly acted all grown-up and wanted to take care of her.

"You can help by staying here," she said gently. "Please, Caleb. Those men are dangerous. Papa and I need you here."

She reached out to him but he pulled back and stalked off.

Lucy watched him disappear inside their father's store. Spotting Jacoby Barnes scurrying away, she promptly forgot about Caleb and followed the newspaper editor back to his office.

Extra, the newspaper's robust marmalade cat, scurried beneath the desk when Lucy entered the small, overstuffed building. The air hung heavy with the smell of ink.

For once Barnes greeted her with a smile. He heaved his bulky body into a chair behind his desk. Rubbing his hands together in eager anticipation, he regarded her through thin-rimmed spectacles.

"What have you got for me, girl?"

"I'm afraid I didn't get a photograph of the white mustang."

He waved her apology away. "Forget the stallion. What about the stage? Where is the photograph of the robbery?"

"Well, I—"

His eyes sharpened. "What? Speak up!"

"I was ready," she explained. "I even had the bandits in my lens."

Barnes leaned forward. "Are you telling me you failed to get a photograph of the holdup?"

"I tried," she said. "But I fell from the tree. I'm lucky to be alive."

His eyebrows rose. "Tree?"

"I was sitting in a tree," she explained. "Fortunately, my camera wasn't damaged and—"

He leaned forward. "A photograph of the holdup would have tripled circulation!" he shouted.

"Yes, yes, it would have," she cried excitedly. At last, he saw the potential.

"Quad-tripled."

Finally, finally, he understood. *Thank you, God.* "Yes!"

Ever since the *New York Daily Graphic* published a photo of Shantytown, Lucy had badgered Barnes to hire her as a photographer. The squatter's camp was the first half-tone photo published in an American newspaper, and it had created quite a stir.

Claiming that photographs were for people too lazy to read, Barnes had fought her all the way. It wasn't until he discovered how the photograph had increased the *Daily Graphic's* circulation that he began to see the light.

"You failed the test," he said.

"But I—"

"You're fired!"

She gasped. "Fired? But I wasn't even hired."

"I told you what would happen if you failed to complete an assignment." His eyes glittered. "No photograph, no job."

Her back ramrod straight, she boldly stood her ground. "Forget the holdup," she said. "Forget the stallion. There're bigger fish to fry."

He pulled back. "Bigger than a holdup?" He shook his head. "There's nothing bigger than that."

"Nothing?" Her lowered voice was no less determined. "What would you say if I told you that I saw the man Trotter said chased him?"

He scoffed. "You failed to get a photograph of the white stallion. You even failed in your attempt to photograph the bandits. Now you're making up stories about the wild man."

"I saw him with my own eyes. Only—"

"Only what?"

"He is *not* wild." Untamed, perhaps, but definitely not wild. *And he kisses like*—she clamped down on her thoughts. "He speaks perfect English and is as normal as you and I."

He shook his head. "Even a parrot speaks English, if it's trained."

"I'm telling you, he's not wild. If we ran his photograph in the newspaper, we could dispel those myths. It's not right for people to have to lock their doors and look over their shoulders. It's time to put the rumors to rest."

Barnes's expression grew hard as granite. "It's not my job to dispel myths or put rumors to rest. It's my job to sell newspapers. A wild man, a *real* wild man will sell newspapers. Dispelling myths will not."

She gritted her teeth in frustration. There was no reasoning with the fool! But reasoning with him was one thing; working for him quite another. And she wasn't about to let her chance for a job, however tenuous, slip through her fingers.

"I'll get your photograph of the white stallion!" she said. "As for the ridiculous wild man rumors, I'll save *that* story for the *Lone Star Tribune*."

She spun around and headed for the door.

"*Miss* Fairbanks!"

She froze, her hand on the doorknob, her back toward him.

"You get me a photograph of this"—he cleared his throat—"*man*, and I'll put it on the front page. That is, if I can figure out the convoluted directions you gave me for printing photographs."

She allowed herself the luxury of a quick smile before turning, face all serious.

"And you'll print the truth about him?" she asked.

He rubbed his chin. "You write the story and I'll print it."

She nodded. "I'll get you your photo," she vowed. *If it's the last thing I do.*

She could barely contain her excitement. She left the office just as the marshal and his motley posse rode out of town.

The marshal's wife, Jenny Armstrong, stood in front of Fairbanks General Merchandise with a frown on her face. As usual, she was perfectly groomed. Her hair was pulled back into a fashionable bun, every shiny blond strand in place, her skirt and waistcoat immaculate.

Lucy glanced down at her own multipatched skirt. Each colorful square hid a hole or rip garnered during a photographic opportunity too good to pass up, even though it meant running through nettle or climbing over fences.

If Jenny noticed the sorrowful condition of Lucy's skirt, she gave no indication. Instead, she greeted Lucy with a worried look. "I heard about your terrible ordeal. Are you all right?"

"I'm fine," Lucy said. Except for a few bruises and a sore shoulder, she was none the worse for wear.

Jenny sighed. "I'm still not used to being married to a marshal. I worry every time he takes off after another outlaw."

Appleby shifted in the rocking chair parked in front of the general store where he spent most of his time and discounted her concern with a well-aimed stream of tobacco juice. "You needn't worry about the marshal. No one can outdraw him"— he shrugged—"except maybe Masie Parsons showin' off her grandbaby's phota-graph."

It was hard to tell by Jenny's demeanor whether Appleby calmed her fears.

Staring at the cloud of dust in the posse's wake, Lucy didn't hold much hope they'd meet with success. The marshal was more than competent, of course, but the gang he'd hastily put together left much to be desired. She kept her thoughts to herself, but if she were a betting woman, she'd place her money on the highwaymen.

The next day was the grand opening of Jenny Armstrong's new store and Lucy had agreed to photograph the event. Though she'd been in Rocky Creek for less than a year, the marshal's wife had done much to improve the town's cultural life. Her husband, however, put his foot down when she suggested converting one of the jail cells into a lending library.

Jenny's Ladies Emporium was already packed with curious onlookers by the time Lucy lugged her equipment through the narrow aisles. She was amazed what Jenny had done to the place. When the owner of The Gold Coin saloon had closed its doors and retired after his wife joined the Woman's Christian Temperance Union, Jenny got to work. She approached Lee Wong and talked him into taking over one half of the building for his laundry while she took over the other half. It was hard to believe that a very short time ago this was one of Rocky Creek's wildest saloons.

Lucy set her tripod and camera on a counter and looked around. Never had she seen such finery except among the pages of *Harper's Bazar*.

Several members of the Rocky Creek Quilting Bee stood in a circle oohing and ahhing at the display of silk camisoles, drawers, corsets, and petticoats.

The preacher's wife suddenly laughed out loud. Never one to follow conventional fashion, Sarah Wells wore a plain blue dress, old red boots, and a black felt hat. Though the current style called for hair to be pinned back with fringe bangs,

Sarah's bright red hair fell down her back in blatant disregard for fashion and propriety.

"There ain't no end to what a woman can stuff under her skirts, is there?" Sarah asked, shaking her head. Out of respect for her preacher husband, Sarah tried to watch her grammar, but sometimes her tongue raced ahead of her good intentions.

"Oh, look at this," Emma Hogg squealed. The usually conservatively dressed spinster pranced in front of the others wearing an outlandish hat and twirling a lace parasol. The other ladies giggled like schoolgirls.

"All you need are these," Jenny's sister Mary Lou called out. She tossed a package over the heads of the others and into Emma's outstretched hand.

It was a package of Zephyr bosom enhancers. Emma blushed and the others roared with laughter.

"That will make Redd notice you," Mary Lou said. Everyone in town knew that Emma had her sights set on Redd Reeder, the owner of the Rocky Creek Café.

Frowning at her younger sister, Jenny took the offending package away from Emma and hid it behind the counter. "Mary Lou, I swear, you'll be the death of me yet."

Lucy laughed. Not even marriage to that handsome mill worker had cured Mary Lou of her scandalous conduct. Nor had her "delicate" condition curbed her preference for low necklines.

Conversation soon turned to the attempted stagecoach robbery.

"Oh, do tell us all about it," Mrs. Hitchcock pleaded, the feathers on her tall hat bopping up and down. "Do tell, do tell." The woman had the annoying habit of repeating herself.

Not wanting to put a damper on Jenny's opening day, Lucy told them about the robbery as quickly as she could, leaving out the part about the rumored wild man.

She was relieved when Jenny clapped her hands, drawing everyone's attention away from the robbery. "Ladies, ladies. I want to welcome you all to my new shop. As you can see, I have the latest fashionable accessories." She held up a pair of silk drawers. "Enjoy your freedom while you can, as I have it on the best authority that bustles are coming back."

A collective groan followed her announcement.

While Jenny pointed out the wide selection of ladies' undergarments and accessories, Lucy set up her camera.

Sarah Wells sidled up to her. She had caused quite a bit of controversy a few years back when she married the pastor of the Rocky Creek Church. She still made tongues wag on a regular basis with her unorthodox behavior, but Lucy liked her and considered her a friend.

"Sounds like you gave those outlaws more trouble than a rattler in a bedroll," Sarah said in a hushed voice.

Lucy smiled. "They gave me a bit of trouble too," she admitted. She'd hardly slept a wink since her ordeal two days ago.

Sarah's expression grew still and Lucy could guess what was on her mind.

Sarah's three brothers were known as the Prescott Gang. Two brothers had gone straight and one brother had even managed to pay back most of the money stolen over the years, but Sarah hadn't heard from her oldest brother George. Having no knowledge of his whereabouts, Sarah worried that he might have resumed his outlaw ways.

"Did . . . did you get a good look at them?" Sarah asked.

"There were three of them," Lucy said. "They had kerchiefs over their faces." She hoped that would be the end of the conversation but Sarah showed no sign of relenting.

"How tall were they?"

"Tall?" Lucy's mind raced. If Sarah knew that at least two of the robbers were tall enough to be George Prescott as described on his wanted posters, it would only worry her.

"Uh, I don't think any of them were more than . . . short." *God, forgive me.* It wasn't exactly a lie. Next to the wild man, the outlaws could be described as downright, "Scrawny."

Sarah blinked. "Scrawny?" She closed her eyes with a sigh. "Praise the Lord."

Lucy patted her on the arm. "You don't think your brother George is still robbing stages, do you?"

"I don't know. I don't think he can change without God's help, and he can be stubborn as a cross-eyed mule." Sarah's worried expression turned to anger. "George ain't one to ask for help unless someone's pointin' a gun at him."

"I'm sure God can arrange that," Lucy said.

Her comment brought a smile to Sarah's face. "Now you sound like my husband." She lowered her voice. "Though not nearly as long-winded." She gave an unladylike wink. Reverend Wells tended to get carried away with some of his sermons.

"I know someone who may disagree with you," Lucy said, wishing she knew the stranger's name. Why, oh why hadn't she thought to ask him?

"Lucy, we're ready for our picture," Jenny called from the back of the shop.

"I'm ready too," Lucy replied, though she had no idea how she would fit everyone into a single photograph.

Sarah hung back. "It don't much matter if it's a camera or a gun. I'm not much for standin' still when someone's shootin' at me."

"I promise you, I'll make it as painless as possible." Lucy squeezed Sarah's arm. "I'll also keep praying that your brother finds the Lord."

Sarah squeezed her hand back and then hurried to pose with the others.

Lucy peered through the viewfinder. The light was poor, giving her no choice but to use her magnesium flashlamp. She wasn't fond of using it in such close quarters as it could cause a fire. "Step back," she called, and the wall of bodies moved back en masse. "Move closer together . . . that's better." Except that Mrs. Hitchcock's hat hid half of the women's faces.

"Mrs. Hitchcock, I need you to switch with Brenda."

She waited while the two women traded places. Now everyone was in the picture, which might not be a good thing. Half the women looked as if they were sitting on a cactus and the other half, a deathbed.

"Relax," Lucy called. "That's the only way a camera will do you justice."

Mrs. Taylor sniffed. "I don't want the camera to do me justice. I want it to show mercy."

Mrs. Hitchcock tittered, which made her hat flop down over her brow.

Lucy waited patiently while Mrs. Hitchcock adjusted her hat. By that time, most of their smiles had turned into frowns.

"Say Rocky Creek backward," Lucy said.

"Yocr Keerk," Mrs. Taylor said

Mrs. Hitchcock made a sound of disgust. "That's not how you say it. The creek part has to come first or it's not backward." She then gave her interpretation, which immediately brought a clamor of disapproval from the others.

"You both have it wrong," Miss Hogg announced. "It's Keekykrock."

"No, no, no," Jenny's sister Brenda said. "It's not that at all. It's . . ."

While the women argued among themselves, they completely forgot the camera. Lucy fired the magnesium powder, producing a bright flash of light and much smoke and ash, but she got her photograph. Not a great one by any means, but it would have to do.

No sooner had Lucy declared success than Mrs. Hitchcock knocked against a shelf on the back wall. Boxes filled with hats, gloves, and all manner of female unmentionables toppled to the floor. A mad scramble was accompanied by squeals of laughter, but somehow amid the confusion Emma Hogg ended up sprawled facedown on the floor.

Jenny screeched in horror. "Miss Hogg!"

At the sound of her name, Emma Hogg looked up from beneath a satin chemise and giggled. Turning her head this way and that as if posing for *Harper's Bazar*, the usually staid spinster showed a side of her personality Lucy had never before witnessed. Emma's usual pale skin was flushed a pretty rosy color and her eyes sparkled. Everyone laughed and clapped.

Smiling, Lucy quickly inserted a new plate into her camera, fired her flashlamp, and snapped a photograph of Miss Hogg's beaming face. For a moment no one could see for all the smoke.

Then Mrs. Hitchcock suddenly pointed her finger and screamed, "Fire, fire, pants on fire!"

All heads swiveled toward a display of undergarments that had burst into flames.

Six

Allow yourself to be photographed with politicians, lawyers, or other scoundrels only under threat of death or other dire emergencies.

—MISS GERTRUDE HASSLEBRINK, 1878

Fortunately the women were able to put out the flames before too much damage was done, but Lucy felt terrible. She should never have used her flashlamp in such close quarters.

"I'll pay for the damage," she said.

"Don't be ridiculous," Jenny replied, sweeping up the ashes.

Mary Lou held up a pair of charred bloomers. "Just think. You're probably the only shop owner who held a fire sale on opening day."

After all the excitement had died down, Lucy gathered up her equipment and left.

Outside she spotted Doc Myers's horse and buggy parked in front of Barrel's barbershop. She carefully placed her camera equipment in the back of her wagon. Then, sidestepping a puddle left by the street sprinkler, she walked past the horses tied to a hitching post. Now was as good a time as any to speak to him about her brother. Maybe that would make up to Caleb for dissuading him from joining the posse.

Lucy liked the doctor, but she was sorely tempted to

take him by the shoulders and shake him. Her friend Monica had carried a torch for Doc Myers for as long as Lucy could remember, but nothing had ever come of it. As far as she knew, the good doctor didn't even know Monica existed. The man was clearly a fool. Years earlier his wife had left him, taking their two children with her. No one knew why she left the kindhearted doctor, though there was speculation about her running off with a tinware peddler.

Over time, the doctor had become a mere shadow of a man. He took care of his patients but otherwise kept to himself. Living alone in a two-story house outside of town, he made his rounds by day and ventured out in the thick of night on occasion to deliver a baby or tend to a medical emergency. He never attended worship, never so much as stepped foot inside the church as far as Lucy knew, though Reverend Justin Wells did everything possible to persuade him to attend.

Why couldn't the doctor forget his long lost love? Monica, the schoolteacher, had so much to offer him.

Lucy pushed her thoughts away. The doctor's personal affairs were none of her business. If he wanted to pine over his deserting wife, nothing could be done about it.

Now the doctor walked out of the barbershop wearing tweed trousers with a matching waistcoat and smelling of soap. His hair was brown but his muttonchop sideburns were flecked with gray.

He looked surprised to see her and she could easily guess why. Bad blood flowed between her father and the doctor for as long as she could remember. Some old-timers insisted they had been childhood friends, but no one could tell her what happened to turn them into enemies. She doubted if anyone even knew.

Rocky Creek was an odd town. At times Lucy felt stifled. She couldn't sneeze without being the topic of conversation. Still, no amount of gossip or lighthearted chatter could dispel the shadows that lurked beneath the surface, or the secrets that whispered from the past.

Now the doctor greeted her with a wary smile and tip of his bowler. "Miss Fairbanks." Though he'd known her all her life, he never called her by her first name. He nodded his head toward Jenny's store.

"It looks like opening day is a success," he said.

She nodded. "It is, indeed." She never thought to see the day Rocky Creek would have a store that specialized solely in women's apparel. Thank God they were able to contain the fire before it did too much damage.

He regarded her with a thoughtful frown. His eye had been injured in a carriage accident in his youth. As a result, one iris was blue, the other brown, giving him a striking appearance that made strangers stare.

"I heard about your latest . . . escapade. You were lucky to escape." He studied her in a way that only a doctor could. "Are you all right? You look pale."

"I'm fine," she said, though she was still shaken by the fire. Obviously he thought she sought him out because of a medical problem. "I bruised my shoulder and have a cut on my foot, but otherwise I'm none the worse for wear."

"I'd be happy to look at your shoulder and foot."

"That won't be necessary," she said. She glanced around anxiously. Her father would have a fit if he saw her talking to the doctor.

"Are you sure?" Doc Myers persisted. "It wouldn't be unusual to have . . . *problems* after your shocking experience. You might notice symptoms like the ones some soldiers suffered upon their return from the war."

That got her attention. The last thing she wanted was to start acting like Timber Joe.

"W-what . . . what kind of symptoms?" she stammered. Maybe the doctor could explain why she couldn't stop thinking about her odd encounter with a certain handsome stranger.

"Sleep disturbances. That sort of thing."

"I hardly slept last night," she admitted. How could she? Each time she closed her eyes, she relived the nightmare. The robbery. The runaway stage. The gunmen shooting at her. But it was the memory of a stranger's lips that commanded the most attention. She finally spent the night pacing the floor and trying to rationalize her own scandalous behavior.

"What other problems might such a shock cause?" she asked.

He thought for a moment. "Hallucinations. A person might start seeing things that are not really there."

She frowned. Could she have imagined the stranger? She hadn't even considered that possibility. She bit her lip. The doctor looked at her with such concern she forced a smile to relieve his mind.

"I'm sure that after a day or two I'll be my old self again."

"Yes, yes, of course. But if you still have trouble sleeping, let me know."

He yawned. It was just the opening she hoped for. "It looks like I'm not the only one who had a bad night."

He rolled his eyes. "Old Mrs. Brubaker is dying again."

Lucy laughed. Mrs. Brubaker had more ailments than was recognized by the American Medical Association and gathered family and friends for deathbed vigils with the same regularity as other women held teas or hosted quilting bees.

Lucy braced herself with a deep breath. "Perhaps it would help if you had an assistant," she said, weighing his reaction. She didn't want to be brash, but she promised Caleb she'd talk to the doctor and she so seldom saw him alone.

Doc Myers' brow furrowed. "An assistant?"

Lucy nodded. "It's not right for one man to work so many hours."

He drew back and studied her. "Why do I get the feeling

there's more to this than simple concern for my working hours?"

"Caleb asked me to talk to you," Lucy confessed. "He wants to be a doctor."

"Really?" He pursed his lips. "I thought his father was grooming him to take over the business."

"Caleb hates working at the store."

He tilted his head. "Your pa know that?"

"Not yet," she said. "But he will." *God help us.*

Doc Myers shook his head. "He won't like it."

Ignoring the doctor's concern, she persisted, "Caleb would make a good doctor. I know he would. He's always bringing injured animals home and taking care of them. He sent away for a brochure from one of those medical schools. One of the preliminary requirements is to read medicine with a doctor."

"Reading medicine" was a fancy term for a doctor in training. Normally a doctor would jump at the chance at having an eager young man serve as nurse, janitor, secretary, and all-around handyman. Still, Doc Myers hesitated.

"I don't want any trouble with your pa."

"There won't be," she said, hoping she spoke the truth. "As long as Caleb continues to work at the store, I don't think Papa will mind what he does in his spare time."

Doc Myers wiped a hand over his newly shaved chin, his initial reluctance seeming to dissipate. "We could probably work something out. Maybe I could put him in charge of Mrs. Brubaker's imaginary illnesses." He winked and Lucy laughed. "Have him come and see me."

"Thank you," she said, resisting the urge to throw her arms around him. *Wait till Caleb hears this!*

It rained for the next two days solid. It was a regular gully washer that turned the roads into rivers of mud.

Lucy paced the floor, anxious for the skies to clear and the warm spring weather of the last couple of weeks to return. She could hardly wait to get started on her newspaper assignment. At long last! A real job. Now if only the rain would stop.

On the third day she got her wish. Waking to find sunlight streaming through her window, she leaped out of bed with a whoop and a holler.

She waited for her father and brother to leave for work before hauling her camera and equipment out to the wagon. Lord help her if Papa knew what she was up to this time. He would surely lock her up.

A photograph of hers on the front page of the *Rocky Creek Gazette*! The very thought sent a thrill down her spine. At long last, her dream of seeing her photographs in print was close to reality. But it wasn't only for professional reasons that she was determined to track down the stranger. She wanted to make certain that the man did indeed exist and hadn't been a figment of her imagination—or what Doc Myers called a hallucination.

If he *was* real, she needed to prove that kissing a stranger was not due to a lack of morality on her part but simply a result of her brush with death. Now that she'd had time to recover from her ordeal, she fully expected that the next time she came face-to-face with him the feel of his lips on hers would be the furthest thing from her mind.

As for Papa . . .

She hated having to go behind his back, but she was certain—more than certain—that he would never understand this compulsion of hers to track the man down.

She recalled with a sigh the frustrated look on her father's face as he ranted at her, and his discouraged look later that same night as he sat in a chair staring at something only he could see.

She didn't doubt for a moment that he wanted what was best for her, but he didn't understand her passion for photography. Whenever he saw her lugging her camera or spending time in the old shed out back—which with Caleb's help she'd turned into a darkroom—he shook his head.

"You shouldn't be working around dangerous chemicals," he'd say. Darkroom explosions were unfortunately common and he never failed to point out any he read about in the news-paper. "Why can't you take up painting, like your mother?" he'd ask time and time again.

She had tried watercolors, had even dabbled in oils, but the truth was painting held no interest for her. She loved the challenge of taking photographs and preserving for posterity a telling look, a certain move, a fleeting moment of time that might never again be repeated.

Her father didn't understand moments in time; he only understood time that could be measured in hours or days. Nor would he understand her need to capture a photograph of a man she barely knew.

Somehow she would have to find a way to make up for all the trouble and worry she'd caused him. Perhaps marrying Mr. Spencer or Mr. Crankshaw wouldn't be as bad as all that.

She grimaced at the thought. What was she thinking? She loved her father dearly, but there had to be a better way to appease him than to marry a man she didn't even like.

Sighing, she looked over her supplies. Wet plates or dry? Wet plates were considerably cheaper and the glass base could be cleaned and coated and used many times over.

Dry plates saved her the hassle of having to pack bottles of negative bath and vials of ammonia, acid, mercury, and alcohol. They also saved her the trouble of coating glass plates with collodion made from explosive guncotton. Dry plates also required less exposure time than did wet plates. After much consideration, she decided to go with the dry plates, despite the additional cost.

The last thing she wedged into the back of the wagon next

to her photo equipment was a basket with cheese, a loaf of bread, and a flask of lemonade.

Heady with anticipation, she harnessed her horse, Tripod, and hitched him to the wagon. Moments later she was on her way.

The road was muddy, which meant she had to drive around large puddles of water, but the warming rays of sun cheered her as did the clear blue sky.

With a little luck, she'd have a photograph of the intriguing stranger by the end of the day, and maybe even some answers to her questions. She felt confident that everything would go according to plan.

Just don't let him kiss me again!

Seven

*Children should be seen—but not necessarily by the camera's eye.
Only children with the mildest dispositions should even be allowed
to enter a studio lest their rowdy antics drive the poor
photographer to distraction.*

—Miss Gertrude Hasslebrink, 1878

Lucy scanned every tree, every bush, every shadow, but nothing stirred. Only the steady rush of the swollen muddy river broke the silence. Still, she couldn't shake the feeling that she wasn't alone, that someone or something watched from the distance. *Please don't let it be the three outlaws.* She glanced around. Was she imagining it? Hallucinating? What?

Pushing her nervousness away, she shifted the satchel holding her camera into the other hand and followed the river upstream. So far, she had no luck. She found the ashes of a campfire but nothing more, and there was no way of knowing if it was his.

Red mud covered her shoes and splattered the hem of her skirt, but still she continued her search. The air hung heavy with the smell of damp earth and wet vegetation. She followed a trail through the woods that led her to a small clearing overlooking the river. Across the way, newly cut trees slithered down a metal chute into the churning water, and started downstream toward the lumber mill.

She set her camera down on a tree stump and lowered herself onto a fallen log to rest. She'd been to this particular spot often, but this time she noticed something that had previously escaped her.

The bend of the river and the boulder shaped like the head of an eagle were identical to one of her mother's paintings. Not the ones displayed on the walls of their cabin, but the painting hidden in the back of the cupboard—the one her father refused to let her hang. The bushes were taller now than when her mother had painted the scene, which is why Lucy had not previously recognized the spot.

Shaken by the discovery, she tried to imagine her mother sitting in this very spot, working her brushes across the canvas, dabbling the yellow and gold on the leaves, the red soil, and the purple hue of distant shadows.

Unbelievable sadness seemed to emanate from the very soil at her feet. It wasn't new, this feeling. Whenever she would sneak a look at her mother's last painting, she felt the same oppressive gloominess. She blamed it on not being allowed to hang the painting on the wall. Maybe it wasn't that at all. Maybe it was something in the painting itself. What was her mother thinking when she painted it? And why was her father so adamant against hanging it?

She set her camera on the exact spot she imagined her mother must have sat. Trees had grown through the years, brush had thickened, the water was higher from the recent rains, but the outline of the rock was the same. She adjusted the lens until the granite eagle was exactly where it was in her mother's painting.

Forgetting her original purpose for coming here, she took photograph after photograph, hoping by some miracle to shed light on the mysteries of her mother's painting.

What were you thinking, Mama, when you sat here? Talk to me.

She sighed. Not only was her life one big question mark, it seemed destined to stay that way.

Much to her dismay she realized she had used up all her plates. Her plan to capture a photograph of the intriguing stranger would have to wait.

She gathered up her camera and lugged it all the way back to her horse and wagon. Tripod whickered and greeted her with a nod of his head. Stroking the gelding's slick brown neck, she sighed. With one simple photograph she could have put the persistent and often frightening rumors of a wild man to rest once and for all.

Since she had set her sights on publishing her photographs in the *Rocky Creek Gazette*, her work had been marked by one failure after another. *God, why are you making it so difficult for me?*

It was the last day of the year for the children's Bible class, and Lucy had agreed to take a photograph of Monica Freeman's pupils. Photographing a stampede of angry cattle couldn't have been any harder.

She barely saved her camera from the flailing arms of ten-year-old Jefferson Parker when little Timothy Hawk plowed into her. Never in all her born days did she imagine that photographing a group of children could be so difficult. She had used close to half a dozen negatives plates trying to capture a decent photograph, with no success.

Though the students got a liberal amount of reading, writing, and arithmetic with their Bible lessons, no one dared call it a school. The Texas constitution required that a separate building be provided for colored children, and Reverend Wells stubbornly refused to comply. He insisted that separating pupils based on the color of their skin went against God's will. Since no such law governed churches, Rocky Creek was able to educate its young beneath a single roof.

Monica reached out to grab a wayward student by the collar, but the boy escaped. "Johnny Trotter, if you don't get up here right now, I'll have a talk with your pa."

Twelve-year-old Johnny made a face, but he scampered back up the steps of the church, which doubled as the school, and took his place next to a boy named Arnold, who immediately punched him. Johnny pulled his arm back to return the favor, but Monica caught him by the elbow and moved him next to a tall girl with long blond ringlets and fringe bangs.

"Don't you dare move," Monica said, her finger practically in Johnny's freckled face.

She then flitted from child to child, straightening collars, arranging hair, and giving stern warnings. "Put your tongue in, Skip," she said. "Jennifer, do hold still. And Willie, don't you dare cross your eyes."

Watching her friend, Lucy couldn't help but smile. When the former teacher, Miss Molly Freemyer, was offered a teaching position in Houston with better facilities and higher pay, Monica was asked to take her place. She almost turned it down, thinking she wasn't qualified, but it was hard to think of anyone who could do a better job.

Now she took her place next to Scooter Maxwell, the tallest boy in the class, and faced the camera. "We're ready."

Lucy ducked beneath the black cloth. For no good reason, she imagined she saw the stranger through the lens, and all at once she remembered the feel of his arms around her.

"What's taking so long?" the boy named Skip whined.

Shaking herself free of the invisible hold the stranger seemed to have on her thoughts, Lucy forced herself to concentrate on the task at hand. "Ready!" she called.

She squeezed the black rubber bulb and captured the image of Monica and all fifteen freshly scrubbed students, including

Skip, who'd waited until the last possible moment to stick out his tongue.

Sighing, she pulled her head out from under the cloth. Since she'd used all but one of the dry plates allotted to the task, Skip and his tongue would have to do.

"All done," she said, and the children, who ranged in age from five to fourteen, let out cries of relief.

Skip Owen made a beeline for the camera. "Can I try it?" he asked. "Can I take a photograph?"

"May I," his teacher corrected. "*May* I take a photograph?"

Ignoring Monica, Skip reached for the camera. Lucy stayed him with a hand to his wrist. At nine years old, he was a handsome lad. His rounded blue eyes peered at her from a freckled face with an innocent look that made it that much more difficult to say no to him.

The Owen family, which consisted of the widow Owen and her three sons, had fallen on hard times since the death of Marshal Owen. Mrs. Owen tutored and took in mending to support her family the best she could, but the boys gave her fits. Fortunately Pastor Wells, fulfilling his promise to Marshal Owen to watch over his family, provided moral guidance and male influence that the boys desperately needed.

"Pleee-ase," Skip begged.

"We've talked about this before," Lucy said.

"Ah, come on. You said you'd let me take a photograph when I got older. I'm older now."

He was in fact seven days older than when they last spoke. "When I said older, I meant years, not days."

He might have continued to plead with her had his teacher not prodded him to get his belongings.

Chaos followed as Monica's pupils ran into the church to grab books bound together with leather straps. Pounding feet rattled the windows. The dilapidated walls of the church seemed to breathe a sigh of relief when at last the children lined up to say good-bye to their teacher.

While Monica was busy with her other students, Lucy took the occasion to question Johnny Trotter. "Could you tell me about the man who chased you?" she asked.

Johnny's eyes grew round from beneath a fringe of straw-like hair. He'd shot up at least six inches in the last few months and could almost look her straight in the eye. He was all arms and legs and moved as awkwardly as a newborn colt.

He scrunched up his face as if trying to recall an image of the man. "He was dressed in buckskin, like a mountain man." His voice cracked and dropped an octave lower as if it couldn't make up its mind if it wanted to be tenor or bass. "And he rode a black horse."

Johnny's physical description fit the man who saved her from the highwaymen. "Did he say anything?"

Johnny shook his head. "He can't talk."

She narrowed her eyes. "How do you know that?"

"Men who were raised with bears or wolves or other wild animals can't talk," he said, obviously an authority on the subject. "Everyone knows that."

She folded her arms across her chest. "And what makes you think he was raised with animals?"

He shrugged his shoulders. "I just know."

She leaned closer. "Johnny, do you understand that making up stories and spreading rumors about others is wrong? Some people are afraid to leave their homes since you started the wild man rumor."

Johnny lowered his eyes. "I didn't mean no harm. I was just looking at his things, but he chased me away. The other boys saw me runnin' away and I didn't want no one to think I was chicken."

"So you made up the whole story? About a wild man?" Lucy asked.

"I was just lookin' at his things. I wasn't gonna take anythin', honest."

"But you did take something away from him, Johnny, when you made up a story that wasn't true."

"It was kinda true," Johnny argued. "He did chase me and he looked really angry." One of the other pupils called to him and he took off without saying good-bye to his teacher.

Lucy watched him until he was out of sight. She should probably talk to his father but she doubted it would do much good. Brad Trotter had his hands full with his invalid wife.

"How come everything's upside down?" a child's voice rang out behind her.

Lucy glanced over her shoulder. Skip stood behind the camera, the black cloth bopping up and down. The tripod swayed and she dived forward to keep it from toppling over.

"Skip Owen," Monica said firmly, arms crossed. Skip peered up from beneath the cloth at his disapproving teacher and took off running.

With a weary wave of her hand, Monica slumped against the door frame. "That boy will be the death of me yet." She shook her head. "Your patience behind a camera never fails to amaze me."

Monica wasn't the only one to express that particular sentiment. Restless by nature, Lucy confounded those who knew her by her ability to wait sometimes for hours to capture a picture of a baby chick emerging from its egg, a young butterfly unfolding its wings, or, in this case, a bunch of restless pupils.

"I like photographing children," Lucy said, though she much preferred photographing them individually.

Monica shook her head as if she couldn't imagine anyone liking such a job. "I have a daguerreotype of my parents as children and they were standing perfectly still. That was when you were required to pose for lengthy periods of time. Do you suppose children were calmer back then?"

Lucy shook her head. "Not calmer—drugged."

Monica's eyes widened in alarm. "What?"

"Children were often given laudanum to keep them still while they were being photographed. *Punch Magazine* even suggested that photographers give children chloroform. Can you imagine?"

"That's . . . that's terrible!" Monica exclaimed.

The shocked look on her friend's face made Lucy smile.

"The town is lucky to have you as a teacher." Lucy felt equally lucky to have her as a friend. Monica's mother died the same year Lucy lost hers. Though Monica was four years older than Lucy, their shared losses brought them together, and they had been close ever since.

Lucy stepped behind her camera and refocused her lens. "Look this way."

"What?"

"I want to take your photograph."

"Whatever for?"

"Practice," Lucy said.

"You don't need practice." Monica eyed her with suspicion. "You're up to something. I can tell. You've been hopping around like you found the mother lode ever since you got here."

"I told you, I'm working for the newspaper," Lucy said, omitting the fact that her job depended on her producing a certain photograph.

Monica looked unconvinced but changed the subject. "Oh, Lucy, I still can't believe how you survived your ordeal."

Monica had arrived on Lucy's doorstep the moment she'd heard about the holdup and demanded to know all the details. Lucy was happy to provide them, except the details of a certain kiss that she kept to herself. Though she told both Marshal Armstrong and Monica that a stranger had saved her from the outlaws, she was purposely vague on the details. She decided to keep it that way, at least until she had a chance to dispel the ridiculous wild man rumors.

"To think that you escaped three outlaws—it's incredible. About the man who saved you . . ."

Lucy quickly ducked behind the camera and yanked the dark fabric over her head before Monica had a chance to question her further. "Hold it," she sang out, focusing her lens on her friend. Monica was dressed in a simple gray skirt and plain white shirtwaist that emphasized her tiny waist. The sun was low in the sky, and the golden red rays softened the sharp angles of Monica's face. Her hair was parted in the middle and pulled back. A few strands of brown hair escaped from her severe bun, blurring the sharp lines of her jawbone. But her forehead was creased and she looked tense and self-conscious.

"Think of someone special," Lucy called.

"What?"

"Someone special. You know. Someone you really care about. What you're thinking will show in your face. Come on, now. Think."

All at once a beautiful, wistful expression spread across Monica's face, erasing the lines of fatigue from around her eyes and mouth. It didn't take a mind reader to know that Doc Myers was responsible for the miraculous transformation.

"Perfect," Lucy called, squeezing the bulb. She had plans for the photograph, big plans. If this photograph didn't cause that stubborn old fool of a doctor's blood to stir, then nothing would!

Anxious to get to her darkroom, she quickly disassembled her equipment, humming to herself. Her plan to bring Doc Myers and Monica together was partly responsible for her high spirits, but no more so than another plan—a more daring plan.

If all went well, she would soon capture the image of the bold yet intriguing stranger.

The next day Lucy drove her brother to Doc Myers's house, the photo of Monica tucked into her satchel. Next to her, Caleb stared at the road ahead. She had never seen him so nervous.

"For goodness' sake, Caleb. You look like you're going to the gallows."

Caleb blew out his breath as if he'd been holding it. "Do you think Doc Myers will agree to be my preceptor?"

"He'd be a fool not to," she said and meant it. Caleb had been interested in medicine for as long as she could remember. When he wasn't working at their Pa's shop, he had his nose in a medical book.

She glanced at him. "What did Papa say?"

"I haven't told him yet."

She grimaced. "Oh, Caleb. You're going to have to tell him sooner or later."

Caleb gave her a beseeching look. "Maybe you can talk to him."

"No." She was tempted to turn the wagon around and head back to town.

"Come on, Sis. Please."

She sighed. She never could deny her brother anything when he looked at her with those puppy-dog eyes of his. "We'll talk about this later," she said, pulling up in front of the doctor's picket fence.

Doc Myers opened the door at their knock. "Come in, come in," he said warmly.

He led them into a small cluttered parlor. The chairs and divan were stacked high with books, so they had no choice but to stand. Lucy hadn't stepped foot in the doctor's house since before her mother's death.

The doctor looked Caleb up and down as if measuring him for a suit.

"You look just like your pa when he was your age."

Lucy studied the doctor's face. What was behind that dark look? Pain? Regret?

"You and Papa used to be good friends." Sensing she was treading on sensitive ground, her voice ended on a tentative note.

The doctor's reply was as quick as it was brusque. "That was a long time ago." He changed the subject, directing his full attention on Caleb. "Your sister tells me you want to be a doctor."

"Yes, sir," Caleb said eagerly.

"It's a lot of hard work with very little pay."

"I know that, sir."

Doc Myers's eyebrows rose. "Do you now?" Arms folded across his chest, he studied Caleb with the same intensity he gave his patients. "It means sleepless nights and tramping through the countryside in the heat of summer and cold of winter."

"Yes, sir."

The doctor continued, "It means inconsiderate people calling you out of your warm bed because of a splinter or some other minor inconvenience."

"I'm aware of that, sir."

"Hmm."

"I know how to treat wounds," Caleb said, anxious to impress. "I fixed my mule's leg wound. I also know that carbolic acid prevents infection and asepsis prevents mortality."

"I'm sure my patients will be delighted to know that at long last we found a way to *cure* death," Doc Myers said with warm humor.

Mistaking the doctor's gentle ribbing for approval, Caleb continued. "I also know that the treatment for melancholia is rose-colored spectacles." He should have stopped while he was ahead. Now the doctor laughed and Caleb looked mortified.

"Mrs. Green has been wearing rose-colored spectacles

for fifteen years and she's not only depressed, she's downright morbid." Myers thought for a moment. "Why do you want to be a doctor?"

Caleb hesitated and Lucy gave him a nod of encouragement. "I want to care for the sick," he said.

Doc Myers stabbed the air with his index finger. "Ah. You didn't say cure, you said care. You've done your research. Only quacks claim to cure."

"Papa says that all doctors are quacks," Caleb said.

"Not all, son. Just the handsome ones. That leaves me out." Myers chortled before growing serious again. "God cures, but we get the credit. Don't you forget that."

"I won't."

The doctor indicated a large cabinet. "It also helps to have a place to hide your mistakes," he said with a note of humor.

Caleb's eyes grew round but Lucy laughed.

"That's what I like about photography," she said. "If I make a mistake I just call it art."

"Ah, you see?" Doc Myers said. "Every profession has its secrets."

His referring to photography as a profession was gratifying. Her father considered it nothing more than a waste of time. Lucy always liked the doctor but never more so than at that moment.

The doctor grabbed a hefty book from a chair. "You can start by reading *Gray's Anatomy*." He shoved the book in Caleb's hands.

Caleb lowered his gaze to the book in his hand. His mouth dropped open when the doctor piled yet another book on top. And then another.

Caleb bent forward to accommodate the weight of the books.

"When you can name all the parts of the body, come back and we'll talk about your hours."

"Yes, sir!" Caleb's uncertain frown as he stared at the volumes was at odds with his enthusiastic response.

Taking her cue, Lucy tipped her portfolio. As planned, Monica's photograph floated to the floor as delicate as a feather. Lucy considered it a lucky sign that the glossy print fell directly in front of the doctor, faceup. Doc Myers bent to pick up the photograph and, without so much as a glance at Monica's image, handed it back.

Undeterred, Lucy held up the photograph and pretended to examine it thoughtfully while making sure the doctor could see it. "I think it's one of my best photos. What do you think?"

The doctor arched back to have a look. "Yes, yes, it's very good."

"I'm afraid I can't take all the credit," she said, watching him closely. Did his eyes linger on Monica's face a tad longer than necessary? "The subject had something to do with it."

"Yes, Miss Freeman has very good structure."

Lucy blinked. Had she heard him right? Structure? *Structure!* "The same could be said for the Taj Mahal," she said, not bothering to hide her irritation.

It was a ludicrous comparison but the doctor made no comment. Instead he casually walked toward the door, a signal that the meeting was over.

She shoved the photograph back into her portfolio. If it wasn't for Caleb, she would have told the doctor what she thought of him and his . . . structure.

Caleb, oblivious to her frustration, practically gushed as he thanked the doctor, then lugged his books out to the wagon. No sooner had he placed the volumes on the seat of the wagon and climbed in after them than he started to read.

That night Lucy was so busy thinking of her plan to capture the stranger's image that she barely touched her food. Caleb and her father discussed an inventory problem at the store. Deep into her thoughts, she paid little attention to the conversation until a full-blown argument broke out.

Caleb jumped up from his chair and yelled, "I don't want to work at the store anymore!"

Her father, seated across the table from her, looked stricken. "Then don't work there," he said, his voice curt. "There are other places you can work."

"I only want to work with Doc Myers."

Her father's face was dark with rage. "I forbid it."

"I'm a man now and you can't tell me what to do."

"You're sixteen."

"I'm *going* to be a doctor." Caleb slammed his chair against the table and stormed out of the house.

For several moments her father said nothing but simply stared into space with his usual dark, unfathomable look.

Caleb no longer needed her to fight his battles, but long-held habits were hard to break and Lucy couldn't leave things as they stood. She leaned forward and tilted her face toward her father's.

"Papa."

The hard lines on his face softened. Encouraged, she continued, "God has given Caleb the gift of healing. It would be wrong for him not to use it."

"I don't want him working for Myers," he said, his voice terse.

"But he's the only doctor in town." She frowned. "Doc Myers wasn't responsible for Mama's death. He did everything medically possible to save her." He was a simple horse-and-buggy doctor, but he was always reading the latest medical books and journals, always talking about the latest treatment or discovery.

Papa lifted his head. Sadness had replaced his anger but it was no less alarming. "There are many ways to kill someone," he said, and Lucy had the strangest feeling they were no longer talking about the doctor. Without another word, Papa stood and left the cabin.

Caleb came home sometime before midnight, but her father still hadn't returned. Though his absence worried her, it wasn't all that unusual for him to stay away all night. Once, curious to know where he went on such occasions, she followed him, keeping a discreet distance. He wandered from place to place with seemingly no rhyme or reason and she feared he was losing his mind. Then it occurred to her that he was visiting all her mother's favorite spots as if trying to find her. It near broke Lucy's heart.

Her heart ached anew. *Why, oh why, Papa, are you always searching for that which can't be found?* It was a long and troubling night.

Eight

The way to a man's heart is through his stomach. For this reason a woman wishing to look appropriately domesticated for her Mail-Order Bride photograph should wear an apron and wield a kitchen utensil (preferably not a rolling pin).

— MISS GERTRUDE HASSLEBRINK, 1878

Though Lucy's father didn't return home until after midnight, he had already left the house by the time she arose. It was a sign he'd had trouble sleeping, and this concerned her. She was worried but nonetheless relieved, for his absence would allow her to leave the house earlier than usual without having to explain her intentions.

Eager to put her plan into action, she raced through her morning chores. She washed the dishes, made the beds, and swept the floors.

She searched her meager wardrobe for something to wear that wasn't patched, ripped, or otherwise in disrepair. She finally settled on a light blue skirt with a draped panier and a formfitting bodice that came to a point below the waist. She brushed her hair until it shined. Working her chestnut locks into a smooth braid, she coiled it into a bun and pinned it carefully into place.

When she was finished, she stepped back and regarded

herself in the beveled glass mirror. She looked like a professional photographer, which, of course, was her goal. Her *only* goal. As if to argue with her reflection, she stuck out her tongue and made a face.

"And I don't care what the stranger thinks of me."

She was just about ready to walk out to the barn and hitch her wagon when Timber Joe appeared on her doorstep.

"I hope I'm not intruding." The former Confederate soldier held his visor cap in one hand and his rifle in the other.

"No, of course not," she said, inviting him in. "Any luck tracking down the outlaws?"

"No, ma'am, but it wasn't for lack of trying. We rode clear to the next town and never found a trace."

"I'm sorry to hear that," she said.

He sat on the sofa, stiff as a soldier on guard duty, his shoulder-length hair tied in back. A wooden leg replaced the one lost during the War Between the States. A far greater loss was his wounded spirit. The Reconstruction of the South was complete but the human heart required more than an act of Congress to heal. It required an act of God.

Lucy sat on a chair opposite him. "So what brings you here today?"

Timber Joe cleared his throat. "No sense beating 'round the bush." He looked her straight in the eye like an actor confident of his lines. "It's high time I got myself a"—he cleared his throat—"a wife."

"Oh," she said, surprised. Timber Joe didn't seem like the type to settle down.

"So what do you say?" he asked.

"What do I—" She stared at him. "Oh!" It never occurred to her that he had come *courting*. In fact, nothing could be further from her mind. "I . . . I hope I didn't lead you on," she stammered, hand on her chest.

He shook his head. "It's nothing you said. The thought

occurred to me out of the clear blue sky." He lifted his rifle upward and tapped its butt against the floor for emphasis. "One moment I'm a happy bachelor. The next moment, I'm pining for a wife."

Lucy didn't know what to say. She had no intention of getting married to anyone, let alone a former rebel fighter who suffered from a postwar condition that made him act strange.

"Aren't you a member of The Society for the Protection and Preservation of Male Independence?" she asked in an effort to remind him of the oath he'd taken upon joining the group. The society and its negative attitude toward women and marriage had caused much controversy around town ever since Old Man Appleby founded it a year earlier.

"I've handed in my resignation," Timber Joe said. "I've heard that getting married is kinda like getting hanged. Neither is as bad as folks say it is."

"I sincerely hope you're right." She didn't want to hurt him, but there didn't seem to be any way around it. "I'm most honored. I can't tell you how much. But—"

He stopped her protests with a raised hand. "I'm the one who should be honored, ma'am. A loose lady such as yourself is hard to find."

She was momentarily taken aback. "Loose?"

"Perhaps liberal is a better word. Nothing tight-laced about you." He nodded for emphasis.

Lucy didn't know whether to thank him or slap him.

He continued, "If I may be so bold as to ask you—"

Intent upon saving them both from embarrassment, she leaped to her feet, interrupting him midsentence. "I don't think that's a good idea."

He leaned back, startled. "I meant no offense, ma'am. I thought you would jump at the chance to make some money."

Hands on her hips, she tossed her head. "If you think I can be bought, you are sadly mistaken."

He slapped his hand on his thigh. "If that's not a rare combination. A loose woman with a heart of gold." He held his hands up, palms out. "But I insist on paying you. I wouldn't think of asking you to take my photograph for free."

"Your—" She flushed. "You . . . want me to take your photograph?"

"Don't get me wrong. It wasn't my idea. I'd sooner face a firing squad than the lens of a camera. But the lady insists."

Lucy slowly sat down. "What lady?"

"The lady from one of those mail-order bride catalogs. Says she won't travel no thousand miles until she knows what she's getting herself into."

"You're marrying someone out of a catalog?" Lucy shook her head. Ordering linens or fabric from a catalog was one thing. But a wife? What was the world coming to?

He shrugged. "What choice do I have? As you know, the pickings in Rocky Creek are pretty slim."

"They're not *that* slim," Lucy protested, taking offense.

He ignored her protest. "So will you do it?" he asked. "Will you take my photograph?"

"I'd be happy to." She hesitated and tried not to stare at his frayed uniform. "It's just . . . some things don't photograph well," she said with every bit of tact she could muster.

The corners of his mouth drooped. "Are you saying I won't take a good photograph?"

"I didn't mean you," she hastened to assure him. "I meant . . . your clothes."

He glanced down at himself. "What's wrong with my clothes?"

"They're a bit . . . intimidating," she said for want of another word. His rifle *was* intimidating.

He stiffened. "I heard it on good authority that women like men in uniforms."

"To a certain extent," she said carefully, not wanting to insult him. "The war has been over for quite some time. You don't want to give the impression that you're . . . stuck in the past."

He frowned. "So you think I should change my clothes?"

"I think it would help." A haircut and shave would help just as much.

Timber Joe scratched his head. "The only other uniform I have is at the laundry and it looks just like this one. I don't own any other clothes. My disability pension doesn't allow for luxuries."

Lucy tapped her chin with her finger. Replacing a threadbare uniform with civilian clothes hardly seemed like a luxury. "You do know that having a wife can be rather . . . expensive," she said gently.

"That's why I got me a job," he said.

"You have a job?"

"The Wells Fargo bank hired me to stand guard during business hours just in case those stagecoach robbers get any fancy ideas."

"Oh, Timber Joe, I'm so happy for you." Her mind raced. She was almost positive that her brother's or father's clothes would be too large.

"Why don't you come back another day? Say, Saturday?" The bank was closed on the weekend, which meant he wouldn't have to miss work. Surely she would have solved the uniform problem by then.

He frowned. "I won't have any other clothes on Saturday, either. I don't get paid till the first of June and that's still a couple of weeks away."

She smiled and gave his arm a reassuring pat. "Leave everything to me."

"Very well," he said with considerably less enthusiasm than he showed earlier. He stood. "You really think changing clothes will land me a bride?"

She glanced at his ever-present rifle and sighed. "It's a start."

~

Close to an hour later, she pulled on the reins of her horse and set the brake on her wagon. This was the exact spot where the stranger had come to her rescue. Recalling her hair-raising ride and terrifying encounter with the bandits, she glanced around in apprehension.

The sun glinted off the Rocky Creek River. In the distance, river drivers fought to break up logger jams with long steel poles. The lumbermen were too far away to come to her aid should misfortune strike, but their presence offered a measure of comfort, however false.

She climbed down from the wagon and followed a path through the woods, careful to watch where she was going. The ground was still waterlogged from the recent rains and made squishy sounds beneath her feet. The area was also prone to sinkholes due to eroding limestone, so she was alert for telltale fissures or cracks in the ground

She followed the same path the stranger took. The trees grew so thick that little sun reached this area. Still, she could find no cabin or campsite. The only building anywhere in the area was the old mission. Would he have been able to make it there and back in the short time it took him to fetch salve for her wound? Possibly.

Convinced he was close by, she found a relatively flat open space away from the road and set up her camera, then slid a dry plate into place.

Taking some deep breaths, she tried to calm her fast-beating heart. "This better work," she muttered.

Confident that the lumbermen were out of hearing range,

she cleared her throat, held her arms rigid by her side, and let out a bloodcurdling scream. She then ducked beneath the black cover and waited.

She didn't have to wait long.

The stranger appeared in the clearing directly in front of the camera lens. Instantly she squeezed the black bulb. She didn't dare allow for more than a few seconds of exposure time and her only hope was that it was long enough. She lifted her head from beneath the black cover.

Standing in front of her camera, he glanced around before leveling his puzzled gaze on her. A muscle flickered at his jaw. "Do you mind telling me what you are doing?" He looked her up and down. "Why did you scream?"

He was every bit as tall and handsome as she remembered. Forcing herself to breathe, she ran her damp hands down the front of her skirt. "I wanted to talk to you," she confessed nervously. "I will only take a couple of minutes and—"

"You screamed because you wanted to talk?"

The incredulous tone of his voice made her blush. "I . . . I didn't know how else to find you," she stammered. "Just so you know—my interest is strictly professional."

He considered this for a moment. "I can think of only one profession that requires a woman to pursue a man."

Her mouth dropped open. Twice in the course of a single day she'd been accused of being a loose woman. Recovering quickly, she drew herself up. "All I wanted was your photograph and to ask a few questions. Rest assured that I have no interest in you personally—"

"Why?" he demanded, cutting her off midsentence.

She tossed her head, mustering as much dignity as she could. "For one thing, we haven't been properly introduced."

He looked momentarily taken aback. "I meant why do you want my photograph?"

"Oh." She took a deep breath. "I'm a photographer."

Though others were either shocked or impressed upon learning of her profession, he showed no emotion one way or the other.

"A photographer?" he asked. "You mean like Mathew Brady?"

"Yes, like Mr. Brady," she said, pleased at the comparison. Not only was the nameless stranger not wild, he was also quite knowledgeable.

Mathew Brady and his crew had done something that had never been done before by photographing war scenes, thus providing a visual history of the War Between the States. Brady's New York exhibit stirred up considerable controversy. No one had ever seen photographs of war, and most people were shocked by the graphic images.

"Except he and his men took pictures before and after a battle, never during," she said. At least that's what she'd read. "A terrible oversight, don't you agree?"

His gaze burned through her. "Sometimes it's wiser to stay out of the line of fire," he said. "Which is something, apparently, you know nothing about."

She glared back, "I work for the local newspaper. It's my job to be in the line of fire."

His lips thinned with annoyance. "That still doesn't explain why you're harassing me."

She blinked. Never before had she been accused of harassment. "I'm doing you a favor." More accurately, she was doing the town a favor by exposing the truth.

He took a step back. "If you believe that, you're definitely in the wrong business." He turned to leave.

She had her photograph and that was all she had. No name. Nothing. Berating herself for the way she handled things, she chased after him. "Wait!"

He stopped so abruptly, she almost ran into him. "There's been talk . . ." she began, hoping to whet his curiosity. "And I—"

He swung around to face her. "What kind of talk?"

"Just t-talk," she stammered. "About a wild man."

He tilted his head. "Sorry, I can't help you there. But if I should I run into one I'll let you know."

"You don't understand," she said. "I believe the rumors are referring to you."

"Me?" The corners of his mouth turned up and his eyes softened in amusement. "So what do you think, Miss Fairbanks? Am I wild?"

The fact that he remembered her name unnerved her. She shook her head. "No," she whispered. Mysterious, perhaps, but certainly not wild. He was, however, all man and that made her very aware of being a woman.

"A boy said you chased him," she explained.

"Ah, you must be referring to the youth I found going through my things."

"He said he was chased by a wild man. I now know that's not true—"

"If you know that then you must also know I'm not news. I would ask that you discard my photograph and forget we ever met." He turned and stalked away.

"Wait!" she called again. "Who are you? You know my name but I don't know yours."

He stopped. "Wolf. My name is David Wolf." He glanced over his shoulder at her, his eyebrows drawn together.

"Is that your summer name?" she asked, using the term for an alias.

"It's my all-year-round name," he replied, not really answering her question.

Still, whether the name was real or not, it suited him. Like a wolf he walked silent as the mist, his bearing as proud as it was commanding.

She took a step back. "The truth is—" She forced herself to breathe. Maybe, just maybe if he knew how important this was to her, he would be more willing to cooperate. "The truth is, Mr. Wolf, my job depends on getting your photograph."

He turned to face her. "If that's the case, then I suggest you do us both a favor and look for other employment."

"That's easy for you to say," she snapped. "You're a man and can get any job you desire. Qualified or not, it doesn't matter. But a woman—"

"Can get a job only if she makes a nuisance of herself." In completing her sentence, he so deftly and effortlessly distorted what she had been trying to say, she could only stare at him.

"Obviously, you know nothing about women or employment," she huffed.

His eyes held a gleam of amusement. "I would love to debate the matter further but I'm afraid I have other things to do." He nodded. "Good day, Miss Fairbanks."

Irritated by his cavalier attitude, she watched him walk away, then turned to retrieve her camera. She had his photograph and his name but that's all she had.

The water-soaked ground beneath her suddenly began to sink. Staring at the web of cracks spreading from beneath her feet, she cried out but didn't dare move.

She wasn't aware that Wolf had returned until he shouted, "Grab my hand!"

She clawed the air frantically. His hand on her wrist felt like steel, but before he could pull her to safety, the ground gave way and she was suddenly airborne. She hit bottom with a jolt and everything went black.

~

She had no idea where she was or how she got there. Gradually coming to her senses, she took in her surroundings. She was at the bottom of a sinkhole at least twenty feet deep and perhaps eight feet wide. Spitting dirt out of her mouth, she scanned the dirt walls all the way to the top and her spirits plunged. The circle of blue sky seemed far away.

David Wolf lay next to her, motionless. Bolting upright, she shook off the fog in her brain and leaned over him.

"Mr. Wolf?" She shook him. Nothing. She shook him harder. "Please, please wake up."

At last he stirred and she was nearly overcome with relief. His eyes fluttered open and he groaned. "Talk to me. Say something."

He gingerly felt the back of his head and groaned. "Are you all right?" he asked.

It touched her that his first thought was for her. "Your head . . ."

"Just a little bump," he said, sitting up.

She sighed in relief. Neither of them was seriously injured and for that she was grateful.

She pulled her muddied skirt down to hide her equally muddied bloomers. It seemed like she was doomed to look her worst in front of him, but that was the least of her concerns. The sides closed in on her and there didn't seem to be any way out. She crossed her arms and shivered.

Wolf rose to his feet, seeming to command what little space stretched between them. Hands on his waist, he tilted his head back. His buckskin pants and shirt were covered in mud. Water seeped over the tops of his moccasins.

Dirt continued to trickle down from the sides. The web of entangled tree roots kept the walls from collapsing altogether and burying them alive.

"What are we going to do?" she asked. Wolf was so near that not even the smell of damp earth could hide his masculine scent, which only added to her nervousness.

He said nothing.

"We can't stay here all night. Papa will be worried, and if we don't get out of here soon, it'll be dark and—" She rambled in an effort to ease her nerves, one sentence running into another.

Wolf gestured for her to stop. "I can't think with you talking."

"I can't help it," she said. "I always talk when I'm upset or afraid or—" She glanced around. "Or feel trapped. Anything could happen. The walls could cave in and bury us alive. A wild animal could fall in with us." Even a stray cow dropping in would be disastrous. Her mind whirled with an endless list of possible dangers. How long did Caleb say a body could survive without water? Without food? "We might be here for days and—"

"If you don't stop yapping," he growled, "I'll have to kiss you again."

She smacked her lips together, cheeks blazing. So that's why he'd kissed her—to make her stop talking. It had absolutely nothing to do with . . . attraction. Irritated at herself for dwelling on something so insignificant, she glared at him.

"You are the most despicable man I've ever met."

"And you, Miss Fairbanks, are clearly the most annoying woman."

She seethed in silence, clamping her jaws tight. Silence stretched between them. She was determined not to speak if it killed her and it pretty near did.

"What would you say the chances are that someone will come to our rescue?" he asked at last.

"About the same chance of you dying midsentence," she muttered.

He surprised her by laughing. The humor on his dirt-smeared face provided an odd contrast to the lethal-looking knife he pulled out of its leather sheath. "The less said, the less need to apologize."

Turning his back on her, he stabbed his knife into the dirt wall. With quick movements of his wrist, he dug out a small indentation and continued to work his way around embedded rock. Pulling himself up by a root, he stuck the muddy toe of his moccasin into a hole he carved out and proceeded to dig another with his free hand.

Approving his plan, she blew out her breath. His progress was slow but his movements were strong and fluid. Never did she think that a man so powerful could move with such easy grace.

He was halfway up when loose soil rained down on him. Icy fear twisted inside her. If the dirt wall collapsed they would be buried alive.

"Oh God, please don't let us die. If we die in this horrible hole, I'll never forgive myself." She walked in a tight circle, wringing her hands together. "I should have just done what my father wanted me to and married that . . ." On and on she went, talking a mile a minute. "Wolf, will you ever forgive me?" Just as she asked the question he vanished out of sight.

"Wolf!" She strained her ears but couldn't hear a sound. He wasn't going to leave her there, was he? She glanced around and shuddered. Somehow the hole seemed more frightening now that she was alone.

"Mr. Wolf," she cried. "Are you there? Answer me!" Nothing. "If you help me out of here, I promise not to bother you again." Still nothing. "David?"

Battling tears, she tried reaching the lowest tree root, hoping to pull herself up high enough to fit her foot into the toeholds he'd dug. The problem was, Wolf was much taller than she and had a wider leg span.

Hands on her waist, she gaped upward. Anger replaced fear. "So help me, when I get my hands on you, I won't be responsible for my actions. You won't get away with leaving me here. I'll . . . I'll—" She continued voicing her threats if for no other reason than to break the alarming stillness. Not a sound came from above. Thinking he was probably far away by now, she fell into a seething silence.

She'd all but given up hope when Wolf appeared over-head, dangling a rope. "Are you finished?"

She almost collapsed with relief, but irked by his mocking tone, she dropped her arms to her side, fists tight, and glared at him. She was covered in mud and shivering with cold. She was in no mood to play games.

"You're enjoying this, aren't you?"

"Not as much as I'm going to enjoy hearing you promise to leave me alone." He cocked his head. "You do promise, don't you, Miss Fairbanks?"

"What choice do I have?" she snapped.

"You could choose to stay down there," he said. "Like you said, you never know who might drop in. A mountain lion. Wolf. Rattler."

Fists at her sides she rasped through gritted teeth, "You win. I won't bother you again."

"Would you mind repeating that louder? I couldn't tell if that was a positive or a negative."

She tightened her fists another notch. His use of photo-graphic terms put her in a worse mood. How dare he? "I said I won't bother you again," she all but shouted, and she meant it.

"Smart lady." He dropped the end of the rope into the pit and she reached up to grab it.

"Tie the rope around your waist."

She quickly did as he instructed. Holding on to the rope with both hands, she then pushed against the dirt walls with her feet and slowly began to rise.

The rope burned into the flesh of her palms and dirt stung her eyes, but gradually Wolf pulled her all the way to the top. Grateful to be alive, she fell into his arms. She clung to him while he pulled her away from the edge to safety.

He released her. "Are you all right?" Concern replaced his earlier annoyance.

She nodded and brushed off her skirt. She was a mess. They were both covered in mud and she suddenly laughed.

He laughed too. A warm, hearty laugh that made her momentarily forget how awful she must look.

Their laughter faded away but the warm feelings it evoked in her did not.

"I didn't mean to cause you so much trouble," she said, self-conscious beneath his steady gaze. "All I wanted was your photograph but I never should have tricked you and . . ."

She was rattling on but couldn't seem to stop herself.

He took a step closer and she lost her train of thought. Holding her tongue, she waited.

He gave her a knowing look. "I have no intention of kissing you again, if that's what you're worried about."

She wasn't worried.

With a knowing smile, he turned and walked away.

"I wouldn't kiss you again if you were the last man on earth," she called after him, but already he had disappeared through the trees.

Shaken, she circled around the sinkhole, treading with care. The last thing she needed was for the ground to cave in again.

She found her camera still on its tripod and relief flooded through her. With a little luck the photograph taken in haste would help secure her job. But it was the annoying and intriguing man named David Wolf who occupied her thoughts as she drove her wagon home.

Nine

A man accused of wrongdoing should never stare defiantly at the camera. And don't for goodness' sake look up. Only choir boys can properly assume the upward innocent look. Others will merely appear guilty as charged.

—Miss Gertrude Hasslebrink, 1878

The next morning Lucy sailed into the office of the *Rocky Creek Gazette*. Without so much as a greeting, she placed the photo of David Wolf on the desk in front of the editor, then stepped back and waited.

It was not her best photograph by any means. It was taken in haste and needed longer exposure. Unfortunately, the blurred quality of the dark image didn't do Wolf's good looks justice, which was better for her peace of mind than it was for the newspaper.

Barnes studied the photograph for several moments, then sat back in his chair. "So, the wild man really does exist," he said, excitement evident in his voice.

"No, no," she quickly responded. No right-thinking person could look at the photograph and think the man was wild. "Mr. Wolf is a very nice man."

The editor's eyes gleamed. "Wolf? That's his name?" He

rubbed his hands together. "This gets better by the minute."

She blinked. "Better how? Johnny Trotter made up the story. He as much as admitted he did. He was not chased by a wild man. He was chased by Mr. Wolf, who was only trying to protect his belongings. It's time we put the rumors to rest. The town has been on edge ever since the rumors began, and there's no reason for it."

She handed him a sheet of paper containing her carefully written copy.

"What is this?" he asked.

"An article I wrote to go with the photograph. You said if I wrote it, you would print it."

"So I did," he said, "but I'm only paying you for the photograph."

She could have argued with him but she knew it would do no good. "I talked with Mr. Wolf. It seems only natural that I should be the one to write the article." Once everyone read how he saved her from the stagecoach robbers, the ridiculous rumors would be put to rest.

She decided it best not to mention that she had been trapped in a sinkhole with him. Nor that she had stayed up half the night trying to turn what little she knew of the man into more than a couple of sentences.

She tapped her toe impatiently while he read her carefully written words. His face remained neutral.

He tossed the paper on his desk. "All right, you're hired," he said. No doubt that was as close to a compliment as she was likely to get from the man, but it was enough. "But I'm warning you, there better be no more blunders in the future."

"There won't be," she said.

"Very well, then." He tapped his fingers together and she could almost see the wheels turning in his head. If he hadn't already hired her, she might have been inclined to think he had something up his ink-stained sleeve.

"I want you to go to Garland and ask to see a prisoner by the name of Phelps."

"Phelps?" she asked.

He cleared his throat. "There's . . . uh . . . speculation that he might be one of the . . . uh . . . stagecoach robbers. If he is, you might recognize him."

Her heart raced with excitement. "I'm sure I will, but only if he's one of them."

Though she didn't get a good look at the bandits without their masks, she would never forget their eyes or voices.

"If it is one of the . . . uh . . . robbers, you can take a photograph and we will run it on the front page."

She couldn't believe her good fortune. It was her first real assignment as an actual employee and she was determined not to mess it up. "It will take a couple of days," she said.

The train did not yet go to Garland, which meant she would have to take a stage. That would be two days there and two days back.

"Take as long as you need." He was considerably more accommodating than usual. Apparently he liked her photograph and essay more than he let on, and she intended to use this to her full advantage.

"I expect the paper will pay for my expenses," she said, bracing herself for the battle that was bound to follow any monetary request.

"Of course," he said without hesitation.

His willingness to comply with her demands surprised her. Obviously, he'd not considered the full extent of expense a trip like that would incur. "I'll need money for stage fare and lodgings, plus food," she clarified.

He opened the drawer of his desk and handed her what could only be described as a pittance.

She continued to hold out her hand. Taking the hint, he

dropped another coin in her palm and, after more prodding on her part, reluctantly parted with several more coins.

Satisfied at last that her expenses were covered, she dropped the coins into her reticule, tightened the drawstrings, and slipped the bag onto her wrist.

"I'm not sure photographs are worth all this trouble and expense," he muttered.

She gave him a reassuring smile. "I promise you'll sell more papers than you ever thought possible."

She was still smiling and Barnes still grumbling when she left the office.

Wolf eyed the flock of grackles that took to the sky with harsh, raucous cries. Something or someone was nearby. The rabbit he hoped to nab for supper knew it too. It froze momentarily, its ears pointing straight up, before quickly popping into a hole.

Saved by a hair. Or was that hare? Grinning at the unintentional pun that came to mind, Wolf crouched down low, straining his ears.

Nothing.

For once, it wasn't a certain blue-eyed beauty that intruded. Unless, of course, she had tracked him down and now stood waiting in the early morning shadows with that infernal camera of hers. However much she complicated his life, he didn't find the thought all that unpleasant.

Spotting a broken branch, he picked it up and examined it. The distinct straight grain and open pores told him it was ash. A cabinetmaker by trade, he enjoyed checking out the wide variety of trees in these woods. He could hardly wait to finish his business and return to his craft and the job waiting for him back in the Panhandle.

In the short time he'd been in Rocky Creek, he'd spotted oak, ash, mesquite, cherry, even mahogany. It was like finding a gold mine. Around the mission where he was staying he'd even found some trees not native to the area but probably planted there years ago by missionaries.

A rustling sound like dry leaves in the wind made him tense. He strained his ears but all was quiet again. Around him the trees stood like sentinels. Not even the call of a bird broke the early morning silence; not a breath of air stirred the boughs.

Convinced it had only been a foraging animal, he tossed away the tree branch, placed two fingers in his mouth, and whistled for his horse. He then stepped through the edge of the woods to the meadow where he'd left Shadow to graze.

Momentarily blinded by the rising sun, it took him a moment to realize he wasn't alone. Three men faced him, two with their guns drawn.

"Drop your weapons and put your hands up," one of the men called. Noting that the man wore a sheriff's badge, Wolf slid his rifle holster down his arm to the ground, along with his knife. He then raised his hands shoulder high.

The lawman walked toward him with a languid stride. "Name's Slacker. Sheriff Abe Slacker."

"It's not against the law to scavenge for wood," Wolf said.

The sheriff stepped in front of him and kicked Wolf's knife into the bushes. "Since you're such an expert in the law, then you must know that we don't tolerate people who go around terrorizing other folks."

"Terrorizing?"

"You near scared the Trotter boy to death."

"I chased him away from my belongings."

The sheriff continued as if Wolf's explanation was of no consequence. "And then you terrorized Miss Fairbanks."

"Miss—" Wolf sputtered. He doubted if anything could terrorize that brash woman. "I can assure you I had no intention of causing Miss Fairbanks any . . . discomfort."

"The *Gazette* referred to you as only Wolf. What's your full name?" the sheriff asked.

"David Wolf." He was in the newspaper? Drat!

The sheriff pursed his lips. "Are you from Indian Territory?"

"I'm not a member of any Indian tribe, if that's what you're asking." Not Indian, not white. He lived in no-man's-land. "And no, I've never been to Indian Territory."

The sheriff scrutinized him. "What brings a half-breed like you to these parts?"

Wolf glanced at the two deputies who continued to hold him at gunpoint. One deputy was flabby, his stomach swollen like a flour sack over his gun belt. The other deputy was so young and inexperienced he kept looking at the sheriff for direction.

"I reckon that's my business," Wolf said, turning his attention back to the sheriff. The man struck him as all bluster and little action. No doubt he depended on his deputies to do the dirty work.

"Is that so?" The sheriff hung his thumbs from his belt. "I have a nice jail cell that might convince you otherwise."

Wolf gave the sheriff a look of disdain. It wouldn't be the first time he'd landed in jail for no other reason than the question of his race. "Out of your jurisdiction, aren't you?"

"My jurisdiction is wherever the good folks of Rocky Creek travel."

Slacker signaled to his men and they closed in from both sides.

Just as those youths had closed in all those years ago.

Instinctively, Wolf stiffened. The flabby deputy shoved his gun in his holster and grabbed Wolf's arm. Reacting purely by instinct, Wolf swung his fist into the man's doughy face and the man dropped his hold. Just as he'd counted on, the man was as slow as he was soft. A second fist and the deputy fell to the ground with a curse. It happened so fast all three men were caught by surprise.

The second deputy poked the barrel of his gun into Wolf's side, and with a glance at the sheriff he said, "Hold it right there."

Wolf stiffened and raised his hands again. The sheriff walked up to him, handcuffs dangling.

Just then Shadow came bounding out of the woods. It was just the distraction Wolf needed. Elbowing the younger deputy with lightning speed, Wolf finished the job with a bone-crunching jab. The man fell back, clutching his nose, blood oozing down his chin.

Wolf twisted around just as the sheriff drew his weapon. Wolf kicked the gun out of the sheriff's hand. By this time the pudgy deputy was on his feet again. He made a flying leap, knocking Wolf to the ground. The two rolled down a short incline. Wolf reached through the bushes for the sheriff's gun with one hand and fired a shot. His opponent rolled off him.

Still on his back, Wolf pointed the sheriff's Colt revolver and the three men froze as he staggered to his feet. He swung the gun in a sidewise arc and stepped back.

Pudgy reached for his holster. Wolf fired another warning shot and the man pulled his hand away from his side.

The deputies looked toward the sheriff, who gave a slight nod. Wolf backed away into the nearby woods. Out of sight of the men, he ran.

He whistled for Shadow and the horse whinnied back, the sound echoing among the trees. Wolf turned in a circle, trying to determine which way to go. A shot rang out and something exploded in his thigh. It felt like he was hit by a rock. He ducked through the brush, breaking into a full run. A river of warmth ran down his leg, followed by a searing pain that stopped him in his tracks. Wincing, he looked down. One leg of his buckskin pants was covered in blood. Limping now, he forced himself to keep moving but it wasn't long before his head began to spin. He tried to hold on to the gun but it slipped through his fingers.

Out of breath, he collapsed to the ground. Shadow approached him slowly, cautiously, and nudged him. Bracing himself against his horse's leg, Wolf tried to stand but darkness washed over him. He shook his head in an effort to chase away the fog. The horse snorted and jumped back.

Hands all over him. Rough hands. Powerful. Just as they had been all those years ago. Feet kicking, arms flailing, he fought with what little strength he had left. Fought the three men on top of him. Fought the nightmare that had haunted him all these years.

In the end, it was no use. Weakened by shock and the loss of blood, he could no longer ward off the darkness that closed in around him.

Voices.

A strange smell permeated the air. Wolf opened his eyes but the light blinded him.

Then another voice, this one close. "Take it easy."

Wolf stilled. Some long-ago memory stirred. He had to open his eyes now. Had to put a face to the voice.

Turning his head away from the light, he forced his lids upward. His vision was blurred and he blinked to clear it.

A rough brick wall. Where was he? More voices. Bars. He was in a jail cell. Several men stood outside the cell, their eyes glued to him like he was a freak show in P. T. Barnum's "Greatest Show on Earth."

"He's a wild man, all right," someone said.

"What are you going to do with him, Sheriff?"

Everyone started talking at once. A nearby movement. He shifted his gaze. He wasn't alone in the cell.

Someone leaned over him, blocking his view of the

others. "I'm Dr. Myers," the man said. "I removed a bullet from your leg. You lost a lot of blood, so you'll probably be weak for a while."

Wolf gaped at him. The doctor had two different colored eyes, one blue, one brown. He knew that face. The face was older, of course, twenty years older. Broader. Fine lines were etched in the forehead, traces of gray in the sideburns that hugged his jaw. Even if Wolf didn't recognize the face, he would always know those eyes.

The doctor patted him on the shoulder. Wolf cringed beneath his touch but the doctor either didn't notice or didn't care.

"I'll be back in a day or two to change the bandage. Blink if you understand."

Wolf continued to stare at Myers. He didn't trust the man. Wasn't about to take his gaze off him, not for a second. Hatred bubbled up like a hot tide, surprising him with its intensity. He never thought to harm another man. Never wanted revenge. That's not why he came back to Rocky Creek after all these years.

But lying there helpless in that cell, dependent on the skills of a man who had caused him such pain, Wolf couldn't help but feel anger. He wanted to make the man suffer for what he did. Make them all suffer.

Dr. Myers asked him again to blink and when he got no response, he picked up his leather bag and turned. "I don't think he understands."

"What do you 'spect from a half-breed wild man?" someone said.

The sheriff unlocked the cell and let the doctor out. Soon they were all gone, their voices fading away with their footsteps. Once again Wolf was alone with the ghosts of the past.

He drifted in and out of consciousness. The doctor's face

swam around in his head. One blue eye. One brown. Rough hands. Curses. Darkness.

Later, much later, he awoke. He felt like he was on fire, his mouth dry. His leg burned like someone had poured acid into it. It was pitch-black in his cell. The only source of light was a single star shining through the barred window over-head. He dragged himself across the cell and held on to the bars with both hands.

Doc Myers, they called him. So that was his name. All these years, he never knew his name. Only the eyes. One blue. One brown. Oh yes. You don't forget eyes like that.

At long last, he'd come face-to-face with his past. It wasn't the end. It was only a start. There had been four of them that long ago night. He had only to find the other three.

Ten

A man with an excess of self-portraits is deemed successful;
a woman simply vain.

— MISS GERTRUDE HASSLEBRINK, 1878

Lucy arrived back in Rocky Creek late in the afternoon. The trip to and from Garland had been worse than she anticipated. The stagecoach was overcrowded and the roads rutted from the spring rains. The trip was a total waste of time and money.

Mr. Phelps was not one of the stagecoach robbers and, in fact, was insulted at the mere suggestion. He did, however, readily admit to shooting a man during a card game, a man he claimed "deserved to be shot."

She suspected Barnes would find reason to blame her for the lack of success, though none of it was her fault. In no hurry to face him, she hoped the editor had not noticed the stage's arrival. She was hot and tired and anxious to change out of her dusty traveling suit. She was in no mood to deal with her employer. Not today.

After supervising the unloading of her camera and equipment, she stooped to pick up her valise.

Her brother Caleb came running out of their father's store. "Lucy! You're back! How was your trip?"

"I've had better," she said.

He lifted the box of photographic equipment with enviable ease.

"Be careful with that," she said, more out of habit than necessity. Caleb knew her camera meant everything to her.

"I know, I know," he said. Hauling the crate in his arms, he headed toward the mule and wagon parked in front of the store. "I'm afraid you're going to have to drive yourself home. I can't leave the store. I'll pick up the wagon when Papa returns."

She groaned. "My back hurts, my head hurts. Every bone aches."

Caleb gave her a look of sympathy. "You'll never guess what part of the body has the most bones."

She groaned.

"Give up?" he asked, barely able to contain his glee.

She sighed. "Yes, I give up."

"The hand," he said. "It has twenty-seven bones. And you'll never guess how many bones are in the feet."

"I don't want to know," she said. Her feet were the only parts of body that weren't sore and she didn't want to dwell on them for fear they would start hurting too. She followed her brother, valise in hand. "Where *is* Papa?"

"His horse threw a shoe. He's at the livery." He took the valise from her and set it next to the crate. He then turned to her with a grin. "I have something to show you."

"What?" she asked, though she was anxious to get home.

"Follow me." He stepped on the wooden sidewalk and ran into the store. The bells on the door jingled merrily.

She hesitated a moment before falling in step behind him. Her brother could be annoying at times, but his enthusiasm never failed to rub off on her.

The aroma of plug tobacco and freshly ground coffee greeted her. She followed Caleb to the counter, ducking beneath a hanging ham and sidestepping a keg of beans and a barrel of pickles.

Caleb reached for the newspaper behind the balance scale and held it up.

At first glance she smiled, hands clutched together in delight. Her photograph in a newspaper was a dream come true. However, her initial response soon turned to disappointment. The lack of exposure time and Barnes' inexperience in printing photographs resulted in a dark, menacing image that did nothing to dispel the rumors. Thank goodness her carefully composed article made up for any pictorial lack.

Caleb's grin practically reached his ears. "We sold every paper within a few hours," he said. "Even people who couldn't read bought one, just to look at the photograph. You're lucky I could save one for you."

She took the paper from him and quickly read the copy. "Oh no!" she sputtered. "This isn't what I wrote."

Not only had Barnes rewritten her article, he'd made it seem like Wolf was a monster. "This is terrible."

"No, it's not," Caleb said, moving from behind the counter to join her. "Because of the photograph, they caught him."

Lucy lowered the paper. "Did you say caught? They *caught* Mr. Wolf?"

Caleb nodded. "He's in jail."

Lucy gasped. "But why? He's done nothing wrong." She blinked. "Has he?"

Caleb looked surprised by the question. "According to that article, he's been terrorizing everyone around here, including you."

"That's ridiculous."

"You didn't tell me you met the wild man," he said, sounding hurt. "You could have been killed."

"There was nothing to tell," she said. Well, almost nothing. "And neither is he wild or dangerous." It all began to make sense now. The trip to Garland. Barnes paying her way without a fight. All for the purpose of selling newspapers. "Why that . . ."

Flinging the paper on the floor, she whirled about and headed for the door.

"It won't do you any good to go to the jailhouse," Caleb called after her. "The wild man is in the county jail."

That was even worse news. Marshal Armstrong was a fair and honest man. The same could not be said for the county sheriff, who would sooner hang a man than see that he got a fair trial.

"I've got to go and explain to him what happened," she said.

Caleb shook his head. "The sheriff won't allow visitors. Only Doc Myers and Reverend Wells are allowed to see him."

"Then you've got to go in my place," she said.

"Me?" Caleb scrunched up his face. "What makes you think the sheriff will let me see the prisoner?"

"You're the doctor's assistant. You have a good reason for being there."

"I don't know . . ."

"Please, Caleb. He's not what the others say he is. What Barnes wrote is a bald-faced lie."

Wolf had no way of knowing that the editor changed her copy. How he must hate her. "You must go to him and explain that I didn't write that article. While you're there, tell the sheriff that Mr. Wolf stopped the bandits from robbing the stage and the stories about him being wild were started by an over-imaginative boy and—"

"Whoa." Caleb held up his hands, palms out. "What makes you think the sheriff will listen to anything I have to say?"

"I don't know. Maybe I should go myself." Even if she wasn't allowed to see Wolf, she could talk to the sheriff and convince him that what Barnes had printed was untrue.

Caleb shrugged in resignation. "I'll go, but I don't think it will do any good."

"Perhaps I should talk to the marshal," she said, though she doubted that would do much good either. Marshal Armstrong was critical of the sheriff's vigilante type of justice and the two were at loggerheads.

Caleb shook his head. "You've had a hard journey. Go home and get some rest. I have to make a delivery to the Foster ranch this afternoon."

Lucy brightened. "That's perfect." The county sheriff's office was only a few miles down the road from the Fosters'.

"If the sheriff won't listen to me, then you can talk to Marshal Armstrong," Caleb added.

"Thank you!" She moved to hug him but he held her off with a can of peaches.

Laughing, she playfully punched him on the arm and turned to leave.

"Twenty-six," he called out.

She glanced back at him. "Twenty-six what?"

"Bones in the foot, silly!"

Leaving the shop, she picked up her skirt and ran the short distance to the newspaper office, her high-button shoes pounding like hammers on the wood plank sidewalk. Without slowing down, she burst inside, arriving in front of the startled editor in a flurry of flying ribbons and swishing petticoats. Extra the cat dived under the desk for cover.

For once Barnes looked pleased to see her. "Ah, there you are," he gushed, wringing his hands like an old miser counting his money. "You were right. The photograph on the front page sold more newspapers in a day than I sold all last year. I had to go back for a second and third printing." He laughed. "What was it Napoleon said? A sketch is worth a long speech. The same can be said for a photograph."

She glared at him. "You have no idea what you've done."

"We sold papers." He pounded a fist against his desk. "By cracker, you're hired permanently."

The words she had waited so long to hear bought her no pleasure. "I wouldn't work for you if you were the last—"

"Say no more." He lifted his arms, palms outward in an act of surrender. "How much do you want? Not that you're going to get it, mind you. But I'm a fair man."

Fair? Fair! She drew back. "I don't want your money."

He rose from his chair like one of those gas balloons Redd kept raving about. "Then what do you want, woman? Speak up."

Placing both hands on his desk, she leaned toward him. "I want you to retract the article."

"Retract?" His eyes bulged. "Retract? Are you out of your mind? A retraction is as good as death. I'll lose all credibility."

If she wasn't so angry she might have laughed out loud. Barnes had as much credibility as a thief. "Not only is the story not true," she stormed, "it's a lie!"

"I'm the editor," he bellowed back, stabbing his chest with his thumb. "True is what *I* say it is."

She straightened. "Even though it puts an innocent man in jail?"

His eyes glittered. "The only reason he's still in jail is because he was shot."

Lucy stepped back, stunned. "Shot?" Caleb said nothing about Wolf being shot, but it did explain why Doc Myers was allowed access to the prisoner.

"As soon as he's fully recovered, the sheriff plans to run him out of town. Now about your salary—"

"Keep your salary," she said, whirling toward the door. "I quit!" The words were out of her mouth before she could stop them. Quitting the newspaper meant giving up a long-held dream and a much-needed source of income. But how could she work for such an underhanded man?

Fuming, she hastened along the boardwalk toward the mule and wagon, anxious to get home.

"Yoo-hoo. Miss Fairbanks."

Hearing her name, she spun around. The thick British accent belonged to Mr. Garrett, a sheep rancher from York, England. Following the death of his wife, Catherine, he came to America intent upon starting a sheep ranch. He soon found out that Texans considered sheep men the lowest of the low, as sheep tended to strip grasslands clean and foul the water. No self-respecting steer would step foot in sheep land. Garrett now toyed with the idea of going into the cattle business instead.

Waiting for him to catch up to her, she felt a surge of guilt. Mr. Garrett had hired her to take his photograph. With all the excitement of the last several days, she'd forgotten all about him.

He tipped his top hat politely. His tweed trousers, cutaway morning coat, and silk cravat made him stand out in a town where most men wore canvas pants and boiled shirts.

"I say, I don't mean to be a bother," he said in his nasally voice, "but I wonder if ye've had a chance to develop my photograph. I wish to send it to Mum for her birthday."

"Yes, I've been meaning to talk to you. I'm afraid there's . . . a slight problem," Lucy said.

His gaze sharpened. "A problem? Oh dear. Was there something wrong with the way I posed?"

"Oh no, nothing like that," she said quickly. He'd struck a pompous pose, but on him it seemed natural. "I'm afraid it was my error."

She reached into her wagon for her portfolio. Digging inside she rifled through her prints until she found the one she wanted. She pulled it out and handed it to him. "As you can see, there's a double exposure."

It was her own careless mistake and she felt terrible. She

ran out of dry plates, which meant having to reuse one of her wet plates. In her haste to accommodate his schedule, she failed to adequately clean it. As a result, the ghostly image of a woman could be seen in the background. It was the remains of a photograph she'd taken earlier of Mrs. Weatherbee.

Mr. Garrett stared at the photograph, his face turning a ghastly shade of gray.

"Don't worry," she hastened to assure him. "It was my error, so there's no extra charge for another photograph."

He looked up, his eyes round. "She doesn't want me to be a cattle rancher," he exclaimed. "I should have known!"

"Who doesn't?" she asked, confused.

"My dead wife, of course," he said, stabbing the ghostly image with his finger. "I know that expression. I've seen it hundreds of times. See how she's looking down her nose?"

Lucy leaned closer to the photograph. "Mrs. Weatherbee always looks down her—"

"I should have known my missus would be against the cattle business. She wasn't even that fond of sheep. Oh, thank you, thank you! You saved me from making a big mistake." He took off, clutching the photograph in both hands.

"Does this mean you don't want me to take another photograph?" she called after him, but he kept going.

Still bewildered by Mr. Garrett's erratic behavior, she climbed onto the seat of her father's wagon and prodded Moses to hurry, anxious to avail herself of a bath and change of clothes. Maybe once she cleared her mind, she could figure out a way to undo some of the damage done to Mr. Wolf.

Eleven

When posing, a small toy is appropriate in a child's hand. A fan is permissible for a woman. But a man must refrain from holding a handgun or other weapon for that would label him a ruffian for all time—and a rose won't do him any good either.

— MISS GERTRUDE HASSLEBRINK, 1878

The day went from bad to worse. Not only was Lucy out of a job, waiting for her brother was like sitting on a pincushion. In an effort to think about other things, she tried concentrating on household chores. She swept and dusted and filled vases full of flowers, but still she worried. She was so distressed she completely forgot about Timber Joe's appointment.

Fortunately, before leaving for Garland, she'd asked Redd and Barrel to help her. As promised, they arrived on her doorstep with shirt and trousers at the appointed hour.

Never would she have guessed that photographing Timber Joe would be such a hassle. It took the better part of an hour just for Barrel to give him a shave and haircut.

Harder still was trying to stay focused. She couldn't stop thinking about Wolf. Surely the sheriff wouldn't refuse admittance to Doc Myers's assistant, though she had little hope of the sheriff believing anything Caleb had to say. Her gaze wandered to the window. Where was he? What was taking her brother so long? And why oh why hadn't she gone herself?

Timber Joe picked up on her anxiety. "Don't you worry, Lucy. That wild man is locked up tighter than a new boot. And even if he weren't he'd have me and old Stanley here to contend with." Stanley was how he sometimes referred to his rifle.

"He's not wild," Lucy said, her voice husky. "What Barnes wrote was wrong."

"Not according to the picture, and pictures don't lie." Timber Joe struck a pose. "What do you think?"

She tried to concentrate. "Timber Joe, for goodness' sake. You look as stiff as a scarecrow."

"I don't know why I gotta have my picture taken anyway," Timber Joe grumbled. "I told Annabelle everything she needs to know about me."

"I sincerely doubt that," Lucy said. She gazed through the viewfinder. "Lower your chin. Now look at the camera."

"The shirt is stained," Barrel said, disapproving Redd's contributions. Barrel's own clothes were always immaculate, but they were far too large for Timber Joe's slender frame.

Redd glared at Barrel. "You can't work around food without getting it on your clothes."

"Never mind the shirt," she said. "We have to make him stand more natural." The newer cameras had shortened exposure times and it was no longer necessary for the subject to stand for long periods of time like stone statues.

"I want a profile," Timber Joe said, turning sideways.

It seemed like a reasonable request until Lucy got a good look at his prominent nose. At the current angle, it looked like the map of Italy. Worse, the hand plastered on his hip resembled a bloated starfish.

Barrel frowned and Redd pointed to his own nose and rolled his eyes.

Lucy sighed and tried to think of a tactful way to get Timber Joe to try another pose.

A woman was so much easier to pose than a man. She could always be given something to do with her hands. She could arrange flowers, hold a fan or parasol, pick up her skirt, or simply strike a delicate pose with forefinger and thumb together. But there was only so much a man could do without looking foppish.

"I think a face-on shot would be much more to your lady's liking," she said. "When you stand sideways your features dominate and she won't be able to perceive your character."

Timber Joe stubbornly held his pose. "This is how Julius Caesar posed for his portraits. What was good enough for Julius is good enough for me."

She sighed and squeezed the air ball that controlled the shutter.

Photograph after photograph she snapped, but none seemed right. The revealing moment she looked for when taking a person's picture didn't materialize.

Timber Joe frowned.

He glared.

He glowered.

He scowled.

Redd tried to get him to relax by telling ridiculous jokes. Barrel sang an aria from *The Barber of Seville*, changing some words to English for their benefit, his strong vibrant voice rattling the windows. A portly man as tall as he was wide, he jumped up on a chair with a dancer's agility, snipping the air with his scissors.

"Figaro here, Figaro there. Figaro up, Figaro down . . ." Barrel had trained as an opera singer but his stage fright kept him from singing professionally, though he did sing in the church choir.

Lucy laughed and clapped her hands. Even Redd chuckled

from time to time, though he had little regard for opera. Timber Joe remained stoic, his spine steel-rod straight.

After Barrel's performance, Lucy threw up her hands. "This will never do. Annabelle will take one look at you and marry someone else."

"It's because I don't look like a soldier," Timber Joe insisted.

"Actually that tomato stain on your shirt looks like you're wounded," Redd said, trying to help.

Timber Joe pulled the bowler off his head and tossed it to the ground. "I don't look like myself. That's the problem. Annabelle will see my photograph and want nothing more to do with me." He reached for his kepi cap and grabbed his rifle.

He placed his hat on his head and struck a pose. "Now you can take my photograph."

Lucy blew a wisp of hair away from her face. "I don't think it wise to emphasize your Confederate affiliation."

"Why not?" Timber Joe demanded. "I'm a Confederate soldier. That's who I am."

"Was," Redd said, which only made Timber Joe scowl more.

"Once a soldier, always a soldier," he insisted.

She tried to choose her words carefully. "Some people think slavery was wrong," she said cautiously. "Maybe even Annabelle."

Timber Joe snapped to attention. "Of course it's wrong. Even General Lee said slavery was a sin. I wasn't fighting to uphold slavery. My brother and I fought to protect our homeland. That's what we were fighting for. If Annabelle finds fault with that, then she's not the woman for me." He then went on to talk about his twin brother who died in the war. His words came slowly as if he was speaking in a language not his own.

"I lost a leg and Tommy lost his life, but he would think my sacrifice greater. That's the kind of man he was."

His voice broke and his eyes grew misty—a window of his soul opened—and Lucy got the moment she had hoped for.

It was a good thing, too, because Timber Joe had about all he could take of posing.

"I have one more plate left. Barrel, would you like me to take your photograph? I'm sure Brenda would be pleased." Brenda and Barrel had been married for less than a year.

Barrel waved both hands in front as if warding off an attack. "In opera, a person stabbed or shot is required to sing. I have the same impulse when facing a camera." And just in case she wouldn't take no for an answer, he quickly followed Timber Joe outside.

"How about you, Redd?" When he didn't respond, she looked his way. He stood by the desk holding up one of her photographs.

"Is this Miss Hogg?" he asked, his eyes wide with astonishment.

She walked over and glanced at the print. "Yes. That was taken on the opening day of Jenny's shop." She smiled at the memory of Emma Hogg lying flat on the floor, giggling like a schoolgirl.

"What's that thing on her head?"

"It's a chemise," she said.

"A ch-chemise." His face reddened.

"Why, Redd Reeder, I do believe you're blushing."

"I'm not blushing. I just don't think people should go around wearing . . ."

"A chemise."

" . . . on their heads." He cleared his throat.

She plucked the photograph out of his hands. The look of pure joy on Emma's face filled her with a strange longing.

"Whenever I look through a lens, I feel like I'm the subject," she said. It was as if another person's joy or dreams became her own—if only for a fleeting moment of time. It was an odd feeling and one she couldn't quite explain.

Redd's already droopy eyebrows slanted another notch lower. "If that's true, you'd best avoid photographing politicians." With another quick glance at the print in her hands, he rushed to the door.

The sun had already set by the time Caleb drove up in the store wagon. Lucy stood by the gate waiting for him. He looked like he was bursting with news. "Whoa!" he called out, but Moses—smelling water, feed, or both—had no intention of slowing down until he reached the barn.

"Did you know that the skin is the largest organ of the body?" Caleb yelled as he sailed past her. Chickens scattered out of his way with furious clucks, feathers flying every which way.

"That's it?" she called after him. "That's what you have to tell me?" She picked up her skirt and raced after him. "Caleb Fairbanks, answer me this minute. Did you or did you not see Mr. Wolf?" She stormed into the barn.

He thrust his medical book into her arms and jumped to the ground. "He wasn't there."

Her heart nearly stood still. "What . . . what do you mean he wasn't there?"

He unharnessed Moses and led the animal into a stall. "The sheriff released him."

"That's good news. Isn't it?"

"I guess so. The sheriff told him to leave the area and never come back."

The news hit her like a blow. Wolf was gone? "What about his leg wound?" she managed to squeak out.

Caleb shrugged. After checking Moses's food and water, he joined her by the barn door. "All I know is that the sheriff said if he ever laid eyes on the man again, he would lock him up for good."

"Oh." Surprised to find herself close to tears, she shoved his books into his arms. She then whirled about and started toward the house.

David Wolf was gone. Now she could never explain the article in the paper. Or tell him how sorry she was. Or how much she—

"If you don't quit your yapping, I'll have to kiss you again."

Startled by the voice, she spun around before she realized she'd imagined it.

Overhead, a star winked in the twilight gray sky as if enjoying a joke at her expense.

Surprised by the way the intrusive memory affected her, she shook her head. Kissing Wolf was the furthest thing from her mind—or at least it should be. Had to be. With this thought she broke into a full run in an effort to escape the memory of him.

In the days that followed, Lucy felt depressed and restless. Even working in her darkroom failed to lift her spirits. She refused to think it had anything to do with Wolf. It was her failure to obtain meaningful employment as a photographer that left her bereft. And why wouldn't it? She would soon be twenty-one and her future looked bleak. She prayed for God's guidance but none was forthcoming, and she felt very much alone. If God had a plan for her, he was keeping it to himself.

More than her own future, she worried about Caleb's. There was no way her father could afford to send him to medical school when the time came. The money she made taking family photographs barely paid for the cost of plates and chemicals.

Seated at her desk, she pulled out pen and paper and

wrote letters seeking employment. She addressed her letters to newspapers in Houston, Dallas, St. Louis, and Kansas City. She even wrote letters to the *Chicago Tribune*, *The New York Times*, and *The Boston Globe*. She hated the thought of traveling so far away from home and leaving family and friends, but she couldn't think of any other way to help pay for Caleb's education.

After sealing her letters with wax, she tucked them into her reticule and carefully slid Timber Joe's photograph into her satchel. She then drove into town. Timber Joe stood guard by the Wells Fargo bank, rifle flung over his shoulder, talking to Redd.

She parked her wagon across from the bank and tucked her leather satchel beneath her arm. She then hurried across the street to join them. Both men turned to greet her.

"What brings you to town so early?" Redd asked. He was dressed in a ketchup-stained apron and wore a floppy white hat.

"I have Timber Joe's photograph," she said. She made no mention of the letters she intended to mail. Pulling a print from her portfolio, she handed it to Timber Joe. She was pleased with the finished picture. The composition, light—everything was perfect. But no more so than Timber Joe. The expression on his face as he talked about the brother lost in the war was pure love, and she had captured it in all its glory.

Expecting a positive response, she didn't know what to make of his stoic face as he stared at the photograph in his hand.

"I can't send this to Annabelle," he said at last. "I look like we lost the war."

"You *did* lose the war," Redd said, in his ever-helpful way.

"No need to advertise it," Timber Joe groused.

Lucy tried not to let her disappointment show. She should have known that Timber Joe would think showing emotion was a sign of weakness. He was a soldier through and through.

"It's a wonderful likeness," she insisted. "Your lady friend will be impressed."

Timber Joe looked unconvinced. "I don't know . . ."

After arguing about it for several moments, Lucy squeezed his arm. "Trust me. I'm a woman and I know these things. Annabelle will love it." She beseeched Redd silently to convince Timber Joe she was right.

Timber Joe was still staring at the photograph and shaking his head when she left and headed for Fairbanks General Merchandise on the opposite side of the street. Her father stood behind the counter helping Mrs. Weatherbee with her order.

Caleb greeted her with a silly grin. "Your wet plates didn't come yet," he said, correctly guessing one of her reasons for being there.

Catching her staring at the stack of groceries on the counter, Caleb whispered, "You won't believe how much food that woman buys. She's in here every couple of days. Do you suppose Millard eats that much?"

"Running for office is hard work," she whispered back. Running for state senator had to be almost as difficult as running for president. "Have . . . have you noticed anything strange about her?"

"You mean stranger than usual?"

She nodded. "She talks to herself and sometimes I don't think she recognizes me. Maybe you should mention it to Doc Myers. Something's not right with her brain."

"Talking to Doc Myers won't do much good unless she seeks his help herself," Caleb said. He broke into a wide grin. "Speaking of the brain, do you know why it's impossible to tickle yourself?"

She laughed. "No, why?"

"Doc Myers said it's because the brain anticipates your touch. A tickle makes you laugh only if you ambush the brain, and you can't do that by yourself."

"Mystery solved," she teased, and since he looked about to regale her with more facts about the body, she quickly stuffed her letters into the bag waiting to be taken to the train station, careful to leave the right amount for postage. She then threw him a kiss and left.

Across the way, Redd and Timber Joe were still arguing over the photograph. With a sigh she stroked Tripod on the neck. "I don't know which are harder to photograph, men or women."

With women it was all about appearances and youthfulness. Men simply wanted to look invincible.

Climbing onto the seat, she slapped the reins against Tripod's behind and the wagon took off. It was a beautiful, clear day in late May. White clouds gathered like sheep on the distant horizon. Trees stretched and swayed in the gentle breeze. Though bluebonnets had faded away with the last breath of spring, an abundance of wildflowers danced across the landscape.

Normally she would have stopped to take photographs, but now that she had switched to the more convenient dry plates, she could no longer afford to take pictures for her own enjoyment alone. At three dollars a dozen, dry plates had to be saved for paying jobs. She did, however, hold up one hand and peer through the frame made with forefinger and thumb.

What a beautiful picture, and how she longed to take it. It was the kind of picture she imagined her mother painting. Sighing, she dropped her hand and forced Tripod to pick up speed.

A cow standing by the side of the road lifted its head and mooed, but not even the steady *clip-clopping* of the horse's hooves and squeak of wagon wheels penetrated her dark thoughts.

Something touched her shoulder and she jumped. Crying out in alarm, she swung her head around and gasped, "*Mr. Wolf!*"

Heart racing, she tugged on the reins and tried to catch

her breath. "Don't ever do that again!" She set the brake and leaped to the ground. Hands at her waist, she faced him. "You near scared the life out of me."

"Sorry." Slumped against the inside of the wagon, he looked alarmingly weak. His eyes were glazed, his forehead beaded in sweat. Her anger evaporating, she moved closer.

"I heard you were released," she said.

"The sheriff couldn't trump up enough charges to keep me any longer." His usual strong voice sounded strained, as if it took every bit of his energy to speak. He continued, "What you wrote . . ."

"I didn't write that article."

"It was your photograph," he said, his voice thick with censure.

"Yes, it was," she admitted. "And Barnes promised to print what I wrote, but he didn't."

His gaze sharpened. "What *did* you write?"

"I wrote that the rumors were false and that you kept the stagecoach from being robbed."

He grimaced but didn't respond. Had he heard what she said? And if he had, did he even believe her?

She stepped forward. It was then she saw the spot of fresh blood on his buckskin trousers. "Your leg."

"It's infected," he said.

"Ohhh!" Her mind scrambled. "I'll take you to the doctor."

"No!"

Startled by the fervor in his voice, she tried to think what to do. "An infection is serious. You could lose your—"

"No doctor!" he said sharply.

"But . . . all right," she said reluctantly, not wanting to upset him any more than he already was.

He groaned. She reached out to comfort him but fell short of touching him. "I'm so sorry you landed in jail. I should never have trusted Barnes."

He said something but she couldn't make out what it was. An insult, no doubt. He laid his head back and closed his eyes, his lips slightly parted.

She reached over the side of the wagon and gently shook him. "Mr. Wolf?"

No answer.

"David?"

Nothing.

Worried, she laid her hand on his forehead. He was burning with fever. What if he died? It would be her fault. Oh, why had she trusted Barnes? She forced herself to calm down.

Caleb! He would know what to do.

Climbing into the wagon bed, she arranged a folded prayer shawl under his head, then gently brushed his hair aside. "God, please don't let him die."

Since he was burning with fever, she didn't dare cover him with the blanket. Instead, she rearranged her photographic equipment to better hide him from view and protect him from the sun.

Climbing into the driver's seat, she quickly turned the wagon around and raced back to town.

One prayer was answered at least. Caleb was outside loading boxes of supplies into a customer's cart. She parked a distance away from the store so her father wouldn't see her.

She called to her brother and when he looked up, she signaled with a frantic wave. He finished loading the last of the boxes before joining her.

He looked irritated. "Now what? Don't tell me you and Mr. Barnes had another argument."

"Shh." She glanced around. Much to her dismay, Mrs. Weatherbee walked out of Jenny's Ladies Emporium. She looked like she was talking to herself. It seemed like the woman grew stranger every day.

In an effort to act normal, Lucy smiled and waved. The

woman looked about to ignore her. She started down the street, then stopped. Apparently recalling that her son was running for office, she lifted her hand in a halfhearted wave.

Lucy turned back to her brother. "Mr. Wolf is in the wagon," she whispered. "Don't look. He needs medical care. His leg is infected. *Don't look.*"

A shadow of alarm flitted across Caleb's brow. "I'll go fetch Doc Myers."

"No!" In a softer voice she added, "I promised him I wouldn't involve the doctor."

His face clouded in disbelief. "Have you any idea how serious an infection can be?" Despite her warning, he glanced at Wolf and shook his head. "He needs medical care."

"That's why you have to help me."

"I'm not a doctor," he said, his voice adamant.

She glanced around. The longer they stood arguing, the greater the chance that someone might walk by and spot Wolf in her wagon.

"I don't have time to discuss this now. I need something for the infection. And bandages and bedding." She ticked off what she needed on her fingers. "Blankets. Pillow. Meet me at . . ."

Where? She needed a place nearby but didn't dare take him home. Thanks to Barnes's article, folks still thought he was a wild man. There was no telling what they would do if they knew he was still in town.

"The church," she said. "Meet me at the church. There's an anteroom off the altar for storage. I don't think anyone uses it now that school is out for the summer. He'll be safe there, at least for a while."

Caleb started to say something but she cut him off. "Please, Caleb, we'll talk about this later. Now hurry. And don't say anything to Papa. Go!"

Just then, her friend Monica walked out of Jenny's store

carrying a package. Upon seeing Lucy her face lit up. "Oh, do look what I bought," she called, stepping off the wooden sidewalk.

"Not now," Lucy called back. She snapped the reins and drove away as fast as she could go, leaving Monica in the middle of the road, staring after her.

Twelve

Thank goodness we no longer must clamp heads in a vise in order to capture an image. Modern technology, however, does not give one license to argue, fight, or otherwise cause a disruption during a photographing session (or any other time for that matter).

—MISS GERTRUDE HASSLEBRINK, 1878

Where was Caleb?

Lucy paced back and forth in front of the church. The coast was clear, at least for now. Fortunately, the sanctuary was empty and there was no sign of Reverend Wells.

So where was her brother? It had been more than two hours since she last saw Caleb and he still hadn't arrived. What was taking so long?

David Wolf lay in the back of the wagon. She had sponged him off with cool water collected from the creek, but he still burned with fever. To make matters worse, the breeze had died down. She'd parked beneath an oak tree, but even though summer was still a couple of weeks away, it was hot in the shade. Hot and sticky.

She had done her best to make Wolf comfortable, but without Caleb's help she had no way of moving him inside.

At last she spotted her father's store wagon in the distance, plodding toward the church. Apparently Moses was giving Caleb trouble again. She greeted her brother with a wave of the hand. "I thought you'd never get here."

"I had to make two deliveries," Caleb explained. He set the brake and jumped to the ground. "And Moses here decided that two deliveries was his limit." He gave the mule's short, thick neck an affectionate pat. Moses gave a slight whinny that ended in a *hee-haw*.

Caleb inclined his head toward Wolf. "How's he doing?"

"Not too good." Lucy sighed. She hated putting Caleb in such a difficult position. "He's in and out of consciousness."

Caleb studied Wolf for a moment. "He doesn't look . . . wild."

"That's because he's not. Oh, Caleb, I've made such a mess of things. If it wasn't for me he wouldn't have been arrested or shot. I don't think I could live with myself if he—" She covered her mouth with her hand.

Caleb patted her back. "Come on, we need to get him inside."

Together, they struggled to lift Wolf out of the wagon.

Wolf was tall and solidly built. It would have been easier to carry the mule. He winced the moment the foot of his wounded leg touched the ground. His body folded, and it was only by Caleb's quick action that he didn't altogether fall.

"I have an idea," Caleb said, straining against Wolf's weight. "Spread a blanket on the ground."

Lucy reached into the store's wagon and quickly pulled out one of the blankets Caleb stowed there. Shaking it, she let it billow to the ground and smoothed out the edges.

With a great deal of difficulty, Caleb half carried, half dragged Wolf onto the blanket. Lucy lifted the foot of his good leg and then ever so gently moved the injured one.

Wolf grimaced, his face damp with fever.

Clutching the edge of the blanket with both hands, Caleb

pulled Wolf up the path. It took both of them to heave him up the two steps and into the church.

The anteroom was located to the right of the altar. Used only for storage, it smelled dusty. School supplies and extra hymnal books were stacked on floor-to-ceiling shelves. A broom and mop stood in a corner. There were no windows but the exterior siding was warped, allowing daylight to pour through the slotted boards, providing a welcome glow to the otherwise drab room.

Though it was late May, the nights were still cool. The cracks would be less of an asset after dark, but Lucy decided to handle that problem when the time came.

After sweeping out the room, Lucy made a bed for Wolf in a corner with the pillows and blankets Caleb had brought with him.

Once they got Wolf settled, Caleb kneeled beside him. "We're going to have to take off his pants."

"I'll . . . I'll wait outside."

Caleb looked up. "Oh, no you don't. I need your help."

"Oh." Lucy covered her mouth with her hand. Having helped raise Caleb since he was an infant, she was no stranger to the male anatomy. But this . . . this was different.

"Come on. Don't be a prude," Caleb said in that teasing way of his.

She snapped her head back. "I'm not a prude."

"I'll lift him up and you pull his trousers down."

She took a deep breath to brace herself. "All right." She could do this. She could.

"Ready?" he asked.

"Ready."

She wouldn't look, she wouldn't look. Oh, dear God, she looked.

Face blazing, she averted her eyes and pulled his buckskin pants all the way down and tossed them aside.

"Did you know that a man's—"

"I don't want to know," she snapped.

Caleb laughed and she glared at him.

Much to her relief, Caleb covered Wolf with a blanket, leaving only his injured leg exposed. The thigh was swollen, the skin an alarming red.

"It looks awful," she said.

Caleb sniffed. "It's infected all right, but there's no almond smell, so it's not gangrenous. At least not yet."

"That's good," she said anxiously. "Isn't it?"

Caleb drew back. "I better fetch Doc Myers."

Wolf's eyes flew open. "No!" His body thrashed around, moving from side to side. It was all Lucy and Caleb could do to hold him in place.

"Don't . . . want Doc . . . Myers. No!"

"Stay still," Lucy cried. She pressed down on Wolf's one good leg in an effort to keep it from injuring the other.

"No doctor!"

She exchanged a worried glance with her brother. "All right," she said. It wasn't the first promise she had made to Wolf, but it was by far the one she most regretted.

A muscle tightened at Caleb's jaw, his young face white with disapproval.

Wolf relaxed as if the last bit of his energy had drained away, and his lids fluttered downward.

"He needs a doctor," Caleb mouthed.

Lucy bit down on her lower lip and tried to think what to do. "Can't . . . can't you take care of him?"

"I'm not a doctor," Caleb whispered, sounding as scared as she felt. "I'm just learning anatomy. I don't know how to take care of an infected bullet wound."

"This can't be any worse than Moses's leg," she argued in a low voice. "You saved that mule's life."

Caleb shook his head. "I'm not a doctor, Lucy. And if Papa has his way, I never will be."

Sighing, she dampened a cloth with water from Caleb's canteen and dabbed Wolf's forehead. "He's still burning up."

"I brought laudanum," he said. He uncapped a bottle of Stickley and Poors Paregoric Elixir and carefully measured out one teaspoonful.

"That will help with the pain and should lower the fever," he explained. Despite his protests he was already beginning to sound like a doctor.

She waited for Caleb to finish forcing the liquid down Wolf's throat, then motioned for him to follow her into the sanctuary. Closing the door behind her, she took Caleb by the arm and led him away so Wolf couldn't hear them talk.

"Go fetch Doc Myers." The softness of her voice did not hide the urgency.

"It's the right thing to do," he said, sounding relieved.

"I know." She hated breaking a promise, but Wolf was half out of his mind with delirium. He couldn't know what he was saying, or how seriously ill he was.

"You better not be here when Doc Myers arrives," Caleb said.

"I'm not leaving him alone," she said.

Caleb's worried expression made him look years older. "Everyone thinks he's a wild man."

"Does he look like one to you?"

"Not at all, but it still won't help your reputation if you're found here alone with a man."

Dear, sweet boy. She'd always taken care of Caleb and suddenly the tables were turned, and he now looked out for her. "I think my reputation is already beyond repair."

The smile she hoped for failed to materialize. "Go," she said, waving him away with both hands.

He strode down the aisle of the church and paused at the door. He looked back at her, a glint in his eye. "Did you know that a baby has more bones than an adult?" he called back.

"Go!"

As soon as Caleb left, Lucy rushed back to Wolf's side. Dropping to her knees, she laid her hand on his forehead, his flesh hot and clammy to her touch. She sprinkled water from a canteen onto a cloth and dabbed his fevered brow and neck. She then sat back to wait. *God, please, please don't let him die.*

She formed a square with her forefingers and thumbs and studied Wolf's handsome face through the make-believe lens. The focusing device wasn't as good as her camera but it still helped her see things she might not otherwise have noticed, like the unmistakable shadow of a beard.

The whiskers gave her pause. Maybe he wasn't part Indian as she had originally supposed.

His skin was unnaturally flushed but surprisingly smooth, except for the lines at his temples and either side of his mouth. Trying not to dwell on the memory of that mouth on hers, she clasped her hands together in waiting silence.

He suddenly cried out. The long harrowing sound sent chills down her spine. He thrashed around so violently she feared he would reinjure his leg. "Let me go!"

It took all her strength to keep him from banging against the wall. "It's all right," she said soothingly, her hand on his forehead.

His body stilled and he fell silent. Satisfied that the crisis was over, she sat back but was still shaken. What would make a man cry out like that? Was it the fever? Or something else?

The sun dipped behind the trees, casting the room in dim shadows. The last strains of daylight inching through the warped boards grew dimmer by the minute, and already she could feel a draft.

She lit a kerosene lamp and stacked hymnals in front of some of the larger cracks to block out the cool air.

Wolf muttered softly.

"What? What did you say?" She leaned over him in an effort to make sense of his rambling words and her heart sank. He was delirious.

She drew back and he fell silent.

Close to an hour later, Caleb returned. He opened the door to the anteroom a crack. The yellow light from the lamp emphasized his worried look. He motioned to her from the doorway.

Rushing from the room, she whispered, "Where's the doctor?"

"His housekeeper said he was out on a call and won't be back till day after tomorrow."

"Oh no." She closed the door to the anteroom behind her so they could talk without disturbing Wolf. "What are we going to do?"

"I just thought of something," he said, his voice sounding hopeful. "Maybe I can ask Slim Parker to have a look. He helped me with Moses's leg."

Slim Parker's real name was Running Cloud. A former Apache medicine man, he was what Lucy's father called one of the shadow people. There were several of them living on the outer fringes of Rocky Creek. Some were wartime deserters. One was a former slave who still refused to believe he was free. Slim was the only one not running from his past. It was his future he couldn't face, and the thought of having to live on an Indian reservation far away from the only home he ever knew.

She nodded. "Go. And hurry!"

It was late by the time he returned with Slim. Wolf's leg looked almost purple in the dim yellow light of the kerosene lantern.

Slim leaned over the leg, examining it closely. He was

a tall, lean man with high cheekbones and skin the color of tanned hide. Though he was dressed in canvas pants and a white broadcloth shirt, he still wore his hair in braids, as was the custom of his people.

He stood. "No save." He turned.

"No, no, wait." Lucy practically dived in front of the door to keep him from leaving. "There must be something you can do."

He glanced over his shoulder at Caleb. "I told you five. No more."

She searched her brother's face. "What is he talking about? Five?"

Caleb quickly explained. "As a medicine man he lost five patients. If he loses a sixth he must be put to death. That's the law of his people. He agreed to help only if Wolf was in no danger of dying."

"He's not going to die," she insisted. "He's not!" She beseeched the tall Indian, pressing her fingers hard against his arm. "Please, you must help him."

"No help!"

"But you're not with your tribe. No one would ever know."

"*I* know." For emphasis, he pounded his chest with his fist. "No help." With that, he pushed her aside and practically ripped the door from its hinges.

She ran through the dark church after him, but it was no use. By the time she reached the double front doors, she was greeted by the sound of flying hooves. She stood perfectly still, trying to think what to do.

After awhile Caleb joined her, patting her on her shoulder. "He gave me salve for the infection. I rubbed it on his wound. I think it will help."

"I hope so," she said, squeezing his hand.

"It's almost time for Papa to close shop," Caleb said. "You better go home."

She shivered against the cool night air. "I'm not leaving Wolf."

"You can't stay here all night. Papa will be furious."

She turned to face him. "Go home and close my bedroom door. Papa will think I'm not feeling well." Her father never entered her room when the door was closed.

Caleb gave a reluctant nod. "There's some dried meat and cheese in the wagon. I'll go and get it."

She waited by the door while he ran to the wagon to fetch the food. She took the small package from him, surprised at how hungry she suddenly felt. "What about you and Papa? What are you going to eat?"

"We'll grab something to eat at Redd's." He hesitated. "I'll be back in the morning."

She hated to see him go. "Should I give him more medicine?"

He shook his head. "Doc Myers said we have to be careful when administering laudanum not to overdose or cause addiction." He seemed reluctant to leave her. "Did you know we have sixty thousand miles of blood vessels in our body? Not only that, we have—"

"Go," she said, recognizing the delaying tactic for what it was. She pushed him out the door and stood in front of the church until the rattling sound of wagon wheels faded away.

Feeling very much alone, she gazed at the bright starry sky and began to pray. She prayed mostly for Wolf but she also asked God's help in another matter close to her heart. *God, Caleb would make such a wonderful doctor—the best. You know he would. Please, please help me land a job so I can help put him through school. Amen.*

From the distance came the sound of a fiddle, but she was unable to pick out the tune. Lights from the various saloons cast the town in a faint glow.

It was a town she'd known all her life. Yet tonight it looked strange to her, almost foreign, like she was an outsider and didn't belong. If only she could talk to her best friend Monica, but she didn't dare. It was bad enough that Caleb was involved.

She hated having to keep Wolf's presence a secret, but she didn't want to put him in any more peril than he already was. Barnes's article made him sound dangerous, and the sheriff did nothing to dispel that notion. Even Timber Joe threatened to shoot Wolf on sight.

Still, she hated being secretive—the isolation of it. The way it separated her from others—her father and friends. Maybe even God, for when she prayed she didn't feel close to him.

Shuddering against the thought, she closed the heavy door and hurried back to Wolf's side. It would be a long and lonely night.

Thirteen

To affect a charming pose, women should strive for a line of grace.
Never wear a fullness of dress that makes the face look insignificant
or a hat that gives undue proportions to the head.

— MISS GERTRUDE HASSLEBRINK, 1878

*L*et me go!" *Wolf fought with every bit of strength he had, but his wiry ten-year-old body was no match for the strapping six-footer whose arms clamped around him with the force of a grizzly.*

"Let go of the box."

"I won't!" Wolf cried, clutching the treasured possession next to his chest. It wasn't much larger than a cigar box but it was his, and he had no intention of parting with it.

"We'll see about that," one of the youths said.

"What's he got in there, gold?" another asked.

With only the stars to guide them, the four youths trampled through the woods carrying him. Two boys held him under the arms, the other two held his feet. The boys' joking voices were soon drowned out by the swift-flowing Rocky Creek River.

They reached the water's edge and someone lit a torch. Startled, Wolf stopped squirming. Though he feared what they had in store for him, he refused to let them know he was scared. It wasn't the first time he'd been bullied. Not by any means. He'd learned through the years not to let on how afraid he was, as that only prolonged the torment.

Shadows danced like frenzied spirits around them, but the tall pines were so still the dark, looming shadows might have been painted against the star-studded sky.

Strong hands lifted him into a small rocking rowboat. In the light of the flickering torch, the faces of the youths became clear. A scar . . . one blue eye, one brown . . .

Then a voice. "No. We can't do this!"

"Relax. We're just having a little fun." One of the youths leaned over the side of the boat. He had a scar that ran from his brow to his chin. "What's it gonna be? The box or a ride down the river?"

Wolf shook his head. "It's mine!"

Scarface rocked the boat back and forth so violently that Wolf was forced to let go of the box and grab hold of the side. The box clamored to the bottom of the boat. One of the other youths reached for it. Wolf dived for it but it was too late. The boy let out a whoop and ran away.

"Come back," Wolf called. He tried to stand but the boat was rocking so hard he was knocked off his feet. He fell with a thud, hitting his head. Dazed, it took him a few moments to realize he was in trouble. The boat had pulled free from its moorings and was now caught in the strong current.

He heard shouts from the distance but was too panicky to make out what anyone said. He searched frantically for oars but there were none. In a desperate attempt to keep the boat from going down the dreaded rapids, he tried paddling with his arms to no avail.

The boat continued down the river, faster and faster . . .

Wolf woke with a start. He was dead. He was certain of it. He could hear the heavenly host.

"God give us strength. God give us hope . . ."

He rubbed his eyes. If he wasn't dead, where was he? And why were angels singing?

The edges of his mind dull as an old rusty knife, he blinked until his vision cleared. He turned his head to look around. Threads of sunlight filtered in through slotted walls. He lifted the blanket and peered down the length of his body. He was naked except for his bandaged leg.

Bits and pieces of the last few days and nights came back to him. He had no idea how long he'd lain there, but he guessed it was at least three or four days, maybe more.

It seemed as if every time he opened his eyes, she was there. Lucy Fairbanks.

Her touch had been as soft as a rose petal, her voice gentle to the ear even as she forced liquids down his throat.

"God give us strength. God . . ."

Slowly he sat up, the muscles of his body protesting every move. Where was he? He couldn't remember ever feeling so weak. He held his head between his hands. The singing stopped, along with the resonant sounds of a tuneless piano. Shuffling feet followed by a booming voice rattled the very walls around him.

"Welcome on this glorious day the Lord has made . . ."

His mind whirled.

The voice continued. "God offers us life through the cross. We accept his offer through baptism."

Wolf fought off a wave of dizziness. The words tumbled around and around in his head but nothing made sense.

"Water washes away our old lives, allowing us to begin anew."

Wolf shook his head. What was the man saying? Wolf knew about water. To him it represented death and drowning, not life.

A baby cried out and Wolf blinked. It seemed like the cries filtered from the very walls around him. Then all was quiet.

Wolf stood. A wave of dizziness washed over him but it passed quickly. Putting as little pressure as possible on his injured leg, he staggered across the tiny room, dragging the blanket with him. Bracing himself against the wall, he cracked open the door and peered though the small opening.

A preacher stood only a few short feet away in gospel mode. Dressed in a black frock, arms raised, he addressed a church full of people.

Wolf quietly closed the door, leaning on it until he gathered enough strength to make it back to his makeshift bed.

The baptism complete, the preacher began his sermon. "Jesus said forgive your enemies seventy times seven!" the preacher's voice boomed.

Wolf pulled the blanket over his head, but there was no drowning out the voice. *"Forgive . . . "*

Easy for you to say, preacher. Easy for you to say.

He had little patience for preachers. Left on the steps of the mission as a baby, he'd had his fill of religion. He never felt like he belonged at such a rigid place. At the mission he was called Patrick after some saint, and the name fit him like someone's loose-fitting hand-me-downs. As a child he spent long hours in front of a beveled-looking glass reciting names, trying to find one that fit. *Michael, John, William, Matthew . . .*

He didn't know who his parents were, but for some reason he couldn't explain, he was convinced his mother had named him before placing him on those mission steps and that the name was buried deep inside his consciousness.

The missionaries said he was half-breed: not Indian, not white, but mixed in a way that was "unnatural." Behavior regarded as normal in the other boys was deemed wild in him.

"You're acting like a savage," his instructors would say when he grew restless during his studies. He soon learned that savage was another name for Indian. Too young to know that they were only following the policy of the Office of Indian Affairs policy to "kill the Indian and save the man" or, in his case, the boy, he rebelled.

He decided to search out Indian names but the mission

library offered no help. He began hanging around the Indians that worked in the mission fields. He studied the way they walked and talked. Though they were forced to speak English at the mission, many would fall back on their own language when they were out of ear range of the missionaries.

Fascinated by how Indians rode without a saddle and mounted their horses from the right instead of the left, Wolf practiced. To this day, he still mounted a horse the Indian way and preferred to ride bareback.

He ran away from the mission at the age of ten. Big mistake. He was cornered by four youths who wanted the box he carried that had been left with him as an infant on the mission steps. After they'd sent him down the river, it was only a miracle that a man named Malcolm Combes happened to be in the area and heard his cries.

A cabinetmaker by trade, Combes took him home and named him David, after the boy who alone fought a giant. It was Combes's way of telling him to fight prejudice and injustice, but Wolf often wondered if a weapon existed that could fell such foes.

Combes taught him to read and write and make furniture. Wolf found he had a talent for wood carving and he enjoyed his work. At eighteen he heard one of Combes's customers object to having a half-breed serve him. Worried that he was a liability to Combes, Wolf left the furniture company and traveled from town to town looking for employment.

During this time he discovered an amazing thing. He could grow a full mustache, something most full-blooded Indians could not do. He became convinced this meant he was supposed to live as a white man. However, he soon discovered the futility of hiding behind facial hair.

He considered traveling to The Nation, hoping someone could lead him to the man who carved the wolf on the missing box. But he couldn't forget what happened after the cavalry left Texas to fight in the War Between the States. Indians burned down the Combes's furniture business along with several farms in the Texas panhandle. Combes never fully recovered from his losses, either financial or health-wise. After that, Wolf had grave doubts about pursuing his Indian heritage.

He was a man who lived between two worlds: one which he rejected and one which rejected him.

Upon hearing that Combes had an apoplexy, Wolf returned home to help care for him until his death. It was the least he could do for the man who had rescued him from the river all those years ago.

Combes's son, Joseph, took over the furniture company and offered Wolf his old job back. Wolf was touched by the offer and would have accepted on the spot had Malcolm Combes not convinced him on his deathbed to return to Rocky Creek.

"Find the boys who did that awful thing. Find the box they took from you. That's your stone," he'd said. "That will help you put the demons of your past to rest." They were the last words Combes said before meeting his Maker.

"Find the box. Got to find the stone." Wolf was hardly aware that he spoke aloud. His mind dull with memories, he drifted off again and was back in the boat. Water all around him.

With a start, he woke. Eyes open, he studied a water stain on the ceiling . . . shaped like a dinghy.

Always, always the boat. It was as if he had been born on that boat and at times like this he thought he would die there.

Lucy insisted upon sitting in the second row of the church, her father and brother on either side of her. It was one of two rows normally saved for the hard of hearing or newly disgraced. Reverend Wells insisted that everyone fell short of the glory of God and sitting up front made you no worse than your neighbors, but few were willing to give up the notion of "sinner rows."

Lucy only wished that "sinners" sitting in the front row didn't wear such outlandish hats.

It was not her family's normal place to sit, and this alone was enough to cause consternation among the congregation. Somewhere it was written that all churchgoers had to sit in the same pew week after week, month after month, unless, of course, one had lost his hearing or had committed an offense that required front pew penance.

Though the handsome young preacher stood center stage, all eyes were on Lucy. Gloved hands raised to conceal gossipy lips failed to drown out the question on everyone's mind: What did Lucy Fairbanks do this time?

Before sliding onto the hard wooden pew, her father glanced at the other worshippers and shrugged as if to say he no more understood his daughter then the rest of them did.

Lucy simply ignored the glares. She had other things on her mind—like trying to stay awake. Between worrying that someone would discover Wolf at the church, and traveling back and forth to care for him, she'd hardly slept a wink all week.

From where she sat, she could keep her eye on the door leading to the anteroom. She'd even gone to the bother of placing extra hymnals on the pews lest church attendance reach unprecedented heights. She didn't want to take a chance on one of the ushers going into the back room for extras.

At one point she imagined that the door off the altar had opened. Thinking she'd failed to shut the door properly, she anxiously peered through the feathers of the outlandish hat in front of her for a better look. It turned out to be only her imagination. Hand on her chest, she sat back with a sigh of relief.

She tried not to think about the man on the other side

of that flimsy door. Some of the townsfolk would have a fit if they knew how close they sat to the rumored wild man of Rocky Creek.

She giggled at the thought and this brought a startled look from her father and a frown from Mrs. Weatherbee, who was sitting across the aisle next to her twenty-eight-year-old son, her pride and joy. The woman still wore her dark hair parted in the middle and pulled back into a tight knot, a popular style during the war. Her outdated hairstyle was an ill-conceived attempt to keep the last semblance of youth from slipping away.

Stifling a yawn and trying not to think of Wolf, Lucy pulled her gaze away from the woman and forced herself to concentrate on the preacher.

Reverend Wells had done much to restore the town's faith. Formerly from Boston, he did have one annoying fault. At times, he got so carried away with preaching the gospel that his poor wife, Sarah, would cough in an effort to get her husband to wrap up his long-winded sermon.

At such times the grateful congregation would follow her lead until the hacking grew so loud that Justin Wells had no choice but to say a closing prayer, even though it was obvious he was reluctant to do so.

Though the church had been built in 1845, the same year Texas became a state, it had been sorely neglected during the War Between the States and the Indian wars to the point of being altogether deserted in recent years. Pews had been recently added, replacing mismatched chairs, and new stained glass windows installed, but the siding was warped and the roof missing shingles.

Prior to the arrival of Reverend Wells, the townsfolk had to depend on a circuit preacher who showed up once every six months, if they were lucky, and who always preached the same sermon.

Reverend Wells had a way of making the Bible come alive, but Lucy felt so nervous she could hardly concentrate on what he was saying. She cleared her throat and that proved to be a mistake. The congregation, thinking Sarah had signaled her husband to stop preaching, imitated her until a chorus of coughs filled the church.

At first Reverend Wells tried to ignore the hacking, until his voice was drowned out and he was forced to sit down.

Behind him, the choir led by her friend Barrel stood like rising flags. One singer started across the altar. Thinking he was heading for the anteroom, Lucy jumped to her feet with a cry of dismay. Everyone turned to look at her with an air of expectancy. Obviously, they thought a public confession was forthcoming.

"Amen!" she stammered, her face burning.

"Amen!" the congregation echoed in unison.

It turned out that the singer was simply retrieving his music stand and had no intention of going into the anteroom.

Gulping in embarrassment, she sat down.

Her father leaned toward her. "What is the matter with you? You're acting very strange."

"I thought the sermon was very . . . moving. Didn't you?"

He turned his head away. "There are some things that can't be forgiven," he said quietly.

Lucy shivered, but whether from the forbidding look on his face or fear that the stowaway would be discovered, she didn't know.

After what seemed like an interminable length of time, the church service finally ended, and her friend Monica pulled her aside. "Lucy, what in the world? Sitting in the front like that." She lowered her voice. "What have you done this time?"

"Nothing," Lucy said. Well, almost nothing.

Monica eyed her with suspicion. "You didn't even sit in front when you caused that stampede or when you—"

"Shh. I can't talk about it right now," Lucy whispered.

Monica gave her an odd look. "I saw your photograph in the newspaper. Does this mean you're working for Mr. Barnes?"

"Not anymore," Lucy said. She quickly explained all that had transpired in the last several days and how the editor had rewritten her story. "There is no wild man."

"Oh, Lucy, I'm so sorry. I know how much you wanted that job. Does this mean you're giving up your photography?"

"Of course not," Lucy said. "I'm just not working for Mr. Barnes." God willing, one of the newspapers she wrote to would offer her a job.

"I'll pray for you." Monica frowned. "What you said about the wild man . . . How do you know so much about him?" Fortunately, the parent of a student waylaid Monica, allowing Lucy to make her escape without having to confess.

It took forever for the church to empty, and it was all Millard Weatherbee's fault. Weatherbee was running for state senator, a daring enterprise given his young age and lack of experience, but not impossible. Former slave George Thompson Ruby was elected to the Texas senate at the age of twenty-eight. Apparently Millard thought if George could do it, *he* could do it too.

A compact man with a deep voice, Weatherbee's clothes were almost as progressive as his politics. The only local to wear celluloid collars that required no starch, his shirts had been banned from Lee Wong's Chinese laundry, even with the collars removed. Not only did the new collars melt when over-heated, celluloid occasionally exploded. Anything that came in contact with Weatherbee's collars was suspect in Wong's eyes.

The candidate's crisp black bow tie with its wide flat knot was every bit as perfect as his neatly trimmed mustache.

Pastor Wells shook the candidate's hand. "I heard they've broken ground for Texas's new capitol building."

Weatherbee nodded. "Yes, and from what I hear, it's going

to be a beauty," he said, adding in his well-modulated voice, "I hope I can count on your vote, Reverend Wells."

Pastor Wells studied the earnest young man. "That depends."

"Depends, sir?"

"How do you feel about the Texas Constitution regarding schools?"

Weatherbee looked perplexed. "Schools?"

"The Constitution states that we must provide separate schools for whites and colored," Pastor Wells explained. "I don't believe God wanted us to separate his children."

Lucy knew this subject was close to the pastor's heart, which explained why Rocky Creek had no official school.

"Ah. You must be referring to article seven, section seven," Millard said, eager to make an impression. "Clearly that needs to be revisited, and if you vote for me, I will do everything in my power to see that it is."

"What about the Chinese Exclusion Act?" Pastor Wells continued. The act prevented Lee Wong from fulfilling his dream of becoming an American citizen.

"That's at the federal level," Weatherbee replied with a nervous twitch, as if he feared his answer would cost him a vote.

Instead, Pastor Wells nodded in approval and shook Millard's hand. "In that case, I hope you one day run for US Senate. Meanwhile, you can most assuredly count on my vote."

Millard's mother beamed with pride. Millard's stepfather was a ne'er-do-well who couldn't even support his own family. Ever since her husband vanished several weeks prior, Mrs. Weatherbee seemed even more determined that her son make something of himself and not follow in her husband's footsteps.

No one knew what happened to her husband. He simply dropped out of sight. Some believed he simply grew tired of his wife's nagging. Others thought he might have drowned. Either way, his wife seemed more relieved than concerned.

Mrs. Taylor made a rude sound. "You'd have my vote, too, if we women were treated like normal citizens." She sniffed in contempt. "Women didn't even merit a mention in the Constitution."

Miss Hogg drew herself up to her full height and her voice rose accordingly. "I heard some people say that we women were lumped with idiots, lunatics, paupers, and felons."

Mrs. Taylor's face grew such a horrible shade of red Lucy feared for her well-being. "All this talk about democracy makes no sense when half of us are denied the vote. It's time for us lunatics and idiots to rise up and show them we mean business."

"I agree," Lucy said and, in fact, she did. At the moment, however, all she wanted was for everyone to leave.

"Hear, hear," added Miss Hogg, making a pumping motion with her right arm.

Millard's mother, quick to see the benefit that women's votes would give her son, clapped her hands in approval. Today, she looked alert and nothing like the woman Lucy often saw muttering to herself and staring at her with blank eyes.

Mrs. Taylor looked pleased. "I'll contact Mrs. Folsom and tell her we wish to join her movement." Erminia Folsom, the wife of a Unitarian minister, had attempted to organize the women's rights movement in Texas. So far, she'd met with little success. "We'll change the name of our quilting group to the Rocky Creek Suffra-Quilters." Her proclamation was met with nods of approval.

Caleb poked his head through the open doorway and motioned for Lucy to hurry. "Papa's waiting," he called.

"I'm coming," she said, though she stayed where she was until everyone had left the church. She had no intention of letting anyone discover Wolf's presence.

Fourteen

A camera cannot turn back the clock. It will not reveal how you looked ten years prior no matter how much you beg, cajole, or try to bribe the photographer.

— MISS GERTRUDE HASSLEBRINK, 1878

Later that afternoon, Lucy waited for her father to settle down for his usual Sunday nap before returning to the church with fresh bandages and hot soup.

She entered the anteroom and set her basket on the floor. Wolf lay still, his eyes shut. She kneeled by his side and laid her hand on his forehead. He was cool to the touch, his skin no longer ashen. She drew back and studied his face. So why wasn't he awake?

"Listen to me, Mr. Wolf. I promised you no doctor but something isn't right. Your fever's gone and your color looks normal. If you don't open your eyes, I'm going to have to send Caleb to fetch Doc Myers." She reached in her basket for the flask of hot soup. "I should have fetched the doctor before now. But no, I had to listen to you, a man half out of his wits and . . ."

"I swear you could talk a dead man out of his grave."

Startled by his voice, Lucy dropped the flask and swung around. "You're awake." She almost fainted in relief. Never

135

could she imagine seeing a more welcome sight. *Oh, thank you, thank you, God.*

Wolf peered at her with one eye. "A man would have to be deaf to sleep around here." He sat up slowly and leaned his back against the wall.

Her gaze drifted down his powerful bare chest all the way to the blanket at his waist and her cheeks flared with warmth. She turned her back to him and righted the flask.

"Where are my clothes?" he asked.

She dug into her picnic basket for the tin cup. "Your trousers were covered in blood and I was unable to remove the stain." She nodded toward his laundered shirt, which was folded neatly on a shelf, next to his knife. "I'll ask Caleb if you can borrow a pair of his trousers."

"Caleb?"

"My brother. He wants to be a doctor. He took care of your leg." She met his gaze and her heart turned over. Even his whiskered chin failed to take away from his good looks. "I brought you hot soup."

He grimaced as if in pain. "Smells good."

She leaned toward him, but kept from touching him. "Are you all right?"

He rubbed his chin. "I could use a razor," he said. "If it's not too much trouble."

"No trouble." She unscrewed the cap of the flask and poured hot soup into the cup. At least she didn't have to feed him. Forcing nourishment down his throat was a chore she'd come to dread.

He looked at her askew. "Do people still think I'm a danger to society?"

She bit her lip. Even though she blamed Barnes for Wolf's predicament, she couldn't help but feel guilty. "I'm afraid so," she admitted.

"Then I better leave before someone finds me here."

She nodded. She was so convinced that someone would discover him during worship service, she had been sick to her stomach with worry.

He glanced around. "Why did you bring me here?" he asked. "To a *church*?"

He made it sound like bringing him to a church was a sin.

"I didn't know where else to take you," she said. "I needed some place safe."

"Safe?" He repeated the word as if it were foreign.

She nodded. "When I was a little girl, I used to hide here whenever I was afraid," she explained. Though at the time, she didn't remember the room being so small or drafty. "The church was deserted back then, but it still felt safe." It wasn't until Reverend Wells came to town that the church was restored.

He looked puzzled, as if he couldn't understand how she would think a church safe. "What were you afraid of?" he asked.

Feeling self-conscious and maybe even a little bit foolish, she brushed his question away with a shrug and handed him the cup of soup. "Every child is afraid of something." She smiled at him, which was a mistake because it drew his gaze to her lips. She recapped the flask, giving it more attention than was necessary.

He blew on the hot liquid and took a sip. After drinking half he handed the cup back to her. "Not only is she a most efficient nurse, but she can cook," he said, his voice warm with approval.

His praise only added to her discomfort. Now came the hard part. "I have to change your bandage." If only Caleb were here.

Wolf started to push the blanket away. Fortunately, he thought better of it and stuck his leg out from beneath the cover.

She kneeled down and probed the area around his wound as she'd watched Caleb do. The skin was only slightly red with very little swelling. It looked ninety-nine percent better than it had a few days earlier. Her eyes locked with his. Something in the way he returned her gaze made her cheeks blaze, and she quickly averted her eyes.

"M-most of the infection is gone," she stammered, keeping her lashes lowered. Hands shaking, she carefully applied salve per Caleb's instructions, then wrapped clean gauze around his thigh.

She was accustomed to changing his bandage when he was asleep. Now that he was awake, the task seemed that much more formidable. Though she tried to focus solely on his wound—and was careful where to look and put her hands— she was totally aware of how close she was to . . . *him*.

Her stomach clenched with nervousness. It didn't help that she could feel the heat of his gaze while she worked. As usual when she felt nervous or anxious, she began to talk, and once started, she couldn't seem to stop herself. After snipping the gauze with her scissors, she tied it in a neat bow. She then pulled her hand away as if it were on fire.

". . . and the sheriff should be ashamed of himself for releasing you when you were naked . . . I mean injured."

Horrified by the slip of her tongue, she tried to avoid his amused smile but her already reddened cheeks burned.

"The sheriff had nothing to do with my current state of nudity. Whereas you . . ."

She stood abruptly, sending her scissors and gauze flying. "My brother undressed you."

"Then I am eternally grateful to him. I would hate to have robbed you of your innocence."

She looked him straight in the eye. "No danger of that. My brother is very discreet."

"I'm sure his patients appreciate his discretion." His

mouth quirked with humor. "Especially those with any . . . shortcomings."

To hide her heated cheeks, she wiped the salve off her hands with a cloth and quickly changed the subject. "I looked for your horse but couldn't find it. I do hope he's all right."

"Shadow takes care of himself. He'll find *me* when I need him to."

Shadow. She knew so little about him that even the name of his horse seemed significant.

He regarded her for a moment. "Why did you help me?"

"Not only was it the Christian thing to do . . ." She glanced at him through lowered lashes. "It was partly my fault you landed in jail." Trusting Barnes to print the truth was a mistake she wouldn't make again.

He gave her a wry look. "Partly?"

"I took the photograph but Barnes replaced my article with his own. Had he published what I had written, people would know the truth about you."

"And what would that be?" he asked. "The truth."

"Like I explained . . . I wrote that the rumors about you were false." *The truth is that your kisses are like fire and your arms are like—*

Chest hammering, she quickly scooped the scissors and gauze off the floor and dumped them into the basket. "You saved the stage from being robbed."

When he said nothing, she moved away from him before meeting his gaze. "Had my article been printed you would have been treated as a hero, not a wild man."

"I sincerely doubt that."

"I'm a very persuasive writer," she said.

The corners of his mouth twisted upward. "*That* I don't doubt."

She smiled back at him. "What are you doing in Rocky Creek?" she asked with more than a little curiosity.

In his delirium he'd said things she didn't understand. There were questions she wanted to ask him, questions about the boat that caused him to cry out in his sleep. And who were all those people he kept mentioning?

He took so long to answer that at first she thought he wouldn't. "I have business here," he said at last.

"What kind of business?"

A muscle clenched at his jaw. "I'm looking for . . . some men. They have something of mine."

"Are they the men in the boat?"

A dark expression flashed across his face so quickly she could barely discern its meaning before it disappeared. She'd seen a similar look on her father's face many times through the years.

"How do you know about the boat?" he asked, his voice not rough, exactly, but jagged.

Fearing she'd gone too far, she quickly explained. "You were delirious and . . . and said things—"

"What things?" he demanded.

"I couldn't really make out much. Just something about a boat."

He studied her as if to determine whether she spoke the truth. His furrowed brow disappeared as quickly as it came. He held her gaze for a moment before looking away.

She moistened her lips. "I know everyone in town. Maybe I can help you find the men you're looking for."

He shot her a penetrating look. "It would be better if we don't see each other after today. I don't belong in your world."

She moistened her lips. "Because of your Indian blood?"

His jaw tightened. "I don't belong in that world either."

The man spoke in riddles. Irritated, she tossed the flask into her basket. "If you don't want my help . . ."

"Forgive me, I . . ." A shadow of indecision scurried

across his brow. "One of the men I'm looking for has a scar." He indicated on his face, running a finger from his brow to his chin.

She stilled. "I know of only one man who fits that description."

He stiffened. "Who?"

"The newspaper editor." She could barely keep the rancor out of her voice. "His name is Jacoby Barnes and you'd best stay away from him. The scar was inflicted by his drunken father. He's the one who wrote the article about you."

"This Barnes—" He frowned. "Is he the man you work for?"

"Not anymore. I quit."

He tilted his head in surprise. "Surely you didn't quit because of me?"

"I quit because he's more interested in selling papers than printing the truth. As the article he wrote about you proved."

A shadow of disbelief flitted across his face. "I thought your occupation was of prime importance to you."

"Truth is more important," she said. "That's why I take photographs."

"You think photographs capture the truth?" he asked.

Confused by the question, she frowned. "Don't you?"

He shrugged. "I guess it depends on which truth you're looking for."

His comment surprised her. Years ago she'd seen a stranger photographing a horse he wished to buy. Never having seen a camera, she bombarded the man with questions. He explained how a camera focused on an object with such intensity it was able to pick out traits in an animal that a human eye might miss.

Intrigued, she could think of little else for weeks afterward. The possibilities seemed endless. She became convinced that a camera would illuminate the secrets that surrounded her.

Help her make sense of the dark looks on her father's face, the shadows that seemed to fill every corner of the house.

During all the time she spent searching her photographs for answers, not once had it occurred to her that there could be more than a single truth.

"Did I say something wrong?" he asked.

"No," she said. "Nothing."

"Then why so silent? It's not like you."

She looked up at him, her finger gripping the handle of her basket. "Do you think Mr. Barnes is the man you're looking for?"

Again the dark expression. She felt the strongest urge to run her fingers over his forehead to smooth away his frown as she had soothed his feverish brow.

"Perhaps," he said at last.

It was obvious by his closed expression that he wasn't about to reveal his business with Mr. Barnes. Not wanting to deal with more secrets, she started for the door. "I have to go."

"When will you be back?"

Hand on the doorknob she hesitated. "Tonight . . . after supper." She glanced over her shoulder. "I'll bring you food and clothes."

"Whatever you can round up will do," he said.

Tightening her hold on the basket, she left and he called after her. "I'd be mighty grateful if you could bring a razor." She kept walking and didn't look back.

Fifteen

If your hands are red and wrinkled, do not allow them in camera
view unless clad in gloves. Better still, clasp them behind your back.
Clenched fists hide nothing and reveal everything.
—MISS GERTRUDE HASSLEBRINK, 1878

After Lucy left, Wolf tried to decide how best to confront the man named Barnes, but he couldn't focus. He didn't have his strength back yet, and the memory of a certain smile and two pretty blue eyes kept intruding upon his thoughts.

He clenched his hands and tried pushing the vision away. He had more important things to think about than Lucy Fairbanks. He was grateful to her, of course, for nursing him back to health, but it was the least she could do. It was Lucy and her confounded camera that got him shot in the first place and pretty near cost him his life.

She talked too much. Was too darn inquisitive. Stubborn. Overly ambitious. The list went on. She was all the things he hated in a woman.

And yet . . .

He was keenly aware of another side of her—a soft, gentle, and compassionate side that pulled him out of his delirium like a lighthouse guiding a ship through stormy seas.

A Christian, she called herself, but even that didn't explain why she looked puzzled when he mentioned that he wasn't of her world. Was she really so naive as to think that his mixed blood was of no consequence? How he wished that were true. He'd tried living as a white man, living as an Indian, but the blood that ran through his veins was like oil and water, keeping him from either world.

That's why he came back to Rocky Creek. If only he could find the box taken from him all those years ago, the box that was left in his cradle with him when he was abandoned. Maybe then he would at least know his real name, where he belonged. It wasn't much but it was something.

It was crazy to think the box snatched out of his hands so long ago still existed after all this time. Or even that it contained answers to his questions. Still, Combes's deathbed plea had somehow triggered David's overpowering need to find his roots.

He was close. He felt it in his bones. Already he knew one of those youths by name and, thanks to Lucy, maybe even the name of a second one. It was a start.

Feeling restless, he looked around for something to do. There wasn't anything to read but a stack of McGuffey's schoolbooks and a Bible. He touched the leather cover of the Bible but didn't open it. Couldn't. When he lived at the mission, the students were required to memorize scripture. Recalling the punishment he endured for misquoting a verse, having to sit on his knees for hours on a hard tile floor, he quickly removed his hand.

Just let Lucy hurry back with his clothes. That's all he asked. The sooner he could finish his business and return to the Panhandle and the job waiting for him there, the sooner he could leave the painful memories behind.

It was dark by the time he heard her ride up to the church on her horse. He had just returned from bathing in the creek and his hair was wet. He quickly donned his buckskin shirt and wrapped a blanket around his waist.

Standing in the sanctuary, he held up the kerosene lantern so she wouldn't have to walk in the dark.

She greeted him with a smile.

"Ah, good, you brought trousers."

"And a razor," she said.

Once inside the anteroom, he took Caleb's pants, turned, and dropped his blanket.

"Ohhh," she cried. "You could have at least warned me."

He glanced over his shoulder. Her back was toward him, her hands covering her face. "Sorry," he said. He'd been so anxious to dress and regain some sense of normalcy, he hadn't even considered her sensibilities, and for that he felt ashamed. "You can look."

Caleb's pants were at least four inches too short but they would have to do for now.

Acting as if she didn't notice, she busied herself setting out his meal, picnic style, while he shaved. Staring at his reflection in the little handheld looking glass she brought him, he lathered his chin with soap and scraped off his whiskers with the straight-edge razor.

Given the way she smiled at him when he finished the task, it must have been a vast improvement.

She'd brought beef stew, and the savory smell made his stomach turn over in anticipation. The stew was every bit as delicious as he imagined, and he couldn't remember ever enjoying a meal more. After he finished he wiped his newly shaven chin with a cloth napkin.

"I have a gift for you," he said.

"A gift." Her eyes widened in surprise.

He pulled a wooden bracelet from beneath his pillow and handed it to her. He'd worked on it for most of the afternoon.

She gasped when she saw it and ran her finger over the engraved picture of a wolf. "It's . . . it's beautiful."

After a moment she handed the bracelet back to him. "I . . . I can't accept this," she said. "It wouldn't be proper."

He took the bracelet in hand and slipped it onto her slender wrist. It looked perfect.

"Considering my state of undress these past few days, I believe you and I have passed the point of worrying about being proper," he said. "Accept it as a token of my gratitude for taking care of me." He released her hand but only because he was afraid of what would happen if he didn't.

She fingered the intricately carved wolf. "Mr. Wolf. I . . . I don't know what to say."

"David," he said. "Call me David." David seemed more real to him than Wolf, a name adapted from the carving on the box left in his cradle. He reckoned the animal held some meaning to the person who left it with him.

"David," she whispered. Holding her hand up, she continued to admire the bracelet. "I'll always treasure this. Thank you."

He grinned. "I'm glad you like it. By the way, don't bother coming tomorrow as I won't be here."

"You aren't leaving town, are you?" Her indifferent voice contradicted her strained expression.

"Not till I finish my business."

"With Mr. Barnes."

He said nothing and her eyes narrowed and mouth twisted in what looked like disapproval.

"I better go," she said, surprising him with her abruptness. She quickly gathered up the empty plate and silverware and placed them in the basket.

"You're upset with me," he said.

She bit her lower lip. "I'm not upset."

He studied her. "After everything we've been through, I

thought we were friends, at least in private. Naturally we can't be seen together in public but . . ."

"Because of who you are," she said. "Half Indian and half white."

He felt a squeezing pain in his chest. With those words she had deftly reminded him that he had no right to ask for her friendship, private or otherwise.

When he didn't answer, she shook her head. "We can't be friends," she said firmly, echoing his thoughts. "But not because of your heritage."

He held her gaze. The light from the kerosene lantern turned her eyes into shining stars. "What other reason could there be?"

"You're a man with too many secrets. Secretive people make terrible friends." As an afterthought she added, "They also make terrible parents."

She looked about to leave, but he couldn't bear to see her go. Not with this strain between them. He rose to his feet. "Are you saying you have no secrets, Lucy?"

"I had to keep your secret," she replied, and he could see how much it cost her.

"I'm sorry." He took another step closer and cupped her face in his hands. "I'll never forget your kindness to me."

She moistened her lips, drawing his attention to the pretty curve of her mouth.

"Lucy." He caught a lock of her shiny chestnut hair and twisted it around his finger. "You saved my life. I've never known anyone like you. You made me feel like I belonged for the very first time in my life." He dropped his hands to his sides, glanced around, and laughed. "A dusty, drafty room in the back of a church, and for a time I felt like I belong here. Now I know why you used to hide here. Crazy, isn't it?"

"It's not crazy," she whispered.

They stood staring at each other.

"This is good-bye," he said at last, and the words felt like acid to his tongue. She'd already agreed they couldn't be friends and yet . . .

Her lips parted as if she, too, felt a need to postpone the inevitable. He recalled her hand on his forehead, her gentle touch as she tended to his wound, her delicate scent as she sat by his side watching over him.

He couldn't remember anyone being that kind to him, that concerned. Taking care of him was the Christian thing to do, she'd said, but the missionaries never showed him any kindness. The man who rescued him from the river had never mistreated him and always saw that he had what he needed, but it wasn't in Combes's nature to mollycoddle.

Looking into her big blue eyes was like looking into a perfect world—a world where prejudice and hate didn't exist. Now that he had a glimpse of such a world he knew things would never be the same. *He* would never be the same.

Like a man dying of thirst, he absorbed every detail until her eyes, nose, and sweet curving mouth were forever ingrained in his memory.

As if to sense the growing tension between them, she said, "I . . . I b-better go before Papa discovers I'm gone. I also promised Caleb to quiz him on the human heart. Did you know that . . ."

He wasn't a praying man. If he was he would ask God's help in resisting the temptation she posed. He would ask for the strength to walk out of that door and never look back. Instead he stood frozen in place, willing himself not to do something he would most likely regret.

I can't do this, I can't. I won't. He didn't realize he had groaned as if in pain until he saw the concern on her face.

"Are you all right?" she asked. Much to his dismay, she stepped so close to him he could feel the heat of her body. She reached up to touch his forehead but he stopped her with a hand on her wrist.

"Yes." *No.* "You better go." He released her hand and lowered his head, meaning to plant a kiss on her cheek—a good-bye kiss. A brotherly kiss. Two acquaintances simply bidding each other farewell.

Instead his lips brushed against hers like a butterfly tentatively testing a flower. She sighed softly and gazed at him, her eyes glowing with tenderness.

Heart thudding, he pulled her all the way into his arms, locking her in his embrace. Since she offered no resistance he knew he was doomed. Instead of pushing him away, she astonished him by stretching her body the full length of his to wrap her arms around his neck. At that moment he wasn't half this or half that. He was simply all man.

This time when his lips met hers there was no holding back. Judging by the way she returned his kisses, she didn't mind. Not one bit.

Pulling his lips away, he pressed his forehead against hers. "Lucy," he whispered, simply for the pleasure of saying her name. No sooner was the word out of his mouth than his lips found hers again. She moaned softly and he deepened his kiss.

Something snapped, the tension in the air dissipated. Her body stiffened next to his. It took him a moment to realize that the door to the anteroom had flown open.

"Oh!" came an unfamiliar voice.

Lucy pulled out of his arms and cried, "Monica!"

Before the intruder could say another word, a stack of hymnals fell from a shelf and the door slammed shut with a bang. More books fell, knocking over the lantern. The smell of kerosene was followed by a bright flash of light and suddenly Monica's cloak was on fire.

Lucy cried out and Monica jumped around, screaming. Wolf grabbed a woolen blanket and threw it over her to smother the flames. By then, a wall of fire had trapped them inside the tiny smoke-filled room.

"Quick, do something," Lucy cried. "Or we'll die and . . ." Words streamed out of her like sand in an hourglass.

He could barely breathe for all the smoke and there she was, talking up a storm.

He grabbed another blanket off his makeshift bed and flung it against the door, but it was too late. Flames shot across the ceiling like an invading army.

Flinging hot cinders off her clothes, Monica covered her mouth with one hand and coughed. Lucy kept talking.

"I don't know who will take care of Caleb and Papa and . . ."

Realizing the futility of trying to put out the fire, Wolf threw the blanket down. "Let's get out of here."

He held his arm out to protect Lucy and gave the opposite wall a couple of kicks with his good leg. Wood splintered with a cracking sound, leaving a gaping hole, but the fresh air made the flames burn brighter.

"Hurry!" he rasped from smoke-filled lungs. He grabbed Lucy by the hand and dragged her outside. Much to his horror, the other woman failed to follow.

≈

The fresh air was almost as painful to breathe as the smoke. Lucy coughed until tears rolled down her cheeks. Her eyes burned. Blinking furiously, she glanced around and suddenly realized she was alone. "Monica? David?"

Panicking, she stared in horror at the flames leaping high above the roofline, sending brilliant sparks into the darkness.

"David!" she screamed. "Monica!"

A portion of the church collapsed inward with a loud crackling sound, sending sparks high into the nighttime sky. She ran forward but the heat of the fire and falling timbers forced her back.

The remainder of the church's roof caved in with a crash, and Lucy let out a gut-wrenching sob. Then she saw him, saw David carrying Monica in his arms, and she practically collapsed with thanksgiving.

He ran a safe distance away from the church and laid Monica on the ground.

Lucy rushed toward them and dropped to her knees next to Monica's side. Monica's body was racked with coughs but she was alive.

"Thank God," Lucy cried, hugging her close. Tears of gratitude streamed down her cheeks.

"She'll be all right," David said. His face lit by firelight was smudged with soot, his voice roughened by smoke.

Choked with relief, Lucy's mouth felt like it was stuffed with cotton. Her watery eyes distorted the flames into a blur of bright light.

David took her hand and pulled her to her feet. He gathered her in his arms, holding her so tight she could feel his heartbeat. "It's okay," he murmured soothingly. "You're safe."

Head on his chest, she clung to him, her trembling body seeking the warmth and comfort he offered.

From the distance came the shouts of men racing up the hill toward them on horseback and foot.

"I have to go," David whispered. He held her face and gazed at her for an instant before pressing his lips against her forehead. "Take care of your friend."

With that he turned, limped down the hill behind the still-burning church, and vanished in the thick grove of trees below.

Still very much shaken, Lucy dropped to her knees. Monica's eyes were open now. "Oh, Monica, if anything had happened to you, I don't know what I would have done."

Monica took her hand and squeezed it. "I'm okay," she rasped.

Lucy squeezed back. "What were you doing here?"

"Caleb—" As if it took all her strength to utter that one word, she laid her head back, breathing hard. "I was worried about you. You've been acting so strange lately. I made Caleb tell me where"—she coughed—"where I could find you."

Marshal Armstrong came running up to them, followed by at least a dozen other men. After that everything was a blur, like an underexposed photograph.

⟨≈⟩

Wolf stayed hidden in the woods and watched the chaos on the hill. All that remained of the church was a blazing framework and a pile of burning debris. No one attempted to put out the blaze, but two men moved Lucy's and Monica's horses a safe distance away. Several others scattered across the church property, shoveling dirt onto any sparks that had landed on the ground.

A man hastened toward the two women with bag in hand. From his hiding place, Wolf couldn't make out the man's face but he was certain it was the doctor.

Satisfied that Lucy and her friend were being cared for, Wolf started through the woods. He still felt weak and his leg was sore. His progress was slow. When he was a safe distance away from the fire, he stuck two fingers in his mouth and whistled.

Nothing. He walked another mile or so and tried again. Still nothing. On the third try, his whistle was greeted with a high whinny—a welcoming sound.

Muffled at first, Shadow's hoofbeats quickly grew louder. The horse flew out of the woods in a black streak, his coat aglow in the silvery light of a full moon.

Sixteen

Persons with generous proportions should make every effort not to draw the camera's eye away from those less endowed. Never speak disparagingly of another's photograph or suggest in any way that your image is superior.

— MISS GERTRUDE HASSLEBRINK, 1878

Lucy couldn't sleep. It was a warm night, and the air hung heavy and still. Even so, she lay in bed shivering. Her throat felt dry and no amount of water could quench her thirst. Nor could any amount of bathing get rid of the rancid smell that permeated her hair and skin.

Doc Myers seemed confident that Monica would fully recover, but she had inhaled a great deal of smoke and Lucy couldn't help but worry.

Fortunately the fire hadn't spread to the nearby woods, but nothing was left of the church save a pile of smoldering ashes.

She should never have hidden Wolf in the anteroom. Pastor Wells and Sarah had worked hard to restore the church and grow the congregation. Now it seemed that their efforts had all been in vain.

She groaned and covered her face with both hands. "The church is destroyed and it's all my fault."

It wasn't only guilt that kept her tossing and turning. She couldn't stop thinking about David. Where was he? What was to become of him? And why did her overactive mind continue to dwell on their last tender kiss? Wolf hadn't kissed her as much as branded her, and the very thought made her heart race.

She reached on the nightstand for the carved bracelet he gave her and held it close to her heart.

"This is good-bye."

It was for the best. He had his secrets, she had her dreams. There wasn't much room left for anything else. Still, she would miss him. Miss that crooked smile of his. The way he tilted his head when she spoke.

From the distance came the sound of a rooster greeting dawn. The familiar crow lulled her into a restless sleep. By the time she woke, her room was bright with sunlight. The events of the previous night flooded back like water from a broken dam.

Papa! She jumped out of bed, grabbed her dressing gown, and ran barefooted through the house.

Too late. Her father had already left for the day. Now he would hear about her latest misadventures from the townsfolk. She'd hoped to save him embarrassment by telling him herself.

Torn between racing to town before her father heard the news from his customers, or checking on Monica's condition, she quickly dressed. A short while later she was in the saddle, heading for Ma's boardinghouse where Monica lived.

The proprietor, Mrs. Stephens, was a grandmotherly woman who insisted upon being called just plain Ma. She opened the door and greeted Lucy with an uncharacteristic frown. The delectable smell of fresh-baked pastry wafted from the house.

"Am I glad to see you. I've been worried sick. Monica never came home last night."

Lucy was alarmed by the news. Doc Myers told her Monica would be all right and she believed him. Lucy would never have left her had she thought otherwise. "Doc Myers must have kept her overnight."

Ma's eyes grew round. "My word, whatever for?"

"There was a fire at the church last night—an accident. Monica and I were there."

Ma's hands flew to her face. "Mercy me. I hope she's all right."

"Me too." Lucy started to leave but then remembered something. "Would you please tell Mr. Garrett that I'll retake his photograph at no extra charge?" Mr. Garrett was one of Ma's boarders. Lucy hadn't seen the Englishman since their strange exchange.

"I guess you haven't heard," Ma replied. "Mr. Garrett has left town."

"Left town?" That was a surprise. "What about his plans to go into the cattle business?"

Ma rolled her eyes skyward. "He had some sort of religious experience. Something to do with his departed wife. Said he's going to join a monastery."

Lucy's mouth fell open. "All because of a double exposure?" she gasped.

Ma's eyes widened. "A *double* exposure? Oh dear. I hope it wasn't smallpox."

"No, no, nothing like that." Lucy was in too much of a hurry to explain how Mr. Garrett had mistaken the ghostly figure of Mrs. Weatherbee in his photograph for his dead wife. She promised to check on Monica and left.

Since the quickest way to Doc Myers's house was through town, she decided to stop on the way and face her father.

Riding down Main Street, she was surprised by the number of people lining the boardwalk. Had something happened to Monica? To David? Were Monica's burns worse than she knew? Did those annoying wild man rumors still persist?

The number of vehicles parked haphazardly in every direction forced Lucy to tie Tripod to a hitching post a distance away from her father's store where a crowd was gathered in front. No one noticed her presence.

"Lucy's gone too far this time," a rancher named Hampton said. "It wasn't bad enough that she stampeded my cattle. Now she's gone and burned down the church."

"And that ain't all she's done," Old Man Appleby added.

Everyone started talking at once. Even those who had never stepped foot inside the church saw fit to lament its destruction.

Town Marshal Armstrong stepped forward. He had done much in his short time as marshal to rid the town of troublemakers, but he had less success in keeping folks from storming his office every time the least thing went wrong.

He raised his hand. "One at a time. Mrs. Hitchcock."

A collective groan rose from the crowd. A member of what was now called the Suffra-Quilters, it took Mrs. Hitchcock twice as long as anyone else to voice her opinion because of her habit of repeating herself.

Seemingly oblivious to the protests around her, she made her way to the front, her outlandish hat serenely floating through midair like a ship at sea.

The marshal stepped back to make room for her generous proportions. Turning around, she looked down her considerable nose at her dissenters. "I say Mr. Fairbanks should pay for building a new church . . . a new church." She then promptly repeated herself before adding, "Lucy is his daughter . . . his daughter. It's only right."

Groans turned to approval and some even clapped.

Alarm flew through Lucy. Papa couldn't afford to pay for a new church.

The woman's strident voice ringing in her ears, Lucy marched in front of the crowd and stepped onto the wooden sidewalk. She squeezed next to Mrs. Hitchcock and turned to face the icy stares. Everyone fell silent.

"I apologize for what happened last night. I can't tell you how terrible I feel. I just want you to know, I will find a way to pay for a new church building."

"How do you propose to do that?" someone called.

It was a question she was not prepared to answer. "I'll . . . I'll sell photographs." Lots of them, she hoped. And, God willing, maybe the mail would soon bring a much-needed job offer.

"That's all we need, more trouble," heckled the owner and namesake of Jake's Saloon.

"Ain't you caused enough trouble with that camera of yours? I say we should ban it!"

"Stop it, all of you!" came a woman's voice from the back of the crowd. The preacher's wife, Sarah, barreled through the crowd like a cannonball, red boots flashing beneath the swishing hem of her skirt.

Silence prevailed as she made her way up front and stomped up the stairs to the boardwalk. No one would be so bold as to show disrespect to the Reverend's wife, at least not to her face.

"Instead of standing up here jawin' like a bunch of ole crows, we should be figurin' out a way to build a new church," Sarah charged. "If we can build a barn for the Bensons, we can build a church for the Lord."

Appleby scoffed. "It costs money to build. Lumber don't grow on no trees."

Heads nodded. No one saw fit to point out the error of his statement.

Sarah addressed her next comments to Appleby who, as far as anyone knew, had never given a single coin to the church or even to charity. "I reckon we'll all have to dig a little deeper in our pockets, won't we?"

Lucy's father walked out of his store. The moment he spotted her he turned and walked back inside. Lucy's heart fell. She didn't know how she would make up to him for all the trouble she'd caused.

Muttering among themselves, folks began to drift away and Lucy chased after Sarah.

"Sarah, wait."

Sarah turned. "Lucy. Are you okay? You weren't injured in that fire, were you?"

"I'm fine." Lucy laid a hand on Sarah's arm. "I'm so sorry. After all the work you and Reverend Wells have done . . . the fire was an accident and I'll do everything I can to make it right."

"Praise God that no one was seriously injured," Sarah said kindly. "But I don't understand. What were you doin' at the church that time of night? It's not safe for a woman to be out so late."

Lucy withdrew her hand. She didn't want to say anything about David, but she owed Sarah and the pastor an explanation.

"Promise you won't say anything?" Lucy said.

Sarah frowned. "It don't seem right for a wife to keep secrets from her husband, if that's what you're askin' me to do."

"No, of course not," Lucy said quickly. "I plan to talk to Reverend Wells myself."

Sarah nodded in approval. "Then you have my word, whatever's on your mind stays with me, the pastor, and God."

Lucy glanced around to make certain no one was eavesdropping. "Remember the article in the paper about the wild man of Rocky Creek?"

"'Course I do. That's all anyone talked 'bout for days," Sarah said.

"His name is David Wolf and he's not wild."

Sarah drew back, hand on her chest. "He sure looked wild in that *picher*."

"He's not." If only she hadn't let Barnes print that terrible undeveloped photograph of Wolf. His gunshot wound, the church fire, Monica's injuries—none of it would have happened. "I wrote an article that explained the truth but Barnes didn't print it. He wrote his own article and it was all lies."

Sarah looked more confused. "So what's he gotta do with the fire?"

"The sheriff said if Mr. Wolf didn't leave town, he'd end up in jail again. The problem was he couldn't leave. His leg was infected and I didn't know where else to take him, so I hid him in the church."

"Oh, Lucy. Why didn't you come to us? You know me and the pastor would have helped."

Lucy did know that. Even though Sarah and Justin lived in a tiny cabin and had two small children of their own, they never failed to open their home and hearts to anyone in need.

Lucy squeezed Sarah's arm. "I didn't want to cause you any trouble," she explained, feeling utterly miserable. "Instead, that's exactly what I've done."

Sarah gave her a sympathetic look. "Don't you worry none about that, you hear?" She lowered her voice. "You might have done us a favor. At least we won't have to spend another winter in that drafty old church. Now folks are gonna have to get together and build a new one."

"But you heard what Mr. Appleby said about money."

Sarah scoffed. "If God wants us to have a new church, he'll help us find a way." She winked. "And just between you and me, lumber sure *does* grow on trees."

Despite her heavy heart, Lucy laughed. "I better go. I want to stop at Doc Myers's house and check on Monica. Ma said she didn't go home last night."

"That's 'cuz Doc Myers insisted she stay at his place until she's fully recovered." Sarah nodded in satisfaction. "Justin says nothin' can happen that God can't turn into a miracle, and I reckon that includes a church fire."

Lucy smiled. How like Sarah to try and make her feel better, and it worked. The thought of God using the fire for good did lift her spirits. *Please let it be true.*

Lucy and Sarah hugged and parted ways. Lucy glanced at her father's store. Should she face him now or wait till later? She sighed. "Oh, Papa." If only she could be the daughter he wanted her to be.

With a heavy heart she turned and walked toward her horse. Facing her father would have to wait until after she checked on Monica.

Wolf stood in the shadows.

It was twilight. Main Street was deserted except for a lone figure who hurried by to light the town's two gaslights.

The top half of a full moon rose in the east as if to bid farewell to the last strains of the setting sun on the opposite horizon.

Rowdy laughter exploded from Jake's Saloon, and somewhere a piano played "Oh Dem Golden Slippers."

Wolf's gaze never wavered for long from the little square window of the *Rocky Creek Gazette*. The yellow light from a single kerosene lamp flickered behind thin curtains.

Leaving the safety of the alley where he had been hiding, Wolf crossed the rutted dirt street. The bat-wing doors of a saloon swung open and a man stepped outside, staring straight at Wolf. Fearing the man would recognize him from the picture in the newspaper, Wolf quickly opened the door of the newspaper office to a flurry of jingling bells.

A big orange cat gave a lazy stretch before streaking through the half-open door leading to the back room.

The small office stood empty. A single desk was stacked high with paper. A coat and hat hung from a peg on the rough-hewn wall.

Wolf walked toward the door behind the desk and pushed it wide.

The man he suspected was Barnes sat at a long table, his head bent. His hand moved quickly to pull letters one by one from a type case and set them in a metal frame stick. It was hard to believe such a large hand was capable of arranging such tiny lead pieces. Such a job required both dexterity and sobriety, and judging by the smell of alcohol, Barnes lacked one if not both.

Because of the intense labor of typesetting, newspapers seldom had more than eight pages. The *Rocky Creek Gazette* averaged only four pages, leading Wolf to discern that Barnes did most, if not all, of the work himself.

After a moment or two, the editor raised his head and regarded Wolf with a combination of curiosity and annoyance, his eyes bloodshot. "Whatever you want, come back tomorrow. I've got a paper to put out tonight."

The spectacles threw Wolf off balance, but only for a moment. Though Barnes had gained weight through the years and his face had grown puffy, there was no mistaking the scar, which ran from chin to brow like an angry red serpent. According to Lucy, the injury had been inflicted by a drunken father.

Fists tight at his sides, Wolf regarded the man passively. The scar only proved that evil could be passed from father to son.

He now knew what he had come to find out. Jacoby Barnes had been the leader on that long-ago night. No question.

Bile rose to Wolf's mouth and he could do nothing but stare. He'd envisioned this moment for years but nothing prepared him for the disdain he felt for the man.

"Well, speak up," Barnes said with impatience. "What do you want?"

"To buy a paper," Wolf said. "There were none left at the general merchandise store."

Barnes dismissed him with a wave of his hand and reached for another metal letter. "Come back tomorrow. You can read all about the church fire then."

Wolf stayed where he was. Slowly he removed his hat. Barnes scrutinized him over the metal rim of his spectacles.

Wolf waited—waited for recognition to show in those dark probing eyes. None came. Victims seldom forgot their tormentors but, apparently, perpetrators had no such compulsion to remember. Or maybe they simply didn't have the capacity.

"I said come back, boy."

Boy. How he hated that word, hated how it implied he was less than a man. Still, that was an argument for another day.

"You don't remember me?" he asked.

Barnes visibly stiffened. He looked confused, maybe even frightened.

"Can't think of a single reason why I should. I don't associate with half-breeds." His eyes glittered and his hand moved toward a glass paperweight. Obviously he felt the need for a weapon.

"The name's David Wolf."

"Wolf?" Barnes squinted as if trying to reconcile the face with the photograph in the newspaper. "The wild man—" he began, but Wolf cut him off.

"I'm the one you sent down the river in a boat."

Barnes rose to his feet, his face drained of color. He was at least six inches shorter than Wolf and this took Wolf by surprise. He was ten years old the last time he saw Barnes and the man had looked like a giant.

"I thought you were—"

"Dead?" Wolf extended his arms away from his body. "Doesn't look like it."

Barnes stood frozen. "What do you want?"

"You took something from me that night." More than Barnes or the others could possibly know. "A wooden box." He held his hands a foot apart to indicate the length. "I want it back."

"I don't know what you're talking about."

Wolf thought back to that long-ago night. He seemed to remember the scar-faced youth taking the box from him but he couldn't be certain. He laid his palms flat on the table and leaned forward. "You helped put me in the boat that night. One of you took something from me. If you didn't take it, then one of the other three did. I want the names of everyone who was there that night."

"I told you, I don't know what you're talking about." Barnes's fingers encircled the glass globe, and Wolf straightened.

"Are you saying you don't have it?" Wolf asked.

"I'm saying I know nothing about a box," Barnes said.

Was Barnes telling the truth? It was hard to say. It was possible that they tossed the box, though he doubted it. The box was hand-carved and etched in gold. Someone would have recognized its monetary worth if not its personal value.

He looked Barnes straight in the eye. "I found you, and I'll find the others—with or without your help."

Having said what he came to say, he turned to leave.

Seventeen

*To photograph well, women should dress in sedate colors
and unobtrusive patterns. Even the most morally challenged
woman can be made to look chaste given suitable attire
and clever lighting.*

—Miss Gertrude Hasslebrink, 1878

Doc Myers's housekeeper, Rosie, answered Lucy's knock.

"Is it okay for me to visit now?" Lucy asked anxiously. She'd stopped at the doctor's house earlier that day but Monica had been asleep and the doctor didn't want to wake her.

"Ar reckon Miss Monica will be happy to see ya," Rosie said. A middle-aged woman with gray springy curls, smooth dark skin, and a ready smile, she walked with a side-to-side rocking motion.

Lucy followed her into the dimly lit parlor and was greeted by the doctor. Monica lay supine on a brocade sofa, her arm wrapped in a bandage.

Lucy hurried across the room. "Oh no, you *were* hurt," she cried in dismay. "I was so afraid of that."

Monica waved away her concern. "It's nothing, really."

Lucy squeezed Monica's hand. "I've been so worried about you."

"She's going to be fine," Doc Myers said. He gazed at

164

Monica for perhaps a moment longer than necessary before taking his leave. "I'll ask Rosie to make us some tea."

Lucy gave her friend a knowing look and fanned herself with her hand. "Whoa."

Monica blushed. "Now don't go jumping to conclusions. I'm just his patient. His housekeeper stayed the night to chaperone." Her voice was still hoarse from the fire, but the soft glow in her eyes was new.

Lucy sat on a footstool next to Monica's side. "Since when has Doc Myers ever opened his house to patients?"

Monica coughed and cleared her throat. "I'm very grateful to him," she said. Suddenly her eyes filled with tears. "Oh, Lucy, the church."

"I know. I feel terrible about it, but it wasn't your fault."

Monica wiped her tears away with her palms. "But . . . but . . . who was that man?"

"What man?"

Monica gave her a strange look. "You know. The handsome man I saw you kissing."

"Shh." Lucy glanced over her shoulder to make sure the doctor was out of hearing range, but she couldn't suppress a smile. "He is handsome, isn't he?"

Monica lowered her voice but refused to be distracted. "So who is he and where did you meet him?"

Lucy sighed in resignation. "Remember the photograph in the newspaper?"

Monica's eyes widened. "That was him? But it didn't look like the man I saw you with."

"I'm afraid my photograph did him a terrible disservice."

"But . . . but you let a wild man kiss you!"

"First, David is not a wild man."

Monica frowned. "David? You call him by his Christian name?"

Ignoring the question, Lucy continued. "The wild man

rumor was started by the Trotter boy and perpetuated by Mr. Barnes. It has no basis in fact. He saved your life. Both our lives."

"I'm very grateful to him," Monica said, looking appropriately chastised. "But that doesn't change the fact that you were kissing him."

"It's not what you think."

"What else am I to think?" Monica regarded her like a wayward student. "It's not like you to be so secretive."

Lucy felt a wave of guilt. "I didn't mean to be. I didn't want to get anyone in trouble. As for what you saw or think you saw . . . we were saying good-bye. That's all. He'd been shot and was grateful to me for nursing him back to health."

Monica made a face. "I know what I saw and that was not gratitude."

Irked by Monica's insistence, Lucy bit down on her lower lip. She didn't want to think about Wolf. Mainly because thinking about him only confused her. "Right now I have another problem."

"You mean the church." Monica shook her head. "What are we going to do?"

Lucy squeezed Monica's hand. "Like I said, it wasn't your fault. I take full responsibility and I'll find a way to pay for the building of a new church. Caleb should never have told you where to find me."

"Don't blame him. I made him tell me," Monica said.

"But why?"

"I was worried about you. I knew you were up to something. I was afraid you were in trouble again. It never occurred to me that you would be with a *man*."

"Shh." Lucy lowered her voice to almost a whisper. "I wasn't with a man. At least not the way you think. He was injured and in no condition to travel. I hid him in the church so I could take care of him. That's the end of it."

Monica folded her arms across her chest. "I know what I saw."

"Wolf saved me from those stagecoach robbers. We've been through a lot together, but it can't be more than that."

Monica lowered her arms and leaned forward. "A woman doesn't kiss a man unless she has feelings for him. I don't blame you, I don't. He is *very* handsome, but the fact that he's Indian—"

"Part Indian," Lucy said, trying not to let her irritation show. "And what difference does that make?"

"Oh, Lucy. Your father would never allow you to get involved with a half-breed."

"I told you there's nothing between us." Startled by the memory of his arms around her, she impatiently pulled her drifting thoughts back to the present. "He's a man with too many secrets."

Monica lay back and studied Lucy. Apparently satisfied for the moment, she nodded. "I know how you hate secretive people. That's why I didn't understand why you were acting so secretive yourself."

"I'm sorry, Monica. I should have confided in you."

"Where is he now, this mysterious man of yours?"

"I . . . I don't know," Lucy said, her voice breaking. "Remember, you promised not to say a word about this to anyone."

Monica's hand dropped to her lap. "I won't." She tilted her head to the side. "Are you sure that's the end of it?"

"He's gone," Lucy said. The only thing she could think about now was finding employment. Perhaps she should query *The Washington Post*. Surprised to find her hands shaking, she hid them in the folds of her skirt. She was greatly relieved when Doc Myers walked into the room carrying a tray.

It was dark by the time Lucy started home in her wagon.

The night was beautiful and clear. The stars were bright and the moon cast a silvery glow upon the narrow dirt road.

Halfway to town, she spotted a man on horseback on the road ahead. Man and horse couldn't have been more than forty or fifty feet away. They stood so still that at first she thought it was the shadows playing tricks on her. Alarmed, Lucy tugged on the reins easing her wagon to a stop. *Please, God, don't let that be an outlaw out to do me harm.*

Her mouth dry, she stared. Something—

"David!" No sooner had she called his name than he took off.

Heart pounding, she listened, but all she could hear was the galloping sound of hooves fading in the distance.

It was David she saw, no question. Not only did he have a black horse, he sat forward, legs long, as only a man riding bareback would do.

The question was, why hadn't he answered when she called to him?

And why was he in such a hurry?

She continued on her way. Apparently, when he'd said good-bye, he'd meant it in every sense of the word. It was for the best, it was; she knew it was. So why did she feel so utterly miserable?

Her father was asleep in his chair when she arrived home, an open Bible on his lap. The Bible surprised her. It wasn't like Papa to read scripture outside of church. Had the fire really caused him that much distress?

Weighed down by guilt, she gently lifted the Good Book off his lap. He woke with a start and rubbed his eyes. "How's Monica?"

After setting the Bible on the table, Lucy pulled off her

shawl and hung it on a peg next to the door. "She's doing very well," she replied.

"Why are all these blasted windows open?" He rose and crossed to the nearest window.

"Caleb says fresh air prevents consumption."

Her father slammed down a sash, and she sensed more than open windows were responsible for his bad mood. "So are we to die of pneumonia instead?" He spun around to face her. "What were you doing at the church so late at night? Tell me that!"

She suddenly felt tired. Exhausted.

"I was . . . helping a friend," she said, praying she wouldn't be required to reveal the friend's name. The one thing she could not do was lie to her father.

"Some help. You almost got her killed." He obviously thought Monica was the friend she referred to and she made no effort to correct his impression. He shook his head. "The church. Of all the buildings to destroy."

"It was an accident, Papa. I'll get the money to build a new one. I will!"

He scoffed. After a moment of silence he said, "Richard Crankshaw came to see me today." He watched her closely. "He asked for your hand in marriage."

Surprised, but no less grateful for the sudden change of topic no matter how distasteful, it took her awhile to respond. "We've talked about this, Papa. You know how I feel about him."

"Things have changed," he said, his voice thin with anger.

"What things? Certainly not my feelings!"

"You have to make things right—you owe the people of this town. Crankshaw has offered to build a new church in exchange for your hand."

Her jaw dropped. "He wants to *buy* me?"

"That's not his intention. It wouldn't hurt you to show a little gratitude, young lady. Right now, he may be the only friend you have."

"Maybe so, but that doesn't mean I have to marry him."

Her father heaved a sigh and his shoulders slumped. "Lucy, think about it. That's all I ask. He's a good man."

His pleading tone melted away her anger but not her dislike for Crankshaw. "If he were that good, he would offer to rebuild the church without demanding anything in return."

Her father turned to close another window. He lingered for a while, his back toward her, before turning. "I have some money put away. Not much, but it's a start. And . . . if we had to . . . we could probably sell one of your mother's paintings."

Lucy's mouth dropped open. Never did she think he would part with anything of her mother's, let alone a painting.

"No, Papa. It's my fault the church burned down and I'll find the money to rebuild it. We're not selling Mother's work. Nor will I marry a man I don't love."

"Love is not the only consideration in a marriage," he said, his voice surprisingly gentle.

"When I was twelve, I asked you if you would get married again and you told me you could never marry except out of love. Why am I not allowed the same consideration?"

"It's different with you. You're a woman. You need a man to take care of you. Never more so than you do today. There was no reason for me to marry again."

Years of resentment welled up inside. "Yes, there was! I was a child," she said angrily. "I needed a mother! Caleb needed a mother! That was reason enough." A tearful sob escaped her. "More than that, we needed a father."

She bit down on her tongue, but it was too late to take back her hurtful words. The mask of indifference left her father's face and he looked stricken.

She started toward him. "I'm sorry—"

He held up his hand. "I don't deserve to be your father," he said. "I never did."

Puzzled by his cryptic words, she didn't know what to say. Not deserving? How could that be? No matter his failure as a father, she never questioned that he was a good man, a kind man. A God-fearing Christian. One who went out of his way to take care of his customers. Never once had he raised an angry hand to her or Caleb, though God knows they'd tried his patience—or at least she had.

By the time she found her voice, he'd already left the house. She closed her eyes and her heart ached. She knew from past experience that he would spend the night riding through the countryside, searching for the woman who was lost to him forever.

Eighteen

*Pet owners beware: If you must subject Fido or even your horse to
the camera's eye, resist the urge to be photographed together. You
will only subject yourself to an unfavorable comparison.*

— MISS GERTRUDE HASSLEBRINK, 1878

Long after he spotted Lucy, Wolf rode Shadow hard through
a meadow with nothing but the light of the moon leading the
way. He reached the edge of the woods, and the trees closed
in around him. Shadow's mane coarse and wiry in his hands,
he hunched down to avoid low-growing branches.

It felt good to ride again, the wind in his hair, his body in
tune to the rhythm of his horse. He had tried using a saddle—
the white man's way—but it felt awkward and unnatural.
Getting a saddled horse to do what he wanted required broad
movements, and he much preferred subtlety. It was easier to
communicate with the animal when riding bareback—a slight
shift, a flex of a muscle. All he had to do was turn his head in
the direction he wanted to go and the horse complied.

His leg began to throb. As if sensing his growing discomfort, Shadow slowed to a smooth gaited walk. Not a good
thing, for it allowed Wolf's mind to wander back to Lucy and
the memory of her sweet lips.

He imagined he could still hear her calling to him. He

ran away from her not because he wanted to, but because he had to. He had nothing to give her except misery. If marrying a half-breed wouldn't cause her trouble enough, he couldn't even give her his name, only Wolf. He had no knowledge of who he was or how he came to end up on those mission steps.

Now, leaving the woods behind, he rode across a moon-lit meadow, scaring off a family of deer. His leg was no longer infected, but it tired easily and still ached. Only when the aching became unbearable did Wolf signal Shadow to stop.

The rushing sound of water told him he was close to the Rocky Creek River. He imagined hearing a young boy cry, the past clawing at him like a pack of angry wolves. But then the strangest thing happened. He thought he heard Lucy's voice—her laughter—and the troublesome sounds of the past faded away.

"Lucy, wake up."

Caleb's insistent voice chipping away at her conscious-ness, Lucy moaned and rolled over. "Go away," she muttered into her pillow.

He shook her hard. "Wake up. It's time to get those two hundred and six bones of yours on the move."

She groaned. The thought of moving that many bones so early in the morning was more than she cared to contemplate. "This better be important."

She opened her eyes a slit and cried out. A furry object sat on the bed staring at her.

Suddenly wide awake, she sat up. It took a moment, but she finally recognized the ginger animal. "Extra?" There could be no mistaking the cat belonging to Barnes. It even smelled like printer's ink.

She glanced at her brother. "What is he doing here?"

"That's what I want to tell you," he said, his voice tinged with excitement. "Your old boss has disappeared."

Confused, she tilted her head. "My old boss—" She blinked away the last fog of sleep. "Disappeared?"

He nodded. "The door to his office was open and there was blood on a paperweight. Sounds like foul play to me and I think Marshal Armstrong agrees."

Foul play? Caleb was beginning to sound like a dime novel. "But . . . but who would want to harm him?"

"I don't know," Caleb said. "The marshal's questioning everyone in town. Even questioned Pa." He tossed a nod in Extra's direction. "Can't let the cat starve, now, can we?"

As if to concur, Extra let out a loud meow.

Lucy lay back and gazed at the ceiling. Barnes disappeared? But why? "Maybe he left of his own accord," she said. "Maybe the blood wasn't human."

"It was human all right," Caleb said. "Doc Myers had me mix it with gum-water so we could view it under the microscope."

She rested her hand on her forehead, trying to think. "Maybe . . . maybe he banged his head and has . . . what do you call it when you can't remember anything?"

"Amnesia," Caleb said.

"That would explain the blood."

Caleb shrugged. "Maybe. Marshal Armstrong took some men out to look for him. Sure hope the same thing doesn't happen to him that happened to Mr. Weatherbee, whatever that was."

Suddenly something occurred to her, a thought so horrifying that for a moment she forgot to breathe. A muffled cry escaped her.

"What's wrong?" Caleb asked.

"Nothing." She sat up and swung her feet to the floor. "Get out so I can get dressed." He made no motion to move and she threw a pillow at him.

He ducked. "Okay, okay." He swooped the cat up with one arm. "Let's get you some milk." He headed for the door and glanced back at her. "Are you sure you're okay?"

"Positive. Now go." She threw another pillow at him and he quickly left the room, closing the door behind him.

One of the men I'm looking for has a scar. She paced about the room. Without a second thought she'd told David that Barnes fit that description. Now Barnes had mysteriously disappeared.

Recalling their conversation, she shivered. Arms crossed, she ran her hands along her cold flesh. No, no, it can't be true. David wouldn't harm Barnes. He wouldn't harm anyone. Not the man who had saved her life and whose kisses made her melt in his arms.

Still, what did she really know about him? Was it only just a coincidence that the man David was looking for had vanished? *Oh, God, please let it be a coincidence.*

She shook her head against her rampaging thoughts. Here she goes again, jumping to all the wrong conclusions. According to Caleb, no one knew what happened to Barnes. The editor would undoubtedly show up with a perfectly rational explanation.

As much as she wanted to think that was true, her worrisome thoughts persisted.

Dressed, she walked to the kitchen to put on the kettle for tea. The cat sat in a circle of sunshine licking itself and paid her no heed.

Three unopened letters were on the counter, all addressed to her. She quickly ripped the first letter open and read it. It was from the *Galveston County Daily News* and it read:

Dear Miss Fairbanks,
    Our newspaper has a reputation for achieving the highest journalistic standards. Photography is for amusement

purposes only. As such, we fear that photographs would hinder our reporters and distract and, indeed, even trivialize the reporting of serious news.

Thank you . . .

The letters from the *Kansas City Evening Star* and *St. Louis Dispatch* were similar in tone and content. She crumbled all three letters into balls and tossed them into the wastepaper basket.

The kettle whistled and she turned off the flame. "*Amusement* purposes. Ha! Shows you what little they know."

She still hadn't heard from *The New York Times* or *Boston Globe*, but she didn't hold out much hope of either one of them hiring her. *So what now, God? What now?*

Wolf walked around the charred square of land. It was all that was left of the church. Far as he could tell there wasn't any other church for a good many miles around. For that reason, the loss to the town had to be that much greater, which only added to his guilt.

"Kind of reminds me of Solomon's Temple," came a voice from behind him.

Wolf spun around. He'd been so wrapped up in his thoughts he hadn't noticed he had company. He immediately recognized the man as the preacher, though he'd only caught a glimpse of the man at Sunday morning's worship service. Today he was dressed in black trousers and white shirt.

"Except for its destruction, the Rocky Creek Church bore no resemblance to the temple as described in the Old Testament."

"Ah, a man who knows his Bible." The preacher held out his right arm. "Name's Reverend Wells."

No one had ever before shaken Wolf's hand. He hesitated before taking the offered hand in his own. "David Wolf."

"Pleased to meet you, Mr. Wolf." The preacher laid a small wooden cross on the ashes and stepped back.

Something in the kind way the preacher regarded him made Wolf feel uncomfortable. He wasn't used to being looked at like . . . like he was a real person.

First Lucy and now Reverend Wells. What were the chances of finding two such open-minded people in the same town?

"Don't look so distressed," the preacher said. "God was apparently tired of us patching up the old place. He wanted us to start over." He stared down the hill at the town below. "Not a bad idea, starting over. That's what I did when I left Boston to come to Rocky Creek. It's the best thing that ever happened to me."

Wolf followed his gaze. The town seemed so much smaller than he remembered. So did the mission. So did everything, even the river. Everything seemed smaller than when he was a child except, perhaps, his regrets. Had he not run away from the mission at the age of ten, his life wouldn't have taken such a devastating turn.

"Sometimes it's not possible to start over," Wolf said.

Reverend Wells regarded him from beneath the brim of his black felt hat. "The Bible is filled with people who failed and started over. Abraham, Moses, David, Paul. The key is that when you start over, it must be with God. That's what baptism is all about. Starting over with God."

Wolf's jaw tightened. *You have no idea what it's like to spend your life as an outsider. To be caught between two worlds . . . not to know where you belong. Who your parents were.*

"Maybe we should change the name of the church," the preacher continued.

"Why?" Wolf asked, his voice taut. It didn't seem right to arbitrarily change a name. Names weren't just labels that could be changed at will. A name designated identity. That's why he hated the name the missionaries had slapped on him like he was nothing more than a jar of jelly. He wanted his own name, his rightful name. The name he was born with. Not knowing it was a thorn in his side.

"Jesus changed the name of his disciples to show that he had big plans for them," Reverend Wells said. "I think he also has big plans for our church." He looked Wolf over. "The Bible says God will one day give each of us a new name known only to us. That's because he has big plans for us too."

Plans? That's what a name was to God? Not a heritage, but a destiny? A calling? Wolf didn't know what to think about that.

"It looks like God *meant* for us to start over," Wells continued. He rubbed his hands together as if relishing the idea.

"God didn't burn down the church. I did," Wolf said quietly. It didn't seem right to let the preacher think something that wasn't true.

Reverend Wells's eyebrows rose. For several moments silence stretched between them. The sound of a distant train whistle broke the quiet.

"I trust you had a good reason," the preacher said at last.

"It was an accident." Wolf studied the man. "There was a rumor that I was a wild man terrorizing people."

"Yes, I read about you in the paper," Wells said. "I must say you look better in person. So how did you burn down the church?"

"I was shot and needed a place to recover. That's what I was doing there." He made no mention of Lucy—the last thing he wanted was for her to be blamed for what happened. "A lantern was knocked over—"

Wells laughed. "Sorry. For a moment there I thought you were going to blame the mishap on a cow." He was obviously referring to the Great Chicago Fire that was reportedly started by a bovine.

"No cow, just hymnals falling off the shelf."

"What a pity. A cow has a nicer ring to it, don't you think?" He shrugged. "Hymnals—I guess God couldn't be any clearer."

Wolf had never met anyone like the preacher. What Wolf considered a disaster, Wells saw as God's plan. It was a whole new way of looking at things, and Wolf didn't know what to think.

"I'll do whatever I can to help rebuild." He hadn't planned on staying in Rocky Creek more than a couple of days but he had to make this right. "I'm a cabinetmaker by trade but I know how to draw up plans. Just tell me what you want."

Reverend Wells rubbed his chin. "Can you draw up a church with a separate classroom?"

"I can do that," Wolf said.

"What about a library?"

A library and a classroom? What kind of church was this? "It will take a lot more lumber."

Wells nodded as if the matter was settled. "This should be interesting. All the other buildings in town have four walls and a roof. I don't imagine you need plans to build a box. How soon can you have the plans ready?"

Wolf frowned. *That's it?* No interrogation? No asking for references? True, the preacher wasn't from around these parts. But that didn't explain why he so willingly accepted help from a near stranger.

"You do know that I'm part Indian?"

Reverend Wells looked him straight in the eye. "Does that have some sort of bearing on the design of the church?" he asked. "You aren't going to give us a pointed tepee roof, are you?"

"No, no, nothing like that. It's just that some folks might object."

"They might," Reverend Wells said in a somber voice.

"Doesn't that worry you?"

"If you're asking if intolerance worries me . . ." The preacher gazed into the distance. "Prejudice is just a quick way to form an opinion about someone without going to all the bother of getting to know him." He gestured toward the town. "When I first came to Rocky Creek, folks judged me by the way I dressed and talked, and they didn't want to give me the time of day. If I wasn't a preacher I'd have probably ended up with a backside full of lead." He laid a hand on Wolf's shoulder for a moment. "The way I see it, drawing up plans for the church is a good way for people to get to know you."

The preacher made it sound so simple, and it was anything but. Most people took one look at a half-breed and didn't bother taking another. It wasn't just an opinion people formed at first sight, but a declaration of war. It was a fact of life that he had to live with. The preacher, now, that was a different story. He could get himself in a whole lot of hot water if he didn't watch out.

"I don't want to cause you any more trouble than I already have," Wolf said, and he meant it. He liked the preacher. He couldn't imagine Reverend Wells punishing a child for failing to memorize scripture or misquoting a verse.

Reverend Wells pushed a piece of charred wood with his foot. "If you expect trouble, there's plenty of people here who will give it to you. Personally, I prefer God's way, which is to expect the best in people. So do we have a deal?"

"You're hiring me just like that?"

"You said you were a cabinetmaker. Are you any good at what you do?"

"Yes, I'm very good. Excellent, in fact."

The preacher nodded. "That's all I need to know. For as a man thinketh in his heart, so is he." After a moment he added, "Proverbs twenty-three seven."

Wolf had the feeling they were no longer talking about cabinetmaking, but before he could think of anything to say, Reverend Wells tipped his hat in farewell.

"If you'll excuse me, I'm on the way to visit Mrs. Brubaker. She's taken to her deathbed again." With a nod the preacher walked toward a horse picketed in the shade of a distant tree. "What about an office?" he called to Wolf after mounting.

"An office?" Wolf called back, not sure he'd heard right.

Wells grinned. "I've always wanted my own office. If we're going to start over, we may as well start over right, don't you think?"

Touching the brim of his hat, he rode away, leaving Wolf to stare after him. He had a job, an honest to goodness job that didn't require him to hide.

If he had anything to say about it, the good preacher would have himself one mighty fine office. One grand enough for Solomon's Temple.

⁂

The disappearance of Jacoby Barnes was the main topic of conversation in town for the next couple of days. It was the same wherever Lucy went. Clusters of people clogged Main Street, speculating as to his whereabouts.

Worse than the whispers was the undercurrent of suspicion.

No one liked Barnes and he'd argued at one time or another with pretty near everyone in town. Even the marshal's wife, Jenny, got into a brawl with the editor when she first arrived in Rocky Creek. There was enough reason to think that maybe Barnes might not have vanished of his own accord.

Lucy tried not to speculate because the more she did, the more she worried that Wolf had a hand in Barnes's disappearance. Instead she forced herself to concentrate on plastering her handwritten handbills all around town to solicit work as a photographer.

She stood hammering a sign on a post when Mrs. Hitchcock walked by, carrying a basket of recently purchased goods. The feathers on her hat waved back and forth like two exotic birds in a courting dance as she stopped to read the sign.

"Would you like to make an appointment?" Lucy asked. "It's for a good cause. All the money will go toward building a new church."

Mrs. Hitchcock's mouth curled as if the very thought of having her photograph taken was distasteful. "It always depresses me to look at my old daguerreotypes and see how wonderful I once looked." She sighed at the memory of lost youth. "I'll think about . . . think about it." She gave Lucy an apologetic smile before hurrying off.

"What about you, Mr. Appleby?" Lucy called. He sat in front of her father's store, rocking back and forth. "A photograph for a donation to the church?"

Appleby spit out a wad of tobacco and ground down on his gums. "I ain't lettin' you take no pit-churs and that's final." He got up and started down the steps of the boardwalk on rickety legs, muttering all the way. "That's all you think about. If I was drownin' you'd tell me to hold on while you ran and got your camera."

Lucy watched him go, then continued posting her hand-bills. Earning enough money with her photographs to rebuild the church was going to be harder than she thought. After she finished plastering one side of Main Street, she started on the other.

Timber Joe came running up the moment she reached the bank. He looked all hot and bothered. "Annabelle got my photograph and now she's coming to town."

Lucy squealed with delight. "She received your photograph already?" She couldn't believe it. It was amazing how much faster mail was since the arrival of the railway. "That's wonderful."

"Wonderful?" He grimaced. "Did you hear what I said? She's coming *here*. On Wednesday's train."

Lucy was confused. "Isn't that what you wanted?"

"I guess so. But what if she doesn't like what she sees?"

His sudden lack of self-confidence touched her. It was so unlike him. "She'll love you, you'll see. She obviously liked your photograph or she wouldn't be coming."

"I'm not talking about me. I'm talking about Rocky Creek."

"Oh." Lucy glanced up and down Main. The town did leave a lot to be desired. "Maybe we could—"

"What? Whitewash the buildings?" He shook his head. "There isn't time."

He was right. It would take weeks to do all the work that needed to be done. "Don't worry," she said, trying for a positive tone. "If she's the right one for you, she won't care what the town looks like."

"She'll care. I know she'll care." Timber Joe walked away, head down, and her heart went out to him.

Sighing, she turned to hang a handbill in front of the bank. Instead she leaned her head against a wooden post. It seemed like one problem after another kept popping up. Now Timber Joe's future was on the line and she didn't know how to help him.

Nineteen

*When posing for a photograph, matrons in a family way should
wear dark and somber clothing for dignity's sake. Jolly colors, low
necklines, and excessive decoration denote inferior character and
cast a shadow of suspicion upon the unborn child.*

— MISS GERTRUDE HASSLEBRINK, 1878

On Sunday Lucy and Caleb followed a caravan of wagons
and shays up the hill to where the church once stood.

"I still don't see how we can have a church service without
a building," Caleb complained.

Earlier, Lucy had a similar conversation with her father,
who chose to stay home. "It's only temporary," she said, hoping it was true.

Caleb yawned and Lucy slid him a look of sympathy. "You
didn't get much sleep last night." It was after three a.m. when
she heard him come home.

"Old Mrs. Brubaker was dying again," he said. "Doc Myers
put me in charge of her deathbed vigils. He said it would teach
me bedside manners."

Lucy laughed. "It'll teach you patience, I'll say that much."

He grinned. "She's okay. She's just a lonely old lady."

Her heart swelled with pride. She could never be as kind
and understanding as Caleb. The thought depressed her but

only because she feared she and her father would never be able to afford sending him to medical school. Not even selling her mother's paintings would fetch enough to pay for his tuition, books, and lodging.

The smell of ashes permeated the air as they drew nearer to the church property.

Caleb wiggled his nose. "Smells awful. Do you know what happens when a body—"

"No," she said abruptly. "And I don't want to know."

Caleb flashed his white, even teeth before growing serious again. "Have you seen Mr. Wolf?"

"Not recently. Why do you ask?"

"I heard some talk that maybe he's responsible for Barnes's disappearance."

She tightened her hold on the reins. "That's ridiculous. Who would say such a thing?"

"Jake for one. He still believes the wild man rumors and thinks Barnes had something to do with it."

Lucy swallowed hard. "Why would he say that?"

"Wolf got shot because of the article Barnes printed. Jake says that's reason enough to kill someone."

"He's wrong," she said, her voice edged in misgiving.

Caleb frowned. "You don't sound that certain."

"I *am* certain," she said a tad too quickly, and because his face reflected her own doubts, she added, "I am."

She pulled up behind a long row of wagons and shays and set the hand brake. Ignoring the glares directed at her, she followed Caleb past the burned remains of the church to an area a short distance away where people were gathered in stoic silence.

A few chairs had been set up in a circle but these were reserved for the elderly or women in a family way. The members of the Rocky Creek Suffra-Quilters stood in a huddle, whispering among themselves.

Lucy spotted Redd and waved, but he was too busy watching Miss Hogg to notice.

Barrel stood next to his wife, Brenda. Her sister, Mary Lou, arrived with her husband, Jeff, manager of the local sawmill. Her neckline shockingly low given her "delicate condition" and the somber occasion, Mary Lou did Lucy a favor by grabbing the limelight.

It was only a momentary reprieve, for all too soon the accusatory glares returned to Lucy.

The treeless area offered no respite from the blazing hot June sun. Lucy wore her usual Sunday-best bib and tucker, but today the high collar and mutton sleeves were stifling. She wished she'd followed Mary Lou's example and opted for less conventional wear. At the very least, she should have remembered to wear a hat.

Pastor Wells stood next to his wife, Sarah. He glanced at his pocket watch and turned to the crowd. "Welcome on this glorious day the Lord has made. Let's begin today by saying a prayer for the safe return of Jacoby Barnes."

Lucy tried to pray—she honestly did. Though she didn't wish Mr. Barnes any harm, he was one of the most obstinate and stubborn men she'd ever met. God forgive her, but it was true.

Keeping her head low, she allowed her gaze to wander. It was clear by the restless feet all around her that few if any felt obligated to pray for the return of the missing man.

To make matters worse, she spotted that annoying Mr. Crankshaw watching her with his usual leer. It was enough to make her skin crawl.

"Amen." Pastor Wells opened the Bible in his hand. "If you would now turn to Matthew—"

"We could do it a lot better if we had a church," someone yelled.

Several others murmured in agreement. One woman's

glare shot daggers at Lucy. "My daughter planned to get married next week and now she can't."

Lucy tried to maintain a calm demeanor but when the complaints continued, she could no longer hold her tongue.

"It was an accident," she cried, but the loud dissenting voices drowned her out. Obviously the townsfolk were more upset about the burning of the church than Barnes's disappearance.

Looking remarkably composed considering the foul mood of the crowd, Pastor Wells lifted his arms. But it was the sound of a rifle shot that commanded attention.

All eyes turned to Timber Joe, who held his rifle aloft, finger on the trigger, ready to fire again if necessary. Timber Joe and his rifle had done more for the church than all the well-meaning ladies and their casseroles put together. Nothing could fill the offering plate faster than a man pointing a rifle. Though Pastor Wells disapproved of such methods, there were times like today when Timber Joe clearly saved the day.

The former Confederate soldier slipped the rifle over his shoulder and nodded to Pastor Wells. "It's all yours, Preacher."

Pastor Wells thanked Timber Joe and turned to the crowd. "The word *church* is mentioned in the Bible perhaps a hundred times," he said, his strong deep voice droning on like a swarm of lazy bees. "It's not a difficult word to find. What you *won't* find is the word *church* used in reference to a building."

Murmurs of surprise circled around him.

"There is good reason for that," Pastor Wells continued. "For a church is not a building. A church is the people. That's right. You. Me. Timber Joe, here. My beautiful wife, Sarah." His gaze traveled over the crowd, addressing individuals by name, one by one.

"Caleb and Lucy Fairbanks. Mrs. Hitchcock. Marshal Armstrong and Jenny. And yes, even Jacoby Barnes, though he's not with us today. We—all of us—are the church."

Everyone fell silent as he spoke, and some even had the good grace to look remorseful.

Having made his point, Reverend Wells lowered his gaze to his Bible and began where he left off.

Fanning herself with her hand, Lucy glanced around.

A flock of birds took flight from the nearby woods and she caught a flash of black through the trees. *Shadow*. She squinted against the sun to make certain but she knew—knew in the very depth of her soul—what she saw. Her breath caught in her chest.

"I ask you to bow your heads once again in prayer," Pastor Wells continued. "This time we'll ask God's help in keeping our church strong and making our hearts pure."

While the preacher prayed aloud, she glanced at Mr. Crankshaw. His head was bowed and, as far as she could tell, his eyes were closed.

Taking her cue, and after checking to make sure no one else observed her, she slipped away, circling the long way around until she reached the woods, Jake's suspicions very much on her mind.

"David?" she called in a hushed voice.

Hands grabbed her from behind and she cried out.

"Shh." David spun her around in the circle of his arms, his handsome head bent so near she could feel his warm breath on her face.

The nearness of him made her heart pound.

"I'm sorry the church fire has caused you so much trouble. I heard what they said. I just want you to know I'll make this right. You shouldn't have to pay for helping me."

"It was partly my fault," she said. She didn't want to talk about the church. Not now. There were too many other more pressing matters. Out of necessity, she pushed him away. It was the only way she could think clearly.

"What have you done with Barnes?" she asked, hands clenched.

Arms at his side, a puzzled expression crossed his face. "What are you talking about?"

"Barnes is missing and the marshal suspects foul play." Now *she* was beginning to sound like a dime novel. "There's talk in town . . ." She hesitated, hating the question that played on her lips. "Did you . . . ?"

His face darkened. "I can't believe you would think such a thing of me."

"What would you have me believe? You asked if I knew a man with a scar and I told you about Barnes."

"I did nothing to harm him," David said. "I didn't even know he was missing."

She wanted so much to believe him, she did, but too many images flashed through her head. "I saw you the night he disappeared. Near town."

"I remember," he said.

A voice floated from the distance. "Lucinda?" It was Crankshaw. He was the only one who called her by her given name, and she hated it.

She covered her mouth with her hand. "Oh no."

David squeezed her arm. "Meet me later at the old mission."

She gazed up at him. Her heart believed him but she couldn't quiet the misgivings of the mind.

"Trust me," he pleaded. "I'm telling you the truth." With that he was gone.

Lucy turned just as Mr. Crankshaw stepped into the small clearing. His long pointed face anchored by a neatly trimmed goatee, he looked every bit an Easterner in his striped trousers, semi-cutaway coat, and tall silk hat.

He patted his forehead with a handkerchief and greeted her with a nod. His family had made a fortune in railroads, which allowed him to dabble in oil, a crazy idea at best.

Though he claimed to have produced several thousand barrels, the price of oil was not high enough to justify his efforts. Everyone expected him to give up and return to New York, and it couldn't be soon enough for her. Unfortunately he was as stubborn in his pursuit of devil's tar, as some called it, as he was in his pursuit of her hand.

"Lucinda?" She cringed.

He glanced around as if he suspected she had not been alone. He stuck his handkerchief in his coat pocket. "Are you all right? You look flushed."

"It's j-just the heat," she stammered.

"Yes, of course. Let me take you home." He took her by the arm with a familiarity that irritated her.

"Thank you for your kind offer," she said, pulling her arm away. "But I came with my brother."

She turned and walked away, but he fell in step beside her. "I spoke to your father," he said. "Did he tell you?"

"He mentioned something."

"Something?" He grabbed her by the wrist. "Something?" He glared down at her. "'Do you think a man's proposal of marriage is some sort of joke?"

Regretting her dismissive tone, she shook her head. "I didn't mean to suggest . . . I do appreciate your offer."

"I don't want your gratitude," he said, moving his hand away.

"What I mean to say is . . . I'm afraid you would find me wanting as a wife. My photography takes up much of my time."

"I'm sure we can allot time for your leisurely pursuits," he said.

She kept her voice even. "I'm afraid my *profession* takes up more time than you know," she said.

"Your profession?" The tolerant look on his face contradicted the dismissive tone of his voice. "It's not like you have regular employment."

That part was true, but it irked her that he saw fit to point it out.

Caleb called to her from a short distance away, waving his arm to gain her attention. Relieved that she had a legitimate excuse for cutting the conversation short, she waved back.

"I'm sorry. My brother is waiting."

She picked up her skirt and ran to her brother's side. Moments later she sat in the driver's seat and took hold of the reins. She glanced back to find Crankshaw staring at the wooded area where she'd briefly met David.

He knows. The thought sent an icy chill through her body. *He knows I wasn't alone.*

Twenty

It was late that afternoon before she was able to sneak away
and drive to the mission. The building had been deserted for
years and had fallen into disrepair. Was this where he was
staying? Is that why he asked her to meet him here?

The adobe Moorish-style building was surrounded by
weeds, a crumbling fountain, and the remnants of an aque-
duct built to transport water from the river to the crops once
grown there. Long narrow windows were carved in between
support columns. The bell tower had toppled, but the out-
door stone staircase used by former bell ringers remained.

In 1716 Captain Domingo Ramón came to Texas with a
small army of soldiers and friars to build and establish mis-
sions. The purpose was to bring Christianity to the Indians.
No proof existed that the captain had built this particular mission but tradition dictated that he had.

Though the sun was warm, Lucy shivered. This was the
closest she had ever been to the mission. She'd heard numerous

tales about the structure through the years, stories about ringing bells and unexplained lights. She didn't believe in ghosts,
but today, even in the bright afternoon sun, the eerie silence
unnerved her.

She sat parked in front for several moments. She wanted
so much to go to him, to believe that his whispered words were
true, that he had nothing to do with Barnes's disappearance.

But if not Wolf, then who?

Afraid to trust her instincts, she snapped the reins and
drove away.

Old Man Appleby obviously did not take kindly to Lucy's
temporary studio outside her father's store. "How's a man
supp'se to git any peace and quiet with all these comin's and
goin's?" he complained.

"I'm sorry, but it is for a good cause." Lucy checked the
money in her box. Funds for the new church dribbled in much
slower than she'd hoped, but she refused to be discouraged.
"To make up for your inconvenience, I'll take your photograph for free."

Appleby grimaced. "This here face stays right where it is,
and I ain't wanting to see it on no paper."

Lucy sighed. There was no reasoning with the man.
"Would you like me to move your chair to another place?
Perhaps in front of the barbershop?"

"You want me to get my ears blasted?" He made a face.
"All the barb'rs in the country, we have to git stuck with one
that sings opera." He glanced up the street and made a face.
"Argh. Would you look at that?"

Lucy followed his gaze. Mrs. Taylor led a small band of
women down the middle of Main Street. The women, all
members of the Rocky Creek Suffra-Quilters, carried signs
and chanted, "Equal rights, equal rights."

Appleby took off, running along the boardwalk like his pants were on fire. Lucy couldn't help but laugh.

The marching women drew near and their chants grew louder. Millard Weatherbee, obviously thinking that supporting women's rights would somehow help him get elected to the state senate, followed close behind. Women didn't have the vote but they did exert influence on the men in their lives.

Other women ran to join them, some dropping their shopping bags en route. Miss Emma Hogg held on to her hat as she ran down the street trying to catch up. Jenny Armstrong came out of her shop to wave, her sisters Mary Lou and Brenda by her side.

Lucy longed to join the march but she didn't want to leave her camera. Instead she called for them to stop so she could take their photograph.

Mrs. Fields, a birdlike woman with drab brown hair and pointed nose, shook her head and frowned. "That might hurt our cause. A camera is so much kinder to men than it is to women."

Mrs. Taylor scoffed. "Nonsense. The camera treats both men and women with equal disdain. That makes it more democratic than our legislature."

She faced the camera and the others followed her lead. Lucy tried her best to get them to smile but her efforts only made the women more self-conscious.

Mrs. Hitchcock straightened her hat. "That nice Englishman Mr. Garrett . . . Mr. Garrett . . . told me that whenever he faces the camera he simply relaxes and thinks of England. Thinks of England."

"How interesting," said Mrs. Taylor. "I believe that's the same advice Queen Victoria gave her daughter on her wedding night."

No one said a word after that but the tittering smiles on their faces spoke volumes.

No sooner had Lucy snapped her photograph than the bat-wing doors of Jake's Saloon swung open and Appleby and the other members of The Society for the Protection and Preservation of Male Independence came marching out.

The men chanted, "No votes for women."

The women yelled back. "Women's rights, women's rights."

The saloons all along Main Street emptied as men ran outside to see what the ruckus was all about.

Mrs. Taylor's voice rose above the rest. "We will fight to have our votes counted until the crack of doom."

"I reckon that makes you a crackpot," Appleby bellowed back.

His remark was promptly met by Mrs. Taylor's banner, which somehow managed to land on top of his head. Suddenly, all Hades broke loose. Hats and banners flew up in the air and several onlookers jumped into the fray.

Lucy watched in horror as Mrs. Hitchcock pushed one of the saloon owners down on the ground and sat on top of him. The town's blacksmith, Link Haskell, tried to grab her arm but accidentally hit Millard Weatherbee in the nose instead. The young candidate responded in kind and the two men fell to the ground.

Lee Wong, the slightly built owner of the Chinese laundry, flipped Redd head over heels as if he were nothing more than a feather pillow. Caleb, who had run out of his father's store upon hearing shouts, stared with open mouth.

Crying out, Lucy leaped off the boardwalk and rushed to his side. "Redd! Are you all right?" She fell to her knees and cradled his head with one arm while motioning to her brother with the other. "Caleb! Come quick!"

"I'm all right," Redd said, though he didn't sound like it.

Caleb slid next to her and she moved away so he could examine Redd.

"Wow," Caleb said, his voice in awe. "Mr. Wong whirled you around like a whirligig. How did he do that?"

Lucy elbowed him with a hush. Just then Barrel ran out of the barbershop and was met by a fist to his jaw. Lucy gasped when her second friend hit the ground.

She started forward but Caleb held her back. "Don't worry," he said. "He'll be fine. The jawbone's the hardest bone in the body."

Something inside her snapped. "Stop it, all of you," she shouted, but no one could hear her for the grunts, groans, and insults.

"You ole windbag." Appleby grabbed Mrs. Hitchcock's feathered hat.

Miss Hogg tripped him with her foot. "You ninny hammering fool."

"You buffle-headed . . ."

Caleb cupped his hands around his mouth and yelled, "Hey, watch the clavicle."

"Don't tell me," Lucy muttered, "that's the easiest bone to break."

"One of them," Caleb said. "Careful," he bellowed, "that's his femur." To Lucy he said, "Remember when I broke mine? It really hurt."

Redd sat up with a groan and grabbed the back of his neck. "I sure hope your brother never has occasion to fight in a war."

Caleb ran his hand up and down Redd's back checking for injuries. "Doc Myers said if more people practiced preventative medicine he would get more sleep." He lifted his voice to address an overzealous lady battering the blacksmith with her fists. "Careful of the ribs."

Marshal Armstrong came running down the street with Timber Joe not far behind.

Timber Joe fired his rifle while the marshal pulled Mrs. Hitchcock off one of the men. "Get up! All of you," Armstrong bellowed. "Now what's going on here?"

Everyone began to talk at once, fingers pointing every which way.

Marshal Armstrong soon ran out of patience. "Not another word out of any of you!" he ordered.

After the marshal restored order and hauled Mrs. Taylor and Appleby off to jail to cool their heels, Caleb tended to the injuries. Nobody was seriously hurt, though several sported impressive black eyes and more than a few had cases of wounded pride.

After most of the brawlers had left, Lucy returned to her makeshift studio. Barrel joined her, hand on his swollen jaw.

"Did you have Caleb look at that?" she asked.

"It's nothing to worry about," he said, moving his mouth as little as possible. "I just wish I knew what I was fighting for."

"Women's right to vote," she said.

"In that case I'm more than all right. Brenda won't mind me fighting as long as it's for a good cause."

She glanced at the broken signs and banners in the middle of the street. "I don't think fists and name-calling are going to get women the vote."

Barrel followed her gaze and shook his head. "Any idea what will?"

"I'm afraid not, but there has to be another way." Ever since 1776, when Abigail Adams asked her husband "to remember the ladies," women had been fighting for equal rights. So far they'd had little success. "I just know they're going about it all wrong."

Nodding, he drew several banknotes from his pocket and handed them to her.

Thinking he wanted his photograph taken, she tried giving some back. "This is too much. Not even big-city photographers charge this much."

"Oh, I don't want my photograph taken. That's the money Brenda and I have been saving to build an opera house."

"In Rocky Creek?" She didn't want to discourage him, but she couldn't imagine anyone in town attending an opera.

"We won't be putting on operas. At least not for a while. We're just calling it an opera house to give it respectability."

What he said made sense. The word *theater* was synonymous with bawdy entertainment.

"We'll put on plays, vaudeville acts, and minstrels. Don't tell her I told you, but Brenda has quite a flair for acting."

"Does this mean you're going to sing?" she asked. Barrel sang in the choir but he still hadn't completely overcome his stage fright.

He shook his head. "I used to say God gave me a great singing voice but forgot to give me the courage to use it. But Brenda said I was wrong. God didn't forget. He just doesn't want me to sing on stage. He has bigger and better plans for me. I think I finally found out what those plans are."

"Barrel, I'm so happy for you." She sighed. "I am. I just wish . . ."

"Wish what, Lucy?"

"I just wish I could figure out what God's plans are for me. It seems like every door keeps slamming in my face."

He indicated her camera. "You have a gift, Lucy, but I suspect your vision for photography is too limited."

"What do you mean?"

"I once thought that the only way I could use my talents was to sing on stage. I now know God had a bigger plan for me. I can do more than sing. I can produce and direct operas and that was something I never even considered. God has a plan for you too. I'm convinced of it."

"But how do I know what that plan is? God hasn't answered my prayers." So far every job application had been turned down.

He tapped her forehead. "Maybe your shutter isn't open wide enough to see God's plan for you."

"My shutter?" She couldn't help but laugh. Like David, her friend spoke in terms he thought she could best understand. "So you think I just have to open my mind and I'll know what his plan is for me?"

"Not just your mind. When looking for heavenly answers, you have to open your eyes and ears—everything. Now I know that my vision of God's plan for me was too narrow. The answer was there all along. I was just too blind to see it."

"I'm so glad you found your answer, Barrel." She looked down at the money in her hand. "I can't take this—I can't. This money belongs to you and Brenda." She tried stuffing the notes in his pocket but he stopped her.

"We're not giving the money to you. We're giving it to God. As for the opera house, we'll get it built. It'll just take us a little longer."

"I'll help you," she said. "Just as soon as we build the church, we'll work on that opera house of yours."

He tried to smile but ended up grimacing instead. His jaw was now more blue than red. "I'll hold you to that."

After he left, Lucy felt unsettled and restless. *God, do you have a plan for me?* She was relieved when the pastor and his wife, Sarah, drove up in their wagon and she could push her troubling thoughts aside. They had both children with them.

"What happened here?" Pastor Wells asked, referring to the scattered pieces of torn banners and signs that littered the street.

Sarah smiled up at her husband and turned back to Lucy. "Have you had much bus'ness?"

"A little," Lucy said. "Not as much as I had hoped for."

"Do you like my dress?" Elizabeth held out her skirt with both hands. She was dressed all in white with a blue satin ribbon tied around the middle.

"I *love* your dress," Lucy said, smiling down at the pretty round face. She tickled Matthew under his little chubby chin and he burst into a wide, drooling smile.

Pastor Wells sat on the chair facing the camera and held

Matthew on his lap. Sarah and Elizabeth stood on either side of him.

"I think we're ready," Wells said.

Lucy ducked beneath the black cloth. "Say Rocky Creek backwards," she called out.

"Rocky Creek backwards," Elizabeth said, and everyone laughed, even little Matthew.

Lucy gazed through the camera at Sarah and her family and a lump caught in her throat. She imagined she could see a halo of love around them like the ring around the moon on a clear winter night.

Would she ever have a family of her own? Know that kind of love and acceptance, even safety? The thought coming out of nowhere filled her with longing. *Oh, David . . .* she missed him so, missed his teasing smile, the tilt of his head, the feel of his lips . . . She tried pushing the painful memories away but they were like rocks in her head that refused to budge.

She swallowed hard and grasped the air bulb. Squeezing it was like squeezing her own heart. Much to her horror, she burst into tears.

"We're all done," she said, trying to hide her weepy eyes, but Sarah was all over her.

"Oh, Lucy. You poor thing. Don't you worry, none, you hear? We're gonna build the biggest and best church in all of Texas."

The mere mention of the word *church* made Lucy's tears flow faster.

"Don't cry now, you hear?" Sarah continued. "That ole fire was prob'bly the best thin' that happened to this town. It's forcin' people to work together and use their God-given talents. Why, I wouldn't put it past God if it was his plan all along. Don't you agree, Justin?"

Before her preacher husband could get a word in edge-wise, Sarah continued, "Why, just this mornin' Ma told me her plan to sell baked goods. Even Jenny agreed to give a portion of her store profits to the cause."

Sarah's efforts to make Lucy feel better had the opposite effect.

"I'm so sorry," Lucy said, her guilt practically choking her. "You and the pastor worked hard on the church. I thought I was doing what God wanted me to do but . . ." She kept talking, barely stopping for breath. "Had Monica been seriously injured, I would never have been able to forgive myself . . ." A sob shuddered through her. She swallowed in despair but the lump in her throat remained.

"You poor thing," Sarah said, tears welling in her eyes.

Seeing her mother upset, Elizabeth started to cry too.

Not wanting to be left out, Matthew let out an ear-piercing wail.

Known for calm in the face of crisis, Pastor Wells jiggled his son up and down and stared at the three bawling females in dismay. He looked about as close to panic as a man could possibly look.

Twenty-one

A man imagines himself more handsome than his photograph;
a woman believes herself more homely.

— MISS GERTRUDE HASSLEBRINK, 1878

Lucy waited for almost an hour after Sarah and her family left, but the street remained deserted. Since half the town had gone home to nurse their injuries, her chance of selling more photographs looked slim.

She counted the coins in her box and sighed. There was nowhere near as much money as she hoped for. At this rate, it would take forever to raise enough to rebuild the church. Maybe tomorrow would be a better day.

She began to pack up her equipment just as a man dressed in a black hat and long cape stomped up the steps to the boardwalk. Thinking he was one of her father's customers, she ignored him until he sat down on the chair in front of her camera.

"Do you wish to have your photograph taken, sir?" she asked.

The man lifted his head and pushed back his dark hat.

"David!" A warm glow washed over her. She glanced anxiously at the window of the merchandise store but could see no sign of her father. *Please don't let him look outside.* "What are you doing here?"

"I asked you to meet me at the mission." He narrowed his eyes. "You didn't come."

"I . . . I've been busy." She indicated her camera with a wave of her arm.

"I need your help," he said. "More important, I need you to trust me."

"I want to," she said truthfully. If only she could ignore the niggling doubts.

"Barnes was alive and well when I left him." He studied her as if to weigh her reaction. "That's all I can tell you."

"Some people think you blame him for being shot."

"He didn't do me any favor running that photograph and lies in the paper," he admitted. "But if I wanted to do him harm, that would have been the least of my motives."

She frowned. "What . . . what else did he do?"

"We can't talk here." Someone rode by on a horse and David pulled his hat down.

She drew in her breath. Except for the Owen boy, Skip, on the boardwalk spinning his hoop, the street was now deserted, but that could change at any moment. "You best go."

He stood and tossed a handful of gold coins in her money box. Leaning toward her, he whispered in her ear. His lips brushing against her flesh sent ripples of warmth down her spine. "The mission—one hour."

She turned her head to look at him and his nearness took her breath away. "I—"

"Please." His eyes pleaded for her to trust him; his voice demanded so much more.

He made it impossible to say no. "All right, I'll meet you," she said.

The sound of her camera startled her. Skip Owen peered out from beneath the black cloth and grinned. "I'm older now," he said by way of excuse. "I just had a birthday and now I'm ten."

He looked about to dive under the cloth again but Lucy leaped forward before he had a chance. "Not old enough to know you can't take two photographs with the same plate," she said, though she didn't have the heart to scold him.

He grabbed his hoop and ran.

"I don't know what I'm going to do with him." Shaking her head, she turned back to David.

He watched the boy with a strange expression. "He's only ten? He looks . . . young. When I was that age . . ." His face darkened. "I don't think I was ever that young."

"I wasn't much older when my mother died," she said. She hadn't felt young then either. Instead she had felt like she carried the whole world on her shoulders.

He stepped forward as if wanting to prolong the moment they shared, or maybe even comfort her. Instead he tugged on the brim of his hat.

"Soon," he said. He glanced around before stepping off the boardwalk.

An hour later, Lucy walked up to the wooden door of the old mission. It wouldn't budge, and she doubted that any amount of knocking on the heavy oak could be heard from inside.

She followed a broken brick path to the side of the mission, hoping to find another way in. David stepped out of the shadows, startling her.

He cupped her by the elbow, which only made her pulse throb. "I didn't mean to scare you." He released her. "I didn't think you'd come."

"I almost didn't," she said truthfully.

He led her through an open door into a long narrow room with a high vaulted ceiling. The domed crossing at the far end above the altar established this as the sanctuary.

She followed him through another door into another

large room. Though it was hot and muggy outside, the mission was cold and damp. A fire burned in the floor-to-ceiling fireplace. It added little warmth but it did provide a cheery note to the otherwise dreary surroundings.

A pinewood chair stood by the hearth. She ran her fingers along the wooden back. An outline of a wolf was so delicately carved on the splat that it looked like a natural part of the wood.

She glanced up at him. "Did you make this?"

He indicated a bag of carving tools on the floor. "I'm working on it," he said. "I'm a cabinetmaker by trade. It should fetch a handsome amount for the church building, don't you think?"

So Sarah was right; the church would be built by God-given talents. She ran her fingers along the back of the chair. She marveled that such large hands were capable of carving a design so delicate.

"It's beautiful," she said, her voice filled with awe. It was similar to the wolf engraved on the bracelet he gave her, though larger and more detailed. "I'd love to photograph it, but Skip used up my last plate." She doubted a photograph could capture the exquisite details.

"It's not finished yet," he said.

"I know. But there's something intriguing, even suspenseful about unfinished work, don't you think?" It left a question that begged to be answered. Like *The Canterbury Tales* or an unfinished symphony. She ran her fingers over the engraved animal. "Your name . . . Wolf . . . I used to think it suited you, but I don't anymore."

"Oh?" He looked surprised. "Why not?"

"Wolves run in packs," she said.

"Except the ones that are ostracized and become lone wolves." He pointed to the chair. "Go ahead, sit. It might be unfinished but it's sturdy."

She sat on the chair and he lowered himself upon the edge of the stone hearth. She'd been so enthralled with the wolf carving she'd momentarily forgotten the real reason she was here.

"What you said earlier . . ."

"It's true. I had nothing to do with Barnes's disappearance." He watched her closely. "I hope you believe that."

"I saw you. On the road. I called to you," she said.

Hands clasped between his knees, he inhaled a deep breath. "I won't lie to you. I saw him that night."

In the light of the fire, his face looked open and revealing. It was the kind of look she had longed to capture on her father's face with her camera but never could.

Fingering her locket, she studied him.

"You said I was a man of many secrets," he continued. "That's because I don't know who to trust."

His words resonated on so many levels. Was that why her father held on to his secrets? Because of lack of trust?

"I think I've more than earned your trust," she said. She leaned forward. "Who are you, David? And why are you here? If you can't trust me enough to answer those questions, then you can trust me with nothing."

Something in his face changed. He had the faraway look of a man used to gazing across long distances. He took so long to answer that she almost gave up hope that he would. She started to rise but then he spoke and she promptly sat down again.

"I was left on the doorstep of this mission as a baby," he said slowly.

She gasped. "Here?" She glanced around. It was hard to imagine anyone, especially a child, living in the cavernous rooms of the mission. "You were left here?"

He grinned. "I guess there are worse places I could have been left."

"I didn't mean that, I meant . . . do you know anything about your family? Your parents?"

He shook his head. "That information was left with me in a box." He held his hands several inches apart to indicate its size. "The priests told me that I wasn't allowed to look inside until I was eighteen."

"What was in it?" she asked.

"I don't know. The box was locked. All I know is that it was engraved with the head of a wolf."

"Your name," she said.

"Maybe." He shrugged. "I reckon it's as good a name as any. That's why I came back to Rocky Creek. To find that box. My hope is that it will tell me something about my parents. About myself."

"And you think it's here somewhere. In this mission?"

He shook his head. "No, not here." He glanced around. The large room with its clay tile floor and high-beamed ceiling made their voices echo. "There were about twelve of us boys living here. Some were Indians, some were white. Then there was me. I didn't belong to either group. And the others never let me forget it. I was only ten when I decided to run away and find my parents. I was convinced that whatever was in that box would lead me to them." He grinned sheepishly. "The problem was it was locked and I couldn't get it open."

"You were so young," she said. Ten. The same age as Skip Owen. No wonder David was surprised to learn of the boy's tender age. "What happened? Where did you go?"

"I didn't get far when four older boys from the town cornered me. They wanted my box. When I refused to give it to them, they put me in a boat. They grabbed the box and sent me down the river toward the rapids."

Dismayed by his ordeal she pressed her lips together. The rapids could be deadly even in the summer when the water was low and the boulders exposed. How could anyone be so cruel?

"No one has ever survived those rapids," she said. "How . . . how did you escape?"

"Someone heard my screams. A cabinetmaker by the name of Malcolm Combes saved me before I reached the rapids. He happened to be traveling through the area."

His eyes clouded with what she suspected were visions of the past. "The man took me home. He educated me and taught me the business. I learned to make furniture and cabinets. As I grew older, my Indian blood became more evident, so I was not allowed to serve customers."

"That's terrible," she said.

"Combes didn't have a choice. Don't forget this was during the Indian wars."

"I don't know what to say," she said. The conflict between the Texas plains Indians and settlers had ended only eight years earlier in 1874, but in many parts of Texas, the wounds were still raw, even today.

He chuckled. "That's got to be a first." He threw another log into the fire and poked at it with a stick until flames chased up the chimney.

Recalling the church fire and their brush with death, she shuddered. "Why now?" she asked. "What made you come back at this particular time?"

"Combes recently died. He was the closest I had to family."

"I'm sorry," she said.

He nodded. "Before he died he encouraged me to come back here. Whenever I got stuck on a problem—whether it was mathematics or construction—he always told me to go back to the beginning. That's what I'm here to do."

She tried putting the pieces together but there were still too many unanswered questions. "None of this explains why you were so anxious to find Barnes."

He tossed the stick aside. "He helped put me in that boat. He was the leader."

Her body stiffened in shock. "Barnes did that?" She never liked Barnes, but she couldn't imagine him capable of such unbelievable cruelty. To think she had wanted to work for him!

David gave a curt nod of his head. "He and his friends. They took the box from me."

Though the fire was warm she shivered. "You . . . you said there were four."

He nodded. "I only know the names of two, Barnes and Doc Myers."

"Doc—" Stunned, she was momentarily speechless. No, no, not Doc Myers. "You . . . you must be mistaken," she said, when at last she could find her voice. "I've known the doctor all my life and he would never . . ." She shook her head, unable to believe such a thing possible.

"There's no mistake," David said, "I haven't talked to him yet."

"But you talked to Barnes."

"Yes. I asked him what happened to the box but he denied knowing anything about it."

"He may have been telling the truth. Twenty years is a long time. They may have thrown it away."

David shook his head. "The contents, perhaps, but not the box. It was engraved with gold. They may have sold it, but I doubt they threw it away."

It was a long shot, of course, but Lucy couldn't blame him for trying to find it. "What if the box is lost forever?"

"Then I'll never know what was inside. Or who left it with me. I may never know my real family name."

Her heart ached for him. Family was extremely important to her and she couldn't imagine how it would feel to be without.

"Barnes refused to name the other two, but I swear to you, I have no knowledge of Barnes's whereabouts."

She took a deep breath. She believed him, but in light of David's accusations, she was no longer certain she could trust her instincts. Could she really have been that wrong about Doc Myers?

"What . . . do you plan to do?" she asked.

"I planned to approach Myers, but now that suspicion has been cast on me, I have to be even more careful than before." He leaned forward, and his nearness made her pulse race. "That's why I need your help."

"I don't know how I can help," she said. Or maybe she just didn't want to help. *Doc Myers?* She still couldn't believe it.

"The boys who abducted me are probably now in their late thirties, early forties. You know everyone in town. Help me find the other two."

"You only want to find the box they took from you, right?" she asked, and when he didn't reply, she asked it of him again. "Right?"

"Do you understand what I'm telling you? They left me to die. It's a miracle I survived. Yet Myers and Barnes went on to lead successful lives and have respected professions. I think it's time the townsfolk know what kind of men they are."

She pressed the palms of her hands together. "What they did to you . . . there's no excuse. But they were young. And revenge will hurt you more than it will hurt them."

"What would you have me do? Forgive and forget? Doc Myers is a pillar of the town. Barnes runs a newspaper. All I want to do is make Myers and the others face up to what they did."

She swallowed hard. "Exposing them won't restore your childhood."

He rose to his feet. "That's not what this is about." He kneeled down on one knee and took her hands in his. "I fear one of the other three may have something to do with Barnes's disappearance."

"But . . . but that makes no sense," she said. "Not after all this time."

"Then why did he disappear the same night the two of us talked?" He paused for a moment. "Maybe he threatened to reveal their names."

"Would it really matter after all this time?" she asked. "Now that they know you're alive?"

"As far as I know Barnes is the only one who knows it. What if he tried to blackmail the others without telling them he saw me? He can't be making much money with the newspaper. Maybe he saw this as an opportunity to line his pockets."

She hadn't thought of that possibility, but she wouldn't put it past Barnes to do such a thing.

"So will you help me?"

She pulled her hands from his and grasped her locket as she tended to do whenever faced with a dilemma. It wasn't so much that she didn't want to help him—she was afraid to help him. Afraid of what she would find. It was hard enough knowing that Myers and Barnes had left a child to die. But who else? She closed her eyes. *Dear God, who else?*

"Lucy," he said softly.

She raised her lashes, meeting his gaze.

"I'm not going to hurt anyone, at least not physically. All I want to do is expose them. Strip away their respectability. Make them face up to what they did. Is that so wrong?"

She didn't know how to answer that question. Pastor Wells often preached God's word on forgiveness, but it never really related to her personal experience. Forgiveness came easily to her, but forgiving a thoughtless word or gesture wasn't the same as forgiving what David endured.

"I don't know how I can help," she said.

"You can start by making a list of men who fit the age group, men who were living here twenty years ago."

"That's a big job," she said. "There could be fifty or more men who fit that description. And how do you know they haven't moved away?"

"If that's the case, and I'm right about Barnes, that would mean that Doc Myers is responsible for Barnes's disappearance."

She shook her head. Committing a horrible, thoughtless act as a teen was one thing. But purposely harming a man as an adult was something else. "We don't know that anything *has* happened to Barnes," she said. "He could have left of his own accord. Maybe he has . . . what do you call it . . . amnesia? Isn't that possible?"

"Anything's possible, but the timing seems too coincidental."

She couldn't argue with him there. "I was at the doctor's house the night Barnes disappeared," she said, "visiting Monica. I never saw Barnes."

"You weren't there all night, but your friend was. She would know if Barnes was there. Will you help me?"

She wanted to help him, but still she held back. "I . . ."

He tilted his head and searched her face as if trying to reach into her thoughts. "Is that a positive or a negative?"

A sense of uneasiness washed over her. How could she say no to him? How could she not? "I'll talk to Monica." She didn't want to commit to any more than that and he didn't press her, though his burning gaze continued to bore into her.

"You mustn't tell your friend about anything I told you. Until we know the whole story, it would be best if you don't tell anyone. If Myers is responsible—"

"He's not," she said.

"I hope you're right." He stood and pulled her to her feet. His gaze traveled from her eyes to her lips. As if to catch himself, he quickly released her hands and moved away. "Meet me here tomorrow."

"All right."

"Don't say a word of this to anyone."

"I won't," she promised. "I hope for all our sakes that Barnes is alive."

His nod was followed by a tentative smile. "Tomorrow," he whispered. Something in his voice made her heart quicken. His eyes glowed with light from the flickering fire.

She'd known Barnes and Doc Myers all her life. It was hard to imagine them capable of putting a small boy in harm's way. And was it possible that the doctor *was* responsible for Barnes's disappearance, as David suggested? She shuddered at the thought. She didn't know what to believe or even who to trust, but seeing the concern on David's face, she knew to trust *him*.

"I'll see you tomorrow," she said, and the warmth of his quick smile followed her all the way outside.

Twenty-two

*When posing for her wedding portrait, a bride's expression
should be demure, never triumphant. A bridegroom should look
composed, his face void of anything suggesting lust, eagerness,
or anticipation.*

— MISS GERTRUDE HASSLEBRINK, 1878

Leaving the mission behind, Lucy drove straight to Ma's boardinghouse. She wanted to go home in the worst possible way. It had been a long hard day. She still couldn't believe that Doc Myers or even Barnes was capable of willfully putting a young boy's life in danger.

According to Caleb, Monica had returned home and, for that, Lucy was grateful. The last thing she wanted was to come face-to-face with Doc Myers. She wasn't even certain she could look the man in the face again after today.

Ma greeted Lucy at the door with a buttery smile, her white hair pulled back into a neat bun. "Come in, come in."

She led Lucy to her tidy parlor, her wide hips swaying from side to side. The rules for her boardinghouse were posted on the wall: No drinking, no cussing, and no courting. "No women" was an unspoken rule of the past, but in recent years Ma had allowed first Sarah and now Monica to board there. Nothing improper could happen under her

watchful eye—improper covering everything from meaningful looks to holding hands.

The smell of freshly baked pastry wafted from the kitchen.

"Sarah told me you're selling baked goods to help rebuild
the church," Lucy said.

Ma nodded and patted her crisp white apron. "My peach
pie even got that old skinflint Appleby to open his wallet."
She rolled her eyes. "It would have been easier to pull teeth
out of a bull. Whoever said a fool and his money are easily
parted never met Appleby."

Lucy laughed. Ma said what others only dared to think.

"I'll tell Monica you're here."

Moments later Monica floated down the stairs and greeted
Lucy with a hug. Lucy was surprised at how well Monica
looked, how absolutely radiant. Not one to pay much attention to how she looked, Monica had obviously taken great
pains with her appearance today.

Her blue dress draped around her hips in delicate folds,
adding pleasing curves to her slender figure. Her blond hair
was pulled back in a riot of curls from the crown of her head
to her shoulders. Her cheeks were pink and her eyes aglow.
If it weren't for the bandage that showed beneath the thin
sleeves of her dress, no one would ever suspect she had been
so recently injured.

"I'm so glad you came," Monica said. Her voice was still
rough around the edges from the smoke. "I have something
to tell you."

She led Lucy to the red velvet sofa and sat, motioning for
Lucy to join her with a pat on the cushion by her side. "Are
you all right? You look rather pale."

Lucy sat stiffly at the edge of the sofa. She should have
known Monica would sense her distress. She forced herself to
relax and even managed a smile.

"I haven't been sleeping well," she admitted. "I've been so

worried about you and the church and . . . the night I visited you, you still had that rasping cough."

It was obvious that Monica was about to pop with exciting news, and normally Lucy would have insisted upon hearing it at once. Today, however, she had something more pressing on her mind. If only she could figure out how to ask about the activity at the doctor's house the night of Barnes's disappearance without making Monica suspicious.

"My throat still fells scratchy, but the doctor . . ." Her gaze dropped to her lap. "He took good care of me."

Choosing her words carefully, Lucy asked, "Did . . . he stay with you all night?"

Monica's lashes flew upward. "What a question." A coy smile touched her lips. "I assure you, he was a perfect gentleman at all times."

With a start, Lucy realized Monica had misunderstood her. "I didn't mean—"

Monica laughed. "Of course you did," she teased. "I can tell by your face that you're dying to know what, if anything, happened, while I stayed at his house. As if anything could happen beneath the watchful eyes of his housekeeper." She sighed with obvious regret. "After you left, Dr. Myers and I played checkers and then Mr. Barnes arrived—"

"Mr. Barnes was at the doctor's house?" Lucy exclaimed.

If Monica noticed the alarm in Lucy's voice, she gave no indication. "Just for a couple of minutes. Isn't it strange how Mr. Barnes disappeared? He was perfectly fine when he left Leonard's house—I mean, Dr. Myers's house." Monica reddened.

Leonard. Monica called him by his Christian name. No one in town did that. Lucy came here originally to help David, but now it was concern for Monica that forced the next question. "Did you happen to hear what they discussed?"

Monica blinked. "Who?"

"Why, Dr. Myers and Mr. Barnes, of course."

"Oh." She thought for a moment. "I think Leonard said something about wanting to advertise in the newspaper."

Lucy's mind raced. It was a logical explanation on the surface but the more she considered it, the more improbable it seemed. Dr. Myers was the only doctor in town and had more patients than he could handle. Why would he advertise for more? Then, too, it wasn't in Barnes's nature to put himself out for anyone. Traveling to someone's home to conduct business was the last thing he would do. Barnes's late night visit to the doctor's house was about David. It had to be. Nothing else made sense. The question was—who else had Barnes visited that night?

Monica tapped Lucy on the arm as if to pull her back to the present. "So are you happy or disappointed that I'm still a virtuous woman?"

Lucy laughed. She hadn't the slightest doubt that Monica would remain chaste until the day she wed. "At least you don't have to sit in the front row at church."

Monica giggled. A glint of sunlight caught Lucy's attention and she stared at Monica's hand.

Following Lucy's gaze, Monica beamed as she wiggled her fingers to show off her shiny new ring.

Lucy took hold of Monica's hand for a closer look. The gold band was engraved with a single heart.

"That's what I wanted to tell you. Dr. Myers . . . Leonard . . . asked me to marry him."

Dropping Monica's hand, Lucy took a quick sharp breath. She'd prayed Monica and the doctor would get together, but that was before she knew what he did to David. He may have also done harm to Barnes, though she didn't want to believe it.

"Well? Aren't you going to say something?" Monica prodded. "Isn't it customary for one's best friend to be happy for her?"

"I'm sorry," Lucy stammered. "It's just, it's . . . so sudden."

"For him, maybe, but not for me." Monica folded her hands in her lap. "You know how long I've loved him. It's a miracle. There's no other way to describe it. I still can't believe it. What Sarah says is true. God does work through bad things to create miracles."

"B-bad things?" Lucy stammered.

"I'm talking about the fire. Who would have thought that the church burning down would bring Leonard and me together?"

"Oh, Monica . . ." Not knowing what to say, she wrapped her arms around her friend and hugged her tight. Monica had carried a torch for the doctor for years. But given her love of children, learning how her fiancé had put a young boy's life in danger would surely break her heart.

David had warned her about the dangers of saying anything. Until they knew for sure what happened to Barnes, Lucy would have to hold her tongue, however much she hated doing so.

Monica pulled away. "Are you all right?"

Before Lucy could answer, Ma walked into the room carrying a tray that she set on the table in front of them. "It's such a hot day, I thought you could both use some lemonade," she said. She winked at Lucy. "I suppose you heard I'm going to lose another boarder."

"Yes, Monica told me," Lucy said, trying to sound enthusiastic but failing.

Ma gave her a knowing look. "Why, Lucy Fairbanks. Is that envy I hear in your voice? Mark my words, your day will come. God made a lid for every pot and somewhere there's a man for you."

Monica laughed and squeezed Lucy's hand. "Let's hope your 'lid' is somewhere in Texas and not in some far off exotic land like China. Or you'll never find him."

A hot flush crept over Lucy's face. "This is one pot that can do without a lid," she said. "However, you, my friend, need a place to wed and it'll be awhile before they'll rebuild the church." With a little luck, it would take weeks, maybe even months.

"Don't be silly," Ma said. "If they can raise a barn in a day, building a church shouldn't take that much more time."

"It doesn't really matter," Monica said. "Pastor Wells came to visit me and he told me that the church is the people. That means we don't have to worry about where we have our wedding." Her cheeks turned a most becoming pink. "Leonard doesn't want to wait. He wants us to get married as soon as possible."

"What's the hurry?" Lucy asked, her apprehension increasing by the minute. "The traditional length of a betrothal is a year."

Hand on her chest, Monica pulled back in mock surprise. "When have *you* ever concerned yourself with tradition?" She shook her head. The fond look on her face gave way to melancholy. "I'm going to miss you so much."

Still reeling from news of Monica's impending marriage, Lucy wasn't sure she heard right. "Why are you going to miss me? Married women can still have friends."

"Leonard wants to move away from Rocky Creek. Not right away, of course, but eventually. He says his practice is getting too big for him to handle now that he's about to take a wife. We'll probably go to Houston."

Lucy's mouth went dry. "But Houston is so much larger than Rocky Creek." According the *Lone Star Tribune*, Houston's population was well over a million.

"Yes, but he would be one of many doctors."

"But . . . but this is your home."

"I know, but Leonard wants to open an office. It's not something he ever wanted to do, but he says times are changing.

Having patients travel to him rather than the other way around will save an enormous amount of time."

"Patients going to a doctor?" Ma exclaimed. She momentarily stopped pouring. "Bless my weary bones, now I've heard everythin'."

"Leonard says that with all the new medical knowledge, he can better care for patients in his office than in their homes," Monica explained. "He told me they've even discovered the bacteria that causes consumption and this could lead to a vaccination. Isn't that wonderful?"

"It is wonderful," Lucy agreed. Both Monica's parents had died of consumption, which was probably why the doctor took extra precautions after she inhaled all that smoke. "But why doesn't he just open an office here?"

"You know that won't work. People here are too set in their ways." Monica indicated Ma with a roll of her eyes. "Some people won't even ride the train."

Ma made a sound of disgust. "If the good Lord wanted us to travel that fast, I reckon he would have given us wheels instead of feet," she muttered. "And don't get me started on those gas balloons Redd is always talking about. Flying, indeed!" She shuddered. "I'll tell you another thing. It's not right for sick people to have to drag themselves out of bed to see a doctor."

Ma's indignant response made Monica giggle, but Lucy was in no mood to appreciate the humor. Frowning, she asked, "What about his patients here? What about your students? If he leaves, Rocky Creek will be without a doctor *and* a teacher."

"We're not planning to leave for a while. We certainly won't leave until the town finds another doctor and teacher. Maybe by then Caleb will be ready to take over the practice."

Lucy smiled at the thought. Dear Caleb. Wouldn't he love that? If only she could figure out a way to pay for his medical training.

"Maybe you can come, too, and open up your own studio," Monica said. "You can stay with us until you got settled."

It was a tempting idea, but Lucy doubted she would ever have the means to afford her own photography studio.

Monica changed the subject. "I plan to ask Mrs. Taylor to make my wedding dress. She did such a good job with Jenny's." She rattled on about what she planned to wear at her wedding and how she would style her hair. "I do hope you'll take lots of photographs. Please say you will."

"Oh, Monica, you know I'll do anything for you."

Monica smiled. "Ma agreed to let us get married in the garden."

Ma set the pitcher of lemonade on the tray. "It's going to be a beautiful wedding." A dreamy expression crossed her face, making her appear years younger. "Why, we haven't had a wedding since the three Higgins sisters got married last summer." She handed Lucy a glass.

"Thank you." The lemonade was cool and sweet.

"Will you be available the middle of July?" Monica asked. "Sarah is certain that Pastor Wells's schedule is clear."

Spilling her drink all over herself, Lucy jumped to her feet. Ma immediately rushed to her side, mopping her skirt and waistcoat.

Lucy quickly apologized to Ma for her clumsiness, but never took her eyes off Monica. "That's only a couple of weeks away."

Monica wiped a small wet spot off the sofa with a linen napkin, a broad smile on her face. "Just think, this time next month, I shall be Mrs. *Dr.* Myers." Then realizing her gaffe, she laughed.

Ma Taylor laughed too, and neither noticed that Lucy didn't join in their mirth. Knowing that Monica's happiness might not last long near broke Lucy's heart.

Cutting her visit short, Lucy headed for home. She

impatiently snapped the reins against Tripod's rump. Dear God, how would she ever find the words to tell Monica that her fiancé wasn't the man she thought he was? Knowing what he did to David was bad enough, but what if he was involved in the disappearance of Barnes? *Please, God, don't let it be so.*

Arriving home she quickly pulled pen and paper from the drawer of her writing desk and set to work listing Rocky Creek residents who had been in their teens twenty years earlier. Some men were too young or too old or had moved to Rocky Creek in recent years and these she left off the list. She circled the names she wasn't sure about. She was certain Timber Joe didn't move to Rocky Creek until after the war. He looked old enough but men who fought in the war tended to age faster than normal. Marshal Armstrong, Barrel, Redd, and Pastor Wells had moved to town within the last couple of years. Old Man Appleby was too old.

She spent the rest of the day and most of the night listing names or crossing them out. It was hard to remember every family that lived in and around Rocky Creek, harder still to know when they may have moved into town, but it was a start.

She copied the names of the men she knew for certain had lived locally at least twenty years, and who were the right age. She then wrote a one or two word description by each of their names. Folding the paper, she slipped it into her pocket.

She planned to question her father over dinner. He would know when various families had moved to Rocky Creek.

That evening her father walked in the door early. "Something smells good," he said.

He pecked her on the cheek and sat in his favorite chair. She hurried to fetch his slippers, as was her usual custom.

Slippers in hand, she stood watching him as he tamped down his pipe.

How much did he know about that long-ago night on the river? Had Barnes or Myers confided in him? Was that what broke up their friendship? Was that why he was so against Caleb working for the doctor? As much as she wanted to ask him outright, she bit back the urge. He would only want to know how she knew, and then she would have to tell him about David.

She sat on the footstool in front of his chair and proceeded to pull off his boots. "Any news about Mr. Barnes?"

"I talked to the marshal today," he said. "Nothing is missing from Barnes's cabin and his bank account has not been touched."

"That's odd," she said, setting a boot on the floor.

"It's only odd if he's alive."

She looked up. "And you think he's not?"

"The marshal suspects he may not be. He's issued a warrant for the last known man to see him alive."

Trying not to appear overly curious, she struggled to keep her voice even. "Anyone we know?" Was it Doc Myers? *Dear God, please don't let it be so.* It would break Monica's heart.

"It was that Wolf fellow you photographed for the *Gazette*," he said. "The wild man."

She froze, her hand on his boot. "How . . . how do they know it's him?"

"Crankshaw saw him outside the newspaper office the night Barnes disappeared and was able to describe him. There aren't too many men walking around in buckskin."

At mention of Crankshaw's name, her blood ran cold. She was almost certain he knew of Wolf's presence in the woods on Sunday.

Forgetting caution, she blurted out, "David Wolf didn't do it!"

Her father's eyebrows shot up. "How would you know that?"

"I . . . I . . ."

"Speak up, girl. What do you know about this?"

"I t-talked to him," she stammered. "I wrote an article and he's the one who saved me from the stagecoach robbers—"

He rubbed his forehead. "Lucy, Lucy, Lucy." He sighed and dropped his hand to his lap. "This man could have done you great harm."

"No!" She jumped to her feet. "I don't care what Marshal Armstrong says, David didn't kill Barnes! Besides, we don't even know he's dead."

Just then the door flew open and Caleb walked in, lugging his ever-present medical books. Seeming oblivious to the tension in the room, he asked, "What is the only muscle not attached at both ends?"

Lucy tossed her father's boot on the floor and ran from the room.

⌘

Later that night, after her father had retired, Lucy donned her cape and quietly let herself outside.

She was in the barn saddling Tripod when Caleb found her.

"Where are you going?" he asked, his face grim in the yellow light of the lantern.

"I'm going to warn David that the marshal is looking for him," she said.

His eyes widened. "Lucy, don't. It could be dangerous."

"He didn't do what they said he did." She had been wrong about Myers, wrong about Barnes. *Dear God, don't let me be wrong about David.*

"Take the wagon," he said. "And I'll go with you."

His offer touched her deeply and she felt guilty for forcing him to help her care for David, but she didn't know who else to trust.

"No," she whispered. "I have to do this alone." She didn't want to get her brother involved any more than he already was.

He frowned. The lines of worry didn't belong on a sixteen-year-old face. Sometimes it seemed that Caleb carried the world on his shoulders.

Myers and Barnes hadn't been much older than Caleb when they put David in that boat. At first she tried blaming their actions on youth, but age alone could not explain the things David accused them of doing. She couldn't imagine Caleb doing anything so cruel.

"If anything happens to you . . ." Caleb began. His unspoken words exploded in her head. *Like Mama.*

She shuddered at the memory of her mother taking off one night on horseback, never to return. "Nothing's going to happen to me," she assured him.

"Please, let me go with you."

"I'll be all right," she said. She moved to hug him but he pulled away. "I give up. What muscle isn't attached on both ends?" she asked, hoping to humor him out of his worry. She was certain it was the tongue, but she didn't want to spoil his fun.

"Your stubborn fool brain," he said angrily and stormed away.

Twenty-three

*A man can fool a woman but never a camera. A woman can fool
both, but only if she puts her mind to it.*

— Miss Gertrude Hasslebrink, 1878

With only the faint light of a gibbous moon lighting the way,
she rode out of town and followed the road that ran along the
river's edge. It was the same road the runaway stagecoach had
taken, and her stomach clenched at the memory, as it tended
to do every time she rode this way.

Determined to warn David that the marshal was looking
for him, she swallowed her fear. A shadow flew past, barely
missing her, and she cried out in alarm. Hearing the comforting cry of an owl, she pressed a hand on her chest to still her
pounding heart. Tripod nickered but stayed the course, head
bopping up and down in a slow but steady rhythm.

She took the fork that led to the mission. Even in the soft
glow of moonlight, the building looked eerie and forbidding.
Dismounting, she tethered her horse to a splintered hitching
post. There was no sign of Shadow, but that didn't necessarily
mean David wasn't around.

She walked to the open side door, its gaping mouth frozen
in mid-yawn. She took one step inside. "David?" Her voice
echoed through the long hall, followed by dead silence.

Nervously she backed out of the building, grabbed the reins of her horse, and froze. What was that sound? Tripod pricked his ears and whinnied, telling her he'd heard it too. It was the sound of a running horse.

Hoping it was David, but fearing it was the marshal, she looked around for a place to hide. She would never be able to explain her presence out here so late at night.

Before she could move, the hoofbeats grew louder and a magnificent white animal burst out from among the trees. She couldn't believe her eyes. The legendary white mustang really did exist!

His lean body was powerful, his coat luminous. In the pale moonlight he looked like polished marble. His silvery tail held high, it cascaded down like spouting water. Stopping no more than twenty feet in front of her, he stared at her with diamond bright eyes. He then rose on hind legs and pawed the air.

Intrigued and strangely mesmerized, Lucy made a frame with her fingers and pretended to look through the lens of a camera. What she would give for such a photograph. Someone had actually succeeded in photographing landscape in the moonlight but it had required nearly eight hours' exposure time, a luxury no living being would allow her.

Some things could not be caught by a camera. Even if, by some miracle, the stallion stood still long enough to be photographed, she could never capture its power or grace. Was the same true of a man's innocence? A man's secrets? A man's soul?

As if suddenly noticing her presence, the stallion looked straight at her. Head held high, ears forward, the amazing animal opened his mouth and whinnied. The high-pitched cry sent shivers down Lucy's spine.

Next to her Tripod frantically tried to escape, and it was all Lucy could do to hold on to him. "It's all right," she soothed. She stroked her horse's smooth slick neck until the stallion galloped back into the woods.

Still Lucy couldn't pull her gaze away from the streaks of silver that flashed between the trees. At last the horse vanished altogether.

With the stallion gone, the mission and surrounding woods seemed more menacing. Was it dark when David ran away at the age of ten? Probably. No doubt he had the same purposeful strides, the same determination as he did now. Ostracized all his life, she marveled at how he still maintained a sense of humor and dignity. A wave of sadness swept through her for the boy he once was, but her feelings for the man he had become were much more complicated.

Anxious to escape the deserted mission, she quickly mounted her horse and rode away as fast as Tripod could carry her.

Fearing David may have already been arrested, her heart was so heavy it was a wonder that her horse didn't cave beneath the weight.

The following morning she made Caleb promise to let her know if he heard any news. Feeling as if her world were falling apart, she paced the floor, stopping every so often to gaze out the window. No news was good news, right?

It was nearly noon before her brother returned. Dreading what he would say, she ran outside to greet him.

He sat astride Papa's circling horse and shouted, "Mr. Wolf hasn't been arrested yet. The marshal and his men are still looking for him."

She sighed with relief and waved him off. Head bent low, he quickly galloped away, both hands on the reins.

She spent the rest the afternoon in the shack out back that was her darkroom. Usually developing plates made her forget her worries, but not today. Today she couldn't stop thinking of David.

The ruby-glassed lantern bathed the room in a soft red

light. Though Caleb had drilled holes in one wall and covered them with a wooden light trap for ventilation, it was still necessary to step outside on occasion to escape the fumes.

Darkroom explosions were a common occurrence. For that reason she purchased her chemicals ready mixed and stored them on a single shelf in clearly marked bottles.

She was particularly pleased with the photograph of the Wells family. Elizabeth had the most endearing smile. Little Matthew with his big blue eyes and chubby face looked good enough to eat. Sarah would be so pleased. After thoroughly washing the print to assure permanence, she hung it on the line to dry and turned her attention to the next one.

Shocked to see her own image emerge in the bath, she lowered her head for a closer look. She'd forgotten that little Skip Owen had snapped a photograph of her with David. It was the first time she had seen her own likeness captured in a photograph. The picture grew brighter and more revealing, like the gradual illumination of an early morning sky,

It wasn't a good photograph. The composition was all wrong and it was underexposed. David stood in the shadows so his expression was lost, but the slanted rays of sunshine made hers perfectly clear. Her white waistcoat was all wrong. Dark colors were more photographic. Her hair, too, was wrong, piled on top of her head in her usual haphazard way. But it wasn't her clothes or hair that captured her attention, not by any means. It was something else entirely, and she was stunned by what she saw.

A photograph was but a moment in a person's life that revealed an inner truth. She always assumed that the lens revealed only those truths known to the subject. How, then, was it possible for the camera to uncover something of which she was not aware? How could she not know her own heart?

The sleepless nights. The lack of appetite. Now it all made sense.

She pulled the photograph from its bath and studied it. Oh yes, it was abundantly clear.

She hadn't recognized the feeling but she certainly recognized the expression. For she'd seen that very same look on Monica's face.

On Sarah's.

On Jenny's face. Mary Lou's and Brenda's too.

It was the look of a woman in love.

⁂

The following day she sat outside her father's store next to her camera, staring at the letter in her hand.

It was from the *Chicago Tribune*. Fearing it was yet another rejection, she took her time opening the letter. "We regret to inform you," she said aloud, and didn't read any further.

Now that she knew she was in love with David, this rejection had less of an impact than the others. She desperately needed money, but how could she leave David in his time of need?

She tucked the letter away in her portfolio, feeling very much alone.

When no one showed up to have a picture taken, she packed up her gear and headed for the mission. Heart in her throat, she wandered from room to room. It was cold inside, much colder than the air outside, and damp. The place smelled musty, maybe even moldy.

She finally reached the kitchen. It was a huge room with battered wood counters, high ceilings, and a wood-burning cookstove. Cupboards and drawers hung open, their shelves barren. A cast-iron sink was anchored by a rusty water pump.

Sun streamed through a tall narrow window, providing a lighted stage for dancing dust motes. She walked back into the main room. David was nowhere to be found. He'd asked her to meet him here today. So where was he? Why wasn't he here? Had Marshal Armstrong already arrested him? Or had David simply left town? Neither possibility gave her any peace.

Feeling utterly miserable and alone, she hurried through the cavernous building intent on leaving, but the unfinished chair stopped her in her tracks.

Eyes closed, she fingered the chair and imagined David bent over it, working. What if she never saw him again? The thought left her even more bereft.

Trembling, she moved the chair closer to the window, turning it until the light hit the exquisite carved wolf just right.

She ran out to her wagon to fetch her tripod and camera, and for the next several moments nothing else existed but the image in her lens.

She had just completed taking her photographs when David entered the room and her heart skipped a beat. Never could she have imagined a more welcome sight.

"I didn't mean to startle you," he said.

"You d-didn't," she stammered. It was her newly discovered secret of the heart that startled her, not his commanding presence. "I was just photographing your chair. I think the light captures it just right, don't you?" She went on to describe different qualities of light and exposure times, knowing full well she was babbling and not knowing how to stop.

He cocked his head. "I'm not making you nervous, am I?"

"No, no, of course not," she said, feeling herself blush. "It's just that . . . the marshal has a warrant for your arrest. He thinks you're responsible for Barnes's disappearance."

David nodded. "I know. He came here yesterday looking for me." He beckoned to her. "Come in the other room. It's warmer."

He led her to a sunny room behind the sanctuary, which, judging by the old desk, was once used as an office. The room was small and his nearness made her senses spin. Irritated at herself for letting her emotions take precedence over every-thing else, she backed away.

"We have another problem," she said, willing herself not to babble.

Quickly, she told him about the doctor's plan to wed Monica. "The wedding is planned for mid-July. If there's the least suspi-cion that the doctor harmed Barnes in any way, Monica has the right to know."

"I agree, but not yet. Let me talk to him first. Did you ask your friend about the night Barnes disappeared?"

She nodded. "Barnes came by to talk to the doctor that night."

His eyebrows shot up. "Interesting. We have to assume the reason for the visit had something to do with me. What time was that, do you know?"

"I left the doctor's house after eight thirty. So it had to be later."

"A couple of hours after I saw him." His eyes narrowed in thought. "It doesn't take that long to drive to the doctor's house."

"Maybe he was working."

He shook his head. "I went to the newspaper office last night to look around. He never finished the headline he was working on the night I was there. So now we have to wonder what he was doing for those couple of hours."

So that's where David was last night when she looked for him. She reached into her portfolio and pulled out a stack of glossy prints. "These are photographs of some people I know lived here for twenty years or more." When she first got her camera she was so excited, she photographed anyone kind enough to pose. "People change over time but I thought you might recognize someone."

A smile ruffled the corners of his mouth. "So you've decided to help me," he said, his voice warm with approval.

Her face grew hot and she lowered her lashes. "I'm doing this for my friend Monica," she said quickly. She wasn't ready to admit to any other reason.

"Fair enough," he said, though she detected a note of doubt in his voice.

She raised her eyes to his and found him assessing her with a bold frankness that took her breath away. *Please don't let him see in my face what the camera saw.*

She handed him the photos, and one by one, he began flipping through them.

"That's Peter Jefferson," she said, tapping one image. "His father owns a ranch outside of town. He broke his leg as a child and it wasn't set right."

He rejected some photographs at once, handing them back to her. He flipped through the ones he wasn't certain about, holding them up one by one in the full light of the sun. In the end, he handed the entire stack of photos back to her.

Feeling her spirits sink, she slipped the stack into her satchel. She wouldn't give up, and she didn't want him to give up either. "I can take more photographs."

He shook his head. "You're right. People change in twenty years. I think it's time for me to confront Myers. He's going to have to tell me what he knows." Before she could respond, he beckoned her to follow him. "I want to show you something." Reaching the corner desk he picked up a roll of paper. "I told Wells I would design a new church."

"You talked to Pastor Wells?" This surprised her.

"Yes, and he asked me to draw up plans." He spread the paper out and ran his finger over the drawing, naming the different areas. "This is the classroom. I put Pastor Wells's office on the opposite side of the sanctuary so he won't be disturbed by pupils. This, here, is the library."

"It's wonderful," she said, though she had serious misgivings. Classrooms? Office? Library? Her heart sank. She

234

would have to sell a whole lot more photographs to build such a fine church.

He rolled up the drawing and set it on the desk. "Come on, I'll walk you outside."

He grabbed her satchel and camera and led the way. They had just reached the courtyard when David suddenly pulled back inside.

"It's the marshal," he whispered. "He's checking out your horse and wagon."

Lucy's heart pounded. How would she ever explain her presence at the deserted mission? Then she thought of something. She took her camera from him.

"I'll talk to him," she said. Without waiting for him to approve or disapprove, she followed the clay tile path to the front of the mission and greeted the marshal with a smile.

Marshal Armstrong lifted his hat. "Didn't expect to see you, ma'am," he said. "What are you doing all the way out here?"

"Taking photographs," she replied. At least that much was true. "It's a beautiful day. Not a cloud in the sky. A perfect day for taking pictures and—" No, she wouldn't babble. He was bound to know she was nervous and hiding something. She forced herself to stop talking.

He hooked his thumbs on his gun belt. If he suspected anything, she couldn't tell. "It's not a good idea for a woman to be alone out here. We might have a killer on the loose."

A killer? A soft gasp escaped her. "You're not serious, are you?"

"I don't want to jump to conclusions but it's been almost a week and there's still no sign of Barnes." Hands still on his waist, he looked around and she held her breath, waiting.

"I do have some good news for you," he said. His gaze returned to her face. "I got a telegram from Houston. They've arrested three men who held up a stage there. The men fit the descriptions you gave me."

"I'm so happy to hear that," she said. Maybe now she could forget about the holdup. She hesitated. "Sarah was worried that one of them might have been her brother. I tried to tell her they weren't but you know how she worries." She was tempted to keep talking but she clamped her mouth shut.

"None of them resembled the Prescott gang," he said. "I reckon I should stop by and put her mind to rest. Meanwhile, I think it would be best if you stay close to town until we find out for sure what happened to Barnes." He made no mention of David.

"I . . . I'll do that," she said. She placed her camera into the back of her wagon and scrambled into the driver's seat.

Marshal Armstrong swung into the saddle of his horse. He touched a finger to the brim of his hat and galloped away.

She waited until he was out of sight before she jumped to the ground and ran back to the mission.

David was nowhere to be found. Even his chair was missing. She ran outside to the back. "David!"

She caught sight of him in the distance, standing at the edge of the woods. Finger to his lips he motioned her to join him with his other hand.

She hurried to his side. With a hushing sound, he led the way through the woods to the edge of a meadow where the white mustang grazed.

She gasped with delight, which brought a grin to his face.

"He's beautiful," she whispered. Even more beautiful in the sun than in the moonlight.

As if sensing their presence, the horse lifted its head. Raising his tail, he raced away and disappeared in the trees. All too soon he was nothing more than a memory.

"Too bad you didn't have your camera with you," David said.

"I couldn't have gotten his picture anyway. There wasn't enough time." She turned to meet his gaze. "Maybe some things aren't meant to be photographed." It was a pity really. The white stallion had a beauty all its own.

"Why do you suppose differences in nature are valued but not differences in people?" she asked. She hated knowing that David and Lee Wong had to fight for acceptance. Or that colored children were required to go to separate schools. As a woman she knew some of what they went through, but not all. She knew what it was like to be judged for her gender but not by the color of her skin.

"People feel threatened by what they don't know or understand," he replied quietly. "No one feels threatened by a white horse."

She smiled up at him. He looked so handsome it was all she could do to keep from throwing her arms around him. "Not even a black horse?" she asked.

They shared a laugh before she grew serious again. "Just think what a wonderful world this would be if everyone learned to love more like God."

"Or like you." She blushed and he continued. "Your photographs . . . they're special."

Something in the way he said it filled her with joy. "Special?"

"That picture . . . the one of the lame man . . . I knew before you told me. Not about his leg but the sadness. I could see the sadness on his face. Your photographs don't just capture an image, they tell a story. You're an artist."

An artist. He called her an artist. No one had ever before called her that. Never could she imagine how sweet it would sound—or how deeply it would touch her.

"You saw the sadness because that's all *he* sees," she said. "In his mind, nothing exists outside his bad leg."

"Ah, so he can't see the forest for the trees," he said.

Like you, she wanted to say but didn't. He saw the barriers that separated him from the rest of the world—from her—but failed to see the bonds that drew them together.

"I can't stay," she said. Biting back tears, she turned, anxious to make her escape.

"Lucy." He caught her by the arm, trapping her with ironlike fingers. "Did I say something wrong?"

His hand on her arm sent tingles down her spine. *Don't touch me*, she wanted to say. *Don't look at me like that. Don't make me love you any more than I already do.* When she finally found her voice she said none of those things.

"What do you plan to do when you finish your business here . . . do you plan to stay?" She was treading on dangerous ground. If there was the slightest possibility they could be together, she would give up her plans to seek employment out of town in a flash, despite her financial problems.

Frowning, he released her arm. "I plan to go back to the Panhandle and help Combes's son. I can't stay here."

She turned to face him. "Because of the bad memories?"

"Because of who I am." His jaw tightened. "I'm part Indian and part white. Together they don't make a whole."

She threw up her arms in exasperation "You're like the lame man," she charged. "You see only one thing."

He stepped back as if she'd slapped him. "That's not true."

"Isn't it?" Without giving him a chance to answer, she added, "Pastor Wells says we're all children of God. We're all the same in his eyes. I know that doesn't change how other people think, but it's a place to start."

"You believe in a kind and forgiving God." He shook his head as if the very idea of a loving God confounded him. "That's not what I was taught." He nodded toward the mission, his face grim. "They used to beat us for reciting a Bible verse wrong or growing restless during prayer."

"That's not the Christian way," she said. She moved toward him and laid a hand on his cheek.

He took her hand in his and held it tight. "Maybe not,

but it's my experience that more people believe in a punishing God than a loving one."

"They're wrong," she said. "God doesn't care if we get the words wrong or we can't sit still. If that were the case we'd all be in trouble. He doesn't care about outer appearances. He cares about what's inside."

He squeezed her hand. "That's why I like your photographs," he said. "Because they show what's inside."

"Some people say the lens of a camera is like God's eyes," she said.

His mouth curved upward and something like a light passed between them. "You'll make me believe in a loving God yet."

"I certainly hope so." She smiled back at him, and for the longest while his gaze held hers. Finally he lowered his head as if to kiss her, their lips barely a breath apart. Instead he pulled away with a groan.

"I can't," he said. "It's not right."

"What's not right?" she whispered.

"Loving you." She held her breath, his words washing over her like the warming rays of the sun. "I can't help how I feel," he continued, "but that doesn't make it any less wrong."

She gazed up at him. He loved her. He actually *loved* her. Her heart leaped with joy. "How . . . how could that be wrong?"

He shook his head sadly. "Lucy . . ." He said her name slowly, as if he didn't want to release it. "You can't possibly know what you're asking."

She pulled her hand away. "I don't care what anyone thinks or says," she lashed out. "That's not who I am."

"Do you think I want it this way? I've been run out of more towns than you can imagine. I've been spit on and shot at for simply being a half-breed. Even while working at Combes's, I can't show my face. I can't put you through that. I won't." His face bleak, he stared at her a moment before turning to walk away.

She stared after him. Had he stomped on her heart it wouldn't have, couldn't have, hurt more. The gloomy future he described couldn't be any worse than the bleak future she imagined without him.

Jaw held tight, David Wolf wielded the ax over his head and brought it down with a quick swing of the arm. The blade hit the chair with a bang, cracking the seat and sending wood chips flying around the room. He struck the chair again and again. He pounded with his ax until the last of the carving had scattered in tiny splinters. The carving—the wolf—had come from a part of him he had come to hate, a part that kept him from the woman he loved, a part he wanted destroyed.

Malcolm Combes said his way with wood was a gift. "Too bad it's wasted on a half-breed." Combes didn't mean to be unkind. He was simply stating a fact. It was his way of saying that such talent would never be allowed to flourish in the open.

That part never bothered him before. He liked working behind the scenes, turning wood into beautiful yet functional pieces of furniture. It gave him great pleasure knowing that his creations were welcomed into people's homes even if he wasn't.

But it bothered him now. Not just the work part, but all of it. He no longer wanted to stay in the background. He wanted to live a normal life, to be front and center in Lucy's life. For once it wasn't his past that mattered. It was his future—the future he faced without Lucy.

Twenty-four

*A lady should have her photograph taken but three times: once when
she's born, once when she weds, and once for posterity.*

— MISS GERTRUDE HASSLEBRINK, 1878

Lucy gathered up her camera equipment and checked her
plates. Timber Joe's future bride was scheduled to arrive on
the eleven a.m. train from Dallas. Lucy had every intention of
photographing the occasion despite his objections.

"One day Timber Joe will thank me," she said, leaning
down to stroke the cat.

As if to agree with her, Extra meowed loudly and rubbed
against the hem of her skirt. Lucy sighed. "I just hope Barrel
and Redd manage to get Timber Joe into proper clothes."

She checked Extra's water dish and grabbed her satchel.
Camera in hand, she ripped open the door and was surprised
to find Richard Crankshaw standing on her porch, his fist
held high.

"I was just about to knock," he said.

He was the last person she wanted to see, but she didn't
want to appear rude. "I'm sorry. I was just on my way out."

"This won't take long." He pushed his way past her and
took off his derby.

The moment Crankshaw entered the parlor, Extra stopped

licking his paw and hissed, ingratiating himself into Lucy's heart.

Ignoring the cat, Crankshaw wasted no time in stating the purpose of his visit. "I came to make a proposition."

Her heart sank. Not again. She set her camera on the table. "Mr. Crankshaw, I already told you I'm not interested in marriage."

He held up his hand and the cat hissed louder. "All I ask is that you give me the courtesy of hearing what I have to say." He glanced around. "Do you mind if I sit?"

"Eh . . . I really am in a hurry," she said, clamping down on her mouth so as to not go into unnecessary detail.

"This won't take long," he assured her. Eyeing the tom, he circled around the sofa to avoid coming in contact with the animal. He sat, hat in hand.

Scooping Extra up with one hand, Lucy patted him on the head and set him outside on the porch. The cat flicked its tail and sauntered away in obvious disgust. Lucy wished she could do likewise.

Crankshaw waited for her to take a seat opposite him. "I just had a meeting with the Weatherbees," he said. "As you know, Millard's running for state senator and it could be a tight race."

She listened politely, more out of curiosity than anything. Politics held no real interest for her. It wasn't as if she could vote. Mrs. Hitchcock insisted that it was only a matter of time before Texas followed the lead of the Wyoming Territory and gave women the vote, but Lucy suspected it wouldn't happen without a battle, and maybe not even in her lifetime.

Crankshaw droned on. "Mrs. Weatherbee expressed concern about the town's lack of a newspaper, now that Mr. Barnes is gone. She believes it will be difficult for her son to get the support he needs in his hometown without one."

"I don't see what this has to do with me," she said, glancing at the mantle clock.

"Let me finish." He sat back. "I'm considering purchasing the newspaper myself."

This surprised her. Crankshaw was an oilman. What did he know about running a newspaper?

As if to guess her thoughts, he continued. "Business is business whether you're running an oil company or a newspaper. The same principles apply. Barnes, as I'm sure you'll agree, was not only a bad editor but a bad businessman. He didn't even have a regular publishing schedule. The *Gazette* is owned by some out-of-town investor who is willing to sell for the right price."

"I see," she said. "But I still don't know what this has to do with me."

He twirled his derby. "Yesterday I walked through the place as a potential buyer. Some of the equipment needs replacing and, of course, I'll need to hire someone to run it." He paused a moment. "I would like to offer you the position of editor."

Lucy could hardly contain her astonishment. She wouldn't have been more shocked had he asked her to drill for oil. "W-why me?" she stammered at last.

"I was aware of your . . . ability to take photographs," he explained, "but it wasn't until I came across an article in Barnes's desk about the wild man that I knew you could write."

"I . . . I don't know what to say." Her mind raced with excitement. Editor? She couldn't believe it. Never in her wildest dreams did she imagine herself an editor of a newspaper. Not only would the job help her pay for a new church, but it would also help with Caleb's education expenses. If only the offer hadn't come from Crankshaw.

She looked at him askew, not sure she could trust him. "I thought you didn't believe in women pursuing occupational endeavors."

"I still believe a woman's *primary* function is home and hearth," he said. "However, times are changing, and I understand other towns employ women editors." Not even his studied composure could hide the look of triumph in his eyes. Obviously he was confident she would accept his offer.

"How much control would I have?" she asked, masking her reservations with a businesslike voice. *Please don't let this be a trick.*

"As much as you want. Providing, of course, the newspaper doesn't lower its standards and become a journal of feminine fashions and household hints."

She raised an eyebrow. "I don't believe a household hint exists that could match Barnes's low standards," she said.

He laughed. "You may be right." He raked her up and down, his gaze lingering a tad too long on her neckline.

She rose abruptly. "Thank you for your generous offer. As you can imagine, I need time to think about it." She wanted to accept immediately but something made her hold back.

He stood too. "Take all the time you need," he said with a magnanimous air that seemed forced.

She walked across the room and opened the door. "I'm sorry, but I really do have another engagement."

"I understand." He donned his hat. "Oh, by the way. My offer comes with one stipulation."

"Only one?"

"Only one," he said with a smile that didn't reach his eyes. "You will have to accept my proposal of marriage."

So it was a trick after all. It didn't surprise her but she was nonetheless disappointed. He had effectively dashed any hope she had of accomplishing her financial goals and pursuing her profession. She already knew her answer, but he had already donned his hat and was halfway down the walkway. She planned to turn down his offer, of course, but she had no intention of shouting after him.

Extra had no such qualms. The tomcat arched its back and gave Crankshaw the full benefit of a hissy fit.

Nodding approval, Lucy muttered beneath her breath. "My sentiments exactly."

⁓

The train hadn't yet arrived when Lucy pulled her horse and wagon behind a long line of vehicles parked in front of the station.

The number of people gathered on the platform surprised her. It appeared as if the whole town had turned out to greet Timber Joe's bride-to-be. Even the ladies of the newly formed suffragette movement were on hand. Even more surprising was what Jenny and her sisters had done to the train station on such short notice. The platform was strung with red, white, and blue bunting and American flags. Baskets of colorful flowers hung from every post. Never had the depot looked so inviting.

Mrs. Taylor led a parade of enthusiastic supporters. Chanting in high-pitched voices, they held their banners high. "Women's rights, women's rights."

Camera and tripod in hand, Lucy fought her way along the crowded platform until she spotted Barrel, Redd, and Timber Joe.

Timber Joe paced in a circle like a dog chasing its tail. She'd never seen him look so nervous.

He came to a halt and greeted her with a frown. "Can't you make those women stop? The way they're carrying on, they're gonna frighten Annabelle away."

"I doubt it," she said, looking him up and down. If anything could frighten his potential bride away it was his faded Confederate clothes. "You're in uniform."

Redd shrugged. "Me and Barrel here tried to get him to change but he would have none of it."

Timber Joe stuck out his chin. "Annabelle can either take me as I am or not take me at all. Besides, she saw my photograph. She knows what she's getting."

"I sincerely doubt it," Lucy muttered beneath her breath. She glanced at Redd and Barrel, but neither man offered a solution.

Sighing in frustration, Lucy set up her tripod and attached the camera, but she didn't have much hope of using it. Annabelle would most likely take one look at Timber Joe and leave town on the next train.

The chanting grew louder and people kept coming. Sarah and Pastor Wells drove up in their wagon, followed by Marshal Armstrong and his wife, Jenny. Even Ma Stephens was on hand to watch the momentous occasion despite her disapproval of trains.

Timber Joe lifted his hat and wiped his forehead with his sleeve. "Can't a man meet his woman without the whole town showing up?" He had to shout to be heard above the Suffra-Quilters.

"We're happy for you," Lucy said. She nudged him gently with her hand on his shoulder in an effort to tease him out of his bad humor.

Barrel poked Redd with his elbow. "Better watch out. Here comes Miss Hogg."

Redd's face turned the color of the ketchup stain on his boiled shirt, but he said nothing.

Emma Hogg threaded her way through the throng and joined them. "I wouldn't miss this day for the world," she said, addressing her comments to Timber Joe. She didn't even look at Redd.

The distant sound of a train whistle drew a ripple of excitement from the waiting crowd and a look of terror on Timber Joe's face. The Suffra-Quilters, led by Mrs. Taylor, continued their loud chants.

The rumbling sound grew louder as the train slid into the station and came to a grinding halt. Steam hissed across the platform and heads craned as a uniformed conductor disembarked, followed by a stream of passengers.

"What does she look like?" Lucy asked, eyeing a young woman in a blue traveling suit who had just stepped onto the platform. The woman was met by a man and a child and the three walked off together. "What color hair does she have?"

"How am I supposed to know?" Timber Joe grew more anxious with each passing moment. He ran a finger along the frayed collar of his uniform. Sweat rolled down his face. "I told her not to send a photograph. I wanted to be surprised."

The newly arrived travelers began leaving the depot. Standing on tiptoes, Lucy craned her neck to see over the fast-thinning crowd. Had the woman named Annabelle changed her mind?

As if to read her thoughts, Timber Joe said, "I guess she's not coming." He shrugged with an air of indifference as if Annabelle's failure to appear was of no consequence. But Lucy could see past his façade.

"Maybe she sent the letter *before* she got my photograph," he said. "Then when she saw what I looked like she changed her mind about coming."

What Timber Joe suggested was a real possibility and Lucy felt terrible. She had been so certain his photograph would convince Annabelle of his fine character. "I'm so sorry."

Timber Joe grunted but said nothing.

One last passenger stepped off the train and Lucy blinked in disbelief. The man was dressed in what looked like an old army suit and flat-visor hat. From where she stood, the traveler looked enough like Timber Joe to be his twin.

The uniformed stranger looked around, then waved and hurried toward them.

"Timber Joe, is that you?" came a voice that was clearly

soprano. It was then that Lucy realized that the uniformed stranger was a woman.

A hush settled over the remaining spectators. Even the Suffra-Quilters stopped marching to stare in silence at the oddly dressed woman.

"Annabelle!" Timber Joe said, his face lighting up. "Is that you?"

"'Course it's me. Who did you think it was?"

He looked her up and down. "But you're dressed like a Confederate soldier," he sputtered.

"That's because I fought in the war. Just like you." She lowered her voice. "I disguised myself as a man and fought just as hard as one. Of course that was before I was found out and discharged for *gender incompatibility*."

"You're joking, right?" Timber Joe asked. "You fought in the war?"

"General-*lee*, I don't make jokes," she replied, laughing at her own pun.

Timber Joe laughed too.

Annabelle looked him up and down and nodded with approval. "When I got your photograph, I knew you were the man for me."

Timber Joe got all red in the face. "I knew you'd like it," he said with a shy grin. He then saluted her and she saluted him back.

"Don't move," Lucy said, stepping behind her camera. This was one picture she didn't want to miss.

Sarah, Jenny, and all eleven Suffra-Quilters hurried forward to greet Timber Joe's future bride. If her unconventional dress didn't win the hearts of the townsfolk, her friendly personality did.

Ma nodded approvingly. "It's like I always said. God made a lid for every pot." She gave Lucy a maternal look. "Even for you."

Lucy smiled but inside she was dying, dying because the only man for her was David and he'd made it clear they had no future together.

While the others plied Annabelle with questions, Emma Hogg inched closer to Lucy. "I wish to make an appointment to have my photograph taken," she said primly. She glared at Redd. "It's high time I found myself a lid . . . uh . . . husband. I've signed up with one of those marriage catalogs. If it worked for Timber Joe, no doubt it will work for me."

Redd frowned and his face grew grim, but he didn't utter a word.

Lucy watched Redd as she replied, "Could you come on Friday? Say around two?"

"Yes, yes, that would be perfect," Emma said.

"Are you sure you want to do this?" Lucy asked.

"I'm positive," Miss Hogg snapped. "A woman waiting for a man around here is likely to end up an old maid." She whispered in Lucy's ear. "Don't you make the same mistake I've made." In a louder voice, she added, "I'll see you Friday." Head held high, she sailed past Redd and kept going.

Barrel slapped Redd on the back. "Looks like you finally got your wish. Miss Hogg has decided to leave you alone." A crease settled between Redd's eyebrows and his face remained as red as a summer ripe tomato, but whatever he was thinking he kept to himself.

Timber Joe and Annabelle walked off hand in hand and Lucy couldn't take her eyes off them. No photograph could tell her more than what she already knew. God brought them together not only to love each other but to help each other heal.

⁓

Wolf removed the loose hair and dirt from Shadow's coat with a wooden currycomb. "You don't like this much, do you, fellow?"

Not wanting to be seen from the road, he stood in back of the mission behind a moss-covered wall. Several yards away was a small cemetery, the gravestones hidden by overgrown bushes. He couldn't see the river for the trees but he could hear the steady sound of rushing waters.

Last night a thunderstorm had rolled through the area. Now the sky was clear but the air felt hot and sticky.

He patted his horse on the rump and exchanged the comb for the soft-bristle brush. Head and neck extended back, the horse watched his every move.

Upon seeing the brush, Shadow nodded and blew out his breath, relaxing.

Wolf laughed. "You like this better, eh?" He sensed rather than heard someone approach. The sheriff? He tensed.

"David!"

Hearing Lucy call to him, he stepped out from behind the wall where she could see him and waved.

Lucy ran toward him. Skirt lifted high above her ankles, she practically flew along the red brick path.

She seemed so anxious to reach him that he feared something was wrong. Still, no amount of worry could mask his pleasure at seeing her.

"Lucy. What is it?"

"Nothing. Everything." She stopped in front him and, in one breathless sentence, blurted out, "Every pot has a lid and Timber Joe found his, and Sarah found hers, and Jenny found hers, and Monica found hers . . ." She continued with name after name.

Puzzled, he scratched his head. All this talk about pots and lids. Was she trying to invite him to supper? Even Shadow looked puzzled.

"I don't care who you are or who your parents were, I don't care what my father will say or what my friends will think or . . ."

She talked so fast, it was all he could do to make hide or hair out of what she said.

"I love you," she said at last and fell silent.

He stared at her. Love? Did she say she loved him?

"Well?" she demanded. "Say something."

He opened his mouth to object, to tell her all the reasons why they couldn't be together. He would have done exactly that had she not somehow ended up in his arms. Once his lips found hers, he was doomed. The glorious feel of her body next to his crowded out any other thought. By the time he finally let her go, she was not only speechless but out of breath.

"I swear you could talk the bark off a tree," he mustered at last.

She threw back her head and laughed. "And you could stop a riot with your kiss."

He grinned like a foolish youth. "I hope I never have to try."

Her pretty pink mouth still swollen from his kiss, she looked even more beautiful today than usual. Her eyes, bright as the sky, were every bit as blue. Tendrils of shiny hair hugged her face as he longed to do. He wanted to show her in every possible way how much he loved her. He wanted to hold her, to explore every curve of her body, every inch of her skin, every facet of her soul. It was wrong, of course, terribly, terribly wrong, but knowing it didn't make it any easier to release her. He dropped his arms to his sides.

Why did she do this to him? Why did she insist upon making it so difficult for him to do what was right? "Lucy . . . what I said the other day . . ." He tried to hold back the words, but it would have been easier to hold back a tornado. "What I said about loving you . . ."

Her face brightened, her eyes sparkled, and he wished to God he'd never admitted what his heart knew was true. "Nothing's changed."

"I don't care," she whispered. "I just want to be with you."

He grabbed her by the arms. "Lucy, listen to me. We can't be together."

Her face paled and her lips trembled. Hating himself for causing her such pain, he slid his hands down her arms. "You must know how impossible this is."

She shook her head. "It doesn't have to be."

"But it is. You know it is. A white woman married to a half-breed. I fear for your safety."

"Rocky Creek isn't like that," she said. "These are my friends. They'll protect us."

"Oh, Lucy, you don't know what you're saying. You're so kind and loving you can't see the world as it really is."

She pulled away from him. "I know how the world is," she said. Her eyes flashed with anger. "Our town has to hide its colored children so as not to build separate schools. Lee Wong can't bring his family here because of the Chinese exclusion laws. Women don't even rate a mention in the Texas constitution. I know how cruel the world can be. But I've grown up in this town all my life. People know me and love me. In time, they'll get to know you, too, and when they do . . ."

"I can't stay here. What happened . . ." He shook his head. "I can't live in the same town as Myers and Barnes."

"Then we'll find another place to live," she said, and he loved her even more for putting his needs in front of her own.

"You know that won't work. Strangers won't be as kind or as unforgiving as your friends," he said. "And what about your father and brother?"

"I'll . . . miss them, of course." She'd hesitated for only a second, but it was enough for him to know how very much it would cost her to leave. "And I'll find a way to put my brother through school."

"Lucy, every town, every city is a war zone for people like me." He swallowed hard. The fight against the invisible barrier that separated him from the rest of the world was not only a daily struggle, it defined him as a man. He reached for her hands.

She yanked away from him. "I don't care. You're the man I love. I don't care about anything else."

"You deserve so much more." His voice grew tight. "You deserve a man with a name, a birthright. A profession."

She shook her head in protest. "You're a cabinetmaker."

"And how many of your friends will be willing to hire a half-breed to build their furniture? I can tell you from experience that few, if any, will."

"So is that it?" She tilted her chin up and swiped away a tear. "Are we supposed to just walk away from each other and forget how we feel?"

It was exactly what they must do, but to hear it put so bluntly was like a knife to his heart. "It's best that way."

"Best for who?" she cried out.

"For both of us," he said. "Lucy, if I could change things, don't you think I would? If I could make myself all white or all Indian, I would do it in a flash. If I could change the hatred that makes people like me live between two worlds, I wouldn't hesitate a minute."

"You're like the man who can only see his lame leg." She backed away from him. "It's your barriers that are keeping us apart," she stormed, "not society's." She whirled around and stormed away.

Stunned, he could do nothing more than watch her go. His barriers? What did she mean by his barriers?

Lucy hurried away from him, seething. She followed the brick path toward the front of the mission, swiping away the low-hanging branches. Fool man. What did she ever see in him? He was stubborn and pigheaded and . . . ohhh. She told herself it was for the best. Telling Wolf how she felt had settled it once and for all.

She'd only gone a few steps when a bough hit her in the face and she brushed it aside. Her locket flew up in the air, the golden chain catching on a limb over her head.

"Oh no!" she cried.

Instantly David came up behind her. "What's wrong?"

"My locket." She pointed up.

It was a stretch, but he managed to grab hold of the branch. Bending it downward, he lifted the golden chain off the leafy limb and examined it.

"The clasp is broken," he said. "But I can fix it." The locket fell open and he stared at it.

Inside the locket was a daguerreotype miniature. "My parents on their wedding day," she said.

Photography had come a long way since the days of the daguerreotype, which required as much as a minute and a half exposure time. Headrests assured the absolute immobility a daguerreotype required, but resulted in stilted postures and pained expressions, which explained the look on her parents' faces.

"It's the only photograph I have of her," she said wistfully. She could barely remember her mother's smile. What she would give for a photograph of her mother that didn't look so serious.

David's eyes remained fixed on the locket in his hand, but he said nothing. Didn't move. Didn't flex a muscle.

Regretting the angry words spoken moments earlier, she stepped toward him. "David?" When he didn't answer her, she laid her hand on his arm.

Usually that brought a smile to his face, but not this time. The eyes that met hers were those of a stranger's. Mouth twisted as if in pain, his face darkened with emotion. At that moment she was more afraid than she had ever been in her life.

Her stomach in a knot, she gaped at him, her mouth open. Hot denial flooded through her. "No." She reached for her locket, but he held his hand over his head, out of reach.

"No!" she gasped. "You're wrong."

"I'm not wrong," he said with a certainty that turned her very bones cold. "The man in that photograph helped put me on that boat."

"No, no, no." She pounded against his chest with her fists. He caught her by the wrists and held her close.

"I'm sorry," he whispered close to her ear. "I never meant for this to happen."

All these years . . . the secrets . . . the shadows . . . her suspicion that nothing was as it seemed had haunted her, but nothing was as bad as the terrifying realization that now washed over her.

"No!" she cried again, as much for her own benefit as for his. "My father . . . he's a good man. He wouldn't—"

A sob caught in her voice. Backing away from him, she held him at bay with an outstretched hand. Shaking, she ran the rest of the way to her horse and wagon.

Twenty-five

Men should avoid looking pained or henpecked while being photographed. Nor should they use the occasion to assert themselves. As a matter of self-preservation, a photographer must never take sides in family disputes (unless, of course, the husband is blatantly wrong).

— MISS GERTRUDE HASSLEBRINK, 1878

Lucy burst through the door of her father's store. It was empty. She ran past the neatly stacked shelves to the storeroom in back. Tin cans crashed to the floor as she raced by. She found her father unpacking boxes of dry goods. There was no sign of Caleb.

Her father turned to face her. "Lucy, what is it?"

"How could you?" she cried. "How could you have put that little boy in such terrible danger?" Her father stared at her with rounded eyes but said nothing.

"Answer me!"

She held her breath, waiting. She waited for him to deny it, tell her it wasn't true. Tell her that he had no idea what she was talking about. Instead some strange half sob escaped him, a sound that was almost animal-like in its intensity. Color drained from his face. His shoulders slumped and he began to crumble before her very eyes.

Hardly recognizing the broken man in front of her, she

was too numb to feel sorry for him. Instead she shut the door behind her, closing them both inside that tiny room, a signal that they could no longer escape the truth.

Her father gave a slight nod as if he, too, knew that the time had come for honesty. "I was young and stupid," he said at last. "We'd been drinking and weren't thinking right."

This surprised her, as she never knew her father to take a drink.

As if to guess her thoughts, he said, "I've not touched a drop since." Dull eyes stared at her. "Don't you think I've hated myself ever since? Don't you think I've paid?"

"There's no way you could pay for what you did," she stormed.

"Oh, there're ways. Believe me, there're ways. Your mother—"

He ran his hand over his mouth as if attempting to erase his last words.

Her mouth went dry. She wanted the truth. She did, of course she did. So why was she shaking so much? She forced herself to speak. "What . . . what about Mama?"

He closed his eyes and took a deep breath. "The painting hidden in the back closet, you know the one."

She nodded. "The painting of the Eagle Rock." The one he refused to let her hang.

"Your mother painted it shortly before—" He cleared his throat. "She said she had a strange feeling about the place. She hoped by painting it, she would understand why that particular spot haunted her."

So it was true what others said. She was like her mother. Her mother painted to illuminate and enlighten. It was for those very same reasons that Lucy took up photography. But any joy she might have felt in knowing how much she and her mother were alike was blunted by shock and sorrow.

Her mind whirled until gradually things began to make sense, and one by one pieces of the puzzle fell into place.

"The painting . . . that was where you put him in the boat." Each word felt like the stab of a knife.

"Your mother had no way of knowing that, of course. Not at first." The resignation in his voice was at odds with the bleakness in his eyes. "I came home one day and found that painting over the fireplace. It was like a knife had been plunged into my heart. I—I begged her to take it down. Finally, I had no choice but to tell her why."

She swallowed hard. "Mama knew?"

He grimaced as in pain. "She left the house, upset. I didn't think she was ever going to come back to me, and I was right."

This was such a shock to her that moments passed before she could find her voice. "Her horse threw her," she whispered. There could be no mistake about that. She was there. She was only twelve, but she remembered the day her mother died like it was only yesterday. Her father had carried her mother's limp body into the house. Bits and pieces of memory flashed through her mind. It was like flipping through old photographs. Her mother's still body. Caleb's high-pitched cries. Her father's ghostly face—everything.

Now his eyes clouded over as if he, too, relived each moment of that long-ago day. "She would never have been on that horse had I not told her what I'd done." He shook his head, his voice choked.

Stunned and sickened, she swallowed the bitter taste in her mouth. Nothing made sense. Everything made sense. He told her mother what he had done. She left the house upset, too upset to ride with care, and she paid with her life.

For what seemed like an eternity, they stood facing each other. The broken pieces of the past loomed between them. Feelings of despair welled inside her. Renewed grief for her mother descended on her like a dark cloud.

She longed to leave, to run away, hide, but she couldn't. She still needed answers and, fearing her father would shut down again as he had in the past, she forced herself to stand her ground.

"Barnes?" she asked. Though she already knew the answer, she needed to hear it from her father.

He nodded. "He was there too."

"Doc Myers."

"Yes."

She swallowed hard. She wanted so much for him to say that there had been a mistake or that it was all a nightmare. "There were four of you," she said.

His gaze sharpened. "How do you know all this?"

She could see no point in holding back. "David Wolf told me."

"The newspaper photo." He blew out his breath. "Barnes told me who he really was."

"You . . . you spoke to Barnes about him?" she asked.

"He came to see me the night he saw Wolf. He told me the boy had lived. I couldn't believe it. All these years I thought—" He broke off and shook his head. "Barnes had this plan to pay off Wolf to keep him quiet, and he wanted to blackmail—" He stopped abruptly. "I thought he was crazy and I wanted no part of it."

"You told Barnes that?"

"Of course I did. It was like an answer to prayer—it was a miracle that Wolf was alive. I wanted to go to him, to apologize. To make it up to him in some way. But then I found out Barnes had disappeared and that Wolf was responsible. It never occurred to me that Wolf would harm Barnes."

"He didn't," Lucy said. "He had nothing to do with Barnes's disappearance."

Her father studied her. "How do you know that?" He grimaced as if in pain. "You're not in contact with Wolf, are you?" When she didn't answer he groaned. "Oh, Lucy."

"He told me he didn't harm Barnes and I believe him." Her mind whirled. "Who . . . who did Barnes want to blackmail?" she asked, though she already suspected the answer. "The fourth one." Her father neither confirmed nor denied it. Who was he? And why did Barnes think he would pay to keep his identity secret? "His name, Papa. I need to know his name."

"I can't tell you," he said. In a softer voice he added, "It would do no good for you to know." He leaned forward. "Lucy, you need to understand . . . what we did was stupid, but we never meant to do harm. The boat got away by accident and we tried to catch it but couldn't. We ran through the woods even though it was too dark to see. By the time we reached the rapids, the boat was nowhere to be found."

"He could have been killed," she whispered.

"We were convinced that he was." His eyes glazed over as if looking at another place, another time. "And all these years we've had to live with that. It's not been easy." He pressed his hand against his forehead and slumped to the floor. "When I heard that the boy lived, I thought the nightmare was over. But it's not. Maybe it will never be over."

It pained her to see him look so crushed, but she didn't know how to answer him. She could picture the four youths searching the river in a desperate attempt to find the boy. What horror they must have felt. What guilt. David had been so certain they meant to do him harm, but he was wrong. Thank God he was wrong.

She kneeled on the floor and placed her hand on his back. She couldn't imagine living with such a dark secret. No wonder he had seemed so withdrawn at times, so sad. How different things would have been for her family had her father known that David had survived.

"Papa," she whispered.

He searched her face, then fell into her arms and wept.

Lucy left her father's shop and raced out of town, practically sideswiping a peddler's cart. The wagon rattled over the dirt road, bouncing Lucy up and down in her seat, but she hardly noticed. Even the narrow wooden bridge over Rocky Creek didn't slow her down. All she wanted to do was go home and try to make sense out of everything that had happened.

She felt physically numb, but still the events of the last few hours kept going through her mind. She was her father's daughter. That's how she defined herself. During her growing-up years he had seemed larger than life. For that reason, she believed him perfect. She imagined his secrets were noble, his actions good and pure.

In recent years she'd resented him for not accepting her artistry, for discounting her dreams of being a photographer. But maybe hers was the worse failure for not accepting him for who he was but expecting him to be who she wanted him to be.

Wasn't that what she did with everyone and everything? With her perfect pictures? With her glossy prints? Try to create a vision of the world that didn't exist? Certainly it didn't exist for David.

Tears blinding her vision, she pulled over to the side of the road and reached for her camera. She held it to her chest with both hands. It felt heavy—almost too heavy—as if it carried the weight of sadness or maybe only the weight of lost dreams.

The leather case felt hard and unyielding and suddenly she wanted no part of it. Eyes shut tight, she lifted the camera over her head with both hands and tossed it off the wagon. It hit the ground with a thud, along with her hopes for the future. Swiping at her tears, she settled back into the driver's seat and drove away.

She didn't notice Redd on his horse until he called to her. "Lucy, I need to talk to you." He waved both arms over his head in an effort to flag her down.

She whizzed past him. "I can't talk now," she yelled. One hand on the reins, she palmed away the last of her tears with the other and kept going.

Redd gave chase on his horse until he caught up to her. "Lucy, stop."

"I told you I can't talk," she said, forcing Tripod to go faster.

Redd urged his horse in full gallop to match Tripod's stride. "It's about Miss Hogg." He shouted to be heard over the pounding hooves and rumbling wagon wheels. "She's about to make the biggest mistake of her life."

"This isn't a good time," she said, lifting her voice to be heard.

"Please, Lucy!" The road narrowed and he was forced to momentarily fall back, but he soon caught up with her again. "She's going after one of those mail-order husbands and it's not right."

She brushed away a lock of hair blowing in her face. "Why is that your concern?"

"Because I love her."

She glanced at Redd. Jostled by his horse, his words were obviously garbled. "What?"

"I . . . said . . . I . . . love . . . her," he shouted.

This time there was no misunderstanding.

"You gotta stop her . . . mail-order catalog. It worked out for Timber Joe and . . ." His last words were lost to her.

His attention directed at Lucy, he headed straight toward a low-growing tree.

"Watch out!" Lucy warned, but it was too late.

The branch sent him flying in one direction while his horse ran off in another.

"Oh no!" Lucy gasped. Quickly stopping her wagon, she jumped to the ground and hurried to his side.

"Redd!" Dropping to her knees, she leaned over him and patted him frantically on the cheek.

His eyes fluttered open.

"Thank God! Are you all right?"

He waved away her concern with his hand but made no motion to stand. "I'm never gonna be all right," he muttered.

"Oh, Redd. Where does it hurt?" She couldn't tell if he was injured for all the ketchup stains on his shirt.

"Right here." He held his hands to his chest.

Lucy sat back on her heels. Obviously, nothing was seriously wrong with him physically, but he looked so miserable she didn't have the heart to leave him.

"I thought you didn't like Emma. That you wanted her to leave you alone."

Redd's slanted eyebrows drooped another notch lower. "I did at first but all that changed the day I saw that photograph of her on your desk. You know, the one with the folderol on her head."

"You mean the chemise," Lucy said.

His face turned another shade redder. "That opened up my eyes and I started watching her. Did you know that she has the prettiest smile?"

She couldn't help but laugh at the earnest look on his face. "Why, yes, I do believe I noticed."

"And did you know that Emma is the one who places those red, white, and blue bouquets of flowers on the graves of soldiers on Decoration Day?"

"I did know that," Lucy said.

"And do you know why she does that?" he asked.

"Her fiancé was killed during the war."

Redd's forehead crinkled. "You knew she had a fiancé and didn't tell me?"

"I thought everyone knew," Lucy said defensively.

"I didn't," he said. "I didn't know anything about her until after I saw that photograph with the—"

"Chemise," she said, when he appeared to be struggling with the word.

"If it hadn't been for that photograph, I would never have known Emma's true nature."

Lucy couldn't believe what he was saying. "But you're a member of The Society for the Protection and Preservation of Male Independence. What about the pledge you took to remain single?"

"It seemed like a good idea at the time. But when you compare members with married men, it just seems that the married men look less miserable."

"Hmm." First Timber Joe, now Redd. She shuddered to think what Old Man Appleby would say about losing yet another one of his members.

"Redd, you've got to talk to her. Tell her how you feel. It's the only way."

"She won't listen. She won't even look at me." He grabbed hold of Lucy's arm. "I've got to do something but I don't know what. Maybe if you take a photograph of me with some-thing . . . I don't know . . . crazy on my head. Maybe she'll change her mind about me."

"I'm not sure that will work," she said with a quick glance down the road. A male garment wouldn't have the same impact as a woman's. Even if it did, she was done taking photographs. Her camera had caused enough heart-break. Not to mention it was lying somewhere on the side of the road.

Redd groaned. "There's gotta be something I can do. Think."

"I *am* thinking." She clasped her hands together. Still in shock from all that had occurred earlier, she was hard-pressed to come up with any good ideas. "You've got to make her listen to you. Sweep her off her feet."

Redd's mustache twitched. "Sweep her off her feet?" He bolted upright. A slow smile inched across his face. "Sweep her off her feet! That's it." He pushed himself off the ground and, without brushing himself off, ran down the road, calling to his horse.

⌇

Moments later Lucy pulled up to the front of her house and was surprised to find Monica waiting on her doorstep. It was obvious by her red eyes that she had been crying.

"Monica, what's wrong?" Lucy asked in alarm.

Monica burst into fresh tears.

Lucy quickly ushered her into the house and made her sit down.

"Le . . . Le . . . Leonard broke our engagement," she sobbed.

"Oh no!" Lucy placed a hand on Monica's back. "But why?"

"He wouldn't tell me." Monica regarded her with tear-filled eyes. "Oh, Lucy, do you suppose there's someone else?"

Lucy shook her head. "No, of course not."

"How . . . how can you be so certain?"

"I just know." Lucy reached into the pocket of her skirt and handed Monica a linen handkerchief.

"What other reason could there be?" Monica asked, dabbing at her eyes.

Lucy's mind raced. How much or how little should she say?

"Lucy Fairbanks, you know something. I know you do. I can tell by your expression."

"All right." She never was good at keeping her thoughts to herself. She wrung her hands together on her lap. "I'm almost positive the reason Doc Myers broke up with you is because of David."

Monica's eyes widened. "The man I saw you kissing the

night the church burned down?" She drew her eyebrows together. "But . . . I don't understand."

"It's a long story," Lucy said. "Twenty years ago when David was ten years old and living at the mission, he decided to run away and . . ."

The whole time she talked, Monica remained motionless.

"Had he not been rescued he might have drowned or at the very least been seriously injured."

"That's terrible," Monica said after Lucy had explained everything that happened that night at the river. "But what has this got to do with Leonard and me?"

Lucy clasped her hands on her lap. This was the hard part. "The youths who put him on the boat. One of them . . ." Her voice grew husky. "One of them was Doc Myers."

Monica jumped to her feet so abruptly that Extra scooted underneath a chair for cover. "I don't believe it. Not for a second."

"And my father."

"I . . . I know Leonard," Monica gasped. "I know your father. They would never—"

"I didn't want to believe it at first either," Lucy said. "And after what happened to Barnes—"

"Barnes?"

"He was one of the four. We think his disappearance had something to do with what happened all those years ago. That's why Barnes went to see Doc Myers that night."

Monica's eyes widened. "If this is true, why didn't Leonard tell me this himself?"

"Maybe he was afraid you would leave him, like his—" She stopped abruptly.

The lines between Monica's eyebrows deepened. "You were going to say his wife, weren't you?"

Lucy took a ragged breath. "It's possible that she found out what he did. Maybe that's why she left him."

Monica sat down slowly, her back ramrod straight. For several moments she didn't speak. Then, "How long have you known about this?"

"Not long. A few days."

"And you didn't tell me?" Her voice was rife with accusations.

"It wasn't my place," Lucy said. "It was Doc Myers's place to tell you. Monica, what happened to David as a boy . . . no one meant to harm him. I really do believe that and I hope you do too."

Instead of answering her, Monica jumped to her feet again and raced out of the house.

"Wait!" Lucy chased after her, but Monica was already in her shay, reins in hand, by the time she reached her.

"They were young and foolish, but they didn't mean to harm David," Lucy pleaded. "It was a horrible accident. They thought he was dead. That's what they've lived with all these years. Don't you think that's punishment enough?"

Monica snapped the reins and took off, forcing Lucy to jump back or be run over by a wagon wheel.

Twenty-six

Doctors, do not regard the camera as if it's a patient needing help through death's door. Such a pose will speak ill of you, and it won't do much for your practice, either.

— MISS GERTRUDE HASSLEBRINK, 1878

The shiny brass plate on the front door read *Dr. Myers*. Wolf stared at it, surprised by the bitterness that rose up from his very depths. The polished sign, the tidy garden, the two story clapboard house and fine horse and carriage parked in front—all evidence of a successful man, a man who knew who he was and where he belonged. Wolf's tormentors had buried the past and gone on to live normal lives. Wolf couldn't help but marvel at their ability to do so.

It was only by chance that he was rescued that night, but there were many days he wondered if Malcolm Combes had done him any favors.

Since Combes's funeral, he was obsessed with finishing the business of the past. Chained to his childhood, haunted, not only by the actions of others but by his own failure to break through society's barriers, he hoped that whatever was in that box would help him better face the future. Now that he knew Lucy's father was involved, he wished to God he'd stayed away.

Pushing his thoughts aside, Wolf rapped the brass knocker.

Myers opened the door within seconds. Judging by the expectancy on his face, the doctor was clearly hoping it was someone else.

His face turned grim, but he showed no surprise. He looked Wolf up and down. "Twenty years is a long time. I didn't recognize you the day I treated you in jail."

"I recognized you," Wolf said.

"The curse of having two different colored eyes, I suppose." The doctor regarded him, his brow furrowed. "I . . . I thought you were dead. We all did."

"When did you find out who I was?"

"Just a short while ago. Fairbanks came to see me. You just missed him. I—I still can't believe it."

"Fairbanks told you and not Barnes?"

"Barnes never said a word about you being alive. He tried to blackmail me. Said he would tell everything if I didn't pay him. Ruin my reputation as a doctor. I couldn't figure out why now, after all these years, he would do such a thing."

"How much did you pay him?"

"Not a penny. I put him off by telling him I'd think about it. But then he disappeared."

That's the part that puzzled Wolf the most. Barnes disappearing. "Wouldn't ruining your reputation also ruin his own?"

The doctor scoffed. "Barnes reputation was ruined long ago with his lies and his greed." Wolf was still thinking about this when Myers added, "That night that you went down the river . . ."

Wolf's muscles tensed. Even after all this time he could still recall the terror he felt.

"We searched for you for hours. We even went back the next day and the next. I didn't think it possible for anyone to survive those rapids."

"I was lucky," Wolf said. More than lucky. "Someone heard my cries and pulled me out of the water."

The doctor's body jerked as if someone had struck him from behind. "Thank God." He gazed upward. "Thank you, God."

Wolf's anger melted away. Until that moment he considered the doctor an enemy, but Myers seemed genuinely glad he was alive. Wolf wasn't prepared for that. "We need to talk," he said.

The doctor's one brown eye twitched but he said nothing.

"I didn't harm Barnes, if that's what you're thinking."

"The marshal is looking for you." The doctor's gaze traveled the length of Wolf. "They call you a wild man and a killer."

"I'm not a killer," Wolf said. "I'll let you decide if I'm a wild man."

Doc Myers studied him a moment before checking the road to see if anyone was watching. Stepping back, he motioned Wolf inside.

Wolf followed Myers into a parlor and glanced around. The furniture was plain but of good quality. It would have to be to hold the stacks of heavy books piled everywhere. A Duncan Phyfe sofa with ornamental legs and plain crest rail faced the fireplace. The rather plain but functional slant-top desk with teardrop pulls took up one corner of the room.

"It looks like you've done quite well for yourself." Wolf turned to face the doctor.

Myers stood in the middle of the room. "If it's money you want . . ."

Wolf bristled. "Money? You think that's why I'm here? For money?"

"If not for money . . . why did you come back? After all this time?"

It was a question Wolf had asked himself countless times since arriving in Rocky Creek. He thought he knew the answer when he first came there but now he wasn't so sure.

"The night you dragged me to the river, you took something from me. A box. I want it."

"I have no memory of such a box," the doctor said without hesitation. "Maybe one of the others . . ."

The *others*. "Barnes, you, and . . . Fairbanks." Wolf waited. The doctor said nothing.

"I need one more name."

The doctor gave his head a wooden shake. "I can't give it to you. It wouldn't help you to know who he was and it would only cause . . . unnecessary trouble."

Wolf clenched his hands. "Why are you protecting this man?"

Myers let out an audible sigh. "I have my reasons." He covered his face with both hands, shook his head, and slid his hands down to his chin. "What we did . . . that night . . . we'd been drinking. Still, there's no excuse. We were young and foolish, all of us. We never meant for the boat to take off. You've got to believe that." His voice broke.

The doctor gave him a beseeching look. "I would do anything—anything—to change the past if I could. To make it up to you—"

"Tell me the name of the fourth man," Wolf said quietly. "That's all I ask."

Myers held up his hands, palms out. "I can't do that."

"I have the right to know."

"I'm telling you, it won't do you any good."

Wolf turned to leave.

"You think you're the only one who suffered because of that night?" Myers said behind him.

Wolf spun around. "You dare to stand there and tell me you suffered."

The doctor didn't even flinch. "We've all suffered. All of us. You most of all."

Wolf gestured in disgust. "I saw Barnes and there was no suffering there."

"He was just better than the rest of us at hiding it." He nodded to the daguerreotype on the mantel.

"My daughters," he said, his voice hoarse. "I haven't seen them in ten years. My family left after Fairbanks's wife confronted me."

Wolf stiffened. *Lucy's mother*. "Was that the same night Mrs. Fairbanks was thrown from a horse?" Wolf asked.

The doctor nodded. "Somehow she found out what we did to you and she showed up on my doorstep. She said she wanted to understand how such a thing could happen. She was upset . . . I should never have let her leave in her condition, but my wife overheard our conversation and . . . I don't think she was ever meant to be a doctor's wife. Knowing what I'd done gave her an excuse to leave."

Wolf felt sick. All these years he'd been caught up in his own world, in his own pain. Never once had it occurred to him that his tormentors had suffered too. He hated knowing that the events of the past had touched yet another generation. Had deprived Lucy and her brother of a mother. Had deprived two little girls of a pa. The invisible chains that bound him to the past just kept getting longer. Who else had suffered? And who was Myers protecting?

Why hadn't he thought to come back and let the town know he was alive? It would have prevented so many problems, so much heartache. It simply never occurred to him. Left on the mission steps as an infant, discarded like an unwanted object, he'd known a lifetime of rejection. Not once had it occurred to him that his being alive would matter to his tormentors. It was a shock to know that it did.

"I didn't harm Barnes," he said quietly. "And I don't think you did either. So that means he either left of his own accord or someone else harmed him. That leaves only Fairbanks and the man you insist upon protecting."

The doctor shook his head. "You're on the wrong track." The doctor sounded oddly confident of the fact. What was he not saying?

"You can't know that."

"I do know it," Myers insisted. "If anything happened to Barnes, it had nothing to do with you. He made a lot of enemies through the years. Any number of people might wish to do him harm."

Wolf considered this possibility for all of a minute before discounting it. The very same night he visited Barnes, the man disappeared. Coincidence? He didn't think so.

"It had something to do with my return," Wolf said. "With or without your help, I intend to find out what."

Shaken by what he now knew, he turned and walked out of the house. Outside he stood and stared at the sky. What the doctor said . . . could it be true? He thought back to the night on the boat. He'd always assumed he'd been purposely sent down the river. Now he wasn't so certain.

⁓

Wolf waited on the porch of the Fairbanks house. He stood in the shadows until Lucy drove up in her wagon, the late afternoon sun behind the trees. He knew the moment she spotted him, sensed her hesitancy in facing him.

She set the brake and climbed down from the seat. "You shouldn't be here. The sheriff is still looking for you." She'd been crying and tears still shimmered in her eyes. It was yet another reminder of his own failings.

"I was worried about you," he said. He held up her camera. "I found this in the middle of the road. The case is strong—it doesn't appear to be damaged." He had been shocked to see her camera lying in the dirt. Knowing how much it meant to her, he assumed it had somehow fallen out of her wagon without her knowledge. The look on her face told him otherwise.

"Don't give up your photography," he said. "You make people see what can't normally be seen." Maybe even what they don't want to see.

She stared at the camera but said nothing. Instead she brushed past him and into the house.

He followed her inside and set the camera on the table, along with the locket he'd fixed for her. It was a small cabin filled with a riot of color. Sunshine filtered through sparkling clean windows. Curtains matched the blues and yellows in the painting over the fireplace. Vases of wildflowers and colorful rugs drew his gaze around the room.

The room waiting for him over at the Combes Furniture Company now seemed stark and empty by comparison.

Barnes's big ginger cat greeted Wolf with a loud meow and weaved in and out of his legs. He stooped and ran his hands along the cat's furry coat.

"I couldn't stay away," he explained, "not knowing how upset you were."

"I *was* upset. But after talking with Papa, I now understand how it happened."

He stood and Extra sauntered away.

She moistened her lips. "It was an accident, don't you see? They never meant for the boat to get away."

Myers had said basically the same thing. Even if it was true, Wolf couldn't entirely pardon what they'd done. Not only had they endangered his life, they had taken something from him. "Are you asking me to feel sorry for these men?"

"I'm asking you to try and understand how it happened," she whispered.

"Understand? Why? So I can forgive them?"

No sooner were the words out of his mouth than he felt

something change between them. Like they were on opposite sides of a closed door. The silence that filled the room seemed to mute even the colorful surroundings.

"Monica knows," she said, breaking the stillness. "I went looking for her but I couldn't find her."

"It's better that she knows," he said.

"You don't still think that Doc Myers did something to Barnes, do you?"

He shook his head. "No." As much as he hated to admit it after all this time, he believed the doctor was an honorable man. He certainly seemed sincere.

She lifted her head, bleak lines of despair on her face. "What they did to you . . . we've all paid for it in different ways. My brother. Me. Doc Myers. My mother most of all. Don't you see how that night has affected us all? Is still affecting us?"

Something dissipated inside him. Not the hurt—not that—but maybe some of the anger. He began to feel less like a victim of that long-ago night and more like one of many actors in a very bad play. He had been so wrapped up in his anger he'd not once considered what that night had done to others—and for that he felt ashamed. Still . . . to forgive . . . how could she possibly ask that of him? How could anyone?

He stepped toward her, hand held out. He intended to apologize for all the trouble he'd caused her, but she didn't give him a chance.

"Don't," she pleaded. "Don't make me choose sides. Don't make me choose between you and the others."

By the others he assumed she meant Barnes, Myers, and her father. Arms by his sides, fists tight, a pain shot through his head. "It would seem you already have." He turned and walked out the door, letting it slam behind him.

She called to him but he kept going. She ran after him but he didn't look back. How could he? Divided loyalties would only rip her apart much as he had been ripped apart by two separate worlds. He couldn't do that to her. Wouldn't.

Still . . . he was used to people siding against him; people had sided against him all his life, but never had it hurt as much as it hurt at that moment.

The following night Lucy had just finished setting the table when Caleb walked in the door.

"Pa didn't show up for work today," he said, his voice strained.

Alarm shot through her. Unable to sleep, her father often wandered the countryside at night, but she'd never known him to miss a day of work. If anything happened to him . . .

She put the last of the silverware in place.

"What did you and Pa fight about?" Caleb asked. "Your photography or my being a doctor?"

"We didn't fight," she said.

Caleb looked unconvinced. "I think it's time you stop treating me like a child and tell me what's going on."

"I . . . can't tell you, Caleb."

"I can." Startled by her father's voice, she turned to the open door where he stood. Never had he looked so awful. Dark bags skirted his hollow eyes. His ashen complexion emphasized an unshaven chin. Her concern for him momentarily overrode everything else.

Her father closed the door and moved to the sofa. "Sit down, son."

Without a word she left to let her father and brother talk in private.

For the next hour she stayed in her room. As if sensing her distress, Extra jumped on the bed and stretched out by her side. She didn't hear a sound from the parlor. Not a peep. Finally she could no longer stand the suspense.

Caleb was alone. He sat in front of the fireplace staring into the dark hearth. She sat next to him and rubbed her hand across his back.

He looked over his shoulder at her. His eyes were red and she tried to remember the last time she had seen her brother cry. "How could they do such a thing?"

"They were young," she said. "They didn't mean to."

"I never thought Pa—" He wiped his nose with the back of his hand. "And Doc Myers . . . I wanted to be just like him. Now—" He shook his head. "I don't want to be anything like him."

She laid her hand on his lap. "You've always wanted to be a doctor."

"Not anymore. Not if it means working with him."

Lucy felt a squeezing pain in her chest. "I know you're confused, but no one meant to harm David."

"He was a little boy," Caleb said. "Only ten."

Lucy sighed. How could she expect him to understand when she, herself, had trouble understanding? "So many people have suffered already for what happened. Please, Caleb. Don't let your dream become another casualty." She glanced at her camera still on the table where David had placed it, along with her locket.

Caleb fell silent. He was a thinker, her brother. He never formed an opinion without first considering all the facts. She left him alone with his thoughts. She no longer had the heart to pursue her own dreams, but she wasn't about to let Caleb give up on his.

Somehow they had to find a way to reconcile the mistakes of the past. What she couldn't reconcile were her feelings for David.

Twenty-seven

When posing for your photograph, never draw attention to your physical attributes no matter how suitable or attractive. And don't, whatever you do, speak disparagingly of another's photograph or suggest in any way that your image is superior. It will only make others feel inferior.

— MISS GERTRUDE HASSLEBRINK, 1878

The banging on the door woke her. Grabbing her dressing gown, she slipped her arms through the sleeves as she ran barefooted through the house. She had no idea what time it was but it was still dark. "Who is it?"

"Lucy, it's Doc Myers. Your father's been injured."

She yanked the door open. "Is he all right?" she asked in alarm. She could barely make out the doctor's silhouette, or the dark form of her father slung over his shoulder.

"I think so," the doctor said, brushing past her. "He fell and hit his head. Jake said he'd been drinking heavily."

Her first instinct was to deny it, even though the smell of whiskey permeated the room. By his own admission her father hadn't touched a drop of alcohol since that long-ago night at the river.

"We need a light," the doctor said, bringing her out of her inertia.

Hands shaking, she lit a kerosene lamp. If anything happened to him . . . memories of her mother flooded back.

She picked up the lamp and led the way to her father's bedroom. The doctor laid him on the bed, then hurried out to fetch his leather bag.

She sat by her father's side and pressed her hand on his forehead. His hair was matted in blood, his skin ashen. What was taking Doc Myers so long?

The doctor's footsteps preceded his voice. "He has a concussion, so we'll have to watch him carefully." He set his black bag on the dresser.

Eyes rounded, she continued to gaze at her father. "Like mama," she said. Her mother had been thrown from a horse but the injuries were similar.

Doc Myers dropped a hand on her shoulder. "Not like your mother," he said. "A man can handle tremors to the brain far better than a woman can. Men have stronger neck stems and backs. He'll no doubt have a headache from the alcohol and injury, but he'll live." He turned toward the dry sink and poured water from a pitcher onto a cloth. He then proceeded to clean her father's head wound.

Caleb appeared at the bedroom door looking disheveled and sleepy-eyed. "What's going on?"

"It's Papa," Lucy explained. "He's had an accident but he'll be all right."

"I need alcohol," Doc Myers said, pointing to his bag.

Caleb crossed to the dresser and reached for a bottle of medicinal whiskey.

"Would you like to do the honors?" the doctor asked.

Caleb shook with anger. "I'm not going to be a doctor," he lashed out. "I don't want to be anything like you."

Doc Myers took the bottle of whiskey from Caleb, unscrewed the top, and poured some on his cloth. "I once had to tend the wounds of a man convicted of killing three lawmen," he said. "It wasn't easy. But a doctor has to put his personal feelings aside and do what's right by the patient. That's what it means to be a doctor." He held out the alcohol-soaked cloth.

Caleb hesitated for a moment before taking it in hand. He then approached his father's side and gently dabbed at the wound on his forehead.

Her father moaned and his eyes fluttered open. He looked dazed. His lips moved but his words were no more than muffled sounds.

Standing by Caleb's side, Lucy reached for her father's hand. "You had an accident, Papa. But you'll be all right."

He didn't try to speak and she had no way of knowing if he understood her. *Dear God, please watch over him.*

Caleb stepped back. "I . . . I don't know what to do next."

The doctor studied him. "Then go back to the beginning. What is a concussion?"

"A concussion is an injury to the brain caused by a severe blow," Caleb replied.

"And what complications can occur?" Doc Myers asked.

"A blood clot can put pressure on the brain."

"And what would be the treatment for such an occurrence?"

"Trepanning," Caleb said. His voice grew stronger, more confident as he went on to describe the medical procedure. "You have to cut or drill into the skull to relieve pressure to the brain."

Annoyed that Doc Myers would use her father's injury to teach a lesson, Lucy was about to protest when she noticed Caleb's expression. His mind focused on the intricacies of brain trauma, he no longer looked angry. Instead his face glowed with eagerness.

"Excellent," Doc Myers said. "And do you see anything that indicates trepanning is necessary in this case?"

Caleb leaned over the bed to examine his father's head and check his pupils. "No, sir."

"What treatment would you prescribe?"

"Bed rest and observation."

Doc Myers turned to Lucy. "I leave the patient in good hands." He picked up his leather case and left the room.

Lucy followed him to the parlor. "Are you sure Papa will be all right?"

The doctor turned to face her. "I wouldn't leave if I thought otherwise. Try to keep him awake as long as possible." He hesitated. "I know you think poorly of me and you have every right to feel that way, but I had nothing to do with Barnes's disappearance."

She studied the doctor as she never had before. He had a kind face, gentle but sad eyes. "I believe you," she said. "I . . . I had no choice but to tell Monica about what happened."

He nodded. "She came to see me and . . ." He shook his head in disbelief. "She still wants to be my wife. She said she's not marrying the boy of twenty years ago, she's marrying the man I've become."

Lucy's heart leaped with joy. "I'm so happy for you both." Most of all, she was proud of Monica.

He stood perfectly still. "I thought the man we now know as David Wolf had died the night we put him on that boat, and I hated myself. More than you'll ever know. My guilt is what drove my wife away. She couldn't live with my moodiness and self-loathing." His eyes grew moist. "Thank God he lived. It's a miracle."

Just hearing David's name filled her with such pain she quickly changed the subject. "You and Papa used to be friends," she said. It was before her time but she'd heard talk around town.

He nodded. "Guilt can do terrible things to a friendship. We couldn't bear to look at each other after that night."

"Maybe things will be different now," she said.

He smiled. "Maybe so." He started to leave but she stopped him with a hand on his arm.

"Thank you . . . for everything. Caleb planned to give up medicine."

He patted her hand. "God has given Caleb a great gift. It would be a shame if he didn't use it. He'll make a fine doctor someday."

She pulled her hand away. "He wants to go to medical school but I'm afraid financially that may be out of the question." She doubted that even selling her mother's paintings would provide enough money for tuition, board, and books.

"I hope to be of assistance in that regard. I would like to pay Caleb's medical school expenses."

Lucy stared at him, not sure she'd heard right. "You want to send Caleb to medical school?"

He nodded. "If your father will let me. I've already discussed it with Monica and she thinks it's a fine idea."

"I . . . I don't know what to say," she gasped. Could this really be happening?

He winked at her. "You don't have to say anything. I'm doing it as much for Rocky Creek as I am for Caleb. For myself. Don't say anything to him. I want to speak to your father first. Make sure he doesn't object."

After the doctor left, she sent Caleb back to bed and sat next to her father's side. Color had returned to his face. He looked slightly confused, his eyes unfocused, but whether from the alcohol he'd consumed or the concussion, she didn't know.

"Get some sh-sh-leep," he slurred.

It was the first he'd spoken since the doctor brought him home, and she was encouraged. "Doc Myers said I have to keep you awake," she explained. "I'm afraid you're stuck with me."

He groaned and touched his head. She sat quietly by his side while he gazed at the ceiling. How long she sat there, she didn't know. At times she thought he'd fallen asleep and she'd have to lean over him to check, but always she found him staring into space, and she couldn't begin to guess what was going through his mind.

At long last, he turned his head to look at her. The redness had left the whites of his eyes, but his lips were dry and cracked. She filled a glass with water from a pitcher. Sliding one arm beneath him she lifted his head to drink.

Head back on his pillow, he spoke. "Crankshaw told me 'bout his . . . offer." He spoke slowly, drawing out each syllable as if each word required his full concentration. When she made no reply, he added, "I 'spect you'll jump at the shance to run . . . run . . . run a newspaper."

At one time that might have been true, but not now. Now the only thing she wanted was to be with David. To love him and be loved by him.

He waited for her to say something and when she didn't, he quirked an eyebrow. "Did you hear what I thaid?"

"I heard, Papa. I can't run a newspaper if it means marrying a man I don't love." Now that Doc Myers had offered to pay for Caleb's education, one very big burden had been removed from her shoulders. The main thing now was to collect enough money to rebuild the church.

For a long while he said nothing. His eyes drifted shut and she gently shook him.

"I'm not thleepin'," he said. "Jus' thinkin'."

"About what?" she asked.

"I've decided to s-shell . . . sell some of your mother's paintin's."

"We already talked about this, Papa," she said. "I won't let you do that. I'll get the money for the church." *Somehow.*

"I'm not talking about the church." He spoke as if he had rocks in his mouth, but he persisted. "I don't know how much they'll fetch, if anything. I hope it's enough for a down payment on the newspaper. It's what your mother would have wanted."

She couldn't believe he seriously considered selling her

mother's artwork to purchase a newspaper business. Was this his way of showing approval for her work? She wanted to think so but deep down she feared it was only the alcohol speaking. Chances were he wouldn't even remember making such an offer once his head cleared.

For the longest while neither of them spoke. Her father was the first to break the silence.

"I've not been a very good father . . . to you and Caleb. I thought I sent a child to his death and I was consumed with guilt."

Alarmed by the look in his eyes, she tried to calm him with a hand to his forehead. "I don't think we should be talking about this now. Your head—"

"Forget my head." He pushed her hand away and she could see him struggle to get his words right. "All these years . . . I didn't feel worthy as a father or a man. As a result, you suffered. Both you and Caleb suffered. Your mother would still be with us—" Something like a sob escaped him. "Let me do this for you."

Lucy didn't know what to say. Her dreams had been big, but never so big as to imagine owning her own newspaper. What editorials she could write! What photographs she could print! The townsfolk deserved so much more than what the newspaper had offered in the past. They deserved honesty and truth.

"Why so sad?" her father asked.

His question surprised her until she realized why the thought of owning her own newspaper gave her no pleasure. Not if it required selling her mother's paintings. But that wasn't the only reason. Without David, she doubted anything could bring her joy or make her smile again. Still, she couldn't altogether discount her father's offer. Now that Caleb's future was assured, the money would help pay for the building of the church and maybe even repay the doctor for his kindness.

"Tell me, child, what is it?" he prodded.

"I'm in love with someone," she said. It didn't seem like the time or place to confess such a thing but she couldn't seem to help herself. "I'm in love with David Wolf."

Her father stared at her for a long while, his eyes suddenly alert. "Do you know what you're in for?"

"He didn't harm Barnes, he didn't."

He lifted his head off the pillow. "I was referring to his mixed blood."

She bit her lip. "I don't care about that."

"You should." He laid back and closed his eyes. "It doesn't end, does it? The boy on the boat comes back to steal my daughter's heart and another generation will suffer because of that one long-ago night."

"Papa, don't say that."

"Why not? It's true."

"I want you to be happy for me—"

"Happy? Because my daughter has chosen to love a man whose blood can only bring her misery?"

"Why does it have to be that way?" she cried. "Why do we have to be judged on things we have no control over?"

With a sigh her father seemed to cave inward like he had nothing left inside. "I don't know the answer to that," he said weakly. "I only know that we are." His voice faded away and, alarmed, she leaned over him.

"Papa?" His eyes were closed. She shook him gently until he stirred. Oh, why did she have to tell him about her feelings for David tonight, of all nights?

After a long silence, he opened his eyes to stare at the ceiling. "There's somethin' I need to do," he said, "but I can't remember." He frowned as if straining to think. "I'm supposed to meet someone—"

"It's after midnight," she said. "Whoever you're supposed to meet can wait."

He dozed off and she shook him again until he opened his eyes.

It was nearly dawn before she decided to let him sleep. Promising herself to wake him in an hour's time, she walked out of his room. Fearing she would fall asleep, she wrapped herself in a quilt, made herself a cup of tea, and sat on the sofa, her camera on her lap.

You make people see what can't normally be seen. David's voice ringing in her ears, she stared at the painting over the fireplace. She recalled thinking the same thing about her mother's paintings. The thought of parting with them was too painful to contemplate but that wasn't the only reason she held back. Secretly she suspected that the paintings held more sentimental value than monetary. Times were tight and most people could ill afford art. Many families could barely afford to pay her for their portraitures.

The *Rocky Creek Gazette* was financially beyond her means but she felt hopeful. Caleb's future was assured and for that she was grateful. Obviously God had a plan for him and maybe, just maybe, he had a plan for her too.

Just please, God, let it include David.

Twenty-eight

"Snapshot" is a hunting term meaning to take a quick shot without careful aim. No worthy photographer would be so careless (unless, of course, a client is particularly unpleasant or uncooperative).

— MISS GERTRUDE HASSLEBRINK, 1878

Lucy woke to loud mewing. Extra sat at her feet, glaring at her. She hadn't even touched her tea. Alarmed by the amount of sunlight pouring through the windows, she raced to her father's room.

The bed was empty. She whirled about to check the corner where she had placed her father's boots hours earlier, but they were gone.

Surely he hadn't left for work.

She knocked on Caleb's door and when there was no answer, she cracked it open. Her brother had already left for the day.

She quickly dressed and pinned her hair up in back. Out of habit she grabbed her camera, though she had no intention of taking photographs. Chickens scattered out of her way as she hurried to the barn.

Caleb had already collected the eggs, mucked out the stalls, and fed Tripod, but there was no sign of him or her father.

After hitching Tripod to the wagon, she rode into town.

Her father's horse was nowhere in sight. Alarmed, she quickened her pace as she hurried up the steps of the boardwalk. Bells jingled on the door of Fairbanks General Merchandise.

Her brother looked up from the counter. "What are you doing here?" he asked. "Why aren't you home taking care of Pa?"

"Papa's not home," she said. "I thought maybe he was here."

Caleb frowned. "I checked Pa before I left this morning and he was still asleep. Do you want me to help you look for him?"

"You stay here. I'll find him. He's probably wandering around Mother's old stomping grounds. Don't worry," she said, more for her own benefit than his.

Outside she queried Appleby.

The crotchety old man spit a stream of tobacco before answering. "Been here all mornin'," he said, the rocking chair creaking beneath him. "And I ain't seen hide nor hair of him."

From across the way, Sarah walked out of Jenny's Emporium and waved. "Lucy."

Carrying little Matthew in one arm, she waved what looked like a letter in the other. She was out of breath by the time she reached Lucy, her face flushed with excitement. "I heard from my brother," she said. "I heard from George and . . . and glory be, he met someone. A young lady and she led him to the Lord."

"Oh, Sarah." She knew how much Sarah had prayed for her outlaw brother. They all had. "That's such good news."

Spotting Jenny's sister Brenda across the street, Sarah excused herself and left before Lucy could ask about her father.

Lucy continued up Main Street, asking everyone she met if they'd seen her father. The number of people scattered along the boardwalk surprised her.

She spotted Barrel standing outside his barbershop. "Have you seen my father?" she called.

Staring at the sky, Barrel held his hand up to shade his eyes from the sun. "No," he called back.

She gazed all the way to the Grand Hotel. Was it only her imagination or was everyone looking up? She tilted her head back but all she could see was clear blue sky with not a cloud in sight.

Emma Hogg raced toward her looking all discombobulated beneath her parasol. "Am I too late?"

"Too late for what?" Lucy asked.

Clearly out of breath from running, Emma folded her parasol. "Mrs. Hitchcock told me that the Suffra-Quilters were planning an important event and I had to be here."

"I don't know anything about that," Lucy said. "Have you by chance seen my father?"

For answer, Emma pointed at the sky. "What *is* that?"

Lucy followed Emma's finger. "It's just a bird."

Cheers rose from up and down the street and some spectators waved their hats. She rubbed her eyes with her knuckles and looked up again. The speck in the sky had grown larger. At first it looked like a mere bubble in the air but gradually the shape and color of it became clear.

"Why, I do believe it's a gas balloon," Lucy said in awe. She'd never actually seen one except for the painting in Redd's café. What an amazing sight. Considering the spectacle it made, it was hard to imagine how Union and Confederate armies used balloons to spy on enemy troops during the war without being noticed.

"My word," Emma gasped, giving her parasol a good shake. "You don't suppose Mrs. Hitchcock or Mrs. Taylor is in that, do you? I'm all for women's rights, but there's a limit to what I'm willing to do for the privilege of voting."

As the balloon approached the ground, murmurs of astonishment turned into cries of dismay. The brightly colored aerial ship looked about to crash into the Wells Fargo bank.

Dogs barked and Sarah's infant boy Matthew let out a wail.

Marshal Armstrong, Caleb, and others ran toward the balloon and tried to grab the dangling cords the aerialist tossed over the sides.

Grasping the cords, the men held the balloon steady while onlookers gave a collective sigh. The shimmering red globe was so large it almost touched the buildings on both sides of Main. The wicker basket hovered but a few feet off the ground.

Lucy couldn't take her eyes off it. It was truly a magnificent sight.

Behind her, Emma Hogg let out an ear-piercing scream. Lucy whirled around just in time to see Barrel fling Emma over his shoulder.

"Put me down at once, do you hear?" Emma yelled. She beat on his back with her fists, her parasol lying on the boardwalk where she dropped it.

Barrel didn't even flinch. Instead he walked right down the middle of Main Street, hauling the indignant woman, and didn't stop until he reached the hovering balloon.

Lucy stormed after him. What in the world was he thinking? "Kip Barrel! You put her down this minute!"

She stopped upon seeing Redd inside the wicker gondola. With a wink at Lucy he leaned over to grab Emma out of Barrel's arms. The upper half of her body inside the basket, Miss Hogg's legs stuck straight up to reveal a shocking display of bloomers.

Then, before anyone could object, the Marshal, Reverend Wells, and Caleb let go of the cords. Gas roared and the balloon rose into the air.

Once her initial shock wore off, Lucy couldn't help but laugh. She clapped her hands in approval. Redd had literally swept Emma Hogg off her feet. "Good for you, Redd. Good for you." She only hoped that Emma liked ketchup.

Her camera! Clutching at her skirt, she raced to her wagon. She had no intention of letting a photographic opportunity like this slip away. But by the time she grabbed her camera, the balloon was a mere dot in the sky.

Undaunted, she hopped onto her wagon seat and tore out of town, almost colliding with Barrel, who flew past on his horse. Others had the same idea, and soon the road leading out of town was filled with horses, wagons, and shays. As the balloon drifted farther away, people began pulling back, and soon Lucy had the road to herself.

The balloon looked like a bubble in the sky. The bright red globe drifted right, vanishing behind the trees. She pulled up on the side of the road, jumped to the ground, and reached for her camera. Maybe she could get a photograph of the balloon over the river. What a prize that would be.

Not even the call of a bird could be heard as she ran through the woods, scanning the sky. As she neared the river, the whooshing sound of water grew louder. She stopped just short of the meadow and peered through the trees. The tall grass was dotted with wildflowers and reminded her of one of her mother's paintings.

On the far side of the meadow, the mission looked less menacing than it had on previous occasions. The red tile roof glistened in the late morning sun. The tall narrow windows seemed less prisonlike.

All at once a huge shadow glided past her and her mouth dropped open in delight. The balloon hovered not more than a thousand feet overhead. Rocking gently in the breeze, the red silk gleamed in the sunlight. Lucy fumbled with the hook of her camera and pulled out the bellows. Shaking with excitement, she set the camera next to a fallen log and aimed the lens upward. She then covered the back with a black cloth and ducked beneath. She gasped at the sight of the balloon in her viewfinder. It looked truly magnificent. If only it were possible to take a colored photograph! She'd never hired a colorist before but perhaps this once she would.

She changed the view from landscape to portrait. The balloon rocked slightly, which required fast exposure time to prevent blurring. She opened the lens wider.

"Hold still," she muttered. She squeezed the bulb and held it as she counted. "One thousand and one, one thousand and two . . ."

She released the bulb and pulled the black cloth away. "Got it!"

She looked up. Redd and Emma Hogg stood side by side, waving and smiling. They looked like miniature dolls.

Lucy jumped to her feet and waved back with both arms. The balloon drifted away until she could no longer see it for the trees.

Recalling her original reason for riding into town that morning, she gasped. "Papa!"

How could she have forgotten? Chiding herself for getting caught up in all the excitement, she quickly retracted the bellows and latched them inside the case.

Startled by a woman's high-pitched voice, she turned toward the river. The voice sounded vaguely familiar but she couldn't put a name to it. Unable to make out the angry words, she walked toward the river's edge and ducked beneath the bushes that served as a barrier.

She followed the winding trail around a bend. The musty smell of decaying leaves permeated the air. Mushrooms poked through the decomposing foliage like little white buttons. A carpet of water hyacinths allowed her to walk faster without making a sound.

The sight of her father's horse startled her. What was he doing way out here?

She suddenly recognized the voice as belonging to Mrs. Weatherbee, which puzzled her even more. Was that the person Papa said he had to meet? And why did she sound so angry?

Confused, Lucy moved closer.

"Millard isn't going to suffer because of you," the woman shouted. Cursing, she continued, "I worked too hard to let the likes of you ruin his future."

Lucy strained her neck but couldn't see her father. All she could see was Mrs. Weatherbee, who appeared to be talking to herself again. Maybe her husband's disappearance had affected her more than anyone knew. Concerned, Lucy stepped around the bend.

"Mrs. Weatherbee?"

The woman swung around, pointing a gun straight at Lucy.

Startled at the sight of the weapon and the wild look in the woman's eyes, Lucy tried to make sense of the strange scene that greeted her. "It's just me, Lucy. I'm not going to—"

Spotting her father in a rowboat, his hands and feet tied, Lucy gasped. The scene in front of her seemed unreal. Her father looked dazed, blood trickling down the side of his head.

"You couldn't leave well enough alone, could you?" Mrs. Weatherbee rasped.

Her father said something, his voice barely carrying above the sound of the river.

Lucy pulled her gaze away from him. "Why . . . why are you doing this?" she stammered.

Mrs. Weatherbee scoffed. "I'll do anything to protect my son."

"Millard?" Why did he need protecting from her father? From anyone? "I don't understand."

"He's got a chance at success. State senate is only the first step. One day he'll be governor, maybe even president. I'm not letting you or anyone get in the way."

A knot formed in Lucy's stomach. The woman wasn't making any sense.

Mrs. Weatherbee's eyes glittered in contempt. "After all these years, he couldn't leave well enough alone."

Lucy shook her head. "Who?" she asked. "Who do you mean?"

"My fool of a husband." She all but spit the words out.

Lucy grew even more bewildered. "What's this got to do with Millard?"

Millard couldn't have been the fourth youth. He would have been too young.

The crazed widow sneered. "Everything," she said, her voice unnaturally high. "If word gets out what his stepfather did, Millard's political career will be over."

"Mr. Weatherbee?" Lucy stammered. Millard's stepfather? Was he the fourth youth? A ne'er-do-well man who couldn't hold a job, she would never have guessed him capable of anything, let alone a dark secret.

So *that's* why her father and Doc Myers refused to divulge the name of the fourth person. They were protecting Millard.

It made sense. Following the scandal and corruption of President Grant's term, anyone running for office was now held to the highest possible standards. The least scandal could derail a political career before it had even begun.

"My husband"—the woman grimaced as if her words tasted bitter—"always harped on what he'd done to the half-breed. Then when that new preacher came to town, Arthur went and got himself all religious. He confessed to Reverend Wells and asked for forgiveness and that ruined everything."

"How?" Lucy asked. "Anything said to Reverend Wells is held in the strictest of confidence."

"Arthur said that confession was good for the soul. He was a new man. After years of not being able to hold down a job, he claimed he finally found his calling. He planned to become a preacher. He said that when people heard what he did and how God had forgiven him, they would repent too. I couldn't let him do that."

Lucy rubbed her hands up and down her arms to ward off a sudden chill. The woman was obviously out of her mind. "What . . . what did you do with your husband?"

"Don't worry about him. Once my Millard wins the election, I'll let him go."

Lucy stared at her. "You're holding your husband captive?"

Mrs. Weatherbee shrugged. "Holding him was no big deal. But then Barnes had to put his nose where it didn't belong—"

Lucy gasped. "You're holding Barnes too?" That would certainly explain Mrs. Weatherbee's large food purchases.

"I didn't have a choice." Mrs. Weatherbee's eyes gleamed in triumph. "The fool man tried to blackmail me. Barnes wanted me to pay him to keep quiet. I had no choice but to stop him."

Shocked, Lucy glanced at her father, who looked as if he'd passed out. Lucy tried not to panic but her mind scrambled.

"Now I've got you and your father to worry about," Mrs. Weatherbee said. "At this rate, I'm gonna have to find a bigger place to hold you all." She gave her head a sideways nod. "Get in the boat."

Lucy rubbed damp hands down the sides of her skirt. Obviously, the woman wasn't thinking clearly, or she'd know that it was too late to save her son's career. She couldn't hold them captive forever and Barnes would see to it the moment she let him go. "You don't need to do this. We'll find a way to protect Millard. I promise we will and—"

Mrs. Weatherbee waved her gun with impatience. "Shut up and get in the boat." She indicated the bobbing craft with a toss of her head. "Don't say another word. You can row."

"You can't do this, Mrs. Weatherbee. It's not right. I know Millard, and he wouldn't want you to . . ."

"Get in that boat," she snarled.

Before Lucy could do as she was told, a shadow passed

over them. It was the gas balloon. Mrs. Weatherbee's jaw dropped and her eyes practically popped out of her head.

With not a moment to lose, Lucy ducked through the trees and ran.

"Wait!" Mrs. Weatherbee yelled, giving chase.

Lucy kept her eye on the balloon as she ran. "Redd! Help!" she cried.

"Hel-loooooooo!" Redd called.

"Hel-loooooooo!" Emma Hogg echoed.

Skirt held high, Lucy raced through the woods, leaping over fallen logs and crashing through the brush. The balloon stayed the course just ahead of her, skimming high over the treetops and tracking her progress. That meant that Mrs. Weatherbee knew exactly where she was. Thanks to Redd and his confounded balloon, it would do no good to climb a tree or otherwise try to hide.

Oblivious to her plight, the aerialists continued to wave.

"Help me!" Lucy screamed.

"Hello!" Redd and Emma sang out in unison.

Redd cupped his hands around his mouth. "We're getting married!"

Lucy ran until she couldn't run anymore. Her side ached and she was out breath. Hands on her thighs, she stopped and gasped for air. Trust Redd to pick this particular time to announce his wedding plans.

The balloon appeared to be rising.

"Did you hear what I said?" Redd called, his voice growing fainter. "We're getting mar—"

A bullet whizzed by, hitting a nearby tree. Mrs. Weatherbee fired again and Lucy dropped down on hands and knees. Thinking she was shot, she frantically checked herself, but it was a piece of bark that hit her.

Head held low she scrambled through the brush and ducked behind a fallen tree. Her skirt caught on a branch and she yanked it free, ruining yet another article of clothing, but with a madwoman on her trail that was the least of her worries. Breathing hard, she tried to catch her breath before peering over the trunk.

The balloon was no longer in sight.

"You can't get away from me, Lucy," Mrs. Weatherbee called.

Crouching low like a frightened rabbit, Lucy tried to think what to do. There was no place to run. The nearest tree was at least twenty feet away. But she couldn't stay where she was.

Seconds passed. Minutes. Time was on Mrs. Weatherbee's side. The sound of a snapping twig made Lucy's heart pound that much faster.

"Luuu . . . ceec," Mrs. Weatherbee called at last, sounding alarmingly close.

Searching the ground, Lucy found a rock. She peered over the log, rock in hand. Mrs. Weatherbee was less than fifteen feet away.

A movement caught her eye. A shadow. Had her father escaped? *God, please let it be true.*

Mrs. Weatherbee stopped moving. "Who's there?" She swung around and fired a random shot.

Heart pounding, Lucy threw the rock as hard as she could. It fell short of her target and dropped mere inches from Mrs. Weatherbee's feet. The woman swung around again and Lucy ducked.

"You think you're so clever, don't you, girl? We'll see how clever you are."

She fired at the log. Lucy stayed down, hands over her ears, eyes closed, and prayed.

Suddenly the earth seemed to tremble with the sound of hoofbeats, followed by a man's voice. "Hold it right there."

It was David's voice, loud and clear. With a cry of relief Lucy opened her eyes and lifted her head. David had confiscated Mrs. Weatherbee's weapon and held her at gun-point. Shadow stood but a few feet away.

With a cry of joy, Lucy leaped up. "Am I ever glad to see you," she cried. "How did you know?"

He scratched his head as if the whole thing was bizarre. "I heard gunfire and I stepped outside the mission. You're not going to believe this, but a voice came from the sky. It said someone was shooting at you." He glanced upward as if he expected to see angels or something.

She grinned. "I do believe it." Thank God for Redd and his crazy idea to sweep Emma off her feet. She suddenly remembered her father and her smiled died. "Papa! He's tied up in a boat."

"Go," David said. He tossed her his sheathed knife. "I'll be there as soon as I tie up our friend here."

Clutching the fabric of her skirt with one hand and the knife in the other, she ran toward the river, her feet barely skimming the ground. She rounded the bend only to find her father's boat gone. Was she in the wrong place? She didn't think so, but she couldn't be sure.

She ran along the riverbank calling his name. She finally spotted the boat.

Caught in the current, the boat moved toward the rapids, bucking up and down like a wild stallion.

"Papa!" she cried, but her voice barely carried over the thunderous sound of cascading water. The boat spun in a circle as if caught in a whirlpool. It snagged in a knot of floating logs before pulling free.

With no time to lose she dropped her skirt and kicked off her shoes. Shoving the sheathed knife into her bloomer waist, she plunged headlong into the water.

Twenty-nine

When sitting for a picture a widow should say "kerchunk" to present the appropriate mournful expression. To assure adequate sympathy, compose yourself to look brave or resigned but never happy. A merry widow will only raise eyebrows.

— MISS GERTRUDE HASSLEBRINK, 1878

Lucy floundered around in circles. Struggling to keep her head above water, she kicked and flailed and thrashed about. A burning pain shot up her spine and she sank, but this time she touched bottom. Sputtering, she rose up on hands and knees, river rocks biting into her flesh. Her hair had fallen from its pins, and she shook the wet strands aside.

Gasping for air, she forced herself to think. She was in a shallow pool. Behind her white water rushed over huge boulders. The roar of rushing water was deafening, the glints of sunlight blinding.

Suddenly it hit her. Papa!

Urgency overcoming the pain that shot down her back, she struggled to her feet. The water was only knee-deep but the moss-covered rocks were slippery, making it difficult to stand, let alone walk. She balanced herself with arms held out to the side.

"Papa!" she called, but the crashing sound of water drowned out her voice.

Splashing around, she spotted her father floating next to what was left of the boat. By some miracle he floated faceup. Slipping and sliding, she worked her way to his side. He was still breathing, but barely.

Grabbing hold of his shirt with bloodied hands, she dragged him to the river's edge and struck him on the back to dispel any water in his lungs. It took several swats before he coughed a stream of water and gasped for air. She lowered his head to the muddied ground. She'd barely had time to free his hands before she saw, in her peripheral vision, the boat plunging over the rapids.

His feet were still tied together. She felt at her waist for David's knife but it was gone. She tapped his cheek lightly and his eyes fluttered open. The left side of his face was badly scraped, the gash on his head bleeding.

"Papa, talk to me. Say something."

"We . . . we made it," he gasped. "We made it down the rapids alive." She could barely hear him over the force of the rapids but tears of relief rolled down her cheeks. If he could talk perhaps he wasn't seriously injured.

"That we did, Papa." Her gaze traveled along the outcrop of dangerous boulders. She said a prayer of thanksgiving. "That we did."

Her feet and knees covered in cuts and bruises, her tattered stockings hung down in strips. Her wet bloomers felt clammy next to her body, and her torn shirtwaist fell from one bare shoulder. But they had indeed survived. God was good.

He groaned. "My arm." A bone protruded just below his elbow.

"I'm afraid it's broken." She anxiously scanned the riverbank. *David, where are you?*

Her father grimaced before managing a faint smile. "That will make Caleb's day."

She returned his smile. "Yes, it will."

His eyes shimmered. "You saved my life."

She blinked back another rush of fresh tears. "Oh, Papa, if anything had happened to you—"

"You could have been killed."

The calm she maintained during the crisis now deserted her. Thinking about what *could* have happened made her words pour out like water through a sieve. "I love you so much and I was so afraid of losing you." She held his hand, squeezing it tight. "Oh, Papa, I'm so ashamed. How selfish I've been. I've been so consumed by my photography and trying to obtain employment I fear I've neglected you." How could she even think of moving away and leaving the people she loved most in the whole world? "I promise to be a better daughter to you. I'll do whatever you want me to do. I will. Just please don't ask me to marry Crankshaw."

He gazed at her for several moments before shaking his head. "I thought we were both going to die and I kept thinking about all the things I've left undone. Things you've left undone."

"What . . . what things do you mean, Papa?"

"All the things you could do with your camera. You're an artist, Lucy. Just like your mother."

A lump rose to her throat. She never thought to hear her father say such a thing and she thought her heart would burst with pleasure.

"You and Caleb . . . you have to follow your own hearts. Your own dreams. That's what God wants. That's what your mother would have wanted. I know that now."

She laid her head on his chest. Her heart was so full of gratitude she could hardly breathe. An artist. He called her an artist.

"Lucy!"

She quickly wiped away her tears. "Over here," she called, scrambling to her feet. It hurt to lift her arm but she managed to wave.

David slid off his horse and ran down the riverbank toward her and suddenly she was locked in his embrace. His breath warm next to her face, he whispered her name over and over as if saying a prayer. "You're alive. I thought . . ." His voice sounded husky. "If anything had happened to you . . ."

"Oh, David," she sobbed, clutching at his sleeve. "I thought I'd never see you again."

"What a fool I've been. There has to be a way we can be together. We'll find a way."

She gazed up at him. If she was dreaming at that moment, she prayed that no one would wake her. "I—I don't know what to say."

He laughed at her loss for words and pulled her closer. She flinched in pain and he quickly backed away. His eyes soft with concern, he cupped her face between his hands. "You're hurt and cold."

"Just a little," she said.

He took off his buckskin shirt and slid it over her head and down her body. It was way too large for her but the warm softness felt like salve next to her bruised skin.

Fingers on her chin, he tilted her head upward. "I love you, Lucy Fairbanks. To think I almost lost you." For the longest moment all they could do was stare at one another.

Her father coughed, finally, reminding them of his presence. They pulled apart like two children caught stealing candy.

David reached for the knife strapped to his leg. He rushed to cut the rope from her father's ankles.

"So you're Wolf," her father said. "I never thought we'd meet again."

"It's been awhile," David said. He glanced at Lucy before

turning his attention back to her father. "What I said to Lucy . . . I'm sorry you heard that."

Her father waved his apology away with his good arm. "Lucy already told me how she feels about you."

"She did?" The two men stared at each other.

"You do know, of course, that any father in his right mind would object to a half-breed courting his daughter."

Cheeks blazing, Lucy sank next to her father's side. "Papa," she whispered. Out loud she said, "His arm is broken."

David nodded. "We're going to have to splint your arm before we move you. I'm afraid it will hurt."

"It already hurts."

David scoured the water's edge for something he could use as a splint. He returned with a branch that he hacked lengthwise with his knife. Lucy held on to her father while David carefully placed the two pieces of wood on either side of his broken arm.

Her father stiffened and cried out, his face a ghastly white. Lucy laid a soothing hand on his forehead. "Hold on, Papa."

"We're almost done," David said. He wrapped his kerchief around the splint and tied it in a knot. "That should hold it until we get you to a doctor."

Her father closed his eyes and she feared he had fainted. She shook him. "Papa?"

He opened his eyes and turned his head toward David. "There were times I wished I had died the night you went down this river."

"Papa, we'll talk about this later."

"No, I want to talk about it now." He never took his eyes off David. "Things were never the same after that. I spent every minute of every day regretting that night. Hating myself. Do you think you can ever forgive me? Forgive all of us?"

The roaring sound of water seemed almost deafening in the waiting silence that followed. "I'm the one who should be asking for forgiveness," David said at last. His powerful bare chest gleaming in the sunlight, he lifted his gaze to Lucy.

"You? What for?" her father asked.

"For not coming back sooner. For not letting you know I was alive. I had no idea anyone would care one way or the other whether I lived or died." He beseeched Lucy with his eyes. "Had I done so, things might have turned out very different."

Lucy suspected he referred to her mother's death and she shook her head. No good could come from dwelling on what might have been.

"You were a child," her father said, as if to guess her thoughts. "You had no way of knowing what the rest of us were going through. You owe us no apology. None."

"Papa's right," Lucy added. "Nothing that happened was your fault."

David's eyes locked with hers. The tenderness in their depths quickened her pulse and turned her mouth dry.

"So what do you say?" Her father held out his good hand. "Do you think we can put the past behind us?"

"I think it's about time," David said, grabbing hold of her father's offered hand.

A cry of joy broke from her lips. It wasn't only forgiveness she saw flow between them, but acceptance. Every bone in her body ached from the battering of water and rocks, but at that moment she felt like the happiest woman alive.

Her father pulled his hand out of David's. "Now kiss her already, would you?"

David stared at him, clearly baffled. "I thought you disapproved of me courting your daughter."

"I said any father in his right mind would disapprove." Her father grimaced and groaned. "You just happened to catch me when I'm out of my mind. So what in blazes are you waiting for? Hurry up and kiss her so we can get out of here."

Two hours later Wolf stood outside a deserted cabin where Barnes and Weatherbee had been held captive.

Both men had been locked inside and were now giving their statements to the marshal. Mrs. Weatherbee had tricked her husband into coming to the cabin. She hit him on the head and, while he was unconscious, tied him up and locked him inside. Barnes had a different story. After hitting him over the head with a paperweight, she then forced him to the cabin at gunpoint.

Lucy had driven her father to Doc Myers's, but Wolf stayed behind. He had yet to come face-to-face with the fourth and last man who put him on that boat. Weatherbee was his only hope in locating the box taken from him.

Barnes had lost weight since Wolf last saw him, and he now sported half a scraggly beard. No whiskers grew on his scar, which now looked more purple than red.

"It's about time you got here," Barnes said, glaring at the marshal. "That . . . that woman is a maniac. I offered to help her son get elected and this is the thanks I get."

"You tried to blackmail me," Mrs. Weatherbee yelled. "You said if I paid you, you'd keep quiet about the boy in the boat."

"Asking for hush money isn't the same as blackmail," Barnes shouted back.

"Quiet! Both of you," Marshal Armstrong ordered. He turned to Mrs. Weatherbee's husband. "What's your story?"

Weatherbee had been held captive considerably longer than Barnes and he looked it. His clothes hung on his thin frame. Dark bags skirted sunken eyes and the skin above his unkempt beard was sallow, but he didn't mince words. He pointed at his wife. "She kept us locked up like animals."

"Quit your griping," Mrs. Weatherbee said, looking

remarkably self-righteous considering the trouble she was in. "I fed you twice a day, didn't I?"

"You tried to kill me!" her husband argued.

Mrs. Weatherbee discounted his accusation with a wave of her hand. "Nonsense. I couldn't kill you even if I wanted to. I couldn't kill anyone. I'm a Christian."

Marshal Armstrong grimaced in disgust and grabbed her by the arm. "Reverend Wells may want to straighten you out in that regard. But he'll have to get in line behind the sheriff."

He hauled his prisoner away and Barnes followed them. Wolf stepped in front of Weatherbee, whose wheezy breathing and concave chest indicated he was asthmatic. A distant memory came to the fore. One of the youths had trouble breathing, but at ten years old, Wolf had had no way of knowing the cause.

Weatherbee looked him up and down. "So you're the boy," he rasped.

"Was," Wolf replied.

Weatherbee pursed his lips. "Barnes told me you were alive. I couldn't believe it." He shook his head. "Still can't."

Wolf waited for Weatherbee to blame that long-ago night on his present circumstances but he made no attempt to do so.

"Did Barnes tell you why I came back?" Wolf asked.

"At first he told me you wanted money to keep quiet. Eventually he told me what you really wanted. Captivity can make an honest man out of pretty near anyone, even Barnes." As if he ran out of breath, he stopped before adding, "I remember the box. Had an animal on the lid."

Wolf felt his hopes rise. "A wolf. Do you know where it is now?"

Weatherbee coughed and seemed to gasp for breath. Alarmed, Wolf reached for the man's arm but Weatherbee waved away his concern.

"Sorry. Wish I could be more help." His voice drifted

away as he gazed at the road. His wife sat rigid in the saddle while the marshal prepared to tow her horse. "What's gonna happen to her?"

"I reckon she'll go to jail," Wolf said. *If she's lucky.* A less desirable option would be an insane asylum.

"Drat! If I go into the ministry like I plan, I'm gonna have to forgive her. Do you think God will give me a pass if I don't?"

"I reckon that's between you and him," Wolf said. Weatherbee's lips were bluish in color. "Come on, you need to see Doc Myers. I'll take you there."

Weatherbee shook his head. "Not till I talk to Millard. I dreaded facing you, but not half as much as I dread facing my stepson. What am I gonna tell him about his mother?"

"The truth," Wolf said. In the end, that's all anyone really wanted to know. "Tell him his mother's lost her way." Ambition could do that to a person. But so could seeing yourself through the eyes of others—a mistake he wouldn't repeat.

Following the Sunday morning service, Pastor Wells held the plans up for the new Rocky Creek Community Church. It was a hot humid day in July and everyone was anxious to go home. Nevertheless, the entire congregation crowded in for a closer look.

Lucy glanced up at David and smiled. "They're going to love it," she whispered. "I know they are." She squeezed his arm.

David patted her hand and gave her a quick grin. "Is that a positive?" he whispered back.

"Absolutely," she said, broadening her smile.

Reverend Wells cleared his throat, and after a short intro-ductory speech he pointed to the drawing. "This will be the classroom," he said proudly. "And here is the library." He glanced at Marshal Armstrong. "Now your jail cells are safe," he said.

This brought a round of laughter from the churchgoers. Everyone knew Jenny had tried to persuade her marshal husband into turning one of the jail cells into a lending library.

"And this is my office," Pastor Wells continued with a fond smile at his wife, Sarah.

Sarah nodded. "If that don't take the rag off the bush. Does that mean I get my kitchen table back?"

"Absolutely, my dear," Pastor Wells said.

Mrs. Taylor clapped her hands in approval. "Oh, this is so exciting," she squealed.

Mrs. Hitchcock concurred. "Oh, it is, it is."

Richard Crankshaw hovered nearby, but no one paid attention to him until he stepped in front of the building plans and faced the crowd. "You do know, of course, that this church was designed by . . . that man, an outsider." He pointed to David. He didn't say it out loud but the words *half-breed* were clearly written in the curl of his mouth.

A dead silence followed and Lucy's heart sank. Already it was starting, everything her father and David had warned her about. She gazed up at David but his thoughts were hidden behind a stone mask.

Crankshaw addressed the gathering as if he had every right to do so. "I asked one of my men to draw up new plans for the church and I believe you will find them much more to your liking." No sooner were the words out of his mouth than he raised his arm and snapped his fingers, signaling to a man at the back of the crowd to join him. The man came forward, held up a set of plans, and Crankshaw spent the next few minutes detailing his design—a basic church setup with none of the unique elements Wells had planned.

Pastor Wells stepped forward. "There's no need to

trouble yourself, Mr. Crankshaw. We already have plans for the church."

Crankshaw gave the pastor a benign smile. "I'm sure that the good citizens of Rocky Creek would prefer a church designed by one of their own."

Anger flashed across Wells's face. "By one of our own, I assume you mean a man of God."

Crankshaw's face turned dark. "Perhaps we should let the people be the judge of which man that is," he said in a clipped voice. "I say we vote on it." He glanced at the Suffra-Quilters. "Men and *women* get to vote equally," he added with a magnanimous air.

"Drat!" Lucy muttered. The women were so anxious to have a say in how things were run, she wouldn't be surprised if they showed their gratitude by voting in Crankshaw's favor.

"All those in favor of . . . Mr. Wolf's design, raise your hand," Crankshaw said. He looked and sounded like a man confident of the outcome.

Appleby shocked everyone by being the first to shoot his hand in the air. Lucy raised her hand next, then Caleb. Her father raised his unbroken arm and Lucy felt like her heart was going to burst with pride.

She glanced around, stunned by the sight that greeted her. Was she imagining all those hands in the air? Even the man working for Crankshaw held a hand straight up, thanks to Timber Joe's strategically aimed rifle.

Lucy shook her head in disbelief and did a mental roll call. Monica and Doc Myers held their hands high. As did Sarah and Emma Hogg. Redd, Barrel, Brenda, and Annabelle. Soon there were too many hands to count. Even the Suffra-Quilters and members of The Society for the Protection and Preservation of Male Independence held their hands up high. It was the first time the two groups agreed on anything.

Pastor Wells couldn't have looked more pleased. "Mr. Crankshaw, I believe you have your answer."

Crankshaw cursed, but seeing that the crowd stood against him, he donned his hat and left, and the entire congregation burst into applause.

Later, much later, Lucy stopped Appleby to thank him. "Why did you vote for Wolf?" she asked. Never had she known him to take part in civil affairs. So why today?

Appleby spit out a stream of tobacco juice. "Do you think mixed folks are the only ones who are discrim'nated ag'inst? Us ole folks know a thin' or two about intol'ance," he groused. "These days it's all about youth and it ain't fair."

Lucy did something that surprised even her. She flung her arms around him and gave him a big hug. Appleby got all red in the face and pushed her away.

"Don't go gettin' any ideas. I'm the president of The Society for the Protection and Preserv'tion of Male Ind'pendence and I ain't meanin' to take no wife. And that includes you."

He walked away grumbling.

Grinning, Lucy watched him go, and she was still smiling when her father joined her.

She tucked her arm into his good one. His other arm was still in a cast. "Thank you, Papa, for voting for David's building plans."

He squeezed her arm with his own. "I wasn't voting for his plans. What do I know about building a church? I was voting for the man."

She smiled and laid her head on his shoulder.

"I like seeing you happy," he said.

She lifted her head. "I *am* happy, Papa." The way the town rallied around David when the story came out made her heart burst with pride. David's plans had generated so much excitement that, after the church service, people practically fell over each other in their haste to make donations. No doubt they would soon have enough to rebuild the church.

Her father turned to face her. "No regrets about turning down Barnes's job offer?"

Barnes had offered her a job at the newspaper but she no longer trusted him enough to work for him. Turning him down meant having to give up her dream, perhaps for good. Now she might never see her photographs in print. Still, she was convinced she'd made the right decision.

"No regrets," she said, though that was only half true. Now that the shadows and secrets that once plagued her were gone, she longed to do something more with her photographs—something significant.

"I just wish I could make the world a better place." The revealing eye of the camera changed people's lives and the way they thought. Mathew Brady's photographs exposed the harsh realities of war, showing that it was anything but glorious. The photograph of Shantytown shamed people into action. There was so much power in photography.

But would she ever be able to do anything that important? Not only did she live in a small Texas town, she was a woman, and that alone worked against her. War and politics, even poverty, were out of her realm.

"Now you sound like your mama. She never saw the world as it was. She only saw the possibilities."

"So what do I do, Papa? Tell me what to do."

He planted a kiss on her forehead. "Don't give up. God will find a way to use your talents." He rolled his eyes upward. "I only hope the good Lord knows what he's in for."

Thirty

Brides, take pity on your photographer. Mathew Brady and his helpers were able to record the entire War Between the States with little more than 1100 photographs. Half that number should satisfy most brides.
—MISS GERTRUDE HASSLEBRINK, 1878

T he building plans spread out before him, Wolf leaned over to add another line with his pencil. Behind him the raw-wood frame of the church rose high into the sky. The sound of hammering filled the air along with children's laughter.

A thunderstorm had rolled through the town during the night and the air hung heavy as thick curtains. The lingering clouds offered precious little protection from the heat of the July sun. But neither the heat nor humidity could dampen the enthusiasm of those who turned out to build or cheer on the builders of the church—which was pretty near everybody in town.

Lucy joined him and he looked up from his work. Dressed in a pretty blue skirt and white shirtwaist, she carried a picnic basket in one hand and fanned herself with the other.

Her hair was pulled back from her face, but already it had worked its way out of its confines to fall loosely down her back. She had been working with her budding young photographers most of the morning.

"Hungry?" she asked. She had to lift her voice to be heard above all the hammering and chanting.

He smiled at her. "A little. Let me just finish here." He added another line to his drawing.

Lucy peered over his shoulder. "That doesn't look like the church."

"It's Barrel's opera house." He tapped his finger against the drawing. "This is the stage."

Lucy squealed with delight. "Barrel and Brenda will be so pleased."

He couldn't help but laugh at her enthusiasm.

A sudden quiet overtook the festivities. The hammering stopped. The chanting ceased and even the children were silent, looking to their parents as if they sensed trouble. Wolf straightened. It was the same silence that greeted him whenever he rode into a new town, and it always meant trouble. Instinctively his hand flew to the knife at his side.

He glanced around, stunned to note that the sudden tension was not directed at him. Instead all eyes were on Millard Weatherbee. No one had seen him since his mother's trial and incarceration, and it wasn't even known that he was still in town.

Wolf felt sorry for the man. He'd been in his shoes more times than he cared to remember. Being an outsider was hard and Millard didn't deserve to be treated like one. None of what happened with his mother was his fault.

Not that long ago Millard had been warmly accepted as he passed out handbills and solicited votes. How quickly divisions could spring up between people, and how difficult it was to tear them down. Today Millard walked alone, holding a rectangular box in his hands, which he offered to Wolf.

Wolf took the box from him and stared at the wolf carving. He never thought he'd see the box again, let alone hold it.

Next to him, Lucy let out a gasp. "That's just like the wolf you carved." She held up her arm to finger the wooden brace-let he made for her.

She was right. It was the same design he'd carved perhaps a hundred times through the years. It surprised him how accurately he'd managed to capture the image from memory.

It was smaller than he remembered, lighter, but then he was a short, scrawny ten-year-old the last time he held it in his hands. The gold inlay shone in the sun.

Millard glanced at Lucy and politely tipped his hat. Without a word he turned to leave.

"Millard, wait," Lucy called after him. "I never got a chance to tell you how sorry I am about your mother. I—I knew something was wrong and I wish now I had said something."

Millard turned, his face shaded by his wide brim felt hat. Gone were the celluloid collars and spiffy bow ties. "I knew something was wrong too. I tried to get her to see Doc Myers but she refused."

"What do you plan to do now?" she asked.

"I'm thinking about traveling to California where I'm not known," he said slowly.

"It's not fair that you should have to give up your career aspirations for something that was not your fault."

Millard gave her a reassuring smile. "Reverend Wells said that God always finds a way to work through bad things. I just have to give him a chance."

Lucy hugged him. "You take care."

He nodded a farewell to Wolf, then walked away, head down. Lucy called after him. "And when we women get the vote, I'll vote for you."

He waved. "I'll hold you to that!" he called back.

After Weatherbee left, Wolf continued to gaze down at the box in his hand.

Lucy laid her hand on his arm. "What are you waiting for?" she prodded. "Open it."

He lifted his gaze to the steeple of the church. It had been an amazing couple of weeks. When the entire story came out, the townsfolk had rallied around him.

He glanced around at the people who befriended him, and he thanked God for bringing them into his life. His search for identity had defined him as a man and almost kept him from the woman he loved, but no more.

"I don't need this box to tell me who I am," he said softly. Thanks to her and her father and all the rest, he knew exactly who he was and where he wanted to spend the rest of his life. He also knew now that God was good. "This box can't possibly tell me more than I already know."

Her eyes filled with tears. "Oh, David." In her rush to throw her arms around him, she inadvertently knocked the box out of his hands. It landed on the ground, the lid open.

For a moment, neither of them moved. All they could do was stare at the empty interior.

She looked up at him. "I'm sorry. I—"

He shook his head and pulled her into his arms. "It's like I said, I don't need to know any more than I already know."

"Say Rocky Creek backwards," Skip Owen called from behind the camera.

Startled, Lucy and Wolf glanced at the camera and then turned back to gaze at each other—and little Skip got his moment.

Later that afternoon Lucy stared up at the frame of the church building. "Do you see the bell tower in the viewfinder?"

Her young pupil nodded from behind the camera, and the black cloth on his head bopped up and down. "I see it," Skip said, sounding older than his ten years. Next to him Sarah's little daughter Elizabeth watched with grave interest.

"Focus, but don't do anything else until I tell you to."

Lucy made a square with her fingers, emulating what Skip could see through the viewfinder. Redd straddled a beam, his legs hanging in midair. David signaled from the ground and a length of lumber was hauled by rope up to the roofline.

"Get ready," Lucy said, dropping her hands to her side. The beam hovered over the rooftop before being lowered into place. "Now."

Skip squeezed the bulb to open the shutter and counted the way she taught him. "One thousand and one, one thousand and two . . ."

"Perfect," she said. She pulled the plate out of the camera and inserted a fresh one. Skip dived beneath the black cloth again and waited for instructions.

She looked up at the sound of chanting. "Women's vote, women's vote." The ladies of the Suffra-Quilters never missed a chance to push their cause. Today they circled around the new building, pumping their signs up and down. It had become a familiar sight.

Somehow Emma Hogg had talked Redd into joining the movement, but given the choice between parading around and building the church, he did what any man in his right mind would do. He grabbed a hammer and ran.

Timber Joe and Annabelle patrolled the perimeter of the church property, rifles in hand. Anyone slacking off got a not-so-subtle reminder to keep working.

"Ouch," Barrel yelled from inside the church door frame.

No sooner had Barrel cried out than Caleb raced toward him with his brand new medical case in hand, a gift from his father. "Did you know that your thumb is the same length as your nose?" he asked.

Barrel held his swollen thumb up. "Not anymore."

Elizabeth tugged on Lucy's skirt, pulling her attention away from Barrel. "Will I get a vode?"

For a moment, Lucy was stumped. "Oh, you mean a

vote?" Not knowing how to answer, she pushed a curl away from the child's pretty round face. How could she tell a three-year-old that some things may not be possible simply because she was a girl? How, for that matter, did you explain a world that keeps Lee Wong away from his family and demanded separate schools for colored children? A world that had, for far too long, turned its back on a man like David Wolf.

She longed to fight the injustices in the world, but how could she? No longer strapped for money now that Caleb's education and the church building were both paid for, Lucy wished with all her heart that she could do something with her photography that would make the world a better place. But no matter how much she prayed, God either wasn't listening or wasn't answering.

Elizabeth stared at her, patiently waiting for Lucy to respond. The little girl's big blue eyes held so much faith and hope and trust it was like looking into an endless sea of possibilities.

"Maybe your shutter isn't open wide enough to see God's plan for you."

Startled by the memory, Lucy was as puzzled today by Barrel's words as she was when he first spoke them.

As if to sense Lucy's confusion, Elizabeth's eyes grew rounder. *"Maybe your shutter isn't open wide enough . . ."*

Then, like a bolt from the sky, Lucy knew—knew without a doubt what God was calling her to do. The answer, of course, had been staring her in the face for weeks. She would bombard every newspaper and magazine in the country with photographs of women saving lives and teaching the young. She would post her photographs in public places and mail them to every state and US senator. The message she would send was that men and women worked and prayed together, so why couldn't they vote together? No sooner had the thought occurred to her than the sun suddenly moved from behind a cloud, and it was as if the very heavens smiled down on her.

Her heart beat with excitement. Her pictures would show in every way possible why keeping the vote away from women not only hurt Texas but hurt the entire country. It might take awhile to convince newspaper editors to run her pictures but she wouldn't give up until they did. Photographer Mathew Brady had his war and she had hers.

"Yes, yes, yes," she exclaimed. "And that, my dear, sweet child, is a positive. One day you *will* get to vote." With God's help and a lot of dry plates.

Elizabeth's face lit up. "Will you take a phot'graph of my vode?"

Lucy tilted her head sideways. "Why do you want me to do that?"

"So that we can keep the vode safe in God's pocket."

Lucy smiled. "Then I most definitely will take a photograph."

"I'll take it," Skip said, stepping out from behind the camera.

Lucy laughed and hugged both children to her. She caught David smiling at her from across the way and knew he would approve her decision. Her heart nearly bursting with happiness, she blew him a kiss in front of God and everyone.

Epilogue

Alas! Some advice simply bears repeating: Never climb higher to take a photograph than you can afford to fall.

— MISS GERTRUDE HASSLEBRINK, 1878

Ohhh," Lucy squealed. Never had she imagined herself flying, but that's what it felt like to ride in a gas balloon.

She held on to the side of the wicker basket and looked straight down. Surely this is what the world must look like as seen through God's eyes.

Above their heads, the massive red silk envelope gleamed in the sun. It rustled in the wind and the gondola creaked out a reluctant response.

"It doesn't feel like we're moving," she said, amazed at the smooth ride.

"That's because we're moving as fast as the wind," the aerialist explained. An older man with white hair and mustache, Eugene Gage kept his hand upon the catch.

She shaded her eyes against the hot September sun. "I do believe that's Barrel." She waved to the man on horseback pursuing them below. Soon they left him far behind. In the distance the Rocky Creek River looked like a narrow satin ribbon, giving no clue of the dangers that lurked there.

The meadows that had been so green following the spring

rains spread out beneath them like a brown velvet carpet. Already a few trees were beginning to turn, dotting the landscape with splashes of yellow and gold.

She moved behind the tripod and dived beneath the dark cloth, prepared to take a photograph of a herd of cattle. However, as soon as the animals spotted the aircraft, they panicked and ran across the field.

She did manage to snap a photograph of a farmer on his plow, and not a moment too soon. The instant the horses saw the aerial ship they took off, dragging the plow and farmer behind. Lucy couldn't help but laugh.

"I bet he never plowed a field so fast," she said. She glanced at David, who stood facing the center of the basket and hadn't said a word.

"David, really, you're missing all the fun," she called.

"If it's all the same to you, I'll wait for the photographs."

"I didn't know you were afraid of heights," she said, teasing.

"Only heights of a thousand feet or more," he assured her.

"Oh, there's the church." She clapped her hands together. The newly built Rocky Creek Community Church looked like a child's dollhouse from such mind-boggling heights, though in reality it was really quite large. School was due to start next week and already the new Mrs. *Doctor* Myers had been busy getting her new classroom ready.

Lucy peered through the viewfinder. "Do you think we can get closer?" she called.

"I'll try to land next to the church," Gage said. "We'll descend slowly so you can get your photographs." He reached up to vent the hydrogen.

The balloon began to descend and the images that had blurred together like a water painting began to separate into individual trees. Lucy snapped her photographs, oohing and ahhing at the shifting shapes in her lens.

Fortunately the church was in full sunlight, which meant

less exposure time was needed and she was able to get photo-graphs from various altitudes. She couldn't wait to show these to Pastor Wells and Sarah.

Just as the gondola grew level with the church, an unex-pected gust of wind sent them sailing toward the steeple.

"Hold fast!" Gage shouted.

Lucy grabbed her camera and David grabbed her. The basket slammed into the top of the church with a jolt. The cow weather vane that David had made special for Reverend Wells flew off the top of the steeple.

"Oh, no!" Lucy cried.

The gondola spun around and struck the church again, this time with such force the bell tower tilted sideways. David pulled her to the floor of the basket, protecting her with his body just as they hit the side of the church for a third time. The loud shattering of glass made Lucy cringe. The balloon then took off again and she peered cautiously over the side of the gondola.

Below them the grappling hook used for landing swung back and forth on a long rope. Overhead, the gas roared like an angry lion.

The pilot called to a man walking a dog and asked for assistance.

The man looked startled. The dog ran circles around him, barking until the owner was hopelessly entangled in his leash. By the time the man was able to free himself the balloon had passed him by.

With a sudden lurch, the bottom of the gondola touched the ground and the three of them rolled over each other. The basket bopped up and down like a frog hopping lily pads.

"We have to jump," the pilot shouted. With that, he dis-appeared over the side.

David grabbed Lucy by the hand, but she pulled back. "My camera!"

By the time she had a hold on her camera, it was too late to jump. Without the pilot's weight, the balloon rose straight up. From the ground the pilot tried to grab hold of the rope but they soon left him far behind.

The balloon suddenly dipped and headed straight for the top of a towering tree.

The impact sent them both flying backward. The gondola swung back and forth before gradually coming to a halt.

"Are you all right?" David scrambled toward her on hands and knees.

Facedown on the floor of the gondola, Lucy lifted herself up. She pushed a tree branch away from her face. "I think so." The balloon hovered high above the top of a bur oak tree, but the basket held fast to the branches.

David peered over the side. "We're in luck," he said. "We're only about fifty feet off the ground."

Lucy picked herself up. "I'm sorry I talked you into this. We could have both been killed."

"Anything for a good photograph," he said good-naturedly, pulling a yellow-brown leaf from her hair. She laughed. How she loved this man, loved everything about him.

"What are we going to do?" She'd climbed her share of trees, but even she wouldn't be so foolish as to climb down this one.

"I guess we hang around for a while," he said.

"You're a big help." She checked her camera but it didn't appear damaged. She then glanced at the ground, which seemed so far away. Fighting back tears, she turned to David.

"I should never have asked you to come today. Ever since you've known me, I've caused you nothing but trouble. I almost got us buried alive and then you were shot because of that photograph and—" The tears did come but there wasn't a thing she could do about it. "And now look at us. We're stuck in a—"

"Marry me."

She slammed her mouth shut and practically forgot to breathe. "What did you say?"

He captured a teardrop on his finger and held it up like it was a precious gem. "I said marry me."

For a moment she couldn't find her voice. "You . . . you can't be thinking right," she stammered at last. "After all the trouble I've caused you."

He gazed at her, his eyes filled with tenderness. "There's nothing wrong with my thinking," he said. "I love you. And that's the way it's been since the first day we met. I didn't think it was possible for us to be together, but the people of Rocky Creek proved me wrong."

Even her tears couldn't hide the sincerity in his eyes. Normally she would have grabbed her camera to capture such a moment, but not today. Instead, she tucked the moment into her heart for safekeeping.

"Are you asking me to be Mrs. David Wolf?" she whispered.

"Actually, I'm thinking about legally changing my name to Combes. That is, if his son Joseph doesn't mind. Pastor Wells says that a name change signals a new beginning, and I can't think of a better way to honor the man who took me under his wing than to begin life anew with his name. So what do you say? How does Mrs. David Combes sound to you?"

Her heart was beating so fast she could hardly speak, and he grinned down at her. "I think you better say *yes* while the church is still standing."

She wished he hadn't reminded her. Recalling how the original church had burned down and the new one sustained damage, she stifled a sob. "Are . . . are you sure you want me for your wife? My photography takes up a lot of my time." Her work with the suffragette movement was of great importance. "And I promised Brenda and Barrel to help them with their opera house and . . ."

She babbled on and on, just as she always did when she was nervous or anxious or, in this case, about to accept a marriage proposal.

"Is that a negative?" he asked when at last he was able to get a word in edgewise.

"It's a positive," she said, then proceeded to tell him all the reasons why she wanted to be his wife.

David patiently waited for her to run out of steam but, of course, he had to know that the only way to make her stop talking was to give her mouth something better to do. And that's exactly what he did.

Dear Reader

This is the third and last book in my Rocky Creek series. I do so hope you like Lucy's and David's stories as much as you liked Sarah's and Justin's in *A Lady Like Sarah* and Jenny's and Rhett's in *A Suitor for Jenny*.

I loved writing about old-time photography, and have nothing but awe for the brave souls who first took camera in hand. It wasn't just men who battled unwieldy equipment and exploding chemicals in the name of art. Women were also photographers, and a few even made names for themselves.

Since female occupations were not listed on the census until 1870, it's hard to know how many professional women photographers existed in America before that time. We do know, however, that some, like Julia Shannon of San Francisco, owned their own studios as early as 1850. Julia took the family portrait to new heights when she shockingly advertised herself as a daguerreotyper and midwife.

Women had an advantage over male photographers, who were often confounded by female dress. This explains why one photographer advertised in 1861 for an assistant, "Who Understands the Hairdressing Business."

Early cameras required long exposure times, which demanded the use of head vises. This accounts in part for our ancestors' cheerless faces (and here you thought they were just plain grouchy). Another reason for the lack of smiles was that a tightly controlled mouth was considered a thing of beauty. In her essay "Why We Say 'Cheese': Producing the Smile in Snapshot Photography," Christina Kotchemidova wrote that photography was once the domain of the rich. "Smiles were worn only by peasants, children, and drunks." She then goes on to explain that fast shutter speed, dental care, and cultural changes began a process of "mouth liberalization."

Did photography have a bearing on the suffragette movement? Indeed, it did, but it appeared to be more of a detriment than a help. The photographs of militant suffragettes or women dressed in bloomers did more harm than good.

If you think America was tough on suffragettes, think again. The women's rights movement was considered the biggest threat to the British Empire. According to the National Archives, the votes-for-women movement became the first "terrorist" organization subjected to secret camera surveillance in the world.

Photography has come a long way since those early daguerreotype days. One can only imagine what the brave souls of yesteryear would think of today's "aim and click" cameras. Nowadays you can't even drive down the street without having your picture taken.

In closing, I leave you with sage advice from Miss Gertrude Hasslebrink, which is just as relevant today as it was in the nineteenth century: "Never leave the house unless you're ready for your close-up—and, as your mother would say, clean undergarments wouldn't hurt, either."

Blessings,

Margaret

Reading Group Guide

1. Lucy believed the camera could see things often missed by the human eye. This proved true when she discovered something surprising about herself. Have you ever looked at a photograph and discovered something new about yourself or others?

2. Having your photograph taken in the nineteenth and early twentieth centuries was serious business. A person might have only one photograph taken in a lifetime. How has the ease of taking pictures today changed your view of picture taking? Do you think we place more or less value on photographs today? Was there ever a time that you felt a camera was intrusive?

3. As a child David was taught that God was harsh and unforgiving. How did your childhood view of God influence your faith? What misconceptions did you have to overcome to grow in your faith?

4. Lucy's plan to be a newspaper photographer met with one failure after another. Still, she persisted until, at last, she discovered God's true plan for her. What are some of the ways that God has revealed his plan for your life?

5. Pastor Wells said that prejudice was a quick way to form an opinion without getting to know someone. Have you ever changed your mind about someone after forming

an initial opinion? Was the way you came to regard the person more favorable or less so?

6. Ma believed that every pot has a lid, which is a way of saying that there is a right man for every woman. Do you agree or disagree? Why or why not?

7. Gaining acceptance is a major theme of the book. David, Lucy, Timber Joe, Barrel, Lee Wong, and even Old Man Appleby (by his own admission) faced some sort of discrimination. John Saltmarsh wrote: "The more we love any that are not as we are, the less we love as men and the more as God." In what ways can we apply this to everyday life?

8. One of the themes of the book is abandonment. David was left on the mission steps as an infant. Lucy felt that her father deserted her emotionally. Describe a time that you felt either physically or emotionally abandoned. In what ways did it affect you?

9. Lucy was deeply touched when David recognized her photographs as art. Has there ever been a time when someone failed to appreciate, acknowledge, or validate your achievements? How did you overcome this?

10. As a child David assumed the boys meant to do him harm. It wasn't until years later that he learned the truth. Think of a hurtful incident from your childhood. Do you now have a different understanding as to how or why it happened, or does your original impression remain the same?

11. Lucy chased the white stallion much as David chased the box taken from him as a child. Both horse and box remained elusive. Has there ever been a time when something you wanted seemed so close but yet so far away? What do you think God is trying to teach us at such times?

12. After a long and tedious battle, the Nineteenth Amendment was finally ratified in 1920, giving women the right to vote on a national level (almost fifty years after women

were able to vote in Wyoming). Why do you think it took so long? Do you think groups like the Suffra-Quilters helped or hindered the cause? How did war slow the process?

13. In what ways was guilt manifested in the men responsible for putting David on that boat? Has there ever been a time when you felt guilty for something you did or didn't do?

14. Neither Lucy nor Caleb shared their father's hopes and dreams for them. In what ways can a parent's aspirations for a child help or hinder?

15. How much influence do you think David's plight had in Lucy's decision to work for women's rights?

Acknowledgments

Have you ever noticed that when you glance through your photographs that some of the same people keep popping up? These are the friends and family members closest to the heart. I guess it only stands to reason that people closest to this writer's heart keep showing up on my acknowledgement—or what I prefer to call my gratitude—pages.

So again I send heart-felt thanks to you, my readers, for the cards, letters, emails, and Facebook messages. Corresponding with you is truly the most pleasurable part of being a writer.

It takes an astounding number of talented and gifted people to produce a book. On the top of that list is my amazing agent, Natasha Kern, the best friend, mentor, supporter, counselor and teacher that a writer could have.

Next is the fabulous Thomas Nelson team starting with editor-supreme Natalie Hanemann. I could go on forever listing the names of those who helped turn my story into a book but special thanks go to Katie, Ashley, Andrea, Ami, Eric, Heather, Jennifer, Jeane, Allen and the fantastic art department and sales team.

No gratitude page is complete without mentioning my family, especially my husband George, who has the unenviable task of keeping me on track. As always I'm grateful to God for leading me down this particular path.

My best wishes to all and may your own gratitude pages be filled with family, friends and countless blessings. Until next time . . .

Margaret
Have a little faith!